E. SCOTT LLOYD

THE UNDER-GRADUATE

A NOVEL

LIBERTY ISLAND
LET YOUR RIGHT BRAIN RUN FREE

A LIBERTY ISLAND BOOK

ISBN: 978-1-947942-32-5

The Undergraduate

Cover design by Logotecture.

Liberty Island

Libertyislandmag.com

Published in the United States of America

To Mary and Ann

CHAPTER 1

We traveled north along a highway from Rome to Florence. Patches of dormant Tuscan farmland waved by in the sullen green hills not far off. At times we passed a pockmarked stone villa or a hamlet from some dot in antiquity as we rode in a blue charter bus with diagonal rainbow stripes on the side. I was the only person awake save Dr. Sellier and the driver. Outside it was cold, but if it snowed it would be rain, or sleet, more likely. The villas, shacks, and chapels that were mostly painted some shade of yellow or beige reflected the late-evening sun and seemed almost to glow. Even the grass looked foreign, which was strange and new, and gave me a tickle in my stomach to go along with the other things.

I fixed my gaze toward the horizon at the tops of the hills and stared through the evening as it became night. When it became too dark to see, I turned and stared at the back of the seat in front of me. I thought about Lily, which before long led elsewhere.

On the seat to my left sat a blue accordion folder containing information about our classes and the like, but I couldn't make much sense of it at the time. For seventeen hours I had been traveling. I was fatigued from the free drinks and the

1

lack of sleep, and my thoughts were in tangles. It was January 20 or 19, and that part of that particular month had a certain significance I wanted to forget, but couldn't at the time.

I shifted around in my seat and looked two rows ahead at Lily for a second. Her thick brown and wavy hair was tied loosely on top of her head and sticking up slightly over the gray itchy fabric of the bus seat. I couldn't tell, but she looked like she was asleep.

I settled again and began nodding off, but fought off the sleepiness since I wasn't sure how much longer it would be before we got to Florence. I wanted to see as much as I could.

Soon enough the lights came on suddenly, and Dr. Sellier stood up at the front of the bus and announced, "We have arrived in Florence."

That woke me up. I tried to look at as many of the buildings and shops as I could. Most of them had stucco or stone on the outside, and were yellow. There were some residences with walls around them and old gates. The shops all had signs on them, only some of which I could translate. There were butchers and bakeries and restaurants that weren't chains. The streets were narrow, a lot of them, and so the buildings felt like they were close-by. The streets seemed to zigzag and loop around.

Dr. Sellier after a few minutes continued with his announcement. We would make a stop to let some of the folks off at a house on the way, and arrive at the train station shortly, he said loudly, intending, I guess, to annoy us awake. I undid the blue string binding my folder and stared at the name of my hostess, Signora Grazie Ridomi. I knew from *The Complete Idiot's Guide to Italian* that her first name meant "thank you," which perplexed what was left of me.

We stopped on a street outside the train station around nine or so, at a curb where the tour buses lined up and their diesel engines coughed and rattled as they waited for passengers to get on or get off. After I stepped onto the sidewalk from the bus, the driver turned off the engine. There was a pause, the first real silence I had heard since home. Then the light at the corner near the commuter buses many yards down changed to green, though, and the *motorini* and little Italian cars came racing by and ruined it.

We unloaded our things from the undercarriage of the bus onto the curb beneath the orange streetlights that glowed with halos in the misty air. The station was a large, uninteresting building behind us with a newsstand and a few storefronts built into it. There were plenty of people around. Several yards down, next to the sidewalk to my left, was a crowd of white taxis, where Dr. Sellier directed us to take our bags. He was average height with rimmed glasses and gray hair that was curly and longish and pushed back. He wore a blazer and a button-down tucked into jeans, in keeping with his campus reputation for being a pretty slick operator.

Beyond the taxis, across the Via delle Belle Donne, was a McDonald's on the bottom floor of an apartment building that was a few stories high. I could see a few people eating and talking, but I wasn't close enough to see which they were doing. I walked in that direction and I looked to my right across the street, where beyond the harried traffic spilling through Piazza Stazione stood the bare brick shoulders of the Basilica di Santa Maria Novella.

Near the taxis stood our program assistant, Julia, who quickly commenced the process of herding and shuffling us in groups into our separate cars while speaking in Italian to the drivers, English to the students. She was thin with black shoulder-length hair and must have been in her mid-thirties. I took the last in the long line of white Mercedes taxicabs, and nodded as she spoke about some things to me. Probably important things, these, but I wasn't quite following. She and I threw my stuff in the back and slammed the hatch.

"We'll be seeing more of you, I hope," I said.

"Pardon me?" she inquired, although I'm sure she heard me. She looked shocked in an amused sort of way, her hands on her hips.

I got in the back seat and slid to the opposite side of the driver so I could see him better. He looked French or Eastern European, with deep folds in the skin at the corners of his eyes and his forehead, which featured a deeply receding hairline, the hair brushed back. He began driving immediately, before he said anything. He smoked and changed the station to some American pop bullshit while drinking a Coke and shifting gears. I appreciated the gesture and then peeked behind us to see if I could discern why he was driving so fast. Caffeine and cigarettes were my best guess. I grabbed the handle on the door, like my mother did when I drove, but he couldn't see it.

"You are staying in Florence," he asked. "I just come to Florence. The women are cold—like ice"—he glanced in the rearview mirror for a second—"but you are an attractive man. You will have no problems."

"Thanks."

"You are American?"

His question was more like a statement, so I did not feel like I had to answer.

"I lived in America, for ten years. Een Manhattan. The Alphabet Deestrict. New Yourrk City. Eet ees a wanderrful city. Eet ees so wanderrful. But my wife"—he waved the hand that had been holding the wheel like he was pushing her away—"she leaves me. So I come to Florence, to be with my brothurr. Also he ees a taxi drrifer." He puffed his cigarette, looked toward the back seat with a grin, and said, "We can't drrife feefty-fife."

4

He cackled and looked in the mirror, and I gave an honest attempt at a good laugh. He deserved it, I figured. I was relieved when he looked at the street again. He looked like the type to be into Sammy Hagar. Not his Van Halen stuff—the straight-up Hagar stuff. I chuckled and trailed off, looked at my lap and tried to think of something to say. My mind was blank from exhaustion, though, so I just looked out the window at the misty streets, storefronts, and eighteenth- or seventeenth- or fifteenth-century apartment buildings, tinted orange in the streetlights. As we shifted and weaved, he recited the names of the streets to himself, and I got the feeling we were lost.

Grazia is Grace. Her name is Grace. That made sense. I felt much better.

"Via Nievo," he said with equal measures of surprise and satisfaction. We sped to midway down the street and stopped hard. We both got out, and he opened the hatchback of the Benz. He was a very thin man of average height in a sweater and pleated gray pants that his legs didn't fill. I dragged my bags out and then dug through my pockets for a tip, although I didn't know how much money to give him. That might have been the first time I had ridden a taxi all by my lonesome.

"No, no, no. The sexy woman—she take care of me. Maybe I go back and take care of her, no?" We both laughed, and it seemed loud in the quiet surroundings. "*Buona fortuna, amico,*" he said slowly.

"*Grazie mille,*" I said as he shook my hand firmly. He had big knuckles.

He got in the Benz and sped off. I stood a bit dazed for a moment on the damp and empty street, and realized I needed to focus. The silence startled me a little, and I wanted to enjoy it. I was surprised to have arrived at where I had been thinking of being for almost a year now. I reached in my pocket and pulled out a cigarette. In Europe, or at least in Heathrow Airport, the Camel Lights come in a pretty blue box with a giant "SMOKING KILLS" across the front. They also cost about nine dollars a pack. I snickered as I pulled one out, because I still had a hint of pride in my carelessness. I lit it and sat on my bags, and it occurred to me this was my first time living in a city, and that the cigarette smoke smelled sort of like a campfire as it blended with the iron-smelling Florentine air. I had never experienced the stillness of a city at night. It felt comfortable, and I thought about that for a minute. I enjoyed the quiet, the mist, the smoke, and the streetlights, but it wasn't long before things started to bother me again. I was a little raw after all of the traveling. I took one last long drag and stomped out the cigarette.

I picked up my bags, turned around, and rang the buzzer at the iron gate painted green. A window opened on the second floor of the two-story building, and the lovely voice of a woman sang out.

"*Pronto?*"

"Hello, it's William," I yelled back.

"*É Ferrguson?*"

"Hello, it's William Ferguson."

"*Sì, uno momento.*"

The gate buzzed, and I opened it, then walked straight, beyond the leafless trees and vines and such lining the short walkway, to the steps leading up to the front door on the side of the building. It cracked open and light spilled onto the stoop in front of me.

The woman leaned her head out the door and watched as I approached. When I reached the top of the steps, dragging my suitcase behind me, she opened the ten-foot-high oak door and shepherded me and my stuff into the space at the bottom of her gray granite stairs.

Signora Ridomi was really the matronly type of woman you would expect to meet while in Italy. She was plump but not fat, with dyed reddish-brown hair and a Roman nose. She wore gold jewelry and was dressed nicely in a light brown blouse and matching brown-gray pants with a smart-looking belt. She looked like she was in her sixties. She greeted me by reaching up and grabbing the back of my head with both of her hands and kissing past each of my cheeks, the way Europeans do.

"Grreetings...eh...*mi chiamo* Grazie."

"*Mi Chiamo* William."

"Sì. *Andiamo, subito. La cena diventa il freddo.*"

Obviously she spoke nearly no English, which was going to make things interesting, since I knew very little Italian. Something was cold, apparently.

We walked up the granite staircase, through two wooden interior doors painted white, down the hall past the den to the second room on the left, which was furnished with two twin-sized beds with two nightstands. The stone floors had simple patterns of green and red worked into them, and opposite the doorway a couple large windows overlooking the street filled the wall, with white curtains pulled to either side. To the left were some cabinets and an entire wall of bookshelves. I couldn't read much Italian, but most of the books seemed to be about socialism. There I put my bags down and met her son, who seemed to be in his thirties and apparently had developmental difficulties. I said hi to Sam, who had arrived on a cheaper flight the day before, and was also staying with the Signora. There was a lot of commotion as she tried to speak to me in bits of English and lots of Italian, Sam tried to interpret, and her son Gabriele repeated, "Mama...Mama... Mama..." to which she responded periodically with a patient, "*Uno momento,* Gabriele."

I gathered that it was dinnertime, as we were processing toward the kitchen at the back of the hall. I was as hungry as I was overloaded. The kitchen was cramped and looked like it was out of the mid-fifties in a charming sort of way. Dinner was on the table, and gave the impression it had been sitting there a while, but not too long. Since it was so late, everyone else had eaten.

I sat across from Grazia. Behind her was the sink, stove, and countertop. Gabriele sat to the left of me, and Sam sat to my right. Sam and I had grown up in Jersey together, went to the same grade school, and were great friends until about middle school. He would always be there with us starting fires or jumping off bridges, or whatever, but he never did any of it. We gave him hell for it, but he remained cautious. He moved out of town in seventh grade, but we went to the same high school. We hung out with different crowds, and really since elementary we hadn't been close at all. We both ended up going to Montpelier University, but didn't see much of each other. We would pass on campus once in a while, but that was about it. He was generally quiet, studious, and smart. When he called to tell me he was going on the Italy trip, too, I figured it was inevitable that we would be rooming together.

Signora Ridomi was a grade-school teacher, Sam told me. She sat up straight and had a very proper manner. The three of them, having already eaten, and probably having used up all of their foreign language skills, trained their curiosity on me.

"What is your name? I do not remember," she said.

"William."

"I am sorry. I do not...eh...know this wourrd."

"My middle name is Edward."

"EDUARDO!" She said with a flourish of her hands and a jubilant look on her face.

"Yes. Eduardo."

"I know Eduardo. I do not know this...othurr name." I didn't understand her through her accent, and I had to ask Sam what she was saying.

"Maybe there's no Italian translation for William," he explained.

"Then I guess I'm Eduardo."

"Yes, Eduardo! It is a name that is very...mmm... *aristocratico*. Do you know...this...ehh...wourrd?" As she spoke she straightened her back and lifted her chin and put her hand on her stomach.

"*Aristocratico? Sí. E la stessa parola negli Stati Uniti*," Sam said.

"What did you just say?" I asked.

"It's the same word in America. Aristocratic."

"Great." By mistake I made a face at the aristocratic thing.

"No, no, it is a good name. Very strong name."

"She wasn't as excited about my name," Sam said.

As I continued to eat—a large bowl of risotto, bread and olive oil, red wine, mineral water, roasted chicken, artichoke hearts prepared like little bowls stuffed with onions, seasoning, and a dash of bread crumbs, fresh slices of parmesan cheese, and a tangerine—she was pointing to the various implements and settings and giving me the Italian names for them. *Coltello...forketta...cucchiaio...piatto....*It was really grating on part of me but the rest of me was interested in learning.

When I finished dinner, she quizzed me on the things she had taught me. I got everything right, but I was tired and it was showing. She recognized this and got up to start clearing the table. Sam and I offered our help but she refused, less so it seemed out of a desire to serve us than out of a desire to keep us from messing stuff up.

We took turns in the bathroom, then I crossed the hall to the bedroom and flopped on the bed. With the scraps of consciousness I had before sleep, I said my prayers, the first of which I hadn't changed since I first started saying them.

There are four corners on my bed, a pillow for my little head. Matthew, Mark, Luke, and John, bless the bed I sleep upon. Amen. God bless everybody. Dear Lord, thank you for getting me here safely. Please forgive us for what we have done. I'm sure you have, but it's something I don't yet understand. Please help me then to stop asking you that. Tell her I am sorry and I love her. Teach me, Lord, please, to forgive myself.

CHAPTER 2

Our alarm went off at 7 a.m. It was an old one with an actual bell, the way it should be. The room was as dark as it was when we had gone to bed. Sam slept on the side of the room with the windows, so he got up and tugged the bottom of the shades, which flapped to the top of the windows. The morning light struck our side of the flat as the shades went up, filling the room, but without warmth.

I got my shower first while Sam ate, and then I ate while he showered. By the time I sat down, Signora had already left, and her housekeeper, Anna, was busy about the flat. Breakfast was bread left from the night before with jam or Nutella. I had a piece with each. Anna poured coffee from the percolator into a cup the size of a bowl. Even sweetened, it was a mighty brew.

I ate and read the sides of the milk carton, trying to translate what I could. As I finished my coffee, Sam came to the kitchen door with his backpack on.

"You ready?"

"Yeah."

As I was collecting things to put in the sink, Anna came in and insisted I stop, yanking the plate out of my hand and standing between me and the table. She said "no" sharply, then smiled and reached up and patted me on the cheek with her hand. She was a tiny and wiry woman who moved swiftly and was very serious about her tasks.

We walked out the giant front doors past the small flower garden that was dead for the winter, and through the iron gate to the sidewalk. The air was cold, and the sunlight was even and white like it is in January. It was much chillier than the night before, but the air was still. Sam had planned our route to school already. As we walked the streets, his guidance left my mind free to wander from the strange cars to the architecture and the smells—mustiness that had turned sweet in the frost.

At the end of the street was a small piazza where school kids passed a soccer ball around. They wore black Invicta backpacks with fluorescent details that I thought were pretty cheesy. Cheese would turn out to be a theme in Italy. The piazza had several bare trees with dirt underneath them, rather than grass, with a little concrete in the middle where the kids were. It hadn't been very well-maintained. When we reached the opposite side, there was a small flower stand like an oversized telephone booth. Standing outside of it was a young, thin, and smart-looking man with a kind face and little round glasses, a flat hat, and a scarf that dangled down to the middle of his black jacket, which had its collar flipped up. He said *buongiorno* to us as we passed in the way that Italians do—that is to say, he made it into a little three-note song.

We crossed the small street that surrounded the piazza. Sam stopped at a bus stop just beyond the corner and explained to me that in the blue folder was a ticket for the bus.

For a few minutes we stood in silence, and then an orange bus rounded the corner. We got on, and it was full of teenage Italian boys on their way to school with backpacks in obnoxious colors and with obnoxious amounts of gel in their hair, being obnoxious. A few of them were talking on cell phones, which were the most obnoxious devices to intrude on the landscape of the infant millennium.

"Do you have a cell phone?" I asked Sam.

"No. Do you?"

"No. I can't stand 'em," I responded.

He stared out the window for a minute, then said, "I thought they seemed pretty convenient."

"Why in the hell would anyone want people to always be able to find them? They're convenient for people who have succeeded in making their lives needlessly complicated. They're like cigarettes."

"Addictive?"

"Well, no. I mean, people do get addicted, but what I mean is that everybody is going to use them and then everybody is going to start dying of brain cancer, then...oops! We find out that cell phones cause cancer, and the cell phone industry knew it all along. By then, the executives, who all have rotary phones, will have cashed out, and we'll all wonder what the hell was so important that we needed a cell phone for it."

"Will."

"Yeah?"

"It's not even eight o'clock in the morning."

"Sorry. These things bother me."

Sam looked away toward the street. "This is our stop."

We got out and Sam took a quick look at his pocket map. We walked down to the end of the straight road along Piazza Santa Maria Novella toward the center of the city. As we headed further *in centro*, near the basilica, the products in the store windows were increasingly placed with a sense of vocation. By the time we made it to Piazza della Signoria, where our school building was, they were truly foreign. The displays in the *dolce* shops, tobacco stands, and cafés, all were works of art in themselves. It was as un-American as mass transit.

The narrow sidewalks on the narrow streets were full of people darkly dressed. The women, every one of them, were decked as boldly and as finely as the *ragazzi* were dressed in the other way, but all without venturing into the realm of the crass and the tasteless. Fur and leopard prints and leather and impossible heels with a stark and fearless walk like steel, forged on the cobblestones. I looked every one of them in their sharp eyes. While I could sometimes get the girls at school to smile, this was useless. I was looking pretty snappy this morning, in my mind, but nothing.

We arrived at another pair of towering oak doors to a building bordering the small, shaded piazza that looked, as many of the buildings did to me, like a castle. In the center of the piazza was a merry-go-round that was lit and attended, but no one was using it. One of the doors was open, and we walked in, where an attendant standing in a small booth by the elevator asked to see our school IDs. We then walked up six flights of gray, stone stairs and entered a small lobby, where a young woman probably a few years older than us with curly red hair, fair skin, brown eyes, and a pretty face sat behind a desk full of papers, a Rolodex, and a phone.

"You are from Montpelier?" she asked.

"Yes, we are," I said.

"Straight ahead, go to the third door on the rright."

"And what is your name?" I asked.

"My name ees Chiara," she responded carelessly.

"I'm Will and this is Sam," I announced.

"Eet ees a pleasurre to meet you. Eet is the thurrd door on thee rright," she said, with not a hint of interest in matrimony.

As we walked down the hall I told Sam about how greatly I favored red curly hair and accents, and that I was in love. He reminded me that she didn't look very interested. No matter, I said. She would come around. As we turned into the classroom, I noticed that she was walking behind us. Sam and I looked at each other and laughed as we sat down in the front row.

To my left was a studly and cheesy-looking guy with spiked blonde hair wearing a leather coat, designer jeans, and expensive-looking leather shoes, and who smelled a little like cologne. His arms were spread out across the backs of the two chairs next to him.

"Mournin', mate. Name is Dudley Ward. Chaps since the ferst form is taiken ta callin' me Doodles." An Australian, apparently.

"Morning, Doodles. I'm Will. People recently are taken to calling me Peachfuzz. This is Sam."

"Plezsha."

Dr. Sellier stood before the thirty-one of us and introduced himself, although most of us had already met him. He mentioned that his wife and his son would be joining us in two weeks and joining us on weekend excursions and many of our other activities. Our group was mostly girls.

He introduced Theresa and me, who had been chosen as Resident Advisors for the trip, which meant we helped him do some things and we got $600. We had to apply separately and have an interview.

As Dr. Sellier continued his introduction to the program, I took in the room. The worn carpet was a deep red. It hadn't faded much, because the giant windows with wavy glass and wooden edges and chipped paint faced out onto a small piazza—so the direct sunlight for the most part couldn't get past the building across the way. The ceilings were maybe

15

fifteen feet tall, and all of the heat in the room rose straight up and collected a few feet above where it could be of some help.

Dudley—Doodles—sat and didn't even pretend to be paying attention. He was looking around, too, but was doing it like he wanted other people to know he wasn't paying attention. He was chewing gum with his mouth open and biting his nails, with his arms still splayed across the backs of the chairs next to him.

The next item on the agenda was a tour of our classrooms, which took up the entire sixth floor. We got up and shuffled out slowly. Doodles, Sam, and I walked together. Our first stop was the computer lab, which was actually a dark room with two computers against a wall and a large table in the middle. The windows faced onto an alley. As Dr. Sellier was explaining things, Doodles, who was standing next to me, leaned over to Maria, a girl with reddish-brown hair, green eyes, a quiet demeanor, and a wide smile.

"Aye see ya looking at me. If this continues, you're going ta have ta buy me a drink."

She giggled politely, but was visibly puzzled. I was shocked myself; it wasn't something I'd ever do sober. We were only forty minutes into things, officially. I looked over at Sam to comment on how I couldn't believe this guy, but he hadn't seen it. He was listening to the tour.

We went on to the library, which was small and had books mostly about the history of art. We took a brief look at the classrooms, and the small room that was actually a hallway between the two wings, where people could come and buy things from vending machines and smoke if so inclined. There were windows above a few benches that one could open.

After that, we broke into our first intensive language class. The four other guys were in intermediate or advanced classes. Lily and I were in the beginner class, along with Ella, Amy, Crystal, and Melanie. The tables in the room were in a U shape, with the teacher's desk in the gap. I didn't want to sit right next to Lily, who had taken a seat already. I didn't want to be straight across from her either, so I sat at the bottom of the U, where I could see her left side. I did a lot of looking at her.

Our teacher introduced himself, Professore Paulo Fortunado. He dressed in a blazer, turtleneck, and khakis. He had dark hair and a full, trimmed beard, about half of it gray. He had clearly learned English from Britons, because when he didn't have an Italian accent, he had a British one, very polished and clear.

"Welcome to Florence," he said, in a relaxed, patient cadence. "This is the beginning of a wonderful adventure. I have lived here in Florence for my whole life, and it is a beautiful city. So many lives and so many of them giants— Dante, Boccaccio, Michelangelo, da Vinci, Raphael, Masaccio, Machiavelli, Galileo..." He sat back and looked around for effect. "Sometimes it boggles the mind." He looked at our faces for a moment. "It is the seed from which nearly all of Western civilization grew, at least so far as visual arts and science are concerned. And much of the literature. And here you are, in the middle. You may find yourself wondering if there is something about this place, and I tell you, it has been the experience of many that they have found Florence to be a place of much mystery. It can be a beautiful place. But at the same time, it is a very harsh city. Mary McCarthy described Florence as the City of Stone. It can be a very harsh city.

"I say this not to trouble you, but to give you a sense of what Florence is. It is beautiful and it is harsh, and thus, it is like man. And I do not mean here to be gender-specific." He looked at us for a second with a smile for his little joke.

"And so, I am quite pleased to meet you all. I can tell by the twinkle in your eyes that you are bright and eager students. I am already proud to be your teacher." He rubbed his beard and looked around at our faces again.

"Well," he said, as he sat up suddenly, like he had forgotten he had a class to teach. "And now, we begin, shall we?"

We started with the basics—"My name is; where's the bathroom? I like..." Most of it I already knew. It was a long class, because it was actually two classes in one; it was *intensive*. After the first hour, we got a break. Some people went into the computer room to check their email; I went into the smoking room.

A lot of the kids were there, including Doodles and Sam. The two of them were talking, and I bought an instant cappuccino and joined them.

"Will, roight?" Doodles asked me.

"Yeah, Dudley," I responded.

"Roight. But I'm more used ta Doodles. I was just asking Sam ova heah if he knows of any strip joints. You know of any?"

"I don't even know where to buy lunch," I mused.

"Shit. Can you imagine the fine-ass Italian women workin' there?"

"I've never been to a strip joint," I said.

"Are ya effin' kiddin' me?" he responded, exasperated.

"No."

"There's a place—many places—where you can go and at almost any time a' day you can watch ladies taike off their knickers an' waive their bare asses in yer face. And ya never been ta one?" he demanded.

"No."

"Neithah has Sam, here. Are you two gay for each other?" he asked with a smile.

"I'm not," I said.

"No," Sam said.

"Well shit. Aye gotta get you two to a strip joint, then," Doodles said.

"Whatever," I said. Sam didn't say anything.

At that I put out my cigarette, as it was time to go back to our classes.

CHAPTER 3

That night was our first official event—dinner at the Selliers' house, or Casa della Veritá, as he liked to call it. The dinner was at 6 p.m. and Sam and I, but mostly Sam, plotted our route to their place.

The two of us left Signora Ridomi's house at about 5 p.m. We decided to walk the whole way, in order to take in the sights. It was cold out and already dark. I put on my knit cap. We walked down Via Nievo to Piazza Indepenza.

"What do you think of Doodles?" Sam asked.

"I don't know. Probably a douche," I responded.

"Hmm," Sam said.

"What do you think?" I asked.

"I don't know. He seems a little annoying," Sam said.

"I'm not sure he can help it," I said.

"Probably not," he said.

"So are you going to go out and have a few drinks after dinner?" I asked.

"Yeah, definitely," he said.

We walked a minute without saying anything.

"So what's going on with you and Lily?" he asked, finally.

"Nothing, why?" I said.

"You were telling me that you two had hooked up..."

"I wouldn't say 'hooked up.'"

"Are you still hooking up?" he asked.

"Nah," I responded.

"Do you want to be?"

"You ask too many questions."

"No, really. Do you?" he asked.

"Probably," I admitted.

"I don't blame you," he said.

"She's a good girl. So who are you interested in?" I asked.

"I don't know yet. Melanie's cute. That girl Maria is cute, too. A lot of them are cute."

"It's true. And there's only five dudes," I said.

"It'll be a good trip," he said.

By then we were down by the train station, passing by McDonald's toward Santa Maria Novella.

All over there were bills posted on construction sites with a black-and-white picture of a woman's ass with the title "Shopping and Fucking." I couldn't tell what the meaning of it was, but I was guessing that it was a show of some sort. I got Sam to take a picture with me and the poster, with my finger pointing strategically. Another poster was an advertisement for a band named Murder Death Maim Dismember, with an upside-down pentagram and some guys with long hair, pointed beards, and leather jackets staring up at the camera.

We walked past the *duomo*, with the wedding cake facade decked in saints and twists and twirls and dandy things—if you saw it, you would know what I mean. I favored the statue of Mary holding the Christ Child that was its centerpiece. We went down past Piazza della Signorina, then across the Ponte Vecchio. Their house was a flat on a street just on the other side of the Arno, which was calm and reflecting the streetlights off of it. We crossed at the bridge and walked to our right down a street. There we found the entrance, which was a small archway in an ancient castle-like building on the west side of a small courtyard with restaurants on each corner.

We rang up and someone buzzed us in. We went up a staircase and found that five or six of the girls had made it before us. Most were helping Dr. Sellier in the kitchen. Sam and I tried to join them, but we weren't much help. The focus was all on Dr. Sellier, who was going on about Italian cuisine and the simplicity yet the boldness. He was jabbing his knife in the air, and holding up the ingredients to have others smell or look. He had our attention, to the woman.

After a minute, Dr. Sellier asked one of the girls to take over for a minute so he could take Sam and me around the flat. It was a pretty impressive place with portraiture, sconces, and giant windows with curtains that had tassels. By the time our tour was done, several other groups of students had arrived.

The meal wasn't that great. Most of us ate standing in the dining room, although some took seats. We were talking in small groups, and Lily and I stayed close since we were both more the type to keep to ourselves, and we knew each other. At first we were making conversation with the others in the crowd, mostly asking what their majors were, and for the people who weren't from Montpelier, asking about their schools—mostly in the mid-Atlantic states.

I didn't feel much like small talk. There was some wine, but not enough. So most of the time I tried to listen in on conversations that were already going on and chewed on my plastic cup.

Lily went to the bathroom, and I joined a conversation with Julia, the program assistant, and the fraternity and sorority people from our school. She had brought her daughter, who looked like she was about six years old. She was running around and being snotty to her mother. She had green eyes and black hair, like her mother, and was missing her two front teeth. Julia was explaining that she had come to Florence because she had had enough of London. She didn't have a job or a place to stay, and she didn't know the language.

Her daughter came up to her and started tugging on her shirt, saying "Mommy" as she tried to speak. Finally Julia acknowledged the girl, turned her around, put her hands on her shoulders, and said, "This, everybody, is my penance for a sinful life. Her name is Veronica."

The girls cooed over her, and her mother continued talking, telling us how it had been very difficult for a long time, especially when Veronica arrived, but that she was doing alright now. She explained it as baffling, how she could leave everything and put herself in the middle of a foreign country, not speaking the language and raising a small child, and find that everything was turning out alright, but it was. She said if there was any advice she could give to people younger than her, it would be to not worry about things too much.

Veronica was ready to leave, so Julia nodded to us all and began saying goodbye to the groups throughout the flat.

I remained with the Greeks, who started talking about other Greeks. This was a conversation I was happy to join, because there was almost no way for me to participate.

They were taking turns naming people from different sororities and fraternities whom they thought the others might know, and if another one of them knew that person, they would begin talking about them—their taste in clothes, their habits, their mannerisms, their drinking habits, their drug use, their performance in bed if it was common knowledge. This was precisely the reason I didn't rush, so my eyes started to wander.

I looked over to my left and saw Lily standing on the other side of the dining room table in front of a hutch. Above it on the rose-colored wall was a mirror with candles flickering from brass sconces. She was wearing a scarlet-colored cashmere sweater with a deep V-neck and a necklace with a diamond that, if it were real, would have been a carat and a half or so. Her left hand was playing with her necklace delicately. The lights from the candles twinkled off her dark eyes.

I walked over to her and asked her if everything was alright.

"Everything's fine," she responded.

"You look like something's wrong," I said.

"I don't know—I suppose I'm just not a person who has a smile plastered on her face all of the time," she said.

"Hmm. Didn't feel like joining the group?" I asked.

"Yeah...that's not my thing," she said.

I had a sip of wine, and Lily continued to play with her necklace, looking around at the decorations. I was watching the lights in her eyes. She looked at me.

"Will," she said, finally.

"Yeah."

"I'm glad I have such a good friend here."

"So am I."

"It's going to be a lot of fun," she said.

"I know," I responded.

CHAPTER 4

L ily and I were old friends who had become close again after a long separation. Our reunion, if you could call it that, happened two and a half years before Italy, at the beginning of freshman year in the unlikeliest of places, in the middle of the "Porn Storm." It was in every way one of those things you just didn't think happened in real life. As for the two of us, I had seen her around; we lived in the same dorm, but Porn Storm was when we really started talking again. You could go as far as to say it was a defining moment of my life, if for no other reason than that I had never been so embarrassed. You could tell from the poster hanging up in our dormitory as an advertisement that it was probably going to be trouble. I remember seeing it in the morning on the second day after I arrived at school on my way to breakfast. It said: "Cum on down and *really* get to know your neighbor at the PORN STORM."

It had an amateur-looking picture of a girl in nothing but white panties with "MU" in block letters written across her butt in red, sitting with her back to the camera and her face turned towards it, her legs straddling a classroom chair. "PORN STORM" was written on a chalkboard just in front of her, and the image had been cut and pasted onto a plain white background. She was a pretty girl with dark hair that complemented the white panties and red letters. Her expression suggested she had been talked into the whole thing. According to the rumor, she was our R.A. Jason's girlfriend. Jason we didn't like very much, for no reason in particular just yet. But it wasn't long before he started writing us up for our antics and stepped into the role.

Porn Storm was planned for a Thursday night at 7. The time was good, because it was early enough to watch some porn, go flog the dolphin, pregame, then go out and party the rest of the night and hopefully get laid. It was in the TV room, which had enough couches and chairs and study tables to hold a good crowd. The walls were made of concrete blocks on two sides, painted a yellowish-beige color. On the other two sides toward the hallway were windows like you would find in an office building or a school, so you could see who was in there watching TV and what they were doing.

A few of us—Brandon, Costigan, Gallo, Petrone, and myself—met at D hall at five thirty, then got back around six and played Asshole until seven and got pretty buzzed. By the time we got down to the room, the place was crammed with people. There was no room on any of the couches or the arms of any couches. There were people on the floor, and sitting on the Ping-Pong table and on the coffee tables. The air conditioning was on full blast in the rest of the building and it was cool, but in here it was hot. There were a good sixty or seventy people, and the mix was about 70/30, guys to girls. Kristen, who we had unofficially decided was Monroe Hall's hottest girl, was there, and a couple of my friends were sitting near her.

There were large plastic bowls being passed around. Some had popcorn, some had condoms. Some people had already inflated a few condoms and were bopping them around at each other. It was raucous. Guys were making moaning noises and pretending to hump the couch and putting their hands across their buddies' mouths and pretending to kiss them by kissing the backs of their hands.

When I saw the seating situation, I walked out across the hallway and grabbed a chair from the laundry room, and brought it in and sat a few feet in from the hallway, next to the couch. A lot of the girls giggled and made comments about the size of guys' packages, and weathered the pick-up lines. Kristen, who had hinted to a few of us that she was into watching porn, was feeding off it all by standing up and lifting her shirt a little and pulling her underwear out of her jeans to show the guys what color she was wearing. Red. Some other girls were sitting there looking like they were ready to leave.

I looked out through the glass to the hall and was surprised to see Lily Marconi walking toward the TV room by herself. At first, I figured she was going to do some laundry, but she walked in through the doorway and stood just to my left a few feet away. A couple guys whistled at her, and she smiled and closed her eyes with her hands on her hips when a condom fluttered through the air and smacked her in the forehead.

It had been years since I had seen her, and I couldn't believe how pretty she had become. Her eyes were still dark, dark brown and sparkled in the lights. Her hair hung wavy just past her shoulders and flopped to one side. She didn't have braces on her teeth anymore. That day she was wearing a shirt that was pink, with thin straps like ribbons that went over her shoulders, which were tanned. She had a white, flowing sort of cotton skirt on that went halfway down her calves. She looked almost bohemian, but she wasn't dirty or anything. She didn't have to try, so she didn't put a whole lot of time into worrying about how she looked.

When I knew her before, there were certain things about her that made me assume she was not the type of girl I would find at Porn Storm. She may have had the same thought about me. When she walked through the door, I guessed she had changed a little. I wasn't sure if I liked that, but I didn't think very much about it.

She didn't notice me immediately, so I stood up, and we were face to face, except she was shorter. Seeing her made me a little embarrassed to be there, but she was there, too, so I was confused about how to feel.

"Hi," I said after a second.

"Oh, hi, Will. How are you?" She flashed her bright smile and looked like she was honestly happy to see me.

"Good, thanks. Did you want to sit down?" I motioned for my chair.

"No, thanks," she said.

"No, please. I can get another chair from across the hall," I said.

She looked down at the chair and seemed to think about it for a second. "Alright," she said finally, without looking up, and sat down. Chivalry, even in the midst of the Storm. My friends looked up at her, and they said hi to each other.

I walked across the hall again and got another chair, and brought it back in, wondering why other people hadn't thought of that. I got in the room and kicked Petrone to get him out of the way. He cursed at me and moved, and I sat next to Lily on the side closest to the door. She was taking in the sights.

I personally had not seen much porn that wasn't scrambled. I had been getting it off the internet since I was thirteen, but only at my friends' houses, and it was before you could get whole movies on the internet. It was also before there was so much free stuff out there, that I knew about at least. To be honest, I was more interested in the girls in real life.

So sitting there, I didn't know what to say to Lily. This was one of the more baffling situations I had experienced.

"So, I didn't know you were coming to MU," I said finally.

"Yeah—I didn't know you were coming, either. This is a pleasant surprise, Will," she said.

"Really?" I asked, surprised.

"Really. I've missed you," she said.

"Thanks. I've missed you, too," I said. I really did. I regretted how things had ended, and thought about it from time to time.

"Didn't think I'd see you at Porn Storm," I said.

She looked at me and smiled again. "Yeah," she said, nodding slightly, and like there was more she wasn't saying. We both giggled a little, nervously.

At that, Jason, the R.A., got up and stood in the space between the huge TV and the students on the floor. Two of the other R.A.s were in the room—one of the guys and one of the girls.

"Hello, Monroe Hall perverts, and welcome to Porn Storm," Jason bellowed above the noise. There was a huge roar, and the guys slapped their hands against tables and the floor, making a thumping sound, and popcorn and condoms flew through the air.

"We have a delightful selection for you tonight."

"YOUR GIRLFRIEND IS HOT!" one voice cried out, and then there were some cheers and laughs.

"She's not my girlfriend...anymore." He smiled, and laughs broke out throughout the crowd.

"Okay. Tonight, I have selected for you five gems from the Monroe Hall Resident Advisor collection. Which...is my collection." There were a few laughs. He held in his hands five

VHS tapes, and looked down at them and shuffled them as he read their names. "There's *Backdoor Angels*." A roar went through the crowd, with a bit of a laugh. "There's *Babysitters with Benefits*, starring Stella Rockefeller." A slightly louder roar went through the crowd. "There's *Kitty Initiation, Episode 19*." The cheering was much louder and more prolonged. Lily turned to me.

"What is *Kitty Initiation*?" she asked.

I hesitated. "I haven't seen any of these."

"Right," she said.

"Seriously. Anyway, *Kitty Initiation* is where it's the girl's first time doing porn. There's a whole series."

Jason held his freer hand out to quell the uproar a little.

"Then there's *Kitty Initiation, Episode 21—Three Kitties on their 18th Birthday*." The room went berserk. Some of the guys were picking up the coffee table things and pounding them on the ground and pounding on the floors, tables, and their chests. The girls were putting their fingers in their ears.

Lily, with her finger in her right ear, leaned toward me.

"Do I even need to ask?"

"This is the one with Kitty Claire."

"Oh," Lily said, nodding.

Episode 21, as the newspapers and tabloids called it, was a national phenomenon. It started when the production company, Twisted Pink Productions, held a nationwide "talent" search for three girls turning eighteen on a certain date in '96. They had casting calls in New York, Los Angeles, and Little Rock, Arkansas, which they picked because it was the Bible Belt and because it had certain political significance at the time. They had thousands of applicants, supposedly, and picked one girl from each location. The winners did photo shoots and interviews after filming for publicity. The girl who became Kitty Claire was the one from Los Angeles. Basically, she was the prettiest, so she had gone on to make four more movies in less than a year. There was going to be another talent search for one of the guys or girls to star in her fifth film, but the project was scrapped after she was hospitalized for exhaustion. Kitty Claire was dedicated, at least.

Because there had been so much controversy over the talent searches, politicians and prosecutors got involved and a few state laws were passed against recruiting girls for the sex industry before they turned eighteen, which the porn industry challenged on First Amendment grounds. There was also a huge dispute about whether she had actually been eighteen in the first one, which only made the demand for it stronger. The Department of Justice got involved, but in an investigation they had trouble verifying her birth date, since she was Romanian, and they dropped it. On top of that, the video got held up because of some distribution dispute, so this one hadn't come out until just a few weeks before. All of this was in the news for more than a year, which could not have been better for the great Americans at Twisted Pink.

This particular video had a limited release in theaters, and then went on to be the best-selling porn video in history, in only a couple weeks. Copies of it were selling on the internet for $250. I hadn't seen it or bought it, for the record. I was curious, though, and maybe not for the reasons you think.

Jason didn't even bother trying to talk over the crowd, which was now chanting, "Kitty Claire, Kitty Claire, Kitty Claire." He turned on the giant TV, which was tuned to ESPN, and looked down at the remote to switch to video access. The screen turned black, and the crowd started to die down. He bent over and fed the cassette into the machine, and the FBI warning came up on the screen. The crowd was now silent, and after all of that noise it sounded eerie. I noticed my leg was touching Lily's, so I moved it.

A cheap computer graphic came up on the screen: *Kitty Initiation, Episode 21: Three Kitties on their 18th Birthday*. The Twisted Pink Productions logo—the silhouette of a naked woman reclining, her hair flowing in the wind behind her, on a strand of pink ribbon—was below it. The title and the logo faded out, and slowly the picture faded in of three girls sitting silently on the edge of what looked like a large hotel bed. Claire was seated in the middle, and although all three were somewhat pretty, she was the prettiest, with large blue eyes and other occasions of largeness. She was wearing a low-cut tank top and jeans. The girl to the left had a black miniskirt on and a white tube top. The girl on the right was in a dress that had a halter-top that crossed at her breasts and became a short skirt at the bottom. It was pink. They looked like three regular girls off the street, which was the point. It was interesting to see Claire pre-superstardom. Her hair was brown in this film and had turned platinum blonde soon after. Her clothes looked plain, and she had no accessories but a tiny silver necklace with a medallion on it. She was beautiful without all of the glitz and the makeup. The girls were smiling and blinking, but not saying or doing anything.

The camera panned out, and from the left, in walked a paunchy middle-aged guy in a three-piece pinstripe suit with a groomed beard and a ponytail. He had become a familiar face, since he was apparently the owner of this production company, but I forgot his name. He had been an activist and a politician for a while, then a music exec, then this.

"Hello, and welcome to Episode 21 of my revolutionary *Kitty Initiation* series," he commanded. "Today we are very lucky to have three gorgeous young ladies here with us...all of them celebrating their eighteenth birthday by putting on a little show for us. All unscripted, all unrehearsed, all for the first time." He looked down at them, and all three of them were looking up and toward him like they were cartoon birds in a nest. "Isn't that right, girls?" They all giggled a little.

Lily shifted in her seat. She seemed a little antsy. I guess I was a little, too.

"Let me start by getting to know you girls a little. Let's start with you, Dollie." The camera zoomed in a little on the girl to the right, but without cutting the other girls out. Looking up at the bearded man, she said, "Uh, hi, my name..."

"Into the camera, beautiful. We want to see your pretty young face," he said.

"Oh," she giggled. "Sorry. My name is Jenny—" The video beeped and blanked out her mouth.

"No last names, beautiful, please."

She giggled, and so did the other two girls.

"Oh, I'm sorry," said Jenny.

"It's okay. Maybe I'll give you a little spanking later," said the talking beard.

"Ooh, uh, okay," she said like she was surprised, then looked at the other girls and giggled.

"When were you born, sweetheart," asked the beard.

"June 6th, 1978," Jenny assured him.

"That makes you eighteen today, right?"

"Yep, that's correct," she responded.

"Tell us what you like to do when you're naked," he said.

"Well, I don't know...I'm *very* open-minded," she responded.

"Like what? What do you like to do?" he insisted.

"Uh, lots...I'm sorry—I'm a little nervous," she said.

"It's okay, sweetie. You're doing great," he reassured her. "Do you like to be spanked?" he asked.

"Not *too* hard!" She laughed nervously. The other two giggled. "But yeah...I'm, uh, naughty sometimes," she said, trying to play it cool.

"Tell me, Jenny, have you ever made love in front of a camera before?" he asked.

"No, never." She paused for a minute, and looked a little confused about what else to say. "I can't wait," she said finally, and looked up at the guy.

"Okay, now on to you, sweetheart," he continued, putting the next girl and then the third girl through the same routine.

"Now—before we start, do any of you know each other?" he asked.

"No," they all said, shaking their heads.

"Why don't you all exchange kisses a little, to get to know one another. Just a quick kiss, nothing else," he said.

At that, the camera panned out a little, and the girls did his bidding. Afterward, the camera panned out to include the bearded man, who was looking down at them.

"Congratulations, you beautiful, beautiful girls. That was your first kiss on camera—your maiden voyage into the adult world. It's a wonderful birthday present, isn't it?" he asked like a proud...pornographer.

They nodded and laughed a little.

"You have beautiful things ahead. I'm proud of you girls," he said.

"Thank you," they seemed to have said. With that, the bearded man took off his jacket and sat down on the left next to Kitty. I really wanted him to shut up.

"Think you could give me a little kiss, sweetie?" he asked her.

She shrugged her shoulder a little, straightened her back, and leaned over and kissed him. She seemed almost like she wanted to impress him with how much tongue she gave him. She moaned a little and he reached up to her breast and mashed it up against her chest. It lasted a few seconds, and he pulled back and smiled.

"I'm so happy to have such beautiful faces here today. Look what you've done." He leaned back and looked down at his lap. "That's a real compliment." They looked at each other and giggled.

"You're going to help me with that, aren't you, Kitty?" he asked.

As that was happening, Lily started standing up. I was glad, because it was getting officially weird with her right next to me. I had always remembered her as a good girl. I figured she had had enough, or maybe that she had to go to the bathroom. She turned around and picked up her chair. In the background I could hear the bearded man giving rather specific instructions to the girls. I was watching Lily with a little curiosity.

She turned around with her chair in her hand and lifted it up high enough not to hit other people in the head with the legs. She had to navigate around several people sitting on the floor, some of whom grumbled. She was walking toward the TV, and I was beginning to wonder what was going on.

She put the chair down next to the huge TV, and by then people were telling her they couldn't see. She sat down on the chair, looked up at the audience, and crossed her legs. Her calf-length skirt slipped to just below her knee when she did that, her sandal dangling off her toes.

What the hell was she doing? I wondered, as whispers started to trickle through the audience. Did she want to join the show? If that was the case, then she had changed *completely*. The crowd was half watching her, and half of them had not even flinched, being so absorbed in the action.

I looked a little above Lily's legs, where she had placed something in her lap—a small cloth bag with a string cinching it. The whispering in the crowd had become a murmur. She was looking down at it and undoing it with her wavy hair dangling a little past her face. I was wondering what it was, and the only thing that popped into my head was a…device. I was embarrassed at myself when I saw her pull out what was clearly a strand of rosary beads. She looked at a place in between the crowd and the TV, crossed herself, and started praying silently, barely moving her lips.

Instantly when people saw the rosary, there was a collective groan. Shouts started coming from the crowd, "Get the hell outta here!" and "Church is on Sunday, bitch!" with some laughs. After that, little bits of popcorn started flying through the air and landing near her, some of it in her lap, some of it in her hair. Then condoms, packaged and unpackaged, started fluttering through the air and hitting her in various places, and one got stuck in her hair.

"Go back to the Bible Belt!" screamed one admirer. "You need some good cock!" was the recommendation of another, probably from the pre-med program.

Cooler heads were yelling to the others, "Just ignore her! She's a dumb bitch! Ignore her; don't let her ruin it!"

The popcorn and condoms were flying through the air with more frequency, as were the shouts. After not too long the crowd began chanting, "Suck it!" over and over again. Others started chanting, "Show your tits!" and gradually that became the consensus.

Costigan turned around and looked up at me.

"You know this girl?" he asked.

"Who?" I responded.

"The one sitting next to the TV, who was sitting next to you, who is now getting shit thrown at her," he said like I was an idiot.

"Kinda," I responded.

The popcorn-and-condom thing was getting worse. Some people started throwing change at her. Her eyes were tearing up. One of the hard plastic popcorn bowls bounced off the floor and hit her in the calf, then wobbled through the air and hit the wall behind her. I could hear Costigan say, "That's messed up." Meanwhile, the girls and the creepy guy on the screen were mostly naked, doing various things, making this quite an interesting scene.

When loose change started hitting her, I knew I had to do *some*thing. I stood up with my knees slightly buckling, not knowing what to do, exactly. Like I was watching myself from somewhere outside my body, I turned around and got my chair, then worked my way through the crowd, putting it down just to the left of Lily. I sat down with her facing the crowd, which was apparently angrier that someone else had joined her, or liberated, because the guys apparently felt they didn't have to try to *not* injure me with what they were throwing. Luckily—for her, at least—people started taking their increased frustration out on me. The popcorn wasn't too much of a bother, except that I had just taken a shower and didn't feel like getting filthy again.

The condom packages were what stung a little, especially when they hit my face, and the change just hurt when it hit any part of my head, but was less frequent. Soon the bowls that held the condoms and popcorn headed my way, one hitting me in the leg, the other in the right shoulder. The popcorn bowl was half full, and it got all over me. I looked at Lily, who was still praying, apparently. Her eyes were closed, and there were a few tears running down her cheeks. She was getting hit, but not as bad. She hadn't flinched, but she looked like she was shaking. I was, too.

Next came the plastic cups people were using for soda, many of them full or half full. I would definitely have to take another shower. When a full can hit the ground in front of me and exploded, to cheers, Jason got up and turned the lights on.

That got a worse reaction from the crowd. People started standing up and heading toward the door, screaming in our direction. Many of them on the way bent over and got inches from our faces, yelling assorted niceties. Guys were walking by Lily and grabbing their crotches and shaking them in front of her face, telling her to suck it. Some other guys pretended to masturbate in front of her and pantomimed ejaculating onto her face. She didn't open her eyes or move; she just kept praying and closed them tighter.

Jason and the other R.A.s started waving people through the door and telling them to go watch something in their rooms. When the people had left, Jason turned to face us, both of us covered in popcorn, soda, and condoms.

"So are you two, like, the God Squad for Monroe Hall?" Jason asked. "This isn't Steubenville."

Lily looked up at him and asked, "If I called you a douchebag, would that answer your question?" I chuckled to myself a little bit. He looked a little mad. I didn't have anything to say, since I was still trying to figure out what had just happened.

"You didn't have to make a scene. You could have just remained with the elect in your rooms. You can clean this shit up." He left.

Lily put her face down in her hands and started to sob softly, with the beads dangling from them. She wasn't making any noise, just shaking from the sobs and the trembling. I brushed some of the popcorn off of myself and scooted my seat over toward her and put my arm around her.

It didn't stay there long, though, because in the background I could hear a cacophony of moans, like cats wailing, and skin slapping. I got up and hit the Stop button and then both power buttons, without looking up at the TV. I walked over to the table set up on the other side of the room and got a handful of napkins and two bottled waters and walked over to her, pouring water on one of the napkins and handing it to her.

She looked up at me and had soda and tears dripping from her face. A popcorn kernel was stuck on her cheek, and I chuckled at her. She laughed, too.

"You haven't changed," I said.

"You have," she said.

"Not really," I responded.

I wet my own napkin and started washing my face off.

"I never got to apologize to you," I said.

"I think you just did, Will." She brushed off her skirt with her napkin. "But I wasn't looking for an apology."

"Hmm." I looked around at the trash that had collected around our seats. "So did that go how you planned it?"

"I didn't plan it," she said, not looking up from wiping things off her skirt.

"Hmm." I wasn't going to pursue it right then. I reached out and offered my hand, and I noticed how soft hers were when she took it after putting her rosary away and brushing some of the wet popcorn off of her lap. I started walking out the door, and she hesitated.

"I need another couple seconds, Will," she said.

"Okay. Did you want me to stay with you?" I asked.

"No, you don't have to. What you did was very nice. Thank you for your help," she said.

"No problem."

I figured she wanted to be alone, so I started walking down the hall toward the stairs, and started thinking about how much shit I was going to get from my friends, many of whom had just been cursing at me and throwing stuff. I opened the door to the stairwell and began going up the stairs, then stopped. I decided it wasn't a good idea to leave her by herself. With all of the booze and sex and anger, who knows what would happen. I turned around and walked down the hall, and when I could see into the room, I saw Lily bent over by the TV, picking popcorn kernels up off the floor and putting them onto a plate.

"What are you doing?" I asked, a bit shocked.

"The place is a mess," she responded.

"Lily—are you nuts? You didn't do this..."

She didn't pause. "Will, I'm okay. It's not a big deal; I figured I'd help out."

I sighed and grabbed a couple paper plates off the floor and bent over by the TV and shoveled popcorn onto one with the other.

When I got to the area in front of the TV, I looked up at the VCR below it on a shelf in the entertainment center, which had the stack of videos next to it. Both the VCR and the videos were drenched in soda, and a puddle had collected. There was about an entire can's worth there, and it hadn't been there when I had turned off the video. I stood up and looked over at her—she was concentrating on picking bits of popcorn out of the Berber rug. She noticed me looking at her and smiled without standing up.

"What?" she asked, her smile getting bigger as she looked back down at the ground.

"Nothing," I said, then wiped up the soda that had collected on the shelf.

After a few minutes, Costigan and Petrone came through the door. I was nervous about what they were going to say.

"You two alright?" Petrone asked.

"Yeah," I said.

"Dude, they were throwing soda cans at you," Costigan said.

"I know—one hit me in the shin. Friggin' hurt," I said.

"That was some crazy shit," Petrone said.

"Petrone, I saw you. You threw your cup at me," I said.

"Yeah..."

I figured he would say something else, so I just kept looking at him. It took him a second. "I don't know. I figured it was the last chance in my life I'd get to throw something at you as part of an angry mob."

"Thanks," I said.

"No, Peachfuzz, thank *you*. For the opportunity." Peachfuzz was my nickname, which they invented for me almost immediately. I hated it.

"Happy to oblige," I said through the side of my mouth.

"Actually, I was kinda glad for that to be over," Costigan said. "It was getting a little creepy."

"Yeah, that dude was creeping me out," I said.

"The girls, on the other hand, were *smok*ing," Petrone said.

"Claire or Kitty Claire or whatever is pretty hot, but I don't know about the other two," I said. I wanted to tell them, but decided against it.

"I liked Kitty Pink. She had a down-home look," Costigan said. At that, Lily, who had been walking around and finishing up, told us she was leaving. We all said goodbye, and Petrone and Costigan said sorry to her for what had happened. I asked if she wanted us to walk her up, but she said no, she'd take the elevator. That way, she'd miss the guys' floor. Once she had gone, Petrone looked at us.

"Dude," Petrone said, "let's pop in the movie."

"Nah, it got soda all over it," I said.

"Really? Dude—Jason is going to be *pissed*," he said.

"Sucks for him," I said, shrugging my shoulders.

"Peachfuzz, how do you know that girl?" Costigan asked.

"Who, Lily?" I asked.

"Yeah."

"She and I used to be close when we were younger, but she moved away," I said.

"She's *hot,* dude," he said.

"She's got quite a shapely ass," Petrone noted. "I saw her going to the gym one time in some shorts, and man, that girl is *fit.*"

"She's got some nice breasticles, too," Costigan added.

"Yeah. She's hot. Definitely hot," I said. "I think she's on scholarship."

"Hmm," responded Costigan.

"So what did everybody do? Are they at that girl Kristen's now?" I asked. Kristen had jokingly said she would do a show for us after the Storm.

"No, everyone's at my place playing Asshole. Kristen went out to some frat," Costigan said. His room was right next door to mine. "Why don't you get a shower, finish telling your beads, and come get drunk?" The two of them laughed.

The three of us walked up and passed a couple guys who had been there and were standing in the stairwell talking, but not about Porn Storm. They glanced at me and didn't say anything, but after I passed, one of them started clapping, mockingly.

When we got up to our rooms, they knocked on Costigan's door. Someone on the other side said, "Who is it?" and came the answer, "Don't be a cocksmooch." It was our secret line to tell the others that we were not R.A.s.

I went into my room, and it was empty. I went into the bathroom, which we shared with the people in the room next to ours, and looked in the mirror and sighed. My hair was all matted down to my head, and my shirt was stuck to my chest, and there were pieces of yellow popcorn all over. I was most concerned with the shorts, which I had just bought and which were now covered with soda and bits of popcorn. I took everything off and put it in my sink, which I stopped up and filled with water, then I took a shower.

When I was done I got dressed and combed my hair and everything, then I walked next door, which still had lots of noise and loud music coming from it. It was one of Tom Petty's greatest hits—"Runnin' Down a Dream." I knocked and was nervous, because I knew I was going to get a bunch of shit.

"Who is it?"

"Don't be a cocksmooch."

The door opened, and on the other side was Brandon, who lived on the other side of me and shared a bathroom with us. He didn't drink because of some family history.

"Peachfuzz, what's up? You alright?" he asked.

"Yeah, fine," I said.

"You got a mark on your forehead," he said.

"Maybe it was from a can," I said.

"Geez, dude. That shit was scary," he said.

"Yeah. It sucked," I responded.

From inside the room someone shouted, "Look! It's the God Squad!" And everyone joined in clapping and cheering. As I walked closer to the circle, a condom flew through the air and hit me in the forehead, and everyone laughed.

"Pull up a seat, Father Peach," Gallo said, moving over on the couch we had stolen from Alpha Kappa Lambda. "Father, I confess I just had sex with your mom. Please, have pity on me."

I sighed, sat down, and said, "Can someone grab me a beer please?" More laughing.

Skeeter, my roommate, handed me a can of Busch Light, which was nice and cold, and I chugged it without coming up for air. I crushed the can and asked for another, which I also chugged. It got some notice from a couple guys. I asked for another, and my stomach was pretty full of air, so I had to take it easy and make sure I burped a little. It was pretty overwhelming, all that had just happened, and a couple times I had to choke back tears, but I was feeling a little better now.

CHAPTER 5

The school newspaper did a write-up of the story—"Good Girl Quells Porn Storm." with the subhead "Who is this girl, whom even the wind and waves obey?" The article was pretty fair, but the mail was insane. The grievance-industry-in-training didn't know what the hell to make of it. Some approved but thought she had spoiled it by doing it in the name of such a patriarchal, patronizing, arcane institution. One of the professors wrote a letter saying basically the same thing, except she scolded Lily for squandering the sexual liberation from our male-dominated society that she and her sisters had worked so hard to achieve. Others said Lily was wrong because the actresses could do what they wanted with their bodies, but then they felt bad for criticizing her, because Lily was a woman, so if she wanted to use her body to pray in front of people watching porn, then she should be allowed to do that with her body. One girl asked that Lily print her address so she could send a video of her having sex with her girlfriend to open up her bigoted mind. In the next issue, five guys offered their addresses. I realized then that college wouldn't be so difficult, because I was surrounded by idiots.

After a few weeks, most people forgot about it. They started focusing on homecoming. More people weren't there than were there, anyway. They tried to do Porn Storm the next month, but a couple girls who weren't Lily started a dorm petition against it, and the petition was popular enough—especially with the girls—to nix it.

Lily did get a reputation, though. Among the guys, it was a joke about who would corrupt her, and how she was like the grand prize because obviously it was so hard to get into her pants. Sometimes I would try to put a stop to it, but that would just get me harassed, so most of the time I would just try to change the subject or leave the room.

She became active with the Catholic group, which had dances and gatherings and that sort of thing. She asked me to go often, but I went only once or twice. She was just notorious enough for people every once in a while to randomly call her a bitch or a virgin whore while I was walking with her around campus. I would have punched them if they hadn't all been girls. Some girls thanked her.

So as one might expect, after that episode Lily and I started hanging out again. I never asked her what she had been thinking that night. I figured she would tell me if she thought it was something worth explaining.

When we were in catechism class as kids together it was annoying, because she would always ask questions and it would turn out that a lot of the time she knew better than the teacher did, and sometimes it looked like she was showing off. I told her that one time, and she told me she had a duty to make sure the other students were informed. I told her she had a duty to stop being such a dork. But I didn't bother her too much, because she would give me the answers to the homework in the time between Mass and class.

She was at my school only for two years—fourth and fifth grade—but we were close then, too. In fifth grade, though, at the beginning of the year, we found out we had Family Life class once a week. It was with Ms. Daphne, the school nurse. She had curly brown hair that went halfway down to her butt. She wore glasses sometimes and these awful pleated khaki pants with Wigwam socks and sweatshirts. We all thought she was cool, though, because she was young and did cool things like write the word "fuck" on the board to tell us that it used to be a legal term that meant "forced unlawful carnal knowledge." The first subject was family relationships, and then the next subject for just a week was how we needed to tell someone if adults touched us inappropriately. Then the next week was the sex unit. I remember the yellow book with the red letters "S-E-X" written on it, and learning about orgasms, and masturbation, and "sex play." Who the hell knew?

This was a small school, and there were only eight of us in our grade. The first class started with Ms. Daphne telling us that for the next month or so we would be talking about sex. We would be going in the opposite sex's bathrooms, and learning about a lot of things that would make us giggle, but it was information we needed to know. It was a long talk, and we were all dead silent. Then she gave us our assignment, which was to draw ourselves naked—what we looked like then—and then what we thought we would look like naked in ten years. She said it wasn't for a grade, and that only she would be looking at it.

Lily raised her hand and told Ms. Daphne she didn't want to participate. She said Lily didn't have to, but that most students would be, and it would be hard to participate in the class if she didn't do the assignment, and since it was such a small class, if there was a student who wasn't participating, then it would make class less effective. Lily said she understood that, and she still didn't want to do it.

It's hard to say, but that might have been the worse decision for Lily. The whole thing made me feel pretty sick and embarrassed, but I also didn't want to make a big deal about it, or to get a bad grade. And I didn't want to get the treatment Lily ended up getting. Two of the other girls in class—Casey and Mackenzie—were best friends and nasty girls at the time. And the fact that Lily didn't want to do it, and the next day got permission not to take the class, led to speculation about why she didn't want to do it, coming from the girls, mostly.

All week, there was talk about her having a hairy butt, or warts all over herself, or hairy moles, being covered in sores or having AIDS. Every day it was something different. The next Thursday at the lunch table we all had our drawings with us, since it was the class after lunch. Randy Murdoch, who was a year older than all of us but in our grade, and fat, was demanding to see everyone's pictures. This started the business of passing our pictures around and commenting on them. Lily was sitting across from me, looking miserable. She didn't have a picture to pass around, but one started going around that somebody else had drawn, and it had a penis and hair and sores and zits with her name on the top. The two of us were sitting on the end of the table and Randy was waving the picture in her face, so she turned away towards the windows, put her face in her hands, and started crying.

This was sort of the beginning of a trend—it opened up the floodgates for everyone, especially Casey and Mackenzie, to treat her like hell. They used to put tacks on her seat and call her AIDS girl, whore baby, or horse face. For a long time Randy pretended he was in love with her and wrote her love notes about how he wanted to get his lips caught in her braces, and got down on his knees and said he wanted to catch AIDS from her. I didn't join in; I didn't laugh; I just didn't do anything to stop it. Over time, we talked less and I hung out more with the guys. I was the only one in the class who had been with her, and when I left her she was alone. Before the end of the year, she left the school. And that's what I regretted over the years from time to time. So I was surprised that when we met again, she didn't hold anything against me. She had every right to.

Katrina Ivanski moved into my school the next year. Katrina Ivanski, whether you believe me or not, is the girl who would become Kitty Claire. She was my second love, I guess, since Lily must have been my first in an innocent sort of way. Not so much with Kat—the innocent part.

She was Romanian but born in Bayonne, New Jersey. After her father and her mother split, she moved to Chelsea and was in the grade below me at my school. She was seventeen when she did the film. How the Justice Department didn't figure this out was a mystery to me. The only thing I could figure was that maybe they knew and didn't care but wanted to look like they were doing something. Maybe they were just incompetent. The Romanian accent was fake.

When she got to school I instantly had a crush on her, but she started dating Kevin, a seventh grader. It used to make me jealous, but every time I saw the first star at night or my eyelash fell out, I would wish to date Katrina.

This wish came true when I was in seventh grade. Over the next few years, even after we broke up, Katrina and I used to hang out together all of the time. All of that changed, though, when Ms. Daphne became roommates with Katrina's mom. Katrina stopped calling me and stopped hanging out with me. Things were bad at home, as they had been for a couple years now, so I felt lonely a lot. When she finally told me that she and Ms. Daphne were spending every Saturday at home making love while her mom was at work, it almost made my head explode. She told me not to tell anyone. The thought that there was something wrong or illegal about that, other than the fact that it wasn't me, didn't enter my head, because Ms. Daphne seemed young and she treated us like adults. She was convicted several years later for doing the same thing to another girl at school.

I thought about telling people at Montpelier that I used to date Kitty Claire, but I knew that nobody would believe me, and then they would make fun of me for thinking that I had.

I told Lily and told her not to tell anyone. She said she was a very pretty girl and wanted to know how I felt seeing her on the video. I told her I wasn't very surprised, but it made me want to pull the guy's nuts out through his teeth. At least I finally got to see her naked, mostly. I thought the fake accent was clever and well-done. But I felt bad for her—really bad. Lily told me she would pray for her, and I hadn't thought of that, so I started, too. I told her to pray for me, and she said that she already did.

CHAPTER 6

It was nearing the end of freshman year, and it had been one of those days, the false spring, when the temperature shoots up to 78 degrees for a day, and you think that finally all of the loveliness of spring is here, but by the end of the week, the frost and the sleet return. The party was at the student apartments just off campus. A few of my buddies—Brandon, who was drinking by then, Johnny X, Petrone, and Costigan, and maybe a couple other guys—were there, and so was Kristen from the third floor. The guys had all walked with me to the party, and Kristen was already there. By the time we arrived, I was pretty drunk, and I think the rest of the group was, too, since we had been to a party already. We had tried for a minute to go to a second, but on our way to walk through the apartment to the beer, we found there were too many people for us to get to the back porch. Quickly we all agreed that we didn't want to deal with the crowd. Kristen ran into us right as we were leaving and decided to come with us to the next one, which was a party at the house of one of the Alpha Kappa Lambda brothers. Kristen, I had gathered, did a lot of hanging out with AKL brothers. None of our friends liked the frats. We saw them as a sign of insecurity. But we didn't mind drinking their beers, it wasn't a far walk, and it was warm outside. On the way, Kristen was telling me how she hoped Tony wouldn't be there. I didn't know who Tony was, and I didn't care, so I didn't pursue the matter.

The next party wasn't as crowded, but there was a decent amount of people. There were plenty of comely sorority chicks and beefy fraternity dudes doing stupid things. We walked to the back of the apartment onto the back porch, got our beers, and stood out there. I had already had a twenty-two-ounce Heineken, so I didn't need any at the time. Some of us lit cigarettes and started chatting. Kristen bummed one off of me.

"So where are you from again?" I had seen her around quite a bit, and sometimes she hung out with me and Lily, but we had never really gotten into a conversation between just the two of us. I couldn't think of anything else to talk about.

"New Jersey," she said.

"Really? I didn't know that—me too. What part?"

"Glen Rock."

"That's right across the bridge from the city right?"

"Kinda."

"So you're the people who come to my town to take a shit on it," I said.

"Where are you from?"

"Chelsea."

"Ew. And, like, keep your families employed and your economy running? Yeeah. That's me," she countered.

"See, that's what I'm talking about. I guess I should thank you."

"You're welcome." She squinted and took a drag of her cigarette. "Our family used to have a house at the shore where we stayed the whole summer. So we're local enough."

"All of you summer families try to pull that shit," I said. "You're not local if you don't stay there through February. It's the most miserable time of anyplace anywhere."

"I came down there once during Thanksgiving weekend with a friend, and it was like—a ghost town. I couldn't believe it."

"Yeah, no shit," I said, warming to her. "It's nice because as a kid you rule the town, basically. We could play in the middle of the street if we wanted to. It made us all very imaginative, in a weird sort of way."

"What do you mean?"

"I don't know. It's like we speak our own language."

"Does it involve a lot of whining and 'How can I help you?'"

I smiled and looked around for a second, taking a long drag of my cigarette. "Man, don't try and talk down to me from your rat-infested hole you call NYC. If it's so bad, stop coming to my town."

"It's *not* bad. As a matter of fact, it would be perfect if there weren't any locals."

I smiled and shook my head again. "I would be defending my homeland right now, but my mother raised a gentleman."

"Your brother? Is he here?"

"Clever."

We both took drags of our cigarettes. "I'm just kidding, but I'd still like it if you roughed me up a little bit," she said after a minute.

I didn't know what to say about that one. I wasn't sure what she meant. I would have been glad to do whatever if that involved her being naked. I just moved on to some stories about growing up in my town—how it's best in September and October, when it empties out, the sunsets last half the day, the water stays warm enough to swim, and the stripers arrive, and the water in the bay stays calm and for the most part glassy when the tide isn't moving.

Even though I was talking a lot, I was near the keg and getting a good amount of drinking done. Around then, a couple guys came out on the back deck. One was no taller than Kristen, with hair that was cut close but curly on top.

"What the hell are you doing here?" he asked, apparently talking to Kristen.

"Why, I'm enjoying this tasty beverage, kind sir," I said. He glanced at me, then looked at her.

"Anthony, leave me alone," Kristen said.

"Kristen, you need to get your skankin' ass out of here."

"Pardon me, but who in the hell do you think you're talking to?" I asked, without thinking.

"And who the hell are you?"

"What makes you think you can talk to a girl like that?"

At that, he threw his beer at me, and missed. That was odd, because he was about six feet away from me. I did not miss, though, when I threw my bottle at him. It hit him in the chest.

At that, my friends took notice and got in between us, and grabbed me and started pulling me into the apartment toward the front door, saying, "No, Peachfuzz, stop..."

"We're getting him out of here, right now," Petrone said to the crowd of guys in front of us. I was kicking and fighting and cursing at the guys and at the fraternity in general as we moved through the crowd.

Once we got outside, Brandon closed the door and turned to me.

"Peachfuzz, you stupid son of a bitch. That whole place is full of people who are right now getting ready to come out here and jump your ass."

"I don't care. They're all a bunch of PUSSIES!!!" I yelled at the door.

"Peach," Petrone said. "I'm leaving your stupid ass here. Kristen is hot, but she is not worth dying for."

"I'm stayin'," Johnny said. Johnny was from the North Shore of Long Island, had tattoos, and wore wife-beaters all the time.

"Look," Brandon said. "There are about sixty of them and four of us. Let's at least start walking in the other direction, and if some of them come to stomp our heads in, then we can do something about that then."

Petrone was already walking; Brandon followed. Johnny and I would walk a little bit and then turn around and yell back at them about how they were wimps and the like. Once we got about a hundred yards away from the building, a group of about seven guys came out. I started walking toward them, and so did Johnny. For me, I think the courage was in the alcohol. I think Johnny was just crazy. Petrone and Brandon were pretty far ahead of us, and it must have taken a minute to figure out what was going on, because they caught up to us right before we confronted the frat guys.

"My friend is a drunk idiot; we don't want to fight you," Brandon said once we were close enough to them.

"Look, I don't have a beef with anyone other than the little man, here," I said. "Your buddy was in there cursing at a woman. I think that's something that cowards do. If you want to try and beat my ass over that, then go ahead."

By now, the one who had been cursing was standing in front of me. Johnny was to my left, Brandon was to his left and behind him, and Petrone was to my right and behind me. The frat guys were in sort of a half circle behind him.

"What makes you think you can get into someone else's business?"

"I was standing there talking to a woman, and you come out and in the middle of it start calling her a bitch. You made it my business."

"You better watch yourself, freshman."

"If you guys want to throw down, let's throw down," Johnny said. "I don't have any beef with any of ya, but I'm not gonna let you guys jump Peachfuzz."

At this, a few of the frat guys, who still had their beers in their hands, decided that this was stupid and tried to get their friend to leave. Two more agreed. One of the guys started arguing with the others.

"You're lucky to be alive right now," the guy in front of me said.

"Right."

I backed up a few paces and then turned around, and my friends did the same. After we got out a ways, we all started bragging to each other about ourselves. Hell yeah, they won't mess with us, they didn't want none of this. That sort of thing. None of us heard them running up on us. Suddenly the back of my skull felt like it got struck by lightning boulders, my head lurched forward, I bit my tongue, my ears rang for a second, and I saw stars. I stumbled forward a little bit and put my hand on the ground but didn't fall. The bottle landed on the street next to me. I saw it was a twenty-two-ounce Heineken bottle.

I didn't have time to figure out what was going on or pick up the bottle, since what seemed to be the little man jumped on my back. I flipped him down on the street on his back. It was him. He had a grimace on his face when he landed, and I hit him across the side of the face. He put his hand in my face, and then I was tackled from the right side onto the asphalt, and I felt my face scrape against the gravel.

Whoever this was, he was big and solid like a steer. He flipped me onto my back, and bunched my shirt up and pinned my shoulders to the ground, and I struggled to get my arms to a place where I could try and push him off and prepared to digest some teeth. It took me a second to see straight.

I looked up to see a familiar smirk shining white from behind a dark face, with bling in his ears.

"Malcolm?"

"You're staying right here, Peachfuzz," he said.

"Funny seeing you here. Thanks for not killing me."

"You're welcome."

"So...you wanna make out?"

"Better watch it, Peachfuzz. Don't push your luck."

Malcolm sat next to me in the back of my business class. Most of the time we played Eights. It was an easy class. He and I joked a lot and would grab lunch every once in a while after class. He was a running back on the football team and could bench-press two or three of me. He was always telling me to rush. I hadn't seen him at the party, or among the group of guys that we had just confronted. They must have gone back and rounded up another couple guys. But there he was, and I knew I would be alright for now. The action continued around us, though, and Malcolm looked up and to his left, just in time to catch the laces of someone's shoe with his teeth. This knocked him off me and to the side. I stood up, and Johnny was now on top of Malcolm.

"Shit, Johnny, stop! He's cool! He's cool!"

While I was saying that, someone ran up and hit me in the same cheekbone that had scraped on the street. My head spun a little bit, but it wasn't a good shot. I saw some blue lights flashing and thought it was from the impact. I caught my balance, and I turned around and saw cops coming from down the street, and started running, like everyone else did. We all split up in different directions. I ran through the parking lot toward a gas station, where a few people pumping gas took notice, through that across Silver Creek Road onto campus. When I got about a hundred yards onto campus, I didn't see anyone coming, so I slowed down and walked panting through a parking lot off the main road going through it. When I made it back to Monroe, Brandon and Johnny were already there.

CHAPTER 7

Johnny was smoking a cigarette, and Brandon was bent over with his hands on his knees catching his breath. I was still out of breath myself.

"Johnny, you're psycho," I said in between breaths.

"What?"

"You kicked my boy Malcolm in the face."

"I thought I was doing you a favor."

"He was just keeping me off his friends. He wasn't going to do anything. You're lucky the cops came—he could wipe his ass with you."

"I realized that when I got on top of him. I think he's alright, though. I didn't get a good shot 'cuz he rolled with it. I think I pulled it a little, too. I'm not the head-stompin' kind, ya know? More inta rib crackin'."

After I caught my breath, I lit a cigarette and we chatted for a minute about how we got back. I was sweaty and my face hurt, so after I finished my cigarette, I went in the building to my room to get in the shower.

I stripped down to my boxers and went in the bathroom and looked in the mirror. There were scrapes on my cheek, and it looked a little like rug burn, but it was fine. There was a knot on my head from where the bottle had hit. I thought about how lucky I was that the bottle hadn't broken, and how lucky I was that Malcolm had somehow showed up, and that he had decided not to kick my ass. I said a little prayer to thank God. God was the only way I could explain any of that.

I took a quick shower and toweled off, then wrapped the towel around my waist and walked out of the bathroom into my dorm room, where I sat on my bed and turned on the TV. I didn't really look at what was on; instead I looked around the room. Above my desk was a huge poster of Jack Nicholson in *The Shining* from when he had axed the door and was looking through saying, "Here's Johnny!" The rest of the walls were papered with thin cardboard cases for canned beer. Most of it was Busch, some of it was Beast, some of it was Keystone. There was one box of Coors Light, which had a prominent place, since it was rare that we drank beer that good.

I had been sitting down for only a minute when someone knocked on my door. I got up and looked through the peephole. I was surprised to see it was Kristen. I wasn't sure if I should get dressed or just answer the door as I was. I decided to crack the door open and stick my head out a little bit.

"Hey, Kristen, what's up?"

"Will, are you alright?"

"Yeah. I'm fine," I said.

"I heard there was a big fight."

"Yeah, I didn't get the worst of it," I said, smiling.

"Holy shit, your cheek is all scraped up." She reached out and touched it gently.

"I'm alright. What was that all about?" I asked.

"He's my old boyfriend's best friend."

"He was a douche."

"Yeah, he sucks. He's got penis envy," she said.

I laughed. "How much longer did you stay?"

"Just a few minutes, then I went with my friend Jennifer to a party at the building next door. I saw Anthony and his friends walking back all bloody, and I knew something had happened. When I heard about the fight, I got really scared for you guys."

"Yeah, I know one of those guys, and Johnny kicked him in the face," I said.

"Holy shit! Which one?"

"Malcolm," I said.

"Aww, Malcolm's a sweetie! Is he alright?"

"Yeah, he's fine. Johnny didn't get a good shot in." I looked down at the ground. "I'd invite you in, but I just got out of the shower."

"Okay." She looked down at the rug, then down the hall toward the lobby. "Are you going back out?"

"What time is it?"

"One thirty," she said.

"I was planning on just going to sleep. All that fighting and running took a lot out of me." I was also thinking about going to church with Lily the next day, but didn't say that.

"Really? That sucks."

"Yeah," I said.

"Well, I just wanted to thank you for being so sweet. Your mother did raise a gentleman."

"Thanks, Kristen."

"Goodnight."

"Goodnight."

She gave me a really sweet smile and bit her bottom lip, then walked away. When I got back in the room, I started to think that maybe I had just missed a golden opportunity there. Then I remembered the "roughing up" comment and knew for sure that I had missed a golden opportunity.

I shook my head and told myself I was an idiot, then put on some shorts and a T-shirt, sat on my bed, and started watching TV again. I really, really started feeling like an idiot. I thought about going up to talk to her, but she would probably think I just wanted to talk to Lily. Then I would have to explain why I didn't want to talk to Lily, and probably to Lily. I thought that Lily might not be there, but I knew that she definitely would be there, because it was one thirty on a Sunday morning. She didn't stay out late, and she went to church in the morning.

I thought about calling their room and if Lily answered, pretending it was someone else. But that wouldn't work, because she knew my voice too well. Man, I was an idiot.

Then I started thinking that it was my imagination. Kristen was out of my league. We had established that she was out of all of our leagues by the end of the first month. She had gone off and become popular among a crowd of people who all weren't freshmen, and who were allowed to have their cars at campus and had their own apartments and could drink legally and had big parties with DJs and black lights and guest lists in the stale-beer-stinking basements of their houses. I was imagining things.

Just then my door swung open and slammed up against the wall, then swung back and hit the figure coming through it saying, "PEEAACHFUZZZ." It was Gallo.

"What up, dude?"

"Effin' Peeeaachfuzzz." He had a thirteen-inch sub from Blimpie tucked under his arm. His eyes looked bloodshot and only half open. He walked past me and flopped on Skeeter's bed and started opening his sandwich.

"What did you get?"

"Effin' steak and cheese, beeotch," he answered.

"You gotta hook me up with some of that shit."

"You gotta hook your mother up with some of this shit," he said, indignantly.

"C'mon, man, I just beat some kids' asses. I'm hungry."

"You got in a fight?" he asked, with interest.

"Yeah, man, we got jumped. Dude hit me over the head with a bottle."

"Aah ooh huckin' hiddin' me?" he said with a mouth full of steak and cheese.

"No, dude."

He paused for a minute while he chewed and swallowed. "Did you get cut?"

"No, it didn't break."

"How do you not break a bottle on somebody's head? This guy must have been a wimp."

"He was. He was cursing out Kristen."

"From-the-third-floor Kristen?" he asked.

"Yeah."

"You were hanging out with Kristen?" he asked.

"Yeah, dude, she wants to hook up with me. I defended her honor."

Someone knocked on the door.

"Gallo, get that."

"Bite me, Peachfuzz."

"C'mon, man. I twisted my ankle."

He got up, and once he did, I grabbed the sandwich and took a huge bite. I looked up and saw him in the doorway talking to whoever it was. I watched the TV and tried to chew as fast as I could so I could take another bite.

"You asshole!" I heard him say.

I looked up and he was walking toward me. Behind him was Kristen. I looked at her, then looked back at him. He raised his eyebrows a couple times and smiled a big, wide smile at me, then flopped down and resumed eating his sandwich.

I was chewing my bite of the sandwich, so I could only grunt to greet her as she sat at the foot of my bed.

"Hey..." she said.

"Mmmm."

"There was some dude in my room with Lily, so I decided I would come back down and see if you were still up."

I chewed and tried to swallow it down quickly.

"A guy in the room with Lily?" I asked.

"Ah, ha, Peechfuuh," Gallo said. He had some sandwich still in his mouth and had to talk with his head tilted back. "All that popcorn on your face and you're not going to be the one to pop her cherry."

"Shut up, Gallo."

"That's rude," she said.

"I didn't know she was dating anyone," I said.

"Neither did I. But I opened the door and he was coming out of the bathroom in his boxers. He turned around and looked at me, and I said hi and I was going to go have a cigarette, and I shut the door."

"Weird," I said.

"Come out, Virginia, don't be late, Cath-o-lic girls start much too late..." Gallo started singing, clapping his thigh with his free hand.

Kristen wasn't even acknowledging he was there. "Want to go have a cigarette with me?" she asked.

"I'd rather laugh with the sinners than cry with the saints," he was singing, louder now, since he saw that we were both ignoring him.

"Sure," I said.

We both got up and walked toward the door.

"Sinners have much more fuunnnnnnnnnnnn..." he was singing as we closed the door.

We walked down the hall of cinder blocks painted white, with posters here and there, and through the little lobby and out the front door.

I sat down first on the concrete steps. She sat next to me. She really was a beautiful girl. She was wearing stretchy black pants and a white button-down shirt with a pink sweater vest on top. Her perfume was sweet—sort of like vanilla. It was cooler than it had been that day but alright out of the wind. She sat down, and I held out my pack of cigarettes and she took one. I lit hers and then took one out for myself. I was getting nervous about what to talk about.

"That was really sweet of you to say something to Anthony," she said as I lit my cigarette.

"I was just doing what came naturally," I responded.

"He's such a prick."

"Seems like it. I got a good shot in for you."

"Thanks," she said.

We smoked and stared out across the street, which was a path that led to the quad. White lamps lined it, and the light shined on the dew in the grass and on the bluish-gray stones of the buildings that had columns painted white.

"Did you get hurt?" she asked.

"I think somebody hit me in the head with a bottle."

"Holy shit! Are you kidding me? Who did it? Was it Anthony?"

"I don't know. I didn't see them. They came from behind," I said.

"What pussies. That's awful. I'm sorry, Will," she said.

"I had it coming to me. I shouldn't have thrown mine at him."

"Where did they hit you?"

"Right here." I rubbed my fingers over the lump on the back of my head. She reached out and rubbed her hand across the spot. When she did that, she leaned in farther than necessary.

"You have to get some ice on that; that's awful." She started to get up.

"Let's finish our cigarettes. It's a nice night."

"Alright." She settled back, but was a little closer to me now.

We looked out at the night again and smoked. It was getting late, and I wasn't going to fish for small talk. After a minute she started breathing through her teeth like they were chattering and pulled her elbows in against her stomach.

"You cold?" I asked.

"Yeah, a little."

I scooted over a little closer to her, and she leaned up against me.

"Will, nobody has ever stuck up for me like that. It felt so...like...chivalrous," she said.

I smoked for a second and let that sink in. "Well, there are a few things you don't do. One of them is call a woman a skank. It's not any more complicated than that," I said.

"I've always wanted to get to talk to you more, but you always act like you're too cool for me." That was a lie. "It's like you like Lily a lot better."

"I always thought you were too cool for me. I mean, I'm no frat boy." I really wished she hadn't brought Lily into this. It was ruining the moment. "Lily is just someone I've known from when we were younger."

"You seem to get along with her pretty well," she said.

"Well, I do. I have *a* relationship with her. It's a relationship that is very important to me. But it's not the type of relationship that's going to stop me from...I don't know, whatever. We're not, like, together. She's one of the few things here I knew before I got here." I really didn't want to be talking about this.

"'Cuz I wouldn't want to interfere with anything between you and her."

"Look, I think you're getting the wrong impression. She's not my girlfriend. We just spend some time together. You wouldn't be interfering with anything."

She stomped out her cigarette.

"Well, do you think I could persuade you to come up to see *me* every once in a while?"

"Maybe." I smiled at her, then threw my cigarette out toward the street. "How would you be doing that?"

"I have some ideas." She put her purse in her lap and rummaged through it. She pulled out a pack of Wrigley's spearmint gum.

"By bribing me with gum?" I asked.

"Want one?"

"No, that's alright."

"No, you want one," she said, smiling. She had white teeth.

"Okay, then I want one."

She handed me one, and I put it in my mouth. We chewed for a second, looking out at the night again. She started doing the teeth-chattering thing again.

"So, did you know when a girl wants a guy's arm around her before you got here?" she asked.

"Uh, I heard they teach you that when you rush. Like I said, I'm no frat boy." I put my arm across her back and my hand on her waist, and we looked at each other.

"Stop with that frat-boy stuff," she said.

"Must be the beer talking."

She looked down and unfolded the gum wrapper that she had been holding in her hand.

"Want to spit out your gum?" she said, while taking hers out from between her white teeth.

"Nah. I'm alright." I smiled at her.

"No, you want to spit out your gum." She laughed a little and shook her head. "They must have hit you hard with that bottle."

I took my gum out and stuck it in her wrapper. She stood up and walked toward the door and dropped it in the ashtray, then walked back and sat next to me again. *How thorough*, I thought. I put my arm back around her, and we looked at each other. She took her hand and touched the scraped area on my face.

"Does it hurt?"

"A little."

She leaned in and kissed me there, then leaned back a couple inches and looked at me. She bit her bottom lip and surveyed my face. I leaned in and kissed her. We kissed for a minute. We both stopped and looked at each other and giggled.

"My knight in shining armor," she said. I smiled and thought to myself that it was a cheesy comment.

"Most of the time guys are looking for a reason to fight when they're drunk."

"Don't ruin it for me."

"Well, I wouldn't do it for just any girl."

"That's better."

We kissed a little longer, and as this was going on I heard the shuffling of feet past us.

"*Peach-fuzz, Peach-fuzz, Peach-fuzz*," they chanted in a whisper. I stopped and looked up, and it was some of my buddies. They were giving me the thumbs-up. She turned around, and quickly they snapped into normal walking mode.

When she looked at me, they started giving me the thumbs-up again and then went inside.

She leaned back on her hands. "I'm cold, Will."

I was a little hesitant to say this, because I didn't want to assume that things were going as well as I thought they might be going, and I had never said it before: "Want to go back to my room?"

"*YES.*"

"Alright."

We went in through the lobby, then down the hall a few feet to my room, which was unlocked. When I went in, my TV was on and Gallo was sleeping on Skeeter's bed with the rest of his sandwich in his hand. He was snoring pretty loudly.

I walked over to him and slapped him on the arm a couple times. I called his name, loudly. I saw that this wasn't getting anywhere, so I put my left hand over his mouth and pinched his nose. He shook his head and jerked up quickly.

"Uh?"

"Gallo, go back to your room."

"No, dude." He had a confused look on his face, and his eyes were bleary and glassy. He looked down in his hand and saw that he was holding the nub of the sandwich, and took a bite. He looked up and saw Kristen sitting on the bed behind me. "Iiii, Kwissen," he said with his mouth full. After a second he seemed to put two and two together, and he looked up at me and smiled with his mouth still full. "Peehfuhhh."

"Get out, Gallo."

He took a swig of the beer that was sitting on the end table. "Peeeeachfuzzz. You dog. You dirty dog."

"Goodnight, Gallo."

He stood up and got lettuce shreds all over Skeeter's bed. He took another bite of his sandwich. "Peehfuhh, I wuvv ooh." He chewed and swallowed. "I look up to you, man," he said as he walked. "You're like a big brother to me."

"Goodnight, Gallo."

CHAPTER 8

Usually on Sunday nights there wasn't much going on, but that night was the semi-finals for March Madness. I really didn't care about it, but I liked having a reason to drink on Sunday night.

For some reason, Farmer Jack's was selling cases of Moosehead beer for about ten dollars. I didn't like the beer that much, but it was a hell of a lot better than Beast or Busch. We got five or six cases. The sale lasted for what seemed like weeks, and it became known as the great Moosehead Rush of 1998.

After getting the beer, I did a little homework and drank a couple to pre-game. I went by myself to D hall to get dinner, then went straight to Costigan and Gallo's room. I knocked.

"Who is it?" asked a muffled voice from behind the door.

"Don't be a cocksmooch."

The door opened, and on the other side was Costigan. "Peeachfuzz."

"What up? Game start?"

"Nah, got a couple minutes."

The dorm rooms all had a small hallway, with closets on one side and a bathroom on the other. Costigan and Gallo had one of the two handicap-accessible rooms, so it didn't share its bathroom with the next room.

As I walked down the little hallway, Gallo saw me from the couch and clapped once, then twice, then a third time, picking up speed. Others looked at him, then looked at me and joined in. Soon everyone in the room was quiet and clapping. Gallo started the chant, *Peach-fuzz, Peach-fuzz, Peach-fuzz,* and the whole room joined in. Gallo stood up and put his arm around me.

"Peachfuzz, you have been to effin' Narnia, the land spoken of but never seen," he said in a loud voice, "in between Kristen from the third floor's long, luscious, athletic legs. A land we can only visit in dreams. You are a sexy bitch, Peachfuzz, but I didn't see this comin'."

Everyone hooted. There was an extra chair, and I sat on that. The chants lasted another minute, and then it got quiet. I asked for a beer and opened it, and looked up and saw everyone looking at me.

"Well?" Costigan asked.

"Well what?"

"What the hell? Give us some details, man. She got big nipples?" Gallo asked.

"Nope. Good-sized."

"Good, I hate that. How was she?" he interrogated.

"Uh, at what?"

"Don't be an asshole. You tapped that ass, right?"

"Affirmative."

Everyone hooted and slapped their legs.

"How many times?" Costigan asked.

"I'm not going to get into that."

"OOOHHHH," they all said.

"You are a lucky son of a bitch," Gallo confirmed. At that, the commercial break ended and everyone turned to the game.

I started looking at the TV but wasn't watching it, really. Petrone and Costigan were sitting next to me on the couch and resuming an argument, so I tried to figure out what they were talking about. It was about rock 'n' roll—which era was better, the early nineties or the early sixties. After a few minutes, Petrone tapped me on the arm and asked my opinion.

I thought for a second. "The nineties. Hands down," I said.

"Oh, what bullshit," Costigan said at the same time Petrone said, "Ah, ha ha. You're in a slim minority, my friend."

"You guys aren't being objective about it. You two are just going by what you know," Costigan said.

"I know how to be objective. It's the nineties," I said.

"In the sixties you had the Beatles, the Stones, and Dylan. The conversation is over."

"Radiohead, Nirvana, and Beck."

"Radiohead is a contender. Nirvana is not the Beatles or the Stones, and Beck is not Dylan."

"Dylan, by 1965, had not released *Blood on the Tracks*, or even *Blonde on Blonde*. Nirvana, if it had lasted, would have done far more than the Beatles. The Beatles ran their course, and Nirvana was cut short."

"That's one of the dumbest things I've ever heard in my life," Costigan said.

"Well, let me put it this way. Nirvana's lyrics were better than the Beatles'," Petrone said.

"Alright, maybe," Costigan said.

"Whatever. It doesn't matter," I said. "All of those bands in the sixties were working with something that was brand new. It's not like everything had been done before. Nothing had been done before. It's like, 'Oh, shit! This song has strings? Wow, how original! What geniuses! Wow, they cut up the tape and taped it back together? Amazing!' You can do anything and it's exciting and it's genius. And if you go back and listen, it's not that great. Then the nineties came along, and rock and hard rock and punk and metal and speed metal and everything else new you could do with rock 'n' roll had all already happened. Look at the music that was popular before grunge. It was half-assed rehashes of Led Zeppelin. All the sixties was about was doing drugs and not fighting in the war." I took a swig of beer. "Like...the war collapsed under its own weight, so really it was just about drugs. And sex. There was an honesty to the nineties stuff. They weren't singing songs about Marxism that they wrote in a penthouse apartment on New York's Upper West Side."

"So Rage Against the Machine redistributes their wealth among their roadies?" Costigan asked.

"True. I didn't think of that."

"If it weren't for the music in the sixties, we'd be living in a much different, much more boring and conformist world. The sixties totally changed pop culture. Without it, the nineties grunge thing would have been impossible. It was about revolution. Revolution against racism, against capitalism, against patriarchy, against militarism. If it weren't for them, we'd all be studying to do market analysis on fiber optics. It was about revolution."

"Fiber optics?" I asked.

"Aluminum. Plastics. Whatever."

Petrone piped up, "Revolution? Yeah—the first time in history that Americans thought to themselves, 'Ah, screw it. If it's hard, it ain't worth doin'. I wanna smoke pot and eat acid and bone hippies. I'd rather die doing that than die saving the world from Communism.' How is that a revolution? How hard is it to sell the idea that you should be lazy and you should have a lot of sex and drink a lot and do a lot of drugs?"

"Dude, we would be drinking out of white and colored fountains. They ended segregation," Costigan said.

"Who did?" Petrone demanded.

"That generation," he responded.

"Dude—'I Have a Dream' was in 1963, the same year as Dylan's first album. *Brown v. Board* was nine years before it. The Civil Rights Act...all that shit happened before Dylan put out his third album."

"True."

"The nineties people weren't fooling themselves into thinking it was about anything other than rock 'n' roll. At the most, the nineties stuff was all about, 'Yeah, we tried that experiment, and guess what, you effed it all up. We're all a mess, and it's your fault, because you refused to be parents.' Those parents happen to be the same people who think that Bob Dylan is a prophet and John Lennon is a martyr."

"But you can't deny that things really changed in the sixties," Costigan said.

"No, you can't deny that. But it wasn't rock 'n' roll that changed anything. It was people being changed who made the music. The people who were actually changing things were too busy," Petrone said. "Think about it. Name a single album that has changed your life."

We sat and thought for a long minute.

"I don't know," I said after a minute. "I started playing guitar after I started listening to Nirvana and Metallica."

"So it influences musicians. That's it."

"I seriously doubt that Martin Luther King was a fan of Dylan. He was a preacher," I said.

"Not Martin Luther King, but his followers. You know what I mean. Plus, it made art an option," Costigan said. "It didn't just influence musicians. It made more musicians."

"That's a huge generalization," Petrone said. "They had jazz before that—the Harlem Renaissance in the twenties. In the fifties they had just got done fighting a World War. You probably want stuff to be safe." He got a little more animated. "You know, *shit.* This black-and-white bullshit. It's so judgmental. They had Sinatra and Peggy Lee and Billie Holiday and...Louie Armstrong and...Fats Domino and...Woody Guthrie and...Hank Williams...all this before rock 'n' roll. All this was real American music! The world didn't start when TV put a camera on it. Think about it. The hippies, they're our parents now. They're our teachers and administrators and our politicians. You—all of us—have been spoon-fed this notion that there was nothing before Elvis came along, and we're supposed to be grateful to the boomers for all the albums they bought and their sock hops and the acid they took and for the Summer of Love. I don't give a shit about the Summer of Love or Woodstock or the Beatles or Bob Dylan. I mean, look at the most popular class in our school right now. It's the history of rock. It's probably some over-the-hill guy in a nappy blazer and a black T-shirt with beads and a nappy beard and a nappy ponytail. It's just self-preserving mythology. They're the man, now—El Jefe is one of them. All our politicians and our classrooms and our TVs are all like a big dick poking a hole into our brains. If rock 'n' roll taught us anything, it's that we should be fighting them and hoping we don't grow up like them."

"So what do you think we should do, gadfly?" Costigan asked.

"I don't know!" Petrone said. "Tune out and drop in? Put in an application? Participate? I'm not saying I have any answers. I didn't fight their cheesedick battles. I'm just saying, what the hell is wrong with getting a job and staying sober and going to church and getting married and having kids? What's wrong with defending your country? From Communism! What's wrong with women who want to stay home and raise their kids? My mom did it. She went to Yale! It's not like families with both parents working have it any better off than the families with one parent working back in the fifties. They fought against stuff that was good, or at least wasn't bad."

"Like racism?" Costigan asked.

"Oh, would you shut up? No, not racism, you asshole. Yes, they were against racism, which is good. But dammit, there's nothing wrong with any of the rest. They were paranoid, which is what happens when you smoke pot. They want us to perpetuate their bad trip so they feel it was all worth it. Wasting all that time and energy and life."

We were all sitting on the edge of our seats and looking at our beers.

"I thought this was about rock 'n' roll," I said.

"It is...sort of. Isn't it?" Petrone said.

"Whatever. You sound paranoid. I just want to drink some beer," I said.

The three of us looked up toward the TV at the announcers talking about the game coming up.

"I'd say this is the perfect weekend. I got drunk with my buddies, got in a fight, and got laid," I said. I was trying to change the subject.

"You're living the dream, Peachfuzz," Petrone said.

"Did you use protection?" Costigan asked. I thought about that for a second. That hadn't crossed my mind, really. A little bit.

"I didn't have any jimmies. I figured she wouldn't have gone there if she wasn't on birth control."

"Better watch it," Petrone said. "You're gonna end up making a little Peach."

"Hmm," I said.

"So are you going to date her?" Costigan asked.

"I don't think so."

"Do you want that?" Costigan asked.

"I don't know. I don't know her that well. I doubt I'm ready for a relationship right now."

"Bop 'em and drop 'em," Costigan said.

"The more you bang a girl, the more she wants a relationship. You might end up living the nightmare," Petrone said.

I thought for a second and took a drink of beer. "I haven't talked to her since this morning. I didn't think it seemed like that. We only have six weeks left, so it's not like there's even a lot of time, really."

"So what does Lily think of all of this?" Petrone asked. I had managed to forget about that for a while. The knot in my stomach returned.

I took a deep breath and blew it out. "I don't know."

"Does she know?"

"I don't know. She came by my room and Kristen was still there."

"*Really?*"

"What did she say?" Costigan asked.

"She just talked about going to church. I don't know if she could tell or not. Kristen might tell her; they're roommates. I doubt she would care that much. It's not like we're dating or anything."

"Yeah, but everyone knows there's something going on between you two," Petrone said.

"Everyone but me and her, apparently." I took out a cigarette and lit it up.

"Or maybe just you," Costigan said.

The knot in my stomach got worse as I thought about that for a minute. I took a long drink of Moosehead. "Maybe."

CHAPTER 9

That week I did a lot of worrying about what would happen, how things would end up with me and Kristen and how things would end up with me and Lily, and if Lily knew. I avoided going up to their room or even to the top floor, but that wasn't a big deal since we were all busy during the week and usually didn't see each other much anyway. On Thursday night while I was getting ready to go to a party with Gallo, Petrone, Skeeter, and Brandon, Kristen knocked on my door. Skeeter was already over in Gallo's room playing Asshole.

I let her in and closed the door, then asked her to have a seat and motioned toward my bed. She wasn't dressed to go out. She was wearing short red gym shorts and a T-shirt, and her hair was up. She looked beautiful.

"So...how have you been?" I asked once she sat down. This was the talk I had been avoiding—what our relationship would be or some such.

"Good, you?"

"Not bad."

She looked around the room, then at me. "I had a great time on Saturday night"—she looked down at the floor—"...and Sunday." She giggled.

"Me too."

She sat very straight with her hands on her knees, and she took a breath in and then blew it out. "Where's Skeeter?"

"He's next door at Gallo and Costigan's."

"Think he'll be back anytime soon?"

"No, I doubt it." She stood up, and I watched how she moved as she walked over and locked the door to our room, then to our bathroom. She turned around and started back, stopping a few feet in front of me.

"Uh, I don't know how to say this...*faire vous aime un...* uh..." She was searching for a word and looking up.

"Sorry, I don't know French. Is that French?"

She looked down at the ground and smiled, then back up at me. "I don't know the word..." She looked up at the ceiling, then back at me. "I'm trying to think of a classy way to say it and, like, 'fellatio' sounds too clinical."

"I don't know Spanish, either."

She laughed and shook her head. "You have no game."

"You have no class," I responded with a smile.

CHAPTER 10

My hometown is a beach resort, where the highest peaks are head-high sand dunes tangled with dune grass. There aren't all that many trees, and there aren't any that are very tall. In order to protect the ocean views, the buildings by law aren't allowed to be more than two stories high. The air smells like salt marsh, and usually you can hear the waves. There's ongoing concern for the marshland and the crabs and herons and egrets, and especially the turtles that have to cross the one road leading in and out of town to lay their eggs. There isn't much concern for the seagulls, though. You hear stories about people feeding them Alka-Seltzer tablets, which supposedly makes their stomachs explode. I had never seen that. I didn't have much of a problem with them, really, but they are drunken, awkward, classless birds, and they would swoop down and take the sandwich right out of your hand, if given the opportunity. In a cartoon movie about birds, they would be the dumb villains. Hearing their squawking, though, preferably from a good distance, always made me feel inside like summer was coming.

Along with the concern over the wildlife comes the concern for property value. For the most part, the houses in my town were all second homes, so the New York lawyers and doctors and dentists and bankers could come down and sit on the beach or go out in their boats or sail on their yachts. The tourist season started the weekend before Memorial Day, when the towns around us would try to have some event to bring people down from NYC.

My personal favorite was the shark tournament two towns south. To enter, each boat team pays a few thousand dollars, and the winner gets the whole pot, which was always well over a half a million dollars. Raising the money to get in was not a problem for most guys, since they were all rich, and their boats were big enough to hold a good handful of guys who would all chip in. Some of these boats were seventy feet long. That might not sound like much, but if you get up near one, it's impressive.

Most years Mr. Henderson would take me down with his son Tim who was a year below me in school. Mr. Henderson was a charter boat captain—tourists would hire him to take them deep-sea fishing. In the winter, he was a bartender. This was sort of his very early retirement. Before I was even born, or I could remember, he was a broker up on Wall Street. He didn't seem like the type to me.

All of the members had to meet a deadline of six o' clock on Sunday. Around four thirty in the afternoon, people would crowd all over the docks and around the bulkhead of the huge marina that used to host it. As I waited, I would note the sweet smell of the sea along with the fish and the barnacles and seaweed.

If the sharks weren't in, Tim and I would walk around and look at all of the yachts backed into their slips. Most of them had corny names like *Wet Dream* or *Great Scott!* or *Summerbreeze* or *Baroness*. When the sharks came in, though, we would stand there and say nothing. We wouldn't even blink. The scrappy marina workers would wrap their tails up in hooks and chains and hoist them up with ropes and pulleys onto this huge scale that looked like a gallows with old leathery weather-beaten sharks' tails nailed to it.

When the big guys got up there—their dead black eyes staring out at the crowd and their jaws gaping open—their guts would slowly ooze out of their mouths. They never spilled out all the way to the ground, just hung out a couple feet beyond their teeth. For a kid, all of this was just the greatest. For the adults, they probably felt like the kids, too. After it was all over, Mr. Henderson would usually take us out for ice cream.

The summer between fifth and sixth grade, a bunch of guys in their early twenties with shaggy hair went out in a borrowed twenty-one-foot Grady-White with a 150-horesepower Merc on the back—just a couple buckets of chum, a couple flats of mackerel, and a few cases of beer. I think you had all week to fish. To go out fifty or sixty miles and then come back in would have been too much gas, so they would just stay out there. Next to the Blackfin and Viking sport fishers with their captains' decks and their teak and their outriggers sticking high up into the air with colored pennants flapping, these guys looked like they had business elsewhere, as in the local head shop.

They got back, though, with about ten minutes to spare, with their boat sunk down low in the water. The shark they pulled off the back of that boat was over six hundred pounds. The guys, all of them drunk and rowdy, walked away with over seven hundred thousand dollars. They were Chelsea natives, and that made it all the sweeter.

All of this was to make up for the winter, when it's like the blood runs out of the place. The big mansions with their vinyl siding and their hard plastic columns just sit and glow in the moonlight like gravestones. The wind sweeps through the streets, and there isn't anything there to stop it. Nor'easters would come through and would sit on top of us for three, four, sometimes five days with nothing but gray clouds and cold rain. In some ways it was good for us kids. When it wasn't raining we could get lost pretty easily and do our deeds, whatever they might be, for the day. Other times, though, it was a lonesome and miserable place to be.

The locals are a different breed from the tourists. Lots are fishermen, lots of them hard-drinking. Not commercial fishermen, really. Most of them are painters or electricians during the day and fishers during the noontime and the evenings, the afternoons, early mornings, holidays, sick days, and workdays. Some of them are surfers or both, but the waves never quite live up to the gusto. The women are all teachers or nurses or work in social services, like treatment for alcoholism. The other option is to work in a store, or own one. Lots of locals own businesses or work at places only in the summer and collect unemployment eight months out of the year. The bars stay open all winter.

It's a family place, but a rich family place. Not as much for the locals—the rich part. Some people respect the town for what it really is. Some vacationers just gave me a knot in my stomach. Their attitudes did, anyway.

In mid-June, the streets would start to get more crowded, especially on the weekends, but for the most part June was quiet, the first half at least. Most people didn't go down yet, because most kids were still in school. It wasn't until Independence Day that things became crowded. In June the water in the ocean was still in the 60s, so it could get a little chilly on the beach, depending on which way the wind was blowing. Then the "Welcome to Chelsea" sign on Main Street would be up again. That's when you knew the tourist season had begun.

One morning, after the end of my sophomore year, the family went to church, and my two younger brothers and I served as altar boys. For me it was the first time serving in years, and Jimmy, my middle brother, had retired as well. I had served regularly until about the age of seventeen.

But that day all three of us were on the altar to serve at a Mass celebrating Monsignor Rinaldi's fiftieth anniversary as a priest. Our parish, St. Augustine's, was made up of the locals—mostly retired folks and a few younger families sitting in the spots they had staked out years ago sprinkled evenly throughout the pews. There were usually about fifty people in a church that could hold about a thousand. In the summers after Independence Day it was usually full.

The church was elegant in a humble sort of way. The floor was done in sand- and green-colored stone of some sort. The wall behind the altar was sky blue with a stale brass-colored decorative panel reaching up halfway, and an undersized crucifix beneath three skinny stained-glass windows like spires reaching up from the tabernacle, which was coated in gold. There were a couple steps leading down from it to a raised marble platform with a mammoth white marble altar with sand-colored marble legs that reminded me of cigarette butts. To either side of the altar were walls in coffee-bean brown paneling with niches containing statues of Mary on the left and Joseph on the right, with fake red clicker candles below them. That the candles weren't real bugged me even when I was little. There were also small chapels on either side of the altar, next to the niches and the candles, built into the side walls—one for the Divine Mercy on the right, the other for Mary on the left. The altar rail, pulpit, and seats for the help on the altar were of the same coffee-bean-brown wood with brass details.

That day, for the first time, I was the oldest altar boy serving a Mass where all of the parish altar boy help participated. It felt odd, but in return I didn't have to do anything but carry the cross up and back during the processions.

Father Grillo, my favorite priest since childhood, was visiting to celebrate the Mass with the man who had been a mentor for the first several years of his priesthood. He had a Brooklyn accent and attitude—brief but not gruff—with looks like a mix between Robert De Niro and Cary Grant. He said Mass with the precision of a neurosurgeon—forty-five minutes flat, complete with plenty of Latin. You could set a watch by him. His sermons were timeless. They were funny, smart, taut, and had genuine depth of learning and expectation. Sometimes they would bring a tear to your eye; sometimes someone would get up and walk out.

His sermon that day was about giving one's life to Christ. Most of it registered, but in the periphery I had other things on my mind. I stared down at the tassel in my hand, which was on the end of the rope tied around my waist. As I thought, I bent the loose strands of rope around the knot so it looked like hair on a faceless, bodiless woman. I tried to get her part just perfect—every hair in place—like I had done during the sermons for ten years or so. I was listening, but it probably did not appear to be the case.

As I flopped the tassels in my fingers, I listened to Father Grillo talk about holiness and giving one's life to God. I thought hard about how my sophomore year had ended—in a gale of insanity.

All of that expectation that college would be this wonderland of booze and women—it was half true freshman year. Living in the dorm rooms, though, we were still under supervision. As freshmen, it was unlikely that the older girls would stoop down, and it was also likely that the freshman girls would go for older guys. The Kristen thing, although we had fooled around a couple times, seemed like a fluke more than anything. But sophomore year we all got apartments close to each other—I had a place with Brandon, Skeeter, and Petrone. By homecoming weekend, it was becoming clear what kind of potential this new arrangement would have. I wasn't stupid enough to think that it didn't have its downsides, but I was stupid enough to try to ignore them.

The drinking had become a ritual petition for catastrophe. In December I was hospitalized for a day. After that I slowed down for a while, especially when I went home, but by the end of the spring semester, the drinking had only gotten worse.

The girls were also part of it. It was unexpected, and out of character, but too hard to resist, or so it seemed. I knew God frowned on it, and likely despised it. I prayed to him and told him how sorry I was. I was really going to try to be a better person. I resolved to drink less and stop hooking up. It was easy at the time. There weren't many girls around town yet, and none of my friends drank, really; they were all too young. I wanted to be closer to God. It turned out he was much closer than I thought.

CHAPTER 11

Church ended and I went home, changed, and walked down and sat on the beach with Tony and Demetrios for two hours. Demetrios we called Trio or the Greek. I didn't call him the Greek, usually, because I thought it was rude. But I was in a band with Tony, and one of our songs was called "The Greek." Mea culpa.

Tim Henderson and Eli were working. Shawn we didn't see that often these days. All of us had gone to grade school together, where the K–8 population never topped eighty. I graduated with seven other kids. I was one of the two oldest of the group of us who still hung out.

Tony and Trio were high school seniors, so mostly I just told stories about college—how when you were a kid and you wished that you didn't have to go home at dark, that you didn't have to go to school, that you could sleep over at your friend's house every night; all of that comes true at college. I told them that everything you hear about the drinking and the women is true, no matter how hard that is to believe. The trouble is striking a balance, which I had not done. When I wasn't talking about school, we sat and watched the waves and dug our feet into the sand.

After about an hour, I left, because I had to go to work at my restaurant job. I went feeling sorry for myself the whole way; I worked a lot during the summer. Usually I made some decent money, but the hours working late as a waiter bothered me sometimes. But it was what I had to do.

That night, a new waitress started, and Rosie asked me to show her around. She had a surfer accent, curly hair, and a tongue ring. She was pretty, and I was happy about that.

I tended to be fifty-fifty when it came to conversations with girls when I was sober. If I had enough to discuss, it would be entertaining enough for the both of us. If I was distracted, or I just didn't find some common ground, it was all dead air. But I was doing alright, much to my surprise. We stood at the back of the dining room.

"Your name was what, again?"

"Christie."

"And, let me guess—you're twenty-two."

"Twenty-six. That was a good guess, though," she said.

"My name is W. E. Ferguson."

"So, what should I call you?"

"W. E."

"Okay. What does that stand for?" she asked.

"Worthy of Esteem."

"Can I call you Worthy, instead of W. E.?"

"Sure. Your Royal Highness works, too. You can call me Will if you're nasty."

"Okay. So how long have you been a waiter, uh...Will?" She smiled at me.

"Have you ever waitressed before?"

"A little bit."

I leaned back against the hutch full of silverware and coffee cups. It was a seafood establishment. It was meant to be a classy place with dark wood and ship's wheels and fisherman's nets hanging from the ceiling. It worked pretty well. The air conditioning was always too low.

"Well, you should know I've been a waiter for a long time, so you can trust me. First, you should tell all of your customers that you are new, and you should do that for the first month. The whole summer if you want. That way, you can mess up, and if you keep reminding them of that fact, they will just feel bad for you. Make sure you're reasonably apologetic at all times. Always compliment children. Tell the parents they have beautiful babies. They love that. Hand the check to one of the kids at the table. Always gets big laughs. But you can only use this material on nights when I'm not working."

She followed me around for the entire night, bummed a few cigarettes in the back room, and took to my stupid sense of humor. She met some of the other waiters. Most of them were college kids or recent grads renting a beach house for the summer, usually not with their own money. At the end of the night everyone was making plans to meet at the bar after work.

"Will, do you mind if I bum another cigarette?"

"You'd be doing me a favor. They're a hazard to my health."

I held out the pack and she pulled one out. "But what about me?"

"What can I say? Quit before it kills you."

I lit her cigarette for her.

"I think I'm going to meet Jason and Brad at D.J.'s," she said as she puffed to get her cigarette lit well. "Did you want to meet us there?"

I was never a good liar, except when lying to myself. Usually I didn't attempt it. So what came out next was going to be the truth, regardless of how badly I didn't want to tell it. "Yeah, I'd love to..." I tried to think of a different way to say this and failed. "But I'm only nineteen."

The corners of her smile dropped a bit, and she sounded disappointed, although she didn't mean to: "Oh..." She took a drag of her cigarette. "You should get an ID."

"Yeah." I looked down at my shoes and scratched my head. "I'm off tomorrow, so I guess I'll see you Tuesday?"

"Okay." She started to walk away. "Thanks for the cigarette."

CHAPTER 12

I left the restaurant and walked home in the dark through the empty and quiet streets. The seagulls in the summer must have spent the night in packs out in the marsh, because you could always hear them squawking by the thousands in the far distance, very faint. There was only a slight breeze, so the ocean wasn't rough enough to be heard on the west side of the island. A block farther east you could, probably. My house was a few blocks to the south, and I didn't run into any people or any cars or anything—just the smell of the ocean. I liked the silence.

When I got home, I still had the waitress on my mind. She wasn't just some college girl; she was a full-blown *woman*, and she still took a nibble.

Our house had been built in the thirties. It was sort of a ramshackle beach rental property with four apartments in it—two in the main house, and two garage apartments in the back. It was white with the old-style asbestos tile siding, with steps on the side leading up to the top apartment. It needed some work, and we didn't really have the money to do that. We moved there because my parents were coming close to losing our other house. Somehow it turned out that it didn't improve our situation very much.

When I walked through the front door, my parents were seated on opposite sides of the couch watching TV. It was turned up too loud, which rattled me after walking home on the quiet streets. The old wooden door with wavy glass panes banged up against the coat tree as I opened it. I walked through the entrance area, which was an old porch that was closed in, and into the family room. The walls were a sandy color, and the room still had the faint smell of varnish that my father had laid down during his recent unemployment.

"Hey, baby."

"Hey, Mom."

"How was work?"

"Fine."

"Did you make any money?"

"No," I huffed. "You ask me this every night. The tourists aren't down yet. Give it some time."

I took a couple steps in and turned to see what they were watching, and began removing my tie.

"A girl from school called," she said. It was about nine thirty at night.

"Hmm," I said in response, as some names bubbled to the surface. I figured it was Lily, since she called me a few times the summer before, in between freshman and sophomore year. It was a nice surprise—getting word from school. After being back at home for a little while, it seemed almost like school never actually happened. At home, it was a lot different. I couldn't smoke around even my friends without getting harassed. I hadn't had a beer in a solid month and a half.

"Kristen—she wants you to call her. I wrote her number down." Mom turned and picked up a pink notecard with the number on it off the table next to her.

I took the card, and as my knees began to buckle and the color ran out of my face, I tried to walk across the family room without looking so rattled. I proceeded to my bedroom at the back of the house, off the kitchen.

The previous summer we had lived in the top apartment of the front house, but this year we lived on the bottom floor. My room was probably an old storage closet, and as the only son not living there year-round, I had to cram all of my crap into it. My bed was a futon that turned into a couch. I never bothered to convert it back and forth, so I couldn't open the closet, and I could hardly open the drawers of my dresser. I piled my clothes and effects on top of the dresser, adding to the claustrophobia. It was like sleeping in a veal cage.

I sat at the edge of my bed, with my knees against the open dresser drawers in front of me. I placed the phone on a pile of sweatshirts inside the drawer in front of me as a sort of makeshift desk. The cord was several feet long, but so gnarled that it didn't quite cover the distance between the phone and my ear. I had to constantly pull the cord straight or hang my head over the phone to talk on it. I grabbed the beige plastic receiver and dialed before I could think about it. Before the last digit, my finger stopped in the space between my fingertip and the phone. I stared at my finger while a bullet hail of thoughts bounced around in the back of my skull. Nothing surfaced but a sense of absurdity. I looked up at my mirror and startled myself—first with the pallor of my face and second with the smirk that resided there. This was so unbelievable, it was almost funny.

Doo doo dee....We're sorry, but...

I slammed the phone down.

"Shit," I muttered.

I snatched the receiver again, dialed the first ten digits, and stopped again. For the next ten minutes I repeated this process. I paused and snorted at how strange this seemed, and out of the urge to weep.

I held my breath and dialed.

On the other end was a busy signal. So far, this was going just as I would imagine it. It was nine forty-five. I waited thirty seconds and tried again.

"Hello?" She sounded tired.

"Hi, Kristen?"

"Hey, Will."

I was surprised she knew who it was. We had never talked on the phone.

"What's up?"

She wasted no time—no small talk or anything. I was curious about how she got my number.

"Do you remember Costigan's party?"

For a moment I felt a bit of relief, because I thought she might be calling about something else. There had been a lot of people at that party.

"Yeah."

"And you know how I stayed at your place that night?"

"Yeah."

She paused, sighed, and ruffled the phone, like she was switching ears. I knew what she was going to say, but the pressure in my gut surged anyway.

"I'm pregnant...and it can only be yours." She paused to let this sink in.

I blew out softly through my lips. I knew she was going to tell me she had a disease or she was pregnant, but this was still—a surprise.

I opened my mouth to say something, but just sighed again.

"And if you want an abortion, I need some money."

I knew on some level that that was an option, but I hadn't felt it until then.

I spoke slowly, my voice shaky. "Can we talk about this?"

"Yeah."

"It's probably not a good idea to do it on the phone, though."

"You're right," she said.

"Are you busy tomorrow morning? I don't have to work until four," I said.

"No, I'm not busy."

"I'll come up. You're up near the city, right?"

"Yeah, Glen Rock," she said.

"Let me get a pen." There were four or five on the dresser from work. "What's your address?"

The next minute or two we spent on logistics—she lived about two hours away. I could hear in both our voices a tinge of relief to be talking about something else. We'd meet at ten the next morning.

I hung up and dropped my face into my hands. On the floor was my alarm clock, which read 9:49. Four minutes.

I shook badly, and I tried in vain to control it. I didn't move for several minutes, except for the shaking.

I got up finally and paced around the bedroom, but there wasn't really enough room to accomplish that, and the clothes on the floor didn't help. I sat back down and put the phone on my knee. I had to talk to somebody.

Kat first came to mind. I had helped her with problems with her mom, problems with her dad, problems with her uncle, problems with her sexual orientation. I called and her mom answered, and she wasn't even in the state.

I thought of Jill, a girl I had dated the summer before, and emailed throughout the year. I picked up the phone and dialed a few numbers, and then decided against it. She and I weren't very close, really. The relationship was mainly physical. I noted the irony.

I got up and tried to pace some more. My body heat was filling the bitty room. I thought of telling Tony, but went back and forth about it because I was two years older and had a chip on my shoulder about that. I paced some more, and then I called Tony.

"Yeah?"

"Tony, what are you doing?"

"I'm studying for my trig final," he answered.

"I have to talk to you," I said.

"What's up?"

"I'm coming over."

"Dude, I have to go to bed soon," he said.

"I'll be there in a minute."

"What's up?" he asked.

"I'll tell you when I get there."

I hung up, and stood still for a minute. I got out of my waiter clothes and put on some clean clothes. I put my hand on my bedroom doorknob, took a deep breath, and stepped out into the dark, cool, empty kitchen, through the dining room, and into the family room where my parents still sat watching TV. It felt like ten years since I had seen them last.

"Where are you going?" my mom asked.

"Just going to Tony's. I might be going to Trio's later."

I bent over and kissed her, then my dad. I was afraid they could sense it, but truly they had no idea.

CHAPTER 13

Tony's house was eight blocks away, so I was there in about two minutes, forty-five seconds. It was a huge house that took up most of the lot, with little patches of perfectly maintained landscaping and a polymer-sealed concrete driveway. The exterior was gray-brown vinyl cedar with hard plastic columns. The front door faced the ocean less than a block away. From the second-floor den you could see it.

His dad had redesigned and rebuilt the house a year earlier, and that, combined with its location, made it worth about two million dollars at a time when million-dollar homes were just coming into fashion. I parked at the curb, walked up the driveway around the back, then through the storm door, which closed like the door of a safe. On the other side was his bedroom. He was sitting on his bed in his underwear, with books on his lap and a small lamp shining next to his bed but not lighting much of the room. His TV glowed a silent blue in the rest of the space.

Tony was half Italian, but as far as he was concerned, he was all Italian. He was about five-foot-four, with a round face, glasses, and a hairline with peaks and valleys. He had gotten a little gut because of his affinity for cheesesteaks, stromboli, and mozzarella sticks. His hair was spiked and brushed back at the time. As early as age seventeen, he was covered in hair on his chest, shoulders, part of his back, and especially his ass. Somehow our body hair—especially his—would come up in almost every conversation from puberty into adulthood. He had a perverted sense of humor, but he was a truly innocent person in most of the ways one could be innocent.

He looked up, and I inhaled like I was going to say something but couldn't decide where to begin. He wore a goofy grin, but concern showed in his eyes.

"I Naired my shoulders today," he said after a long pause. He laughed, because he thought all of his jokes were funny.

"I thought you were going to wait for me."

"I couldn't wait."

I paused for another minute. "Did it burn?"

"Yeah. And it smelled like avocados."

"Weird." I stood and thought about what to say. "I need something to drink."

I walked through his bedroom and out into the dark foyer with precise doorjambs, French doors, and tiles. The moonlight streamed through the giant picture windows that filled the wall above the staircase leading up to the second floor. His mom kept a closet there stocked with drinks for Tony and his friends—iced tea and lemonade, sports drinks of all flavors, and bottled water. I grabbed a Lemon Ice Gatorade.

I walked back into the room and began pacing, stopping every couple seconds to drink or to try to talk. He watched me like a puppy would watch a tennis match.

"Are you okay, dude?" he asked, finally.

Tony always loved to hear stories about my getting drunk or fooling around with girls. Just a couple weeks before, I had ridden for eight hours with him to bring his prom date back to Pennsylvania. The entire ride back I had told him about our stunts and about the girls. It was still novel. Since high school, whenever Tony knew I was going to be in the company of a girl, he would tell me, "Make me Uncle Tony!" with a shit-eating grin.

So I said, "I made you Uncle Tony."

His jaw flopped open, and his whole upper body lurched forward as he said, "Whaaat?"

"I got a girl pregnant."

"Holy shit..." He paused and stared at me, his glasses reflecting the television screen, his jaw reflecting shock.

"Who?"

"Remember that girl Kristen from school?"

"You got her PREGnant?"

I stared at him and took a swig of the Gatorade. He stared at me for a minute, mouth open.

"Willie, don't you know that girls get hornier when they're fertile?" Tony was a suspect source of information, especially when it came to sex. It made sense, though.

"Tony, why are you telling me this now?"

"I don't know. What are you going to do?"

"I have no idea. I think she wants...to get an abortion."

He looked at the wall for a second and contemplated this, mouth still open. "Is that what *you* want?"

"No...I don't think so...I have no idea." I paced and looked at his floor. "I know I can't be a dad right now. I'm nineteen years old. And my parents are going to kill me." I was walking four or five steps, stopping, and changing direction. His room was considerably larger than mine.

"I'm sorry, Will."

"It's not your fault," I said.

"Well, I mean..."

By now I had put down the Gatorade, stopped pacing, and was staring at the foot of his bed, with one elbow in the hand of the arm crossing my stomach, chewing the thumbnail of my other hand.

"I can't believe this is happening to me, dude. I can't freakin' believe it."

"It sucks," he said, also staring at the foot of his bed.

We stared for a solid minute, the TV lights playing on the walls.

"You can't tell anyone, dude," I said finally.

"Who would I tell?"

"I dunno, Eli, maybe."

"I'm not—"

"Well, I'm going to tell him. I just want to be the one to do it."

"I'm not going to tell anyone," he reassured me.

I sat on the foot of his bed and stared at the carpet while taking intermittent swigs of Gatorade, but then got up and started pacing again.

"I'm going to go up to talk to her tomorrow morning," I said.

Another pause.

"Do you need anything?"

"No. I just"—I trailed off for a beat—"don't know what to do." I rubbed my hand across my mouth. "Stop with the Uncle Tony jokes."

I chugged the rest of the Gatorade. Everything I drank now I chugged. Before I got to college, I used to hold things in my mouth for a moment before I swallowed. Now, everything went straight to the back of my throat.

"Well, I guess I'm going to go."

"Dude, if you need me to do anything, let me know."

"Alright. Wish me luck."

"Good luck, buddy."

I left the Gatorade on his dresser, because I knew it would make him angry. I liked getting a rise out of him. He probably wouldn't realize it until the next morning. I walked out his storm door into the silence. It was actually more of a whisper, because I could hear the ocean. The sounds helped me think. The air was humid and forming halos around the streetlights. It was a bit chilly. When I got to my car, I leaned on it and lit a cigarette and stood there smoking until I was done.

CHAPTER 14

It was sophomore year, and again I was waking up in a strange place. From the look of the ceiling fan, I could tell I was in an apartment in my own dorm complex, but from the way the sunlight was coming in, I could tell it was not my apartment. It was as though I had blinked at some point the night before, and on the other side of my eyelids was the next day. I stared at my watch for a solid minute and a half, because it had hands and no numbers, and I couldn't think straight. It was 11:13 a.m. This was to be the day Kristen would become pregnant, that I would become a father.

I stood up and nearly fell forward. I braced myself on the couch—the type that came with the apartment, with a tough wooden frame and hard foam cushions made to withstand college kids—then flopped down in it. My stomach felt a little raw, but it was invincible except for that time that it had started bleeding. The tolerance of an ox, as one girl put it. I stood up and I went in the kitchen and realized this was Megan, Jess, and Melissa's apartment. I had my blue shirt on. I walked outside and down the two flights of treated wood steps into the blazing sunlight glaring off every metallic surface in the parking lot. I stopped and urinated in one of the bushes on the side of the apartment building, and then shuffled and swayed through the lot to my car—a bone-white aging Oldsmobile Delta 88 with a burgundy interior and a three-speed automatic transmission. I called her Bess. I lit a cigarette as I backed out, and drove in the direction of Mr. Bagel.

As I drove and smoked, I realized that I was still a little drunk, but I was good at driving drunk so it didn't matter. It took a couple minutes to remember how the night had ended. We had had a party the night before, and it was packed. A genuine hazard to all of us, considering the quality of construction in our apartment complex. One floor in another building had collapsed a few weeks before. Not completely; it had just sunk in a way. Secretly, the fact that it wasn't our party made me jealous. Nobody was hurt, so it was alright to feel that way.

The night before, we had had four kegs, which had become our default and was an order of magnitude larger than most at MU. At homecoming we'd had six, which was probably what put us on the map as the guys who wore bowling shirts and played Gang Starr at their parties.

Scenes from the night before were coming to me as if from a comic book. I remembered finally why I was at Megan's. She and her roommates lived in the building next to Costigan, Johnny, Jeremy, and Eli. When the girls discovered how much weed those guys smoked, they became official groupies.

I arrived at the bagel shop in a strip mall off Route 11, which went west into the mountains and east into...the mountains. Mr. Bagel was one of the few places within a couple miles that wasn't a chain of some sort. I walked through the parking lot thinking how badly I needed a pair of sunglasses. The line was out the door, but I squeezed past a few people, walked in, and stood near the drink refrigerator. Tommy at the cash register looked up and spotted me. He finished helping his customer, asked someone else to take the register, and shuffled up to me.

"I can't believe you made it to work today," I said.

He sort of mumbled at my chest, though usually he's pretty animated. "I just stayed up, yo. Me and Davie were doing gravity hits until about six in the morning, and I just said fuggit, if I go to bed I'll just get tired." He swayed like the weight of his head might pull him down. "So what do you want?"

"Bacon, egg, and cheese on everything, poppy seed with scallion, home fries, and a large coffee."

"A-ight. Just chill right here."

He went back behind the counter, and I sat at one of the tall tables. Nobody was sitting there because it was too close to the line to eat there comfortably. The place was getting hot from all the people. I took a salt packet someone had left and broke it open onto the table, because I liked the way they popped. With the edge of it I collected the salt into lines like I was going to snort them. A few minutes later Tommy walked out with sagging white paper bag and a Styrofoam cup.

"Get some sleep before tonight; you look like you're lunchin'."

He perked up. "Peach, you gotta lotta nerve walkin' up in here in your blue shirt from last night tellin' me I look like I'm lunchin'. At least I took a shower, dawg."

"I just woke up, what can I say."

"That's right, beeotch, I already got, like, a full day's work in. I'm like the effin' Army in this joint."

"Then I guess you better get to work."

"Whatever, man, I'm about ta git fired anyway. But I'll hit you up later, Peach."

I fixed my coffee—lotsa cream, lotsa sugar—and left in Bess toward the Campus Commons apartments. When I opened the heavy white front door, the stench from the night before hit me. Plastic cups with stale beer and cigarettes fermenting together covered every flat and raised surface in the apartment. Our table had a sticky layer of beer and water on it from the beer pong. The apartment stunk of hops, wet carpet, wet cigarettes, perfume, and cologne. It made me proud in a way. It had been a great party.

CHAPTER 15

After breakfast I changed out of my clothes from the night before, left the apartment, and got back in Bess and drove to the convenience store at the edge of campus where Petrone worked. I pulled into the parking lot and walked into the store.

Petrone had become what was probably the closest thing our group had to a genuine rock star. He was skinny and had a big Adam's apple, big lips, and a deep voice. None of that really registered with me until he grew out his hair and started wearing the clothes he had slept in the night before. Then somehow it all clicked. He didn't play any instruments, and he didn't sing, but his knowledge of music was unmatched. Even though he agreed with me that the nineties stuff was better, he was just as effusive about all of the other stuff. At the beginning of sophomore year, he got a record player and started getting tips on good albums. A couple times he would make a few calls and go on a Saturday out to the next state to find a record he wanted. It wasn't the sort of thing like he joined a band and suddenly his hair got longer and he would start shopping in thrift stores and getting armband tattoos. He was the people those people were trying to look like. He would wake up and drink a beer when he was by himself, not to impress anyone but because that's just how he was living. He smoked like it was his vocation, and he carried with him a perpetual sense of having been wronged, usually by a woman. He was his own worst enemy and he knew it, and he hated himself for that.

As I walked in, he was leaning over a textbook. His work shirt was unbuttoned, and he was wearing it over his blue shirt, which was also a button-down and unbuttoned, and a Jim Morrison T-shirt underneath that. Except for the work shirt, the clothes were from the night before. His curly hair was hanging over his eyes.

"Peachfuzz. What's up?" he said, without looking up. The store was quiet, no customers.

"Nothin' man. What are you up to?"

"Reading my Women's Studies homework."

"I forgot you were taking that."

"Yeah." He put a pen in the book, closed it, looked up at me, then out the front door to his left. "I thought it would be a good way to meet some girls."

"What's it about? I mean, besides women. What about them?"

"We're supposed to read a chapter from a book or an article or something, then the class is mostly discussion, which is a stupid way to teach. I don't pay ten grand a semester to have my classmates teach me. They're all idiots and they can't teach me shit. The teacher at the beginning told us there was no such thing as politically correct and we could say anything we wanted, then anytime I speak up, I get fustigated for being sexist. If I've learned anything, it's that the women's movement isn't a women's movement; it's a phony, stupid, bitchy women's movement."

"Fustigated? What did you say to piss them off?"

"The latest was the other day. I said that I thought it didn't make any sense that somehow women's liberation became about birth control. I said it seems like women sold out, because if they really wanted change, they should have changed society to fit them, rather than changing themselves to fit into society. I was sort of thinking out loud, you know?"

"What did they say?"

"Nobody actually argued about what I said; they just told me it would take a man to say something like that, and that I was threatened by their sexual liberation or whatever. They're a bunch of idiots, and the worst part is that I'm probably going to fail."

"I don't know. My grandmother did whatever the hell she wanted to do."

"Exactly. It's like, to them, women are nothing if they're not victims who need the women's movement. It's such shit. In my religion class we're talking about Islam. We should ship these women to frickin' Saudi Arabia and show them what oppression is really about. They can't even drive a car there."

He took out a cigarette and lit it.

"You want one?"

"Nah."

The store was still empty. He looked out the front door again.

"You know that they believe you get seventy-two virgins in heaven?"

"The feminists?"

"Muslims."

"I know. Yeah, I've heard something like that before. Sounds like fun."

"Not my vision of heaven, having dinged four virgins, and having had every one of them go psycho on me."

I looked down and shook my head. "That's just wrong on so many levels."

"It's the truth, man."

"Did you use birth control?"

"Shit, yeah."

I looked at him for a minute.

"Hey, man," he continued. "They didn't come to me looking for liberation, and that's not what I was offering. My point was that I would never take a pill that made my balls shrivel up into my stomach. So if I was a woman and cared about being a woman and hearing me roar, I wouldn't take pills every month to make my man happy. That's me. If they want to, that's their problem."

"No vasectomies for you?" I asked.

"Dog surgery? Are you effin' kidding me?"

I looked out the window for a minute.

"You're so pleasant in the morning."

"It's one thirty in the afternoon, Peachfuzz."

A car pulled up, and before the people came in and started milling about the store, I went to the back where they kept the good beer. I grabbed a four-pack of stout, a case of microbrew, two six-packs of imported stuff, and a thirty-pack of dregs. I stood in line and had a bit of difficulty managing. I waited for a minute, then it was my turn at the register. There were still a few customers in the back, but there was nobody in line behind me.

"I'll also need two packs of Camel Lights," I said.

"Can I see some ID?" Petrone answered in his store clerk voice.

I put the beer down by my feet and took out my library card.

"Okay, Mr. Jones," he said.

"Also this pack of gum," I added.

"You're well read; it's well known. There's something happenin' here, and you don't know what it is," he sang sort of under his breath as he entered three things into the register and voided each, then rang up the pack of gum. The little screen said forty-nine cents. "Do you, Mr. Jones?"

I gave him a dollar and he gave me the change.

"To live outside the law, you must be honest," I responded.

"Have a nice day, Mr. Jones."

I picked up the beer carefully, went out to Bess, and loaded her up. Her hindquarters were sagging a bit.

CHAPTER 16

The last time I had seen Kristen was that night at Golden's party. About halfway through our sophomore year, we befriended those guys, who lived next door to Costigan in the Campus Commons. The party was three kegs. Not quite our caliber, but not bad. It was the weekend before the weekend before finals—really the last weekend everyone could, in good conscience, drink their faces off.

Golden had told the blue shirt crowd we could come and pre-game at their place around 8 p.m. Around then I met Brandon at Golden's apartment. I had gotten there a few minutes before he showed up with his girlfriend, and gave the requisite high fives and manly half hugs. The air conditioning was blasting in anticipation of the body heat; the tables, chairs, and couches were against the wall, and the beer mugs and shot glasses were hidden so they wouldn't get stolen. There were two Ping-Pong balls on the wooden table. The first keg was in their utility closet, the second in Golden's shower, and the third was across the hall at Tommy's, in case the cops came, and in case the line got too long for the regulars. Beast Light, the beer of champions. It tasted like fermented aluminum.

Brandon gave his requisite slaps and whatnot.

"Peeeachfuzzzzzz. You ready to get your drink on, nee-agh?"

"Howdyboutcha, beeotch!"

"Let's get some beer pong goin' on up in heah, sukkas! Let's GET DRUNK; GET CHICKS NAKED!" I joined him on the last three words.

I had been trying to figure out Brandon's accent since I met him. He was from Virginia Beach, and among him and his friends, the accent was a blend of equal parts Southern good-ol'-boy drawl and ghetto speak. When we all had first gotten to school, he was this quiet, sweet, nice-guy sort of kid with long hair. But at the beginning of sophomore year he cut the hair off and broke out of his shell. By the end of the year he was by far the most sparkling personality of the bunch. It was like he was a frickin' Mouseketeer. He would get the keg tapped, the beer pong started, the music on, the ladies dancing. He and I had become good friends living together. Before the girlfriend, we used to chase girls together. He was as clammy about it as I was when sober. We provided encouragement and excuses for one another in equal measures. We used to talk about everything—high school, family problems, school problems, girls. We both had three boys in our families and money problems growing up. We would talk about everything except God and death. One time the both of them came up, and he told me that he didn't like thinking about those things.

This was an electric part of the night. This time of the year, the mountain air was perfumed and dewy, the girls were tanned. The gel and the cologne were fresh, the buzz was light, and the pack of cigarettes was full, the interior packaging foil balled up and thrown at the nearest douchebag. The room was empty and cool, black lights on. We had just spent the year building our reputation as the illest sons of bitches on campus, and we didn't have to prove it anymore. We were going to trash this fine evening properly. I was a chrome-plated hurricane.

The first game of beer pong was against Brandon's girlfriend, Heather, who was the only person who wasn't showering, getting changed, brushing their teeth, smoking weed, or otherwise occupied. Usually there would be another person on her team. She didn't drink that much, so anytime we got a ball in one of her cups, we would chug it for her. So it was like we were playing against ourselves, which meant we had to drink twice as much beer. It got the evening started properly.

"Dude—Peachfuzz—you hooked up last night."

"Who told you?"

I hadn't told Brandon that I had hooked up with a girl because after I dropped her off at her apartment, I went to church. The Gospel had been the story in which Jesus wept at the death of Lazarus. As I was leaving, I began thinking to myself about how it seemed unfair that Jesus wept for certain friends. I wanted to know whether he would have wept for me if I had been around then. The answer startled me when it appeared like someone was speaking over my shoulder: *he does*. I was a little shaken up by this. I decided then that I wouldn't brag about girls anymore; I would try to hook up less, and try to put a brake on things in general.

"Skeeter."

"Skeeter is full of shit," I said.

After a few minutes of chatting and grab-assing, Khan and Petrone were ready to play us. We racked up the cups; they had to go fill the pitcher of beer to fill them. We got the first two shots and sank them both. When one team makes two in a row, they get one of the balls back. I took the bonus shot and sunk it. Brandon and I were pretty happy about all of that.

Khan was madly competitive, so this irked him. They made their first two shots, and he missed the bonus shot. He started pacing a little bit.

"Khan, did you hook up with Danielle last night?" I asked as Brandon was taking his shot.

"Nah, Danielle sucks."

"What do you mean?"

"She's just not that hot."

He prepared himself carefully and missed the next shot.

"I was trying to get into Monica's pants last night," he continued.

"You mean Kristen's roommate?"

"Yeah, dude. She's dumb as a brick, but she's got some biiiiig-ass knockers."

Brandon piped up: "I think those girls are coming over tonight."

"Did you talk to them?" I asked.

"I ran into Katie on campus."

"That must have been fun."

He blew out and shook his head. Heather was across the room talking to Costigan. Still he lowered his voice a little. "Dude, I *hate* talking to that girl. She is such a little bitch. She always eyeballin' me like I'm the daddy that left her."

"Dude, you threw it to her and then you stopped talking to her. I'm guessing she's not too happy about that. You just feel bad because you were a dick to her."

"Thanks, Reverend Buzzkill."

"Whatever, dude."

Brandon and I won. We told them to stay on the table, because we were tired of it.

I exited and stood outside in the night. I lit a cigarette after some consideration.

A few feet away, Gallo and Jesse were arguing about something, and a few people were watching and drinking beers. They had gone to high school together, and the two of them along with Costigan and Petrone were like brothers. Usually they'd be arguing about something that happened in high school. Costigan was watching from a distance, smoking a cigarette. I walked up and stood next to him.

"What's up, Black?"

"Black" was short for "Black Irish." He had a plume of unkempt black hair that waved here and there, and blue eyes. He was born on St. Patrick's Day and would often in the wee hours drape the Irish flag over his shoulders and walk around his apartment. He was one of the biggest drinkers in our league.

"Howdyboutcha, Peachfuzz."

"What's this about?"

"Jesse said some shit about Gallo's sister being a stripper."

"Jesse can't keep his mouth shut sometimes."

"That's Jesse for ya."

"You ever seen Gallo's sister strip?"

"Dude, that would be like watching my little sister strip."

"She's pretty hot, dude."

"Yeah, you're right. She is pretty hot."

Costigan was always unhurried. He always seemed collected, or if not, he wasn't letting it bother him. He had wrecked cars and lost his license once or twice. I felt sure he would do anything for me or any one of us at any time.

"We were doing keg stands earlier, then this started," he said, watching.

"Did you do one?"

"Nah. Petrone did one for a minute."

"Straight?"

"Yep."

"He's going to regret that."

"Maybe."

We puffed our cigarettes for a minute and watched the mayhem. The argument was over. Gallo had now brought one of the chairs that came with the apartment outside and was smashing it, screaming and yelling the lyrics to "Welcome to the Jungle" as a few people stood around and cheered. We had sort of unofficial musical themes—interest in a band or a song that spread throughout the blue shirts and lasted for a while. This month it was *Appetite for Destruction* by Guns N' Roses.

"That's gonna cost us," Costigan said.

If it were my apartment, I'd be angry, and I would have tried to stop him. Gallo was a time bomb, though. There were family problems, and the younger of his two sisters had died in a car accident earlier in the year. Some of the blue shirts went to the funeral, but I didn't. I convinced myself that I had too much work. Really, it was because I was a coward. Not being there was one of the bigger mistakes of my life to that point.

We sipped our beers and smoked. I stomped out my cigarette. Around then, an unmistakable sound pierced the night air murmuring with laughter and conversation.

It was a G chord on an acoustic guitar with a chord on an organ. It was all the blue shirts needed to hear. Jeremy was the first to recognize it out loud—

"FREE BIRD!!!"

The rest of us, one at a time, all chimed in, issuing the same call: "FREE BIRD!" I ran to pour myself another beer. By now, the apartment was full, so I went to the keg in Golden's bathtub.

When I got back out, the blue shirts had all circled up in the middle of the common area, and were singing along. The beer from beer pong had caught up with me, so I was pretty tipsy. I got in between Skeeter and Costigan, putting my right arm around Skeeter, leaving my left arm free to drink.

Skeeter gave me a kiss on my cheek. The group of us was yelling along at the top of our lungs, swaying with our arms around each other, some of us bumping into the next guy, which was a hint of what we were all waiting for.

People who weren't part of the bowling league of intoxicants stood and watched. "Free Bird" had become our song freshman year, when Costigan and Gallo used to blast it in their dorm room at least once a day.

The slow part of "Free Bird" was almost too much for us to bear. As the second verse wore on, we started getting rowdier, pushing each other and spilling each other's beers.

As that last "cha-ee-a-ee-a-ee-a-ee-a-ee-a-ee-a-eenge" came on, we all started jumping up and down, and no one missed a note of the next part:

"LOOOOORRRRD I CAN'T CHAEEEENGE WON'T YOU FLYYYYY HIIIIIIIIIIGH FREEEEEEE BIRRRD, YEAH!"

At that, as the power chords and lead guitar started in, we went berserk—slamming into each other and throwing beer at each other. I threw my plastic cup of beer across the mosh pit at Jabba, and it exploded all over him. In turn he ran across the pit and slammed into me, knocking me backwards over a coffee table, my head slamming against the couch. A couple girls screamed, and I saw stars, but I got up and jumped back into the pit. I could tell I had a few bruises, and probably a knot on my head, and maybe a concussion, but I was more interested in screaming and slamming into everybody. Gallo started overturning chairs, and I grabbed Brandon and threw him into Skeeter. We were throwing elbows and not trying not to hurt each other. Jeremy climbed on the coffee table and did a stage dive on top of us. We didn't catch him very well, because nobody noticed him doing it, really, and he fell pretty hard onto the floor, his foot jamming up in the ceiling fan on the way down. A few of us dog-piled onto him.

Some non-blue shirts were joining the fray, and a lot of girls were screaming in amusement and horror. It was pure madness, pure bliss. We were happy to be alive, to be drunk, to be young, to be listening to Skynyrd. We were happy to have found each other, and to dance shitfaced on the dusty frontier of eternity. It turned out to be more of a precipice.

The rockin' part of "Free Bird" is long, and we slammed into each other the entire time. By the time it was done we were all panting like sprinters, soaked in beer, hoarse, and hysterical. Some were a little bloody. We were giving each other hugs in a sort of congratulatory gesture, I guess for surviving the year so far. I had to go get another beer.

As I was walking to the keg, I ran into Lily, Connie, and Molly.

"My GIIRRRRRLS!" I was still panting, and bent over and put my hands on my knees.

"Will, are you alright?" said Lily, with her bright smile.

"Yeah, I'm fine."

"I saw you hit your head on the couch."

"There's a cushion."

"Still, it sounded bad."

"Really? You could hear it?" The other girls looked at me and nodded. "Cool. Hope it doesn't make me stupider."

"More stupid," Connie said.

"I just figured out the difference between stupid and ignorant today," Lily said.

"How did you figure that out?" I asked.

"It always bothered me when people called someone else ignorant, but then somebody said I was ignorant about something today, and they weren't trying to call me stupid. So I just sort of educated myself."

"Interesting."

"I wasn't stupid about it, I was just ignorant. Now I'm not ignorant anymore, just stupid." She started laughing.

"Stupid with like a 4.8 GPA."

"Whatever."

"How have you studied philosophy for two years without knowing the difference?" I asked.

"I've been called stupid, but not ignorant until the other day."

"We should all be so lucky," I said.

"I'll drink to that," Molly said. Connie held her cup up, and they all had a sip.

Lily's eyes were catching the light just right. She was laughing at herself, and biting her bottom lip. For all of the serious thoughts she had going on in her head, she could make herself the punchline. And for all of her confidence, she remained very mild and modest. She spoke and moved thoughtfully, nothing wasted and nothing done without pausing to consider the truth. A lot of people who didn't know her well thought she was snotty, but she really just had some respect. I admired that.

Molly had shoulder-length brown hair and blue eyes, and was about the same height as Lily. She had transferred from Columbia at the beginning of our sophomore year. She had been friends in high school with Marie, who was their other roommate. She was a little more practiced at boozing and conversation. Her swank came from her North Jersey roots. She and Lily were becoming inseparable.

Connie was a head shorter than the other two. She was pretty but not fussy about it. She could belch like a man, which was funny.

I straightened up and gave them all a hug at the same time. They smelled freshly showered and perfumed, and they made faces as I hugged them, smelling of tobacco smoke, sweat, and beer. I stepped back, and Lily put her arm in mine as I talked.

"So you girls are looking hot! Are you hanging out, because I hope to get y'all drunk and take advantage."

"Okay," Lily said with enthusiasm.

"Well, get to drinkin'!"

"I'm first. I don't want to catch anything from Molly," Connie said, flashing her eyes in her direction.

"Whatever I have I got from Dave." Dave was Connie's boyfriend.

Lily was taking a sip of her beer through her straw, which she used so she didn't taste the beer. She had to spit it out into her cup from laughing.

"You alright?"

Then suddenly, everyone got quiet. The cops had arrived.

CHAPTER 17

From the back door of the apartment I looked past all the people at the front door. When I saw Golden open the door only partway, I knew what was going on. I stopped and waited to see whether it was cops or security, and a bunch of people started heading in my direction out toward the parking lot.

He turned around and told everyone they had to get out. I walked back through the muddy grass toward the parking lot and made a wide circle by myself around a few adjacent buildings to the other side of Golden's building, where Tommy's apartment was. I saw there were people there, but the slider was locked. I knocked on it, and the person nearest didn't know me. He looked to be one of Tommy's friends from home. He looked at Tommy, who looked at me and waved me in. It was a little annoying, the scrutiny, but it wasn't the kid's fault.

I went into the hall closet that housed the keg and cups, and poured myself two beers. I figured more people would be coming after the cops left Golden's, and I didn't want to have to wait in line. When waiting tables I had learned to carry two cups in one hand, so I was good at it. I walked toward the kitchen and saw Johnny X.

"Johnny—you shaved your beard."

"Yeah..."

"Did you mess up trimming it?"

"Just figured I needed a change, yannow? Don't wanna get too comfortable."

"I hear you. In high school I had nice hair and I shaved it off. I hated it but I figured it built character."

He hadn't shaved it all off, just the part between his sideburns and the hair on his chin and lip. Johnny looked Italian, and was half so. The rumor was that he was at Montpelier on a large scholarship, that he had perfect SAT scores, and that he and his dad butted heads. When he had first gotten to college, he was a hard-ass New York stomper wearing wife-beaters and cammo shorts all the time. In one of the first conversations I had with him, he said he wasn't homophobic because he wasn't afraid of fags, he just hated them.

But he had softened up quite a bit. By now he was well on his way from stomper to mussy-haired street-corner café author or philosopher. Some people thought his thoughtfulness was an act. I didn't believe that, though, and I didn't think anyone else had the right to. He was an utterly sincere guy.

"It looks good. You look a little younger."

"Thanks, thanks."

"I saw you at church on Sunday. I didn't know you were Catholic."

"I'm not anymore; I'm Rastafarian. Jah Rasta." He said this looking quite serious.

"Hmm." I took a sip of beer, then took out a cigarette and lit it. "Are you serious?"

"No, I'm not serious." He laughed.

"You never know with you, Johnny. You're a man of many interests."

"Peachfuzz, I'm Italian and Irish. Of course I'm Catholic... what else would I be?"

"I guess I didn't think about it. And you shouldn't practice a religion just because you were raised in it. That's just a habit."

"True, true. I didn't know you were Catholic."

"Weren't you at Porn Storm?"

"Nah. I heard about it. I figured just because you were up there didn't mean you were Catholic."

"You're like the only person who didn't assume that. I guess it's because Lily had a rosary. Yeah, I was raised Catholic." I wrinkled my nose a little bit. "I like going to church, but I..." I was hoping he would pick up on what I was trying to say, because I figured he felt the same way.

"What?"

"I don't know. I don't like how a lot of Christians act, you know?"

"What do you mean?"

I didn't expect to have to explain it.

"Like, I don't know. Like the moral majority and whatever, how they're all Republican and call themselves Christian, but sixty cents to every dollar of taxes goes to bombs and shit.... At the same time, they cut welfare and demonize poor single mothers. And all of this crap with the intern—who cares, really? I'm so sick of hearing it. If they're so Christian, why don't they forgive him? I mean, the president is as big of a douche as the rest of them, but get over it. All of the money pumping into their campaigns from oil companies and insurance companies and banks? They're the slutty interns."

"Yeah, like if you're a fifty-year-old guy and some girl in her twenties is giving you peeks at her thong, you're going to say no? There isn't one of them who wouldn't do the same thing."

"I know, did you hear what Larry Flint did?"

"Nah."

"He offered a million dollars for proof that a Republican was sleeping around, and a congressman voluntarily stepped down from office."

"No shit. That's some funny shit."

I sipped my beer a little more and started up again.

"And how somehow to be Christian means you're supposed to hate gay people—like 'God hates fags.' I mean, if God is the loving God the Bible says he is, then his love has to be a lot better than my mom's love, and if I ever told my mom I was gay she'd still love me."

"I know—I mean, I love you and I know you're gay." We both laughed.

"And Jesus said it's easier for a rich man to pass through the eye of a needle than to enter into the kingdom of Heaven. How did that turn into the Republican party? Shit. I don't know. Who got me started on religion?"

"I think you did, Peach. And I think you're talking about politics."

"Maybe. I don't know."

I took a sip of beer. I was just trying to rant, not really get into a very deep discussion.

"I don't know. I just figure, since it seems to me like it's about greed."

We sipped our beers for another minute and looked around.

"At least Father Bob is getting it right," I said.

"Yeah. Fathah Bob is the shit."

We both stopped and took a sip of beer. I felt funny that all that had spilled out of me, because I didn't talk about religion much. But I thought about it all of the time, and I got talkative when I was drunk.

"Peachfuzz..."

"Yeah?"

"I'm nevah goin' tah caul you Peachfuzz again."

"No, no, it's alright. I know you guys are just kidding. It used to bother me. A lot, actually. But not anymore. Don't worry about it."

"Nah. I'm fourreal, Will. I'm nevah gonna caul you that again."

"Well thanks. But really, it's alright. You don't have to do that."

"I'm fourreal, Will."

CHAPTER 18

It wasn't long before I found myself rather drunk. A decent amount of people showed up at Tommy's from Golden's. There weren't that many girls there.

Kristen was around, though. I had succeeded in avoiding her since December, with only a few transgressions. But tonight I was feeling rather inclined toward taking a stab at it.

And it never seemed to take much effort, for either of us. I never got her number, I never called her, I never gave her a goodbye kiss, and she never seemed to be very interested in any of that. We seemed to get much of the same information about which parties to attend, so we ended up seeing each other often. If we were in the same room together, the chances were good that something would happen. I wanted to be stronger than that, but I wasn't.

We sat next to each other on the couch and talked and teased about nothing. Her outfit was quite revealing, and it looked like she had been working out. That lent an air of inevitability to the course of things.

I got up and stood next to Tommy, who was leaning against his wall watching beer pong. His brother was on his other side, back against the wall. His eyes were closing, his head falling forward, his arms hanging at his sides and his shoulders slouched. He would startle himself awake, shift a little, then his eyes would close, his head would fall forward, and the process would repeat itself.

"Looks like your little brother is hurtin'."

"I warned him. I told him that young blood don't be tryin' to keep up with us. I told him he gotta pace himself because his ass'll be dead before any of us iz even buzzin', know what I'm sayin'? I'm just gonna let his ass stand here so I can tell him how much of a dumbass he is in the mornin'."

I laughed a little. "Well, at least he got to see how the blue shirts get it done."

"Hell yeah."

"Cuz we're the baddest sons of bfitches on this campus."

"Damn straight."

It was getting late and things were beginning to thin out severely, and my mind started to wander. If Brandon had been there, he would have talked me out of it like he had on a few other occasions. But he had left long ago with his girlfriend. I wanted to be talked out of it.

I stood sort of in the middle of the room and looked at the floor in front of me. The room was spinning a little bit. I knew I had to stop drinking.

Kristen came up beside me and spoke flatly. "Everyone's going home. Are we going back to your place?"

I didn't look up.

"Yeah. Let's go."

I said goodbye to those in my vicinity, then we stepped out into the misty, perfumed, and lukewarm air. The streetlights were orange and diffused in the haze. From Tommy's apartment it was a climb to the summit of the parking lot. Our building was situated at the highest point for a couple miles. It was a few hundred yards away.

We walked together in silence up the hill, which felt like an undertow. I took out my last cigarette and lit it.

CHAPTER 19

The next morning I woke up angry that she was there. I wanted better for us. Already my fingers and wrists were trembling, and it was 11:49, hours later than I wanted to wake up.

I got up and urinated. My stomach cramped badly and my thighs ached. My contacts were still in and felt like drops of glue. I put some solution on them and brushed my teeth.

The sun glared hot on the Berber rug and filled the room. I put on a clean pair of underwear, found my jeans, and put them on. I got my crucifix from the end table and put it back around my neck, and pulled on one of my thrift store T-shirts. I sat at the foot of the bed, near her, so by brushing up against her I would wake her up.

She was twisted up in the sheet, her hair plastered against her face in parts, the top of the sheet covering only one breast. Her arm was laid across the pillow above her head. As I put my shoes on she stirred.

"Hey," she said.

"Hey."

"Ugh...my head hurts."

"It was that friggin' weed we smoked."

"I don't smoke usually anymore."

"Neither do I. It was Kind Bud. It kicked my ass." Skeeter had some that he had shared with us when we got back to the apartment.

"Yeah, I've got soo much work to do today."

She was getting up and began looking for her clothes. I handed her her bra and her shirt from the floor. Usually we laughed a little bit about where we found our clothes the next day, but not today.

We walked out and nobody was up yet. We went down and got into Bess. It was a warm day, and we put the windows down. We didn't say anything to each other for the entire ride. Part of it was out of enjoyment of the morning, but most of it was because of the night before. The hills closer to us were blanketed in budding grass, the trees on the mountains in the distance in full bloom. The buds had already dropped off the trees in most parts, but the whites, pinks, and reds still remained in patches. This was the second spring I had spent in the valley, where the roads were lined in cherry trees, blossoms in white or pink that dropped and left a skirt on the grass around them, crisp blue sky without mist, and lingering fragrance.

Campus was about two miles away. The groundskeepers had painted the practical campus landscape with accents from the native palette. For that, and the care with which the janitors kept the toilets so pristine, they deserved an award. They were my people.

We arrived at Monroe Hall, where she lived, and this had me feeling slightly nostalgic. I pulled into the crook in the curb that served as a bus stop.

"See ya later, Kristen."

"This is probably the last time we'll see each other this year."

"I'm sure we'll see each other around before we go back home."

I was bad at goodbyes in general, but especially so with her for reasons that should by now be obvious.

She began to reach across the seat, and we gave each other a hug and a peck on the lips. It was the first time we had kissed goodbye.

CHAPTER 20

When I got home I had a bowl of cereal and brewed some coffee. While it was brewing, I stripped the sheets off my bed and put them in the washing machine, like I did every time I had a girl over. I found the condom on the floor by my bed. I took a quick shower and brushed my teeth. When I got out, the coffee was done. I poured myself some but didn't drink the whole cup. I had already started shaking pretty badly.

Nobody was up yet, and it was one o'clock in the afternoon. I wasn't settled enough to start on the paper, so I grabbed my keys and walked across the development to Megan's apartment. I had a feeling that I had to apologize, not for anything in particular, but in general. As important or more so was the feeling of having a chunk missing from my memory of the night before last. I always went out of my way to make sure somebody told me what I had done and could not remember.

I knocked on the door and let myself in. Megan yelled, "Hello?" from her room. I went in, and she was lying on her bed. I had obviously woken her up. She was already fully dressed, and so this seemed to be a nap.

"Hey, Peachfuzz," she said.

"Hey."

"What's up?"

"Nothin'. What did you do after Golden's?"

"We were at Tommy's for a minute. You were playing beer pong."

"Oh, that's right. I saw you there."

"Then we just came back here."

"Losers."

"Whatever, Peachfuzz."

I looked around her room for a minute. She had lots of posters from movies—Audrey Hepburn from *Breakfast at Tiffany's* was one of them.

"I love Audrey Hepburn," I said.

"Isn't she beautiful?"

"Yeah. I want my wife to look like that."

"If she were still alive, I'd marry her."

"Really? I didn't know you swing that way."

"I don't. But I would totally dyke out for her."

"Well, if I was a chick I would, too."

I looked around for another minute. I checked her bulletin board of pictures to make sure I was featured. I was, in my blue shirt.

"I was stopping by to apologize."

"For what?"

"I dunno, Friday night, I guess. I blacked out, and I hate it when I do that. I know things were getting pretty rowdy, and I was kissing you."

"It's not a big deal, Will."

"Yeah it is. I just...I don't want anything to affect my friendship with any of you girls."

"Aww, that's sweet, Peachfuzz." She wasn't being sarcastic.

"So I'm sorry."

"Don't worry about it."

One of her roommates came home and we talked a little while longer, smoked a couple cigarettes on the porch.

I left after about forty-five minutes, and on the way home I stopped at Lily's apartment. I walked up the three flights of steps to the front door, knocked, and covered the eyelet. Whoever it was opened the door and it was her roommate, Marie.

"Hi Will!"

"Hello, Marie." Marie was about five-foot one with a kind face and blue eyes. She had a nurturing demeanor and seemed wise beyond her years. All of our girls did.

"Lily's not here."

"Dammit. Why do you girls always say that? I'm here to see all of you."

"Okay. Sorry. Come in."

"Thanks." We walked toward the common room.

"So what's going on?"

"I don't know. I have a paper to write, so I figured I'd not do that. I'm having a little trouble concentrating. I smoked weed last night."

"Will!"

"I know. I hate it when I do that. I can't think the whole next day. Skeeter smokes it to study. I don't know how the hell he can do that. He smokes it to do everything."

"I don't know either."

"Have you ever done it?"

"Smoked weed?"

"Yeah."

"No."

"Good. Don't. Don't smoke either. Don't drink. Just do your homework."

"I *do* do my homework."

"Good." I looked at the TV which was turned to MTV, but muted. "Were you doing something when I got here?"

"My homework."

"Oh. Right. So nothing."

"Right. Nothing." At that point, Lily walked in. I looked up from the couch and saw her walk past the kitchen into the room.

"Oh, hi, Will!"

"Hey, what's up?"

"Not much."

"Where were you?"

"I just went to Mass, and then they had an end-of-the-semester brunch for everyone."

"Oh, that's right. I should have gone. That sucks."

"It was nice." She looked up at the TV then back at me. "I have to check my email. Did you want to come chat?"

"Sure."

I went in her room and sat on her bed, and she sat at her computer.

"I'm waiting to hear from one of my teammates on this project I'm doing for art history."

"That's cool."

I looked around the room for a minute while she clicked around on her computer.

"So how are you?" she asked.

"Unsettled."

"Is anything wrong?"

"Nothing in particular, I don't think. But I was wondering what happened last night."

"What do you mean? About Jonathan?"

"Yeah. It's weird to hear you call him by his name."

"Petrone, then."

"Did something happen?"

"He made a crass comment about...whether I've remained chaste at college."

"Did something happen that made him upset?"

She stopped and looked at her computer blankly for a minute. "Maybe."

"Like what?"

"Well, a couple things, I think."

"Go ahead."

"Well, I didn't want to talk about this, but he did ask me out a few times."

"Really?"

"Yeah."

"When?"

"The most recent was last weekend."

"This happened more than once?"

"Yeah, a few times."

"And I guess you didn't go."

"No, I did once."

"You didn't tell me that!"

"You didn't ask." She was still facing the computer screen, but she was smiling.

"How should I know to ask something like that?"

"Well, I just didn't want it to be common knowledge."

"But I'm not going to tell anyone!"

"Well, whatever. I'm sorry. Anyway, we went out for coffee, and it was a pleasant time, and then at the end he drove me home and I think he tried to kiss me."

"You think he did?"

"Well, I don't want to be presumptuous."

"So what did you do?"

"I cleared my throat and told him thank you, I had a really nice time, and I may like to do something in the future, but only as friends."

"What did he say?"

"Well, what could he say? He said okay, and I left and that was it."

"When was this?"

"About a month ago, maybe."

"Wow. I had no idea."

By now she had turned around in her seat and was facing me with her legs crossed playing with her hair. I was noticing how she looked around the room, and how it seemed like there were at least one or two more things going through her mind.

"And then...there's the other thing."

"What's that?"

"I kissed a boy."

"You *what*?"

"I kissed a boy."

"What the hell? When was this?"

"Two weeks ago."

"Who is he?"

"He's a boy in my philosophy course. Very Kantian. In spite of that, I thought he was cute, and he had asked me out a couple times. We went to a movie, and we ended up kissing a little bit."

"Who is this guy?"

"You don't know him."

"How do you know?"

"It's Chase Covington."

"Doesn't sound familiar. Sounds like a douchebag."

"Well, he kinda is. I thought he was cute, though."

"Is this going to continue?"

"Oh, *no*."

"Why not?"

"Because, like you said, he is a douchebag." She smiled. "There is, of course, hope for his conversion, and I'll pray for that."

"But for now it's a no-go."

"Right."

"Don't you see him in class?"

"Yes, and it's awkward, but that's what I get, I guess."

"Has he asked you out again?"

"Yes, a couple times."

"Have you gone?"

"Yes, once."

"Are you going to go again?"

"Maybe."

"I thought you said he was a douchebag."

"I'm praying *really* hard."

I smiled and looked around the room.

"What about you?" she asked. "Any prospects?"

"No."

"What about Kristen?"

"What about her?"

"You two could be cute together."

"I don't think so."

We stopped and looked around. There was a lot to be said right then. So much that I didn't say anything.

"I miss this," I said. "I feel like we don't talk anymore."

"I'm always here."

I looked around some more. "You're right. You are. It's me, I guess. I'm not," I said.

"Sounds very post-modern."

"I have no idea what that means."

"Neither do I, really."

I sighed. "I guess I should go."

"You can hang out here, if you want."

"No, I have work I have to do."

CHAPTER 21

The nine days since learning of the pregnancy had all passed like seasons. The day after Kristen called with the news, I drove up early in the morning to her town. At the very last part I got lost and called her from a pay phone. She gave me directions from there, and I still couldn't find it. I called her from another pay phone outside a little store on a wooded street. It was a pretty suburban place close enough to commute to the city. She told me to wait there, and she would come to me.

I sat in Bess with all of the windows down and flicked absently through the radio stations, wondering if I would pass my sense of direction on to any kid I had fathered.

It was about 10 a.m. The leaves glowed like gems in the sunlight as it passed through the trees on the neighborhood street. The little parking lot was empty and well-shaded. It was June in its quintessence.

A black '95 BMW 3-series pulled in two parking spaces down from me, windows down and pop music playing, with Kristen in the passenger side. I was surprised to find that as she pulled up, I was excited to see her. It was strange considering how petrified I was.

She exited the car, a worried look in her eyes. She was different, with a tan and her light brown hair lighter from the sun. She had just taken a shower, and her hair still looked a little wet, and was pulled back. My mind whirled a little.

We both smiled and said, "Hey" as we walked toward each other, then embraced. As much as the moment before had rattled me, this rattled me more. After the night I had just spent worrying about getting a girl pregnant, to feel warmth and peace and to feel a little tingly was a pleasant shock. I was a dad, and she was the mother of my baby, who was right there, inches from me. I hadn't experienced anything like it. We held each other for a long time.

As her friend pulled away in the BMW, we let go. I opened the passenger side of Bess for her.

"Where did you want to go?" I asked.

"There's a park that's probably pretty empty; it's down this way a bit."

I began driving as she directed. We chatted about how summer had been so far, about her friend's summer house in Long Beach that she had visited. She pointed out her grade school as we passed it, and noted where her friends lived. It felt nice getting to know her roots. But most of the time we remained quiet.

We parked and got out of the car and walked beneath a weeping willow past a baseball field to a wooden bench facing an empty playground. It was well shaded and there was a lazy breeze. I sat on the edge of the seat to her right, with my elbows on my knees. She sat back with her arms across her stomach and her legs crossed, the top one kicking back and forth.

I knew I should begin the conversation.

"So how have you been?"

"Alright," she said, like she was happy I asked.

"Does anyone know?"

"No, just Camie."

"How did you find out?"

She spoke with thoughtful pauses. "I just started feeling sick every morning, and I was throwing up every day for two weeks. I told Camie and we went to get a pregnancy test. It was positive, but I already knew. I wasn't sure if I should call you, but I thought it would only be fair."

It was strange and new to hear her talk about morning sickness.

"I'm glad you did."

We sat and stared at the empty swings for a minute. There was a jungle gym made of wood with a bridge and a small slide. The seesaws were to the right. It was a decent playground.

Morning sickness. It was like "menstrual blood." It made me feel very male.

I spoke slowly, because my voice was shaky. "Well, there's three options." I held my hand out to keep track, starting with my thumb. "We can raise it, and I don't think I'm ready for that."

"No way," she said, before I could finish.

"So we could put it up for adoption...or..." She knew what I was not saying.

"How do you feel about that?"

I thought for a minute while I rubbed my temples. I wasn't used to talking about convictions. And I didn't want to hear what hers were.

"I guess you could say I had really strong pro-life feelings... before this. I figured if I ever found myself in this situation, I would suck it up." By "before this" I didn't mean I had changed my mind. I meant "up until now, so in theory they haven't changed."

"Me too."

We stared for another spell.

"I just can't believe this is happening," she said.

"I know."

She uncrossed her arms and held them palms up, shaking them as she spoke out in front of her toward nothing, "I just want to know, why me? I have so many friends that are... just"—her voice stumbled like she didn't want to say the next part. She pulled her hair back and let it flip forward—"so much *worse* than me. I mean, I'm a good girl, I get good grades, I'm good to my parents..."

"I know."

"It's just not fair."

I dug in the sand with my sandals.

"We can't waste our energy on that, Kristen. It's not going to do us any good."

She sighed. "You're right."

I rubbed my temples, then looked up at the jungle gym. "I don't think I'm the only person you should talk to about this. You should talk to an adult that you trust." I was thinking a priest, but I didn't say that. I didn't know if she was religious or not.

"I know," she said, nodding. "There's a place in the phone book that I'm going to make an appointment at. They give help to pregnant girls."

"Good."

"I've been so stressed out, and I stopped smoking when I started getting sick. It's killing me."

"You didn't smoke that much anyway."

"I've been trying to eat well. It's so weird."

At that point, a car pulled up to the parking lot on the opposite side of the playground. We both stared in its direction, and it felt sort of like we had been caught making out. A brown-haired boy of about three or four and a light-brown-haired girl of about five, both with large green eyes, darted out of the back seat, not closing the door behind them. Their tall, handsome father stepped out of the front seat. The kiddies sprinted to the jungle gym and started climbing up opposite ends of it, the boy going up the wrong way on the slide. The dad looked over at us and nodded a greeting. I nodded back. I'm sure it looked like we were breaking up. If only. The kids kept looking over at us, either because they wanted us to see their stunts, or because they could tell there was something wrong.

I looked over at Kristen, who was staring blank-faced straight at them.

"This is so ironic," she said, barely moving her mouth.

"I know."

"God doesn't have to rub it in."

I chuckled. "They're cute kids," I said. She was always a funny girl. "Time to go?"

"Yeah."

We got back in the car and she directed me back to her house. I told her again to talk to somebody, and I asked her if it would be okay to call her in the coming days. She said yes, but to try to do it at night, and don't call too much, and not too late, because she doesn't have her own line, and late calls from a guy would raise suspicions. I told her it would be hard to get in touch, then, because I worked so much and got home late sometimes, but I would try.

CHAPTER 22

That night I went to a graduation party for Lauren Snider, who was two years behind me at our high school. She was popular, and most guys thought of her as attractive. Eli, Tony, and I showed up sort of late, and I immediately felt uncomfortable because her entire family was there along with a bunch of kids from my high school grade and below. I didn't really have much to say to most of them.

The three of us stalked around and ate as much of the food as possible and talked to as few people as possible. I had never really had much of a conversation with Lauren, but another Chelsea kid, Emily, was a mutual friend. Emily was like a little sister and wanted to set the two of us up. Most of the night she and the girls talked and squealed and group-hugged while we stood in the corner and ate their food.

Em at one point brought me over to talk with Lauren, who had curled her hair and was wearing a short, white, flouncy dress. She had been to the beach quite a bit already. Em brought me over, asking Lauren if she remembered me. I put on my best face, chatted about this and that, thanked her for inviting me to the party.

I excused myself when I sensed it was getting stale. Me, Tony, and Eli went outside to get some sodas at the little tent

146

they had set up, when Tony asked if I was going to tell Eli. I said yes, and we walked out to the parking lot near Tony's car.

"Eli, I'm about to drop a bomb on you."

"Okay." He had always spoken very precisely. I looked past him as I thought about how to put it, and then struggled to say it.

"I got a call from a girl from school yesterday...and...I"—I stopped and took a few breaths—"got her pregnant."

"Holy shit."

Tony chimed in, "You believe that shit? He made me Uncle Tony!"

"Shut up, Tony," Eli and I said in unison. Tony liked to watch the drama in his friends' lives.

"I'm sorry, Will."

"Thanks."

"What are you going to do?"

"I don't know. I don't know what to do."

"If there's anything you need, Will, let me know." Eli was a friggin' rock. No matter what it was, I could be sure that would be his response.

"Thanks, dude."

They both kind of watched me for a second, and nobody knew what to say. But that wouldn't last long for Tony.

"We always knew you were a strong, virile young man, Willie. You got da Super Sperm, you know what I'm sayin', my nigga? You gotta watch where you put that lightning rod, fo' real."

We laughed a little more, and then found ourselves looking at the ground in front of our feet.

"I've never been this scared in my life," I said.

"We know, Willie," Tony said as he put his hand on my shoulder. "You know we're there for you."

"I know."

We started staring again, so I figured I would break it off. I knew they had no idea what to say.

"I'm going to go say hi to Kat," I said. "Did you guys want to come?"

"I have to work at Buck's tomorrow morning."

"I'm going to give Eli a ride home and eat the rest of the cheesesteak stromboli in my fridge."

"Tony, you just ate like three plates of food."

"But I've been waiting *all day* to eat it."

"You're going to have a heart attack."

"Not with the miracle gene, Willie. Grandpa eats McDonald's every day, and he's eighty."

"Whatever, Tony."

CHAPTER 23

Katrina, since leaving L.A., had changed back to a hippie, which was what she had been before she started...acting. She dyed her hair back to its original brown and had dreads and all. They were skinny ones, and they looked good on her. They bothered me in principle, though, and I would never admit liking them. She got an eyebrow ring, too, and she wore eye makeup, which she hadn't done before.

She decided after doing a few more movies that she had had it with Los Angeles and porn, and so she moved back and stayed with her mom and her stepfather. She had been accepted to film school in New York for acting and directing and would be starting in the fall. She was still only nineteen.

Kat had to be careful where she went, because people recognized her, even with the dreads. It wasn't so easy, but still they recognized her. Luckily, most people wouldn't say anything once they recognized her, because this was a family town and people didn't want to admit it. It was a disgrace watching the dads do double and triple takes. She tried her best to blend in, which the dreads didn't help, or she just stayed home. I was only one of a few people she hung out with regularly.

When I first got back home from school I asked her about it, but there was a lot I didn't want to know. I knew from knowing her so well that she had been with only one guy before her first movie.

All of it had come about because she had been in a prolonged fight with her mom, so she bought a ticket on Greyhound and went and visited a girl two years older who went to UCLA. Her name was Katie. She had wanted to visit Katie for a long time, and this gave her an excuse. It was the end of her junior year in high school. For money and for fun, she responded to an ad for a nude photo shoot. They took a couple photos and didn't even ask her to take her clothes off, just bend over a little bit and show some cleavage. They told her to come back the next day. When she did, they asked her if she was interested in doing a movie, and she said yes when they told her they would give her $3,000. They had her sign a few forms, and they pricked her finger for an AIDS test, which was one of the ones that gave results in an hour. They had a nurse on hand.

After the results, they started shooting. They were going to do only two girls, but after seeing her they added her. The contests were mostly shams from what she could tell. She said she had watched a lot of porn with Ms. Daphne, so basically she knew how to act. She thought it would be fun, and she doubted it would get released anyway. Even if that happened, she figured she would do only one, and she definitely didn't think it would be the type of thing that would make her famous. She didn't think about it all that much. She didn't even tell Katie where she went that day. Altogether, she made, she calculated, between ten and fifteen thousand dollars during her career. With it, she paid Katie some rent, and bought a "shit ton" of weed and an old Vespa scooter that later broke. The rest she gave to a soup kitchen and used for food and a bus ticket home. She just wanted to be a hippie—free love but with benefits, as she put it—but found herself hanging out with fellow pornographers, and being expected to be a porn star off screen, although she didn't put it like that. I couldn't believe it. She always was such a smart, smart girl—a beautiful girl, a beautiful person—and this seemed just so stupid and so cheap. It didn't make any sense to me.

She was the only one home when I got to her place after walking back to my car and driving there. We decided to get a movie, which would require us to drive to the next town up. The two of us had done this a couple times since I got back into town. A week before, we had made this same drive to the video store, and we were counting how many people we had hooked up with. I beat her by one, but she didn't accept the results.

As we were driving I told her I had something big to tell her. She was skeptical, because surely she figured that despite her tender age, she had been though everything, and she could scoff at whatever piddly problems I had.

"You're really not going to believe this."

"Will, please. Just tell me and stop this crap."

"Kat, I got a girl pregnant."

She opened her mouth and coughed in disbelief. She stared at me and couldn't get a word out for a while.

"Holy shit."

"I know."

She was turned toward me with her mouth open, bracing herself with her one arm against the door and the other against the back of her seat.

"Stop looking at me like that."

"Holy...shit."

"Stop saying that."

"How did this happen?"

"I had sex with her, Kat."

"Holy shit!"

"You're a real help."

"Give me a cigarette."

I gave her one and took one out for myself.

"What does she want to—wait—who is she?"

"It's a girl from school. I don't know what she wants to do. I went up to talk to her today. We just kinda talked about our options."

"Does she want to keep it?"

"I don't know, Kat. I told you I don't know what she wants to do."

"What do you want to do?"

"I don't know. I can't raise a kid right now, I'm nineteen. And I'm scared to talk to my mom and dad about it."

"Your mother would kill you, Will."

"Worse, she'd be disappointed in me."

We sailed along the perfectly flat, straight, empty road with the dunes on the left and McMansions on the right. The windows were open and I was driving about twenty-six miles per hour. We blew smoke out the windows.

"A fine Boy Scout you turned out to be."

"Bite me, Kat. I wore a condom. I was prepared."

"Did it break?"

"I don't know. I was wasted. And high."

"Doesn't a Boy Scout walk a girl home, then go spank it?"

"What, to a Kitty Claire video?" I said with a Romanian accent. She rolled her eyes. "And would you shut up? I don't need you rubbing my nose in it."

It got quiet for a little while.

"Are you thinking about an abortion?"

"I don't know, Kat. It doesn't seem like the kind of thing I see myself doing." I flicked my cigarette out the window. "But then again, neither is getting a girl pregnant at nineteen." I looked over at her, and she was staring out the window.

"What do you think I should do?"

"Will, you need to figure that out for yourself."

"What would you do?"

"I wouldn't get pregnant."

"I'm sure you've been Ms. Safe Sex. I didn't see a condom on any of those guys."

"Oh, so you watched? I'm flattered."

"Just the one, and I didn't want to. So I guess it was just the one guy."

She took a drag of her cigarette. "We had tests and I used Depo. And besides, Will, I'm a born-again vagina. I mean virgin."

I cackled purposefully to mock her. "A born-again vagina? Can I be one?"

"You're whatever you want to be. Virginity is a state of mind."

"What about pregnancy?"

"I guess it depends on your politics."

"What would Noam Chomsky say?"

"Pregnancy is a lie the government manufactured, and we have been indoctrinated into believing it."

"Hmm....It's more of a moral thing, though, isn't it?"

"What would the pope say?"

"I don't know. Probably keep it in my pants. Not in so many words."

"You should know, Mr. Altar Boy." Kat was baptized Catholic, but had outsmarted us when she was twelve.

"When can I be Will again?"

"Oh, shit. Stop bitching, you know? Dammit. People get pregnant every day, Will. You're not so special."

We stared and drove a little more. I hadn't expected that.

"When can I get you pregnant?"

"You can't get me pregnant until you marry me. Or the Depo wears off."

We were at her house. We went in and watched an artsy movie, smoked a bunch of cigarettes, and I went home after I was sure my parents were in bed. I went in my room and read *The Student Bible*, which my parents had given me for Confirmation. It had little sections about all of the modern issues, including abortion. I had read that section a long time ago, and I read it again now. It didn't say anything I didn't already think would be there. I took out my tattered journal, but didn't feel like spilling the whole story. Instead, I wrote a prayer:

> Lord, take this cup from me
> With the tears of consequence it teems
> But if it cannot be passed,
> Then upon my soul its contents cast
> And may it wash my tomorrows clean

I turned off the light, lay on my back, and forced my eyelids closed. I slept like a downed wire in a hurricane.

CHAPTER 24

For the next two days I told a handful of my closest friends. At first, I expected some advice, but soon realized it wasn't going to happen. After a while it just served informative purposes. It was like they were watching modern art. They knew they were supposed to feel or do or say something, but they weren't sure what, and after a minute they just wanted to leave.

It was early evening and I knew Kat was home, so I drove to her house. I knocked on her door, and her mom answered. She and her mom were hot and cold. Over petty things, usually. Her mom was a nurse and had a clinical way about her. She knew about the movies and the fame, but never said anything about it to her, which I thought was bizarre. When I walked into their living room, Kat was standing in the kitchen. They appeared to be getting along. Her mom didn't know what was going on, and I sort of wished she did.

Kat and I went to her back room, which smelled like patchouli oil. I made my way through the clothes and art projects on the floor and sat on her bed. She sat on a seat she had made with one of her artsy friends that was intended to have the perfect shape for taking bong hits, which I thought was asinine.

We were across the room from each other. It was four days after Kristen had called. I had barely slept, and I had not been able to get in touch with her. I called a couple times, but we missed each other. By now I had told most of my closest friends, but Kat was the one I talked to most about it. She was handling it with grace.

"So what are you thinking?"

"I don't know, Kat. I can't decide what to do. I can't be a dad right now. We could put it up for adoption, but *shit*. I'll have to tell my parents and it will wreck them. I'll be that kid, you know? The kid in town who had to drop out of school because he got a girl pregnant."

"You're talking to the porn star in town."

"I know, but...I don't know. That almost seems better."

"Of course it does, because it's happening to *you*."

"Right. Anyway, my parents will be embarrassed, my brothers won't be able to look up to me anymore. I mean, I've failed them. I feel like I've failed all of these people. I'll miss a semester or a year of school, I'll miss my buddies, I probably won't be able to go to Italy in the spring...

"But what else can I do? You know my family. My parents have always told me family comes first. This is my *kid*. The other option seems like it will take care of things and we can pretend like nothing happened. But Kat, I won't be able to do that. You know that. I'm not going to be able to go through that and then pretend like it didn't happen, and it's stupid for me to think it would be any different. It's my kid, and there's not anything that can change that, whether we do that or not. I'd feel like I killed my own kid, and I wouldn't be able to live with myself." I thought for a minute.

"It would be hard. Really hard. Probably the worst thing we'd ever have to go through," I said.

"Which, the abortion?"

"No—I mean yeah, but no—I meant telling my parents and putting it up for adoption....But we made the mistake, you know? They both suck. So I don't know. I just don't know what to do."

"It sounds like you've made up your mind, Will."

I stared at the wall behind her for a minute. I hadn't at any point thought that to be the case. "I guess you're right."

"You know what's right for you, and you want to do it. That's the Will I know."

I huffed in protest, because I wouldn't be having this conversation if that were true. But she was right in the way only a person who knew me when I was younger could be. "Well, thanks." I had my arms folded across my stomach, and I was staring just past her head. "I guess we'll just have to suck it up."

"I'm sure you'll be fine, Will."

"Will you help me?"

"Will, I'm not sure I want to be in the same state when your mother finds out you got a girl pregnant."

"Great."

"It's something that's between you and your parents."

"You're right."

"Let's have a cigarette."

We went out front and sat on the lawn chairs set up in the pebbles below their stoop. It was near sunset, and we could see the sun setting over the bay down the street if we leaned forward to peek around the house. Her new stepbrother, Rob, pulled up. He had just been accepted to Harvard Business School. We had been in the same after-school science league when we were in grade school.

He played two or three sports in high school, had the same girlfriend he met there sophomore year, made Eagle Scout a year before me. I really liked him, but it was shit seeing him right then.

"Willie, you smoke?"

"No."

"Oh, I see. Just holding it for someone?"

"Yeah."

"How's school going?"

I smiled a little bit to myself. I took a long drag and blew it out. "It's going alright."

"What are you studying? Political science?"

"Engrish."

"'Engrish,' huh. So you're going to be a teacher?"

"That's about the extent of my options."

"That's cool, that's cool."

"So you're going to HBS, huh?"

"Yeah, looks like it."

"Isn't the suicide rate really high there?"

"That's what they say."

"Well, I hope you don't kill yourself." I was actually being sincere. It didn't come out that way.

"Uh, thanks, Willie."

CHAPTER 25

In the days after that, I continued to work and try to get in touch with Kristen. I thought about how I was going to tell my parents.

I thought a lot about how involved I would be in the kid's life. I figured the adoption people would let us have a hand in picking a couple. It would have to be a good Catholic couple.

I was sure it was a girl. She'd have her mother's green eyes and light brown curly hair. She'd spend a lot of time at the beach. She would like *Sesame Street* while she was small, like her dad did. Or no. She wouldn't be allowed to watch TV.

I guessed I wouldn't be allowed to see her too often, if at all, but I would want to write a letter to explain everything. I would want a letter from the couple every once in a while. And some pictures.

I figured at some point it would be okay for us to meet each other. When she got to be about my age she would come looking for me, and we'd catch up at a diner. I would explain everything. There would be some tears shed, but I'd be proud of her for the person she had become, and sad that she didn't need me to do it. She'd learn to understand our decision. She'd be grateful for the life X and Y provided for her, and that Kristen and I did our best in our situation.

As time went on I'd share stories about my parents and my parents' parents. She'd be sweet and inquisitive. I'd see things in her nature that a lifetime of nurture couldn't take away, or put in her. I'd make it to her wedding and sit in the back. I would visit my grandbabies, but as a family friend or something. Maybe she'd babysit for my other kids once in a while, and she would be their favorite.

She'd take her husband and her kids to my funeral. At the reception she'd talk with my wife, who would tell her stories of the good things I did in life. I would have lived it from then on in a way that made her proud to have my blood in her.

But I couldn't let myself think like that for long. There was a lot of work to do.

CHAPTER 26

That Sunday morning I spent with the family. We didn't go to church because sometimes we fell out of the practice in the summer. Our routines were all out of whack. We had breakfast together. I had been sleeping a little better since deciding, but not much. It was taxing to be in their company—I was going to delay telling them until it seemed right.

Tony and Eli came over after breakfast. The moment the three of us were alone, Tony came up to me and reached up and put his hand on my shoulder.

"Willie." He was wearing his grin.

"Yeah, Tony." I knew what was coming next.

"Happy Father's Day, dude." He laughed a little. I shook my head at him. Eli smiled and shook his head from beneath his black Pirates hat.

"You're such a dick," I said.

"I'm serious, dude," he responded.

"So am I. You're a dick. That's been bothering me all day."

"Did you decide what you're going to do?"

"We're going to suck it up and put her up for adoption."

"It's a girl?"

"No, I don't know. That's what I'm guessing."

"Did you tell your parents?"

"Did it look like I told my parents?"

"No."

"Did she?" Eli asked.

"I haven't been able to get in touch with her all week. I've been working too much."

"If you raise it, you might be able to go on welfare, dude."

"Tony, really. Shut up. I haven't been sleeping much, and I'm not in the mood."

"Why aren't you sleeping?"

I stared at his eyes.

His smile waned a bit, and he lowered his eyes. "Sorry." He walked over to the fridge and looked through it. He grabbed some string cheese that I hadn't been eating because I thought it was old.

"You want to go on the boat?" he asked from inside the fridge.

"I have to work in a couple hours."

"We'll be quick, dude."

"I'm not in the mood. I'm just going to try to take a nap before work."

"C'mon, dude. You gotta get your mind off things."

"Sorry, dude. I'm not interested."

CHAPTER 27

When I got home that night, my mom told me Kristen had called. I went back into the room and dialed.

"Hey, Kristen."

"Hey, Will." Her tone had darkened.

"How are you?"

"I have an appointment for the abortion on Tuesday at ten o'clock. I need half of the money."

For some reason, it didn't occur to me, at any point, that she might be thinking anything different than I was.

"Can we talk about this?" I managed to say.

"Yeah."

"I'm working until about nine thirty tomorrow. Should I come up to your place?"

"Did you want to meet halfway?"

"That would probably be best."

"Okay. Is it alright if we meet in Long Beach?"

"Sure. How will you get there?"

"Camie can drive me."

"Where in Long Beach?"

"Let's meet at the McDonald's. It's on Ninth Street and Ocean Drive."

"Alright. Is eleven okay?"

"That's fine. See you then."

I was too tired at that point to go out, to brush my teeth, to do anything. I undressed and lay beneath my sheet. I said my prayers: *There are four corners on my bed, a pillow for my little head. Matthew, Mark, Luke, and John, bless the bed I sleep upon. Amen. God bless everybody. Dear Lord, I'm sure you know what I need. I pray that you help me.*

CHAPTER 28

Work the next night was slow. I didn't need to do much running around, and I didn't get too much food on me or anything. When I got home I took my shirt off and washed my arms up to my elbows in the bathroom. It was a cool night, so I put on my jeans, my sandals, and my blue, worn-out Wharf T-shirt. I put on my red Phillies hat backward.

I took a look in the mirror to try to look my best. Part of me thought it was important for that to be so.

I walked through the house to the front room.

Dad was working. This was a new job for him—security guard in the next town over.

My mom was out on the couch sleeping in front of the TV in her waitress uniform, with the apron balled up in her lap. She had just gotten back from working at my cousin's restaurant. She worked one or two jobs in addition to her regular one during the summer. I walked up and kissed her on the cheek.

She lifted her head a little and opened her eyes for a second.

"Where are you going?" She put her head back down and closed her eyes before she got the sentence out.

"I'm going out. I love you."

"I love you, too, my baby."

"You should go to bed."

"I'm going. Just a minute."

"Go to bed, mom. C'mon."

"Alright, I'm coming." Her green eyes opened and were glassy and unfocused.

"Goodnight, mom."

"Goodnight, my son."

I stepped out into the chilly air and into Bessie. This time of June, by ten o'clock at night on a weekday, all of the Jersey resort towns were dead and empty. I drove with my windows down and listened to my car's swish bounce back at me off the vacant homes, and listened for the ocean. The salt air was a bit thick, like silk.

Usually I loved the quiet. Tonight, though, it was just blank. I drove through the orange haloed streetlights against the moonless sky, through the main part of the main street, which was only a block long, out toward the bridge.

When we used to live close to the bridge, we always had the windows open in the summer. The hum of tires on the drawbridge grates always intrigued me. I would notice it only at night when the wind died down and I was trying to go to sleep. The source of the sound was the greatest mystery of my youngest years. When I figured it out, it was a letdown. But I still enjoyed it until we moved out.

The McDonald's in Long Beach was about thirty minutes away. I didn't go there much. It's a pretty classy place—dry, with a boardwalk that wasn't yet infested with budding inmates. The houses were built right up next to each other. Down the middle of it is the same road that goes down the middle of all the shore towns all the way up to

Maine, according to legend. Or maybe it was the Intracoastal Waterway that did that.

The road was wide, flat, and straight, with evenly spaced streetlights. Houses lined both sides of the street, with clusters of shops in different parts. During the endless drive I didn't see any other cars on the road, or notice them at least.

As I lumbered along, my face became hot. At the same time, though, I trusted that I would be able to handle it. All she had to do was look at things from my angle for a minute.

I went over my reasons, but not what she might say. My gut was wrenched up, and still I felt the pressure to weep. After a while, though, the thoughts just sank away and the rest remained. It was like I was underwater.

My chest burned when I saw the golden arches off to the left in the distance. A lone black BMW was sitting in a parking space as I pulled up. I fixed my hat in the mirror, got out, and stood as straight as I could. She got out and looked worn down. She spoke first, very matter-of-fact.

"Hi." We gave each other a brief hug.

"Were you girls waiting long?"

"Only a couple minutes."

We walked around to the other side of my car under one of the streetlights and sat down on the curb between the sidewalk and the parking lot. She was to my left.

Again it was my turn to start the conversation. I hated that. I took deep breaths and looked at the vacant homes across the street at the other end of the parking lot. I had come here a few times when I was small after going to the pediadontist. I felt bad then eating right after getting my teeth so clean. My mom said it was okay, though.

"I don't know what to say. I think we should put it up for adoption, Kristen."

"Will, I can't have this baby." She had been practicing this. There wasn't even time for her to have registered what I said. I waited a second. I hated arguing, too.

"Why not?"

"Will, first of all, my father will kill you. Then he'll kick me out of the house. My mother will disown me. We both have school we have to think of."

I sighed. "Kristen, I'm willing to accept whatever your father does to me. It's my fault." I really hadn't thought about it from the dad angle yet. If I were him, I'd kill me, too.

"Will, listen to me. I'm telling you he will literally kill you. You don't know my father."

"Kristen, I don't care what your dad does to me. I don't care. I deserve it."

"What about your parents?"

"My parents are going to freak out. But once they're done freaking out, they'll help us."

"Will, I can't take time off of school."

"Then don't!"

"And what? Walk around pregnant? I can't be the pregnant girl walking around campus!"

"Then take a semester off."

"I can't take a semester off! And go through a pregnancy by myself while all of my friends are down there?"

"I'll take a semester off, too. It's not a big deal."

"Will, yes it is a big deal. Yes it is. You can't miss school. We can't ruin our whole lives for this."

"Kristen, it's not our whole lives; it's nine months."

"This is going to ruin all of our schooling. All of our friends will go on without us. We can't ruin all of our studies."

"We have to! We got ourselves into this!"

"Will, I can't carry a baby for nine months and then give it up to somebody I don't even know. I can't do that."

168

"Why not?"

"You have no idea what this is like. I can't carry a baby and give it away. I can't do that."

"So it's better to abort it?"

She huffed in frustration. "Will, I can't carry a baby and put it up for adoption."

"Then I'll raise it."

"Will, you can't raise a baby right now. You're not ready. You're only nineteen years old. You have school to finish, and you have your whole life to think about."

"Then we have to put it up for adoption."

"Will, I can't. My parents will kill me. They'll take me out of college."

"They'll get over it. They'll help you; you're their daughter."

"I can't, Will! I can't! My dad kicked my sister out of the house for the same thing! They took her pictures down!"

"Really?"

"Yes!" Her eyes were tearing up.

That was foreign to me. I thought for a minute.

"Then come live with me at my parents' house. They'll take you in."

"Will, your parents aren't going to take me in. They don't even know me."

"Yes they will. They're like that. They're good, loving people. All of my friends love them. You can stay in one of our apartments if you want. We have a property with four apartments. They're empty in the winter. My mom's a nurse; she'll help you out. She had three kids of her own. She's a good woman. My dad's a great guy."

She put her hand on her forehead and didn't talk for a moment.

"I can't have this baby, Will."

"We have to do this, Kristen. We got ourselves into this."

"Will, we have school to think about. Everyone is going to know. I'm going to be that girl who got pregnant. I'll be taken out of school and kicked out of my house. There's no way I can do this. I'm only nineteen. I can't do this to my family."

"But you *are* that girl who got pregnant. It happens, Kristen. I mean, I feel the same way, but this is what we have to do."

She started to whimper.

"Will, why are you making this so hard on me? Why? Camie didn't even blink an eye. She just said, 'Let's make an appointment with the clinic.'"

"But this isn't Camie's baby. This is our baby, and I think we should put it up for adoption."

"But I have to carry it! This is *my* choice! I wasn't even going to tell you!"

"That's not fair, Kristen! It's my baby, too!"

"You can't make me carry this baby for nine months."

"It's a life, Kristen. This isn't fair."

"I know it's a life! I can feel it inside of me! I saw the ultrasound! You have no idea how hard this is for me!!"

She saw our baby.

"There are three people we have to think about!" I said. "This is our *kid*!"

"Will, I know there are three lives, but there are two main lives!"

I stopped talking, because I couldn't believe what she had just said.

"There are two main lives, Will."

If I would have said anything at that point, it would have been something well short of charitable. And I couldn't piss her off, because then I would be the enemy. But I figured the stupidity of what she had said was self-evident, so I let it hang out there. She was a smart girl. But I'm not sure she noticed.

I looked ahead again across the street at the dark and empty homes. Behind them was the unlit bay and the black marsh. I rubbed my face with the palms of my hands and sighed. This wasn't going anywhere.

"What time do you want me to pick you up?" I didn't look at her.

"Around nine thirty."

"Then I guess I'll see you tomorrow."

I stood up and we hugged briefly. I got in Bess, turned her on, and drove out of the parking lot.

As I drove, the pressure in my head and my gut swelled, and things were quiet, like I was underwater. I felt like I was somebody else watching myself. The orange lights seemed whiter, and to be getting more so, until they seemed to be glaring off the street. I was following a silver car, which also appeared to be getting brighter. And at some point it disappeared.

Like I had just blinked, I found myself in Chelsea.

CHAPTER 29

I had to talk to Kat. It was a little after 2 a.m. I pulled up to her house and saw the TV still glowing in the living room. I walked up the concrete steps and peered through the window. She and her mom were both sitting on the couch. I tapped on the glass-paned door, and they both looked out. Kat got up and came to the door.

"You scared me," she said.

"Sorry."

"What's up?"

"Can I talk to you for a minute?" I asked.

"Yeah." She turned to her mom. "I'm going outside, Mama."

She shut the door behind her, and we walked down the steps and sat on the metal patio chairs out front. She was facing the house and I was facing the street.

"She wants to do it, Kat."

"Put it up for adoption?"

"No. The other thing. I don't know what to do."

"Shit. When did you talk to her?"

"She called on Sunday and told me she had an appointment for tomorrow. I just went up to Long Beach to try to talk her out of it. I told her I would do anything. She's afraid her parents will kick her out. I told her she could come live down here. She doesn't care."

I was using my arms and speaking fast.

"She doesn't want to carry the baby, and I don't know what to do about it, Kat. How do I make her? I can't! Our baby is going to die, Kat. I told her! I told her there's three lives, and she said there's two main lives. What the hell does that mean? A life is a life. Dammit, if you're going to kill someone, kill me! I don't care! Not our baby! I'm the one who deserves it. I said *everything*, Kat!

"Will"—she paused to make sure she had my attention, and looked straight into my face—"you're a good person. And you would make a wonderful father."

The tears came, instantly. I sobbed hard with my whole body. It wasn't something I thought I would hear. It was the very last thing. It hurt a lot to hear it, but I needed it. Every moment, it looked more and more like there was nothing I could do. For some reason what she said offered some comfort, which I had not felt since all this had begun. I covered my face, because I was embarrassed, but my whole body was shaking. When I thought I could talk, I looked up and said, "I know. That's what makes this so hard."

It didn't come out very well, though. I tried to hold back the sobs, or at least make them quieter. But they kept coming in waves. I kept my face in my hands until I got a hold of myself. It took several minutes. I wiped my face and tried to breathe normally.

She offered me a cigarette, and we sat and smoked in silence. My stomach muscles ached and cramped.

"I have to be up in a few hours. I have some thinking to do. Thanks for the cigarette."

"You're welcome, Will."

I got up, walked over to her, and gave her a hug. I remembered Jesus saying whenever two people ask something in his name, it will be done. As we let go, I looked at her, "Kat, please pray for me."

She hesitated. "My spirit is with you."

"No, Kat, please pray for me."

"My spirit is with you."

I sighed. "Goodnight, Kat."

CHAPTER 30

At 7:30 a.m., the cackle of my alarm clock filled my room. My eyelids ached from forcing them shut the entire night. I nearly fell out of bed while lunging to hit the snooze button, but it was too late. I had heard Mom clumping through the house on the hardwood floors, getting her breakfast in the next room, brushing her teeth, filling the dog's water dish. Today she would go do what she had been doing for the past ten years at Ocean County Heart Clinic—mend broken hearts.

Why I had not thought to turn the alarm clock off was a mystery to me at the time. I had all night to think.

After I found the snooze button, there was just dead air, except for the *clump-clump* of her white nursing sneakers with a little green heart imprinted on the bottom getting nearer to my bedroom door. She knocked politely.

"Will." She didn't have a morning voice.

"Yeah." She opened the door and looked down on me as I lay on my back beneath the single white sheet with my limbs jutting out. Her freshly sprayed Calvin Klein Obsession filled the room in an instant.

"I thought you were off today."

"I am...but me, Eli, and Tony are going out to breakfast."

"Where are you going?"

I sat up and rubbed my eyes to make it look like I had slept. The open door coaxed an ocean breeze through the drapes behind me that tickled my back and gave me goosebumps. The silence was thick in the air as I struggled to get something out.

"I don't know." I sounded annoyed so maybe she would stop asking questions.

I didn't look at her. I had been lying to her, silently and out loud, for over a week now. It never got any easier, and it felt that morning like my ribs were splintering under the deceit. But in my mind I had decided that I had gotten myself into this mess, and I would get myself out. I'd tell them after I convinced Kristen.

"Well, you really should take your brother. His girlfriend is out of town and he has nothing to do on his day off."

I merely shrugged my shoulders and lowered my head as my heart clapped against my ribs. I couldn't believe she hadn't figured it out.

I didn't have the energy to think of an excuse. The din in my chest reached a crescendo as I sighed and I just said nothing. Part of me couldn't believe I didn't have the guts to tell her.

"He's your brother. It wouldn't kill you."

I could feel her glare of disapproval burn through my skull for a moment before she, with her dramatic flair, turned and stomped away, closing the door with purpose but not hard enough to wake anyone.

The pressure in my chest spilled throughout me like something had broken. I wanted to claw the tears out from behind my eyes, but they wouldn't come. I swung my legs around and by mistake banged my knees against the open dresser drawers. I put my elbows on them and dropped my face into my hands. When I heard the front door close, I turned the alarm to the off position and noticed I was ten minutes behind schedule. I picked my Young Seducers T-shirt up from the top of the pile in my drawer. Off the floor I picked up my green cargo shorts, and from the top of my dresser I grabbed a handful of cash wads, each of which represented a night's take from seafood peddling. It was mostly ones. I hoped it was enough. I put on my gray sweatshirt, because my room still felt cool, and my glasses from the dresser. I wore sandals.

I called Tony. His phone rang seven times, and I knew on the eighth the machine would pick up, so I hung up and hit redial. Nothing again. The third time, I let the machine pick up.

Jes. My name ees Diego Puntana. Please leave jour name at dee message.

"Tony, wake up.

"TONY.

"Wake UP!" I didn't care if I woke up his parents.

"TONY!"

I slammed the phone down, picked it up, and slammed it again. And again. I stepped out into the sleeping blue kitchen, cool and quiet. It was perfectly still. I walked through it to the front of the house.

As I opened the front door, I felt for the first time how piercing that day's sun would be, as it bored through the gray fabric on my chest from its low position in the sky. I got into Bess, whose burgundy interior had already begun to grow warm. I backed out of the driveway and drove toward Tony's. This was going to make me late. But he needed to know my parents thought I was with him.

More important, I was thinking of the passage about two or more people asking something of Christ. Tony was my only close Catholic friend. We used to pray together before we went surfing.

I raced to his house, and his and his dad's vehicles were in the driveway. Usually he parked on the street, but I figured he was home. I jammed the car into park and sprinted around the side of the house, up the stairs of the back deck, and to the sliding door next to his bed. I banged on the storm glass and yelled his name. Part of me was wondering what the rush was for. It was 8 a.m., but I didn't care if I woke anyone up.

I ran to the front door up the granite steps and rang the doorbell. I would invent some reason for being there so early. I began to dry-sob and knock on the solid oak door like I intended to break my knuckles. I looked at my watch, swallowed, and decided it was time to leave. No tears came.

When I got in the car and began driving, I realized how hungry I was. I took out a cigarette and lit it, even though I never smoked that early. But I would not be eating today. I drove down Third Avenue at forty miles per hour, which in Chelsea is like pissing on the mayor's lawn. Out of habit I took a right on 21st Street past the house I grew up in, which the new owners had remodeled, and it looked like hell. There wasn't a thing wrong with how it had been.

As I crossed the bridge out of town and my tires hummed on the drawbridge, I noticed steam hanging over the grasses in the marsh. After crossing, I skidded into the parking lot of the boatyard at the foot of the bridge. It was made of broken shells and dust. I left the car running and the door open as I scrambled to the pay phone on the outside of the large tin warehouse. I dialed Tony once again as the dust swirled around me in the still air.

Jes. My name ees Diego Puntana. Please leave jour name at dee message.

"Tony. Don't come to my house, because my parents think I'm with you today. I don't know where you are, but if you're home, you're an asshole."

CHAPTER 31

An hour and forty-five minutes later, I arrived and pulled into the driveway. I had no trouble with the directions this time. Her house was nestled in a cul-de-sac with white vinyl siding and a red brick foundation and steps with black shutters on the windows and a red front entrance. The growth around the homes here was mature and lush, and all the houses looked to be about the same size and were similar in design. They were nice but not ostentatious. I honked the horn from where I was.

The door cracked, and she was the first person I saw, and out with her came two more people—a guy and a girl. I didn't expect that. It just didn't seem right to have to argue about this stuff in front of people. It didn't seem right having them there at all; they had no business.

She was wearing a white T-shirt with some blue or black writing above the left breast, and some writing on the back. She had on navy blue mesh gym shorts. I wondered how one picks out an outfit for an abortion—if she had laid it out the night before, or if she was wearing the first thing she had picked in the morning, or what.

The other two were clearly a couple, and they looked like they might have just graduated high school. The guy looked sort of like a baseball player or wrestler. I didn't even notice the girl.

Kristen opened the passenger door and sat down; the lovebirds got in the back. She was freshly showered, and her soft hair was still wet.

"This is...these are my friends from home."

"Glad they could make it."

My mind was racing, but there was no quality thought going on. I just wondered what the hell I could do now. I looked as miserable as I possibly could and didn't look at her.

She told me which way to go. We drove out of her neighborhood onto a busy four-lane road with just yellow lines in between. There were fast-food restaurants, strip malls, and the like all over the place on both sides of the street, with gnarled grass, pebbles, and dust against a curb littered with hubcaps and broken glass. The road was patchy with filled-in potholes, unfilled potholes, and irregularities of every species.

"I need the money," she said in a flat voice.

I slid my hand into the pocket of my cargo shorts and dug out a handful of mostly ones, crumpled like a fistful of dead leaves.

I handed them to her, and she sorted and counted them while I stared straight ahead. She tried to hand me back some extra, which I didn't take at first.

"Take it," she insisted.

I took it and put it back in the pocket.

We kept driving on the road, which felt like a demilitarized zone. My nerves were so exposed and I was so tired that every bump in the shit car sent shocks through me to my fingertips and toenails. I thought about what to do, but it never went beyond that. I simply asked myself what I should do, over and over. No part of me was really working on the answer.

"It's up there at the next corner. Take the next left."

We had been driving for a good ten minutes, but it still seemed soon. I had forgotten there was a destination. In my chest, I started to feel panicky.

"Oh, my God, there's protesters!" she said.

She put her face in her hands, and her friend put her hand on her back. "It's okay, honey." It was awkward to see that out of the corner of my eye—a young girl comforting her friend going off to abort her baby. It doesn't come naturally.

I didn't even see the protesters before we took the left, but I was glad they were there. The building was on a corner across from a fast-food joint. It was big in the front, with a brick facade and white columns, like a library. The parking lot was in the back with a chain-link fence around it, barbs stretched across the top.

We parked and got out of the car. The sun bore through my sweatshirt and torched the asphalt. The three of them were in front of me. I knew it was the last chance to say the last thing to change her mind. It was either say something or pass out.

"Can I talk to Kristen alone a minute?"

"Yeah, no problem."

The guy knew his place, which was miles the hell away from me. He was making an extra effort to be cool with me. He had clearly been sucked into this, and I sort of felt bad for him about that.

She turned around like she didn't want to be bothered. The two of them walked ahead; the two of us toward my car a few paces. This was it.

"Kristen, the right thing to do here is the hard thing. The wrong thing to do is the easy thing. We have to do the right thing." The words came out soft and like sighs, and they were everything I had left.

"I'm not going to have this baby."

"I can't go through with this," I said.

"You can leave."

I looked down at the hot tar and didn't really think about what I was going to do. I didn't say anything for a while. She got impatient.

"I'm going in. You can leave if you want." She paused. "I'm not going to have this baby."

I sighed and stared at the asphalt. That was it. There was nothing else to do. "I can't leave you here," I found myself saying.

We started walking, looking down at the ground. I had that feeling of being underwater. The air was hot and still, and it raked across me as I walked, and it smelled of tar and weeds from the property beyond the fence. She had her arms crossed.

We turned the corner, and at the end of the walkway up to the building near the street were a handful of protesters with signs. Most of them held the signs down by their feet and were talking to each other, drinking water, or protesting toward the traffic, not noticing us much. They were older people, mostly. I didn't read what any of the signs said.

A middle-aged security guard with a mullet, a mustache, and a gut greeted us with a clipboard. His sweat dripped on it as Kristen told him what time she had the appointment. He asked her to confirm her name and she said yes. I had meant to listen to what he said, but I didn't.

He walked with us to the door, which I thought was a useless gesture. The girl went in before us, and the wrestler, whom I had nicknamed "Sporty" in my head, held the door.

Walking the last ten feet felt as though I was chest deep in wet sand. I had felt that only once, when skydiving, and probably one other time when leaving the womb. When we stepped into the lobby, which was frigid, wicked, and dim, the taste in my mouth changed. My blood turned to ink.

CHAPTER 32

It took a minute for my eyes to adjust. The lobby had a high cathedral ceiling with two blonde doors of the type that are hollow inside, with cheap brassy knobs, in the wall across the lobby from the front door. Above them was a large square vent, centered on the wall between the eaves. There were rows of blue padded seats screwed together and in place like in an airport terminal. There were clusters of grim and impatient people sprinkled throughout.

To the left of the blonde doors was a receptionist window with fluorescent light staring out from the inside, and a large woman in a nurse's shirt sitting behind it. In front of the window was a retractable nylon strap to herd us properly. There were windows on three sides of the lobby, with shades drawn nearly to the bottom. The outside glared in through the cracks at the bottom and seemed to freeze in the dark air just beyond.

The lovebirds found a seat, and Kristen and I stood in line, me behind her. There was one girl ahead of us.

We processed up to the window, and the large woman with the curl in her lip pointed to the clipboard in front of her, then looked back down at a magazine. She told Kristen to sign her name, and I strained to see over her shoulder as she did. Kristen DeLonge. I never knew her last name until then. Pretty, I thought.

"Go through those doors and take a seat in the first room on the left."

"Can he come with me?"

"He can come if you want," she said, without looking up, like she didn't want any more questions.

We opened the two blonde doors, where a hallway went straight back into a tiny room to the left.

Inside, the walls were stale and beige, and there was a couch, where we sat on opposite sides. Across from us was a desk with a swivel chair on rollers facing the wall. There were posters of rainbows and waterfalls and kittens on the wall.

A Latina woman about chest high with sleepless eyes came in with her brown curly hair pulled back loosely, wearing a nurse's smock with flower patterns on it. She looked to be in her late thirties and was not overweight. She was carrying a clipboard.

Without saying anything, she pulled the chair on rollers from behind the desk and sat. She turned and took a folder from the desk, and handed Kristen a paper from it.

"Hi," she said, looking at her clipboard.

"Hi."

"We're going to take a minute to explain the procedure to you, and have you sign a few documents."

I stared at her eyes. She glanced over at me and back at Kristen.

"Okay," Kristen said.

"You're about nine weeks, so the procedure will be what is called a vacuum aspiration, which is the second procedure on the sheet."

I glanced at the sheet, which was blanketed in small words. I looked back at the woman's eyes.

"You will be asked to lie on the table and put your feet into the stirrups, like a standard gynecological exam. You will then receive a mild sedative. The doctor will then insert the speculum into the vagina, to open it up, like when you're getting a pap smear."

In my head I kept daring her to look at me. I stared at her eyes and tried not to blink. She wouldn't look at me.

"The cervix will be dilated using an instrument. Some women experience a pinching sensation that lasts a few seconds. Then the doctor will insert the vacuum aspirator. You'll feel a slight pressure, and some women experience some cramping while the doctor removes the tissue."

A wave of anger flashed through me at that last word, and I almost lost it. From the look in her eyes, though, it seemed that she was used to that sort of treatment. This must have been how she threw her weight around. But who in the hell was she, really?

I kept trying to look in her eyes. She wouldn't look at me.

"It will take about ten seconds for all of the tissue to be removed, where it will travel down a tube into a collection jar. The doctor will remove the instruments, and you will have to wait in the recovery room for about a half an hour." She paused and seemed almost to count to five before speaking again. "Are there any questions?"

"No."

"Sign here, then. From here you'll go into the room down the hall, where you'll change and wait before the procedure. Nobody is permitted to accompany you beyond this point."

She glanced at my chest, and I continued to stare at her as the three of us stood up. I was closest to the door, so I stood aside to let the ladies through. Kristen walked out, but the lady bent over the desk and filled out some papers. I left and took a right and went out the two blonde doors into the veiled lobby with the windows glaring white from the outside.

I walked to my right and to the front corner of the lobby, and sat facing the receptionist's window. The kiddies sat in front of me. They were fondling each other like in a school hallway before class, which made me want to throw up. They must have been uncomfortable. I almost said something to them, but figured it didn't make a difference what they did. What reverence did they owe any of this?

Behind them and to the left against the wall was a fish tank, brightly lit with green plastic seaweed, a fake brown and gray shipwreck, colored stones, filter running, and no fish.

I picked up a copy of *Cosmo*, opened the pages to look like I was reading, and I started praying.

Dear God, I believe that you can do anything that you wish. I know that you want my baby to live.

Dear Mary, Mother of Jesus, I ask that you pray for my baby. I am a great sinner, but I know that you are sinless. Please, I ask that you pray for me to God our Father, that he might save the life of my baby.

Dear Jesus, please save the life of my baby. I believe you are the Son of God, and I believe that you can do anything you desire. I ask you to save the life of my baby. I ask you to change Kristen's mind and save my baby. Only say the word and it will be done.

Please, God, if blood must be spilt for our sins, take mine instead.

I said an Our Father and a Hail Mary.

For an hour, I stared at the same page in the magazine and repeated prayers like these. The kiddies were talking about this and that, each putting an arm in the other's, giving kisses here and there.

In the first hour I got a glimpse of the first girl to come out since I had gotten there. She was a thin young Latina girl with dark, straight hair. She was clutching her stomach and proceeding slowly out the two blonde doors. Her nose was wrinkled like she had smelled something foul. Her eyes were blank, and across the entire lobby she noticed nothing but the doors ahead. Some kids got up and went out after her.

I put the magazine down and stared at the floor. Every few seconds I would look at the two blonde doors to see if Kristen had changed her mind and was leaving.

Dear God, please save the life of my baby. If you must, take me instead. Please do not punish my baby for my sins. Dear Mary, please pray for the life of my baby.

It was getting near lunchtime, and my new friends were starting to talk about getting something to eat. I sat with my elbows on my knees staring at the floor.

Dear God, I know you want my baby to live. Although I am a great sinner, please hear my prayer—please, God, save the life of my baby.

"Hey, man, we're going to go to Wendy's to get something to eat. Did you want anything?" asked Sporty.

"No, thanks."

"Are you sure?"

"Yes, I'm sure."

"Anything to drink?"

"No."

"Okay, man. You'll be here if Kristen needs anything?"

"Yes."

They left, and I went back to staring at the floor. I heard the blonde doors burst open and slam against the walls, and a black girl of about seventeen, a little pudgy, ran to the front door. Halfway across the lobby, she started sobbing. A group of four or five other kids got up and scrambled after her, but she was already out the double doors. I could hear her sobs fade as she made her way to the parking lot, her friends yelling after her.

I stared at the blonde doors and continued praying, as someone from inside closed them. My arms and legs were trembling slightly, and my stomach ached from hunger.

God in heaven, please save my baby. Jesus Christ, Son of God and worker of miracles, please grant a miracle for my baby.

I noticed that there were times when the words came but my mind was wandering. I would shake my head and try to align the two. I tried to pray with my whole body, staring at the doors.

God in heaven, please save my baby. Mary, please pray for the life of my baby.

I leaned back in the chair and crossed my arms, staring at the two blonde doors.

More women came out, all of them in a hurry to get to the front doors. Each time the two blonde doors opened, something perked up in me to see if it was Kristen.

I kept praying, and part of me wondered when it would be too late. But I figured I had a duty to keep praying until I knew.

After a while, which was maybe an hour or maybe fifteen minutes, the kiddies came back. The prayers had become shorter and the same, over and over again.

God in heaven, please save my baby. Take me instead.

I stared at the two blonde doors. They cracked open, and Kristen poked her head through. She didn't come out, and it looked like she wanted something. I pointed to myself, but she wasn't looking at me. The girl who came with us cranked her neck around and hurried to her aid when she saw it was Kristen.

They talked for a minute, and Kristen glanced at me. I hadn't moved. I was confused about what to do. They nodded at each other, and Kristen closed the door. The other woman sat back down.

"What did she want?"

"There were a lot of women waiting, and she said her turn was coming up soon."

I looked back down at the floor and started praying with renewed fervor. I looked at my watch, and it was about one o'clock. I stared at the two blonde doors and continued to try to pray without stopping.

CHAPTER 33

An hour later she opened the right of the two blonde doors, and turned after she closed it carefully. She walked across the lobby deliberately, as if across a lake on lily pads. The three of us got up and walked toward the exit, and Sporty held the door.

The heat had saturated the earth. The sun was doing its dirtiest work, and the air felt insufficient. It was about two o'clock. I was walking in front and a little to the left of Kristen, and the other two were just ahead of us in a staggered procession. Kristen walked holding her stomach, swaying. I looked over my right shoulder at her. She looked at the tar.

"Are you alright?" It was difficult for me to ask her that right then.

"Yeah." She didn't look at me and didn't even seem to hear the question.

"Are *you* alright?" asked Sporty. The question struck me as a little funny, and I chuckled for a breath. He must have felt perverted, standing there watching. This was full penetration.

"Yeah."

I looked down at the tar. I was underwater. There was no sound and there were no thoughts; I couldn't feel the ground or anything else.

"I'm such a bad person," Kristen said to herself.

"Shh." Her friend came to her side and rubbed her back.

We got in the car.

"You have to tell me where to go," I said.

"I'll tell you," said Sporty.

The radio was off, and the A/C took a while to begin cooling the car. We all had our windows down.

"I'm such a bad person."

"Kristen, honey, don't do this to yourself," the girl said.

"I'm such a bad person. I'm not like them. The lady I was next to—she was married, and her husband beat her up and drank. She didn't want to have any more of his kids, and she wanted to leave him. She said if he found out she was there, he'd kill her. He thought she was looking for a job." She looked down at her lap. "What did I do?"

We drove in silence, except for the directions and the hot wind through the windows, smelling of diesel exhaust and dust. She started to weep softly, the tears splashing onto her shirt and her shorts. She sunk into her seat and looked out the window with her arms across her stomach and tried not to make too much noise. Her hair was blowing into her face, but she didn't try to brush it away.

CHAPTER 34

We pulled into her driveway. She held her stomach and shuffled from the car to the front door. We all walked into her house, down a hall leading back to the sunken den, another room, and the kitchen, all dark because the afternoon sunlight was hitting the front of the house. We settled in the den.

She flopped onto her side on a grand leather couch looking out toward us but not seeing any of us. Above her on the wall were portraits of her mom, her dad, and her in a Catholic school uniform, probably from the second grade. She was twinkly-eyed and eager and smiling, and missing her two front teeth. She looked like her mom.

She spoke slowly and to no one, "I'm such a bad person..."

She started to sob bitterly.

"I'm such a bad person...oh, God." She lay on her side and curled up with her knees up near her breasts.

"Kristen, honey, please stop. It's okay," said the girl.

"Nooo... noooo...you don't know. You have no idea," she said, sobbing but managing to talk pretty quietly. "It's not okay. I'm such a bad person...oh, God...oh, God, how could I?" Her sobs shook her whole body.

The three of us stood watching her like we were watching a fish struggling to get back into water. A fog of a notion that I didn't want to see her like this passed through me, but I wasn't capable of thinking that I should be doing anything. Her friend sat down in an adjacent recliner and began to stroke her hair. After a few minutes she was only whimpering and staring at a point between her nose and my knees.

"C'mon, honey, let's go up to bed," said the girl.

She went willingly, and swayed with her head down and her arm over the girl's shoulder. They became silhouettes as they entered the hallway. I followed them out to the foyer full of afternoon light.

The girls went upstairs. I stared out the screen door. I was thinking it was odd that it was so hot out, that the air conditioning was on and the front door was open. The thoughts moved slowly through my head like storm clouds. Sporty came up next to me before I could figure out what to do about that. He closed the door.

"You should probably go up with her," he said.

"Hmm."

I stared at the door for another few seconds. I took a deep breath and turned to go upstairs.

The décor was very country-like, and the house was very clean and in order. Lots of pictures on the walls and knickknacks, with the faint smell of cinnamon and potpourri. The girl was in the hallway.

"Where's her room?"

"It's the second one on the left."

"Thanks."

I walked in after them. It was a little girl's room with splashes of teenager. The walls were a light, peaceful, European-looking blue. There was an antique-looking dresser, a desk with a bulletin board, and pictures of her friends tacked up. There were stuffed animals all over, ballet shoes hanging up in a corner. She was tucked in neck high in her bed, which was in the middle of the wall to the left with an ornate wooden headboard painted white and a crucifix above it. There were two windows on the wall to her left overlooking the backyard. She stared out the windows, tears leaking from the corners of her eyes.

I sat down on the bed on the side with the windows and looked out. Something caught my attention, and I sat for a while before my thoughts gathered around where I was and what I was there to do. I did not know what to say. I didn't have anything to say.

I looked above her at the crucifix, and thought about what Christ wanted of me. I looked down at her, but she kept looking out the window.

"Kristen." I waited for her to look at me, and she did after a minute.

"I don't think you're a bad person. I don't blame you," I said. I looked out the window for a second, then back at her. "I'm not angry at you."

I wasn't sure if I meant it, on account of being numb. I thought it would be like me to mean that, but it was impossible to tell anymore. I put my hand on her forehead, brushed her brown hair back, and kissed her forehead.

"I'll call you later tonight," I said.

"Alright."

"Try to get some sleep."

"Okay."

Her unfocused gaze wandered back out the windows. I got up, and I walked through the hall down the steps. The kiddies were in the foyer.

"I think she's going to try to sleep now. I'll call her tonight."

"Okay."

I walked out the front door into the heat, and into Bessie, which was even hotter.

CHAPTER 35

The route back to the highway was easy, but I really didn't like being anywhere near the city, especially in the summer—the exhaust, the kicked-up gravel, the heat and stench of concrete, tar, hot plastic, exhaust, and gasoline.

Just before the highway, I pulled into a decrepit gas station. The service guy asked me what I wanted. I asked him to fill it with regular.

While he pumped, I took the money out of my pocket and counted it. I still had forty-two dollars in ones left over. I stared out the windshield at the traffic spilling in all directions and deep down felt a dull rage. I turned on the radio, and it was the Talking Heads.

And you may ask yourself
What is that beautiful house?
And you may ask yourself
Where does that highway go?
And you may ask yourself
Am I right?...Am I wrong?
And you may tell yourself
My God!...What have I done?
I turned it off.

"Twelve dollars please, sir."

I paid the guy, started the car, and pulled up to the street. As I waited for an opening in the traffic, I lit a cigarette.

CHAPTER 36

Soon I was able to concentrate on driving. I felt lighter, like there was ash in the hollows of my bones. There was a finality to it—no more worrying about what might happen. I was looking at it. I didn't have to try much to put off thoughts of consequences. Not at all, in fact. I don't think I ever believed it would actually happen until it did, that people actually did such things. There had been no way for me to process that then, though. The drive passed quickly.

I got home at about four o'clock. I walked through the wooden doors with wavy glass, and my father was sitting on the middle of the couch in his uniform. He had just gotten off work. I bent over and gave him a kiss on the cheek.

"Hey, Dad."

"Hey! It's my eldest son! We're all home together for dinner!"

When I stood up, I made myself glance at myself in the mirror above the couch. I just looked like myself. I didn't know what I was looking for, exactly, but I had an idea. I guessed what it was would come later—leathery skin and grayness in the eyes. I looked as soft and pink as I had up until then.

"I'm tired, Dad."

"Well go take a nap. We'll wake you up for dinner."

"Okay."

"And Son."

"Yeah."

"Why in the hell are you wearing a sweatshirt in this heat?" We had no air conditioning except for window units for our bedrooms. Even though the ceiling fans were on, it was very hot, but I hadn't noticed.

"I don't know. I was cold this morning."

"Are you out of your ever-lovin' mind?"

"No, Dad. Just tired."

I walked through the house. My mom was in the kitchen.

"Hi, baby."

"Hi, Mom."

"Why are you wearing a sweatshirt?"

"I don't know. I put it on so I wouldn't have to carry it."

"You're going to get heat stroke."

"Sorry, Mom, I'll take it off. I have to take a nap. I'm really tired."

"You've looked really tired. You work too much."

"Well, I'm off today."

"You should ask Mr. Campbell to cut back your hours."

"I know, Mom."

We both knew why I worked so much. But still I guess she couldn't help the instinct to want it to be different. I went in my room, took the sweatshirt off, eased onto my bed, and slept.

CHAPTER 37

A month after the abortion, I tried going back to church. Dad was working the eight-to-four shift, mom was cleaning houses, my brother Zack was selling newspapers, and Jimmy was working at the store around the corner. I was off in the mornings. I got up and took a shower, put on a polo shirt and some khakis, and walked out the front door into the hot sun across the street to St. Augustine's. It was ten-thirty Mass in July, so the place was packed. I sat in the very last pew; a couple older people were off to my right. I had gotten there a little early and knelt down, and I couldn't look up toward the altar. I had never felt that awful in church. The Mass began and I didn't listen, just told God how sorry I was, over and over again, that I was sorry. The people next to me had taken notice of me, probably originally because I was a young kid by myself, then later probably because I looked miserable. I couldn't pretend for their sake, though.

The readings, the prayers, everything rolled by, and I just stared at the back of the pew two rows up. I mumbled some of the prayers in an automatic way. I felt as though I was clashing with the whole deal. At the sign of peace, I reached out to the people next to me but didn't look up at them. When I returned to my place I could see them in my periphery, looking at me. When time came for Communion, I got up, walked out of the pew, and left.

I walked back home and changed into shorts, went into the kitchen and got a piece of bread, buttered it, and drew a glass of water. As I sat there and ate, I thought about God, and where I stood with him, if he existed. A loving God would love me and Kristen and our baby, and he would have wanted to save the baby. He didn't, so he either didn't exist, or he wasn't loving. Or if he was, he didn't love me. I figured it must have been the last one. He could have been a fable, but that was too easy. There were times in my life that, as sure as I knew I loved my mother, I knew God existed. To pretend now would be to just take the easy way out. And there was a good chance he was loving. He clearly loved some people. But he knew that now I was dismantled and empty, and he could have prevented it. But I couldn't be mad at him, because clearly I deserved what I had, which was nothing.

I finished the bread and called Tony. I asked him if he would take us out on his boat, and he agreed. He had to get a shower, call Eli, and pick him up, then he would come get me. I said fine, I would go to Wawa in the meantime.

I left and walked down Third Avenue, which was lined with shops of every sort, most selling things related to the seashore in one way or another.

It was the type of day all the tourists paid the big money to spend near the seashore, so they were all out in their white shorts and Docksiders and tourist T-shirts, with their beautiful children in their Cadillac strollers staring at me.

In between whiffs of fresh seashore air, I got whiffs of carbon monoxide from passing sport utility vehicles driving places that people a generation before would have walked to. There were about three places to get breakfast on the way, with lines out the door and families full of kids. Like I was a seven-foot bird, every one of them, it seemed, was morbidly curious about where I was going.

I got to Wawa after a few minutes, and I bought a pack of cigarettes and a cup of their coffee from the same woman who wouldn't sell me whip cream in high school because she suspected I would use it to get intoxicated. She was wrong, though. The whip cream was for sundaes; the cough syrup for intoxication.

I walked back on the other side of the road and drank my coffee, squinting in the sunlight and trying not to look people in the face. I walked quickly, because I thought the sight and sound of the stupid cars idling by below the twenty-five-mile-per-hour speed limit might make me go insane.

Three quarters of the way there, Tony pulled up next to me and honked his horn. I threw the rest of my coffee out and climbed in the passenger side. He drove a sport utility.

"Hey, Willie."

"Hmm."

"What's up?"

"Nothin'." I took out the pack of cigarettes and started packing them.

"You're not smoking them in my car."

"C'mon."

"No, you're not smoking them in my car."

"I'll put the window down." At that, he put on his brakes and pulled to the side of the road.

"Will, I'm not moving until you put them away."

"Fine, douchebag." I put them in my pocket.

"What's your problem?"

"I dunno, I'm not quite one hundred percent, I'd say."

"Why?"

"Are you kidding me?"

"You're still stressed out about that?"

"Tony, can you conceive any possible way that I couldn't be stressed out about it?"

"Did you go to church today?"

"Yeah."

"Didn't you feel any better?"

"No. I felt worse. I left early, and it felt like the place shat me out."

"I'm sorry, Willie." He drove for a while, and we didn't say anything. "Willie, God will forgive you."

"Where's Eli?"

"He had to go pick up his paycheck and take a shower, so I figured I would come get you first." We were heading in the direction of his house.

"Are you going to his party?"

"Hell yeah, homie. You are too, right?"

"Of course."

"That will cheer you up, Willie."

"Maybe."

We got to Eli's house, and he was waiting out front for us. He got in the car and climbed in the back seat. There were only two doors, and I monopolized the passenger side.

"What's up, Will?"

"Not much."

"Did you end up going out with Lauren Snider?"

"Yeah, I did."

"You went out with Lauren Snider?" Tony asked.

"Yeah."

"How was it?"

"It was fine. We just went and got some coffee and talked for a while, then she drove me to get my car, which was parked behind the theater."

"Then you drove to her house and banged her, right?" Eli asked.

"Nah."

"Why not?"

"I've developed this, like, too-little-too-late sense of morality. It's been messing with my game."

They both chuckled a little bit.

"I think I was sort of a boring date. All I could think about doing was apologizing to her, because I was going through a rough time in my life. I didn't, though."

"She'll probably still do you, Willie," Tony said.

"Enough, Tony."

"Sorry, Willie."

CHAPTER 38

I had been looking forward to that night for a little while—a chance to relax a little. I had to endure work, though.

Sunday nights were typically pretty slow, especially compared to Friday and Saturday nights. I had told Luanne, the manager, that I wanted to leave early. I never asked for that sort of thing, so she didn't have a problem with it.

The night started out with a few tables, and my mind raced so madly that I was getting things all wrong. I brought the salad out before the appetizer for an older couple, who gave me shit for that, and on top of it, I had the wrong dressing. Luanne came up to me before they even got their entrées and asked me what the problem was. I forgot their rolls, too, and they complained.

"Will," she said, "this is only your first table." I apologized.

The next table arrived before the entrées did at the first table. It was a young couple with, of course, their baby, who had large green eyes and was situated right across from me, and was staring at me.

"Good evening, my name is Will and I'll be your waiter tonight. Tonight's special is a surf and turf—two lobster tails and filet mignon served with potato, vegetable, and salad for $24. Our soup tonight is mulligatawny, and our vegetable is sautéed zucchini. Can I start you off with something to drink?"

They ordered.

"You two have a beautiful baby. What's her name?"

"Sophia."

"That's beautiful," I said. They were looking at me like I was odd. I hadn't meant to sound insincere.

"Thank you," the wife finally said.

At that, I felt a tug on my pants. Behind me was the table with the old couple with the messed-up salads.

"We still haven't gotten any rolls, sir, and I must say I've been very disappointed in you so far." He said it loud enough for the other table to hear.

"I'll be right back with your rolls, sir. I apologize."

I walked straight to the roll warmer in the blazing kitchen, cursing at the old man and myself the whole way. I came back and placed the basket on the table, resisting the urge to bounce one off his forehead.

As I was walking back to the computer to enter the order from the second table, Luanne caught up with me.

"Listen to me, Will. You're a good worker and you're a good, nice boy. But lately you've looked like a sad, sad young man. I just don't like to see you like this. It may be none of my business, but I want you to feel like you can talk to me if you need to. You're a very nice, cheerful person, but lately it looks like there is something very wrong." She looked at my face, but I just looked past her.

"I'm not alright, Luanne, but I don't think it's something I should talk about. It's something I have to deal with on my own. Thanks for your concern, but I have to enter this stuff into the computer."

"Well, I think it's usually best to talk about things. You can talk to me, but I understand if you choose not to."

I nodded and walked toward the computer. I looked down hard at the rug, because I was about to break down in front of everyone. I blinked back tears as I walked and stared at the corner in the back room until it was my turn at the computer. I entered the order, but I could not shake the feeling. I went to get the salads, and a tear or two escaped. I opened the refrigerator door and stood behind it for a minute, while I got my composure. It only got worse for a minute, but then when I sensed someone behind me, it retreated. I grabbed the two salads and a basket of rolls and brought it to the table with the baby.

"Thanks! One thing, though—our drinks."

"Oh, I'm sorry." I turned around and asked if everything was okay at the table with the rolls.

"Everything is fine, but I'll be expecting some money off my check for your poor service."

"That's fine, sir. I meant no disrespect. I'm tired and I have a lot on my mind."

"Well, that's not my problem."

"Excellent."

I walked away and got the drinks for the other table, then I went in the bathroom and washed my hands, because I wanted to be where no one else was. I didn't look in the mirror.

That was really the only rush of the night—the first two tables. There were a couple more, but they were easy. As I stood by the hutch during the slow times, the waitresses told me I could talk to them if I needed to. Thanks, I would say, but I'm fine.

Luanne sent me home early, which was the plan originally, but I may have been sent home even earlier. I took a shower and got dressed in a T-shirt and shorts, and got on my bike and rode down Second Avenue to Eli's house. By then it was about eight. The weather had been hot and humid, and the next day was supposed to be worse—going from the lower to the upper nineties. There was no relief at home, since we didn't have air conditioning. I didn't want it, anyway. I was beginning to sweat by the time I got to Eli's, which was about a mile away. There things got out of hand.

CHAPTER 39

I woke up at home the next morning without enough time to take a shower or eat breakfast. The temperature was in the mid-eighties, and the humidity was like a wet quilt. By the time I had walked the two and a half blocks to work, sweat was beading on my forehead and collecting under my arms.

I walked into the lobby of the Summerbreeze motel, which was air conditioned.

"Hi, Will, you look like hell!" said Mr. Campbell. He was an average-height guy with a bald head and wrinkles on his face. He had a bunch of kids; one worked with me. He was off that day.

"I couldn't sleep last night. I was too hot." I knew I stunk like booze and that I looked hungover and he knew exactly why I looked the way that I did. I didn't know why I was lying, because I didn't care what he thought.

"Well, go ahead and start on the pools."

I walked back out into the wall of heat and over to the first pool. At each of them, I had to vacuum the sand out of the bottom, get the leaves off the top. I also had to check the chlorine levels. I started by dragging the vacuum out, then testing the water. It was low on chlorine. I went into the bucket full of chlorine cakes to get more. In this heat they baked in the sun, and opening the top was always accompanied by a cloud of pure chlorine, which, being hungover, I forgot about, and inhaled. As it tore into my lungs and burned my eyes, and as I coughed and gagged, I thought about how stupid we were with our stupid chemicals and how stupid I was for forgetting about them.

I brought the chlorine cakes back to the pool and dropped them in their container with my eyes still burning and watering. I thought about how it would be interesting to see what would happen if I took a bite out of one. I then hooked up the hose to the pump in the pool and began vacuuming the sand out of the bottom. As I stood in the white-hot heat on top of the white concrete with the sun blaring off the pool's surface into my face, the air was so thick I couldn't breathe enough of it, and my chest was tight from the cigarettes and the pot and the chlorine, and my boxer shorts stuck to my pubic hair, and my head swam and my brain swelled, and I could smell the alcohol evaporating out of me, and feel the urge to puke the nothing in my stomach.

I heard the air conditioner motors running, and one of them whined with a pitch that bored right into the center of my brain and vibrated. I thought how stupid it was that we were cooking in our own attempts to avoid the heat. I wondered what the hell ever happened to shade, and why that wasn't enough. As the cars drove by I thought how stupid it was that we had to endure this heat for the pleasure of being lazy. I thought about how stupid it was that my baby died for this. She would have been smarter than we are. I was a speck. I was the stink on the crotch of humanity.

I went and finished the first pool, then the second pool. Usually it took me an hour, but today it took me an hour and a half, and I was twenty minutes late, so I was nearly an hour behind.

Usually there was a lull between the time I finished the pools and the time I had to gather the dirty towels and bath mats the maids left outside of each room. I walked, soaked in sweat, into the lobby where there was a couch. There we would sit and await our next chores.

I sat down and my whole body ached. I had managed to get drunk and get a chick naked, as the cheer went. Complicating this most complicated of situations was the fact that she was Kat's ex-girlfriend, Alice. I prayed.

God, I am sorry for what I have done again. I do not deserve anything. I am nothing. But God, please, please, spare me the consequences of my actions. I am sorry with all of my heart, which beats only to displease you, it seems. Spare me the consequences, Lord. Do not let someone else die or be harmed because of me. My God, I beg you. I cannot handle the consequences. Please, God, I deserve nothing.

I started falling asleep, so I got up and went back outside and started picking up the dirty towels, and ached.

We could leave when we were done, which was usually between 1 and 2 p.m. I didn't finish until a quarter to three, which annoyed Mr. Campbell. After collecting dirty laundry on top of the sweat and everything else, I felt filthy and disgusting. I walked home in heat so intense that it waved in the streets. The temperature was over 100 and would remain so for days. The sweat dripped off my forehead and into my eyes.

As the cars drove by, I heard the air conditioners in the windows of the homes, and I smelled the exhaust and nothing else.

When I got home, I needed to sleep but I couldn't. I needed to shower, but my mind raced, and the thoughts like bullets bounced and pinged and ricocheted and clashed inside my skull so loudly that I forgot. I had a feeling like someone raking their fingers across the back side of my liver—there was heat in the insides of my elbows, and the palms of my hands. I felt like I was running a marathon in a padded telephone booth, like I had lead in the marrow of my bones.

I stood in the middle of my family room and my eyes were unfocused, but I knew I was losing my mind. I put my hand on my forehead and then smacked it four or five times hard, then again. I asked myself what a sane person would do. I reached in my pocket for my keys. I turned around and walked out the front door and got in my car with my hand on my forehead. I drove without air conditioning to Kat's house. About a block away I saw her walking. I did a U-turn in front of an oncoming car that honked loudly and slammed on its brakes. I pulled over next to Kat.

"Get in."

"Fuck off!" She knew.

"Get in, Kat."

"Help! This man is trying to abduct me!" she yelled. I looked around.

"Get in."

She got in and we started driving away. Immediately she started punching me in the shoulder and slapping me in the face. When I could see the road again, I was well into the oncoming lane. Luckily, nobody was coming.

"What the hell?"

"You fucked Alice? You fucked her? What's the matter with you, asshole!"

"She fucked me!"

"Fuck you!"

"It was quick, Kat. I knew there was something wrong, and I stopped."

"Oh, you stupid shit! Haven't you learned your lesson?"

I just got quiet and started clenching my teeth.

"Kat, I..." I was trying to talk, but words couldn't come out of me. The ensemble of hate in my brain just continued to drown out everything. "I'm having a nervous breakdown."

"What's wrong?"

"I'm having a nervous breakdown. I'm sorry, Kat."

"What do you mean? What's wrong?"

I couldn't talk. I just mumbled, "I'm having a nervous breakdown" a few times. "What's right? Look at me. I didn't want to do that shit. I didn't want to hurt you, or her or me. It's not worth it."

"What's not worth it?"

"Me, Kat, life. It might be time to check out. I have nothing to give but hurt. This is a perfect example."

"Will, stop the car right now." I didn't listen to her. She raised her voice. "Stop it now, or I'm jumping out." She opened the door. I pulled the car over to the side of the road. "Don't do this, Will." She threw her cigarette out the window and turned to look at me. "Don't do this. Don't talk like that. Don't you dare. Look at me. Look at me." I did. "You are worth it, Will. Don't you do this to me. Don't you do this to your family. You have your brothers. You have your parents. You have your friends. I know you are hurt, and I know all you feel is who you lost, and I wish I could do something about that, but we just can't. Don't you be a coward, Will. You suck it up. You're not the only person in this world. People need you. I need you."

"Kat, I don't know why. I keep failing them."

I smoked my cigarette a little longer, then threw it out because it was too hot to smoke. I put my head down on the steering wheel. "I'm so tired."

"Go home, Will, and sleep."

"I have to, because I think I'm going to die if I don't."

"I have to get to work."

"Do you want a ride?"
"Yeah, if you put the A/C on."
"Fine."

CHAPTER 40

The first time I saw Kristin again was a Friday. Junior year was still brand new. The mountains in the distance were full and lush with leaves on virgin Appalachian woods; the mountain air was warm but not too hot—fresh and dry. The week before, there had been a thunderstorm on a Saturday, and Costigan and I watched it advance—the blues and grays spilling over the weathered mountain peaks. The two of us sat in lawn chairs in the parking lot, drinking Heineken and watching the lightning stretch across the sky, along the breadth of the mountains. When the rains finally came, we just got wet.

The fields were tall and green and brilliant in the late-summer sunlight. The air wasn't sweet like it was in the spring but fragrant from cut lawn. Everyone was tanned, the sorority girls and frat boys excessively so.

It had been a rough summer. Upon returning to school, I had resolved not to drink, which was something I knew probably wouldn't last, but at least I had to try. The first night I tested the not-drinking thing, I had six beers simply to shut my friends' mouths. After that I figured I would just keep it in check.

One of my classes was developmental psychology, and the professor was a thin, old-fashioned sort of man, like the hapless sheriff of some sleepy frontier town. He was a farmer from Tennessee and talked about it as much as he did psychology, and about his farm out in the mountains down Route 11 beyond the reservoir where the students swam when it was hot. There he raised chickens. He was probably an Evangelical Christian, but he never said anything overtly in that regard. He did, however, overtly show a documentary over the first three classes, chronicling the abortion debate. It was a little dated, but showed in-utero development through birth, footage of protests and clinic bombings, a press conference where an activist had gotten hold of a late-term aborted fetus and held it up before a crowd of reporters, and a segment with a mother giving birth and breastfeeding. It seemed almost comical that I was in his class. I could see that some of it had to do with psychological development, but it wasn't clear why he thought the abortion debate was relevant. Maybe it was the best video on in-utero development he had. He probably knew he was hammering somebody, though.

At the end of most days I would find myself with a headache, and it wasn't until a month or so had passed that I figured out it was from clenching my teeth. My roommates were beginning to bother me about being negative all the time.

That day, though, I was feeling not particularly upset. I was getting a meal at the new dining hall, which was well designed with lots of open space and floors made of giant slabs of green stone, and had a lot of light coming in through the giant windows from the late summer in the mountains.

I had gotten a roasted chicken dinner with macaroni and cheese and a small side salad. I was walking from the cashier to the top of the steps leading down to the lower seating area.

There at the table just to the right of the steps were Kristen and her roommates, Maggie and Monica. Every one of my joints went limp at the sight of them, but not long enough to drop my tray or fall over. Almost, though.

The table was situated so that Maggie was right in front of me, and there was no way I could avoid being seen.

"Will!" Maggie called out.

"Hey! What's up, girls?"

I stopped and turned toward their table, standing behind the empty seat, with Kristen straight across from me, the roommates on either side.

All three of them looked quite good—tanned, lighter hair, outfits showing lots of skin. Kristen sort of looked up at me—at my chest, not my eyes—and she looked unsettled and ready for me to leave. Maggie was the only one who spoke.

"How was your summer?" I asked.

"Pretty good, I guess. How was yours?"

"It was alright. I worked a lot," I said.

"Yeah, me too. Classes good?"

"Yeah."

"Cool, cool. Any good professors?"

"I got a couple."

And that quickly, everyone ran out of things to say. I knew she had probably told both girls and that they felt they weren't supposed to know. I could feel them noticing how I was reacting.

"Well, I have to get back home soon, so I gotta eat and run," I said, finally.

"Okay."

"I'll see you girls later."

"Bye!" they all said, including her.

I went down the steps and picked at the food. I was trembling and holding back tears. I had thought I was getting used to being around the reminders of my situation, and that it was somehow going to just be part of the landscape. But when it wanted to be there, it was there and nothing else was there. I figured I would give it more time, but it was becoming clearer that something was going to have to go.

CHAPTER 41

A couple days later, Sunday, I sat in front of my computer, with plenty of work to be doing, but I could not concentrate. We'd had a party the night before, and I was shaky, but that wasn't what was bothering me at the time.

I walked out to the kitchen to get the phone, past Khan and Skeeter, who were both sitting in front of the TV watching baseball, textbooks in their laps.

I brought it back into my room and stared at it for a minute. I took a deep breath, and dialed the number.

"Hello?" She had a very polite voice.

"Hi, Lily."

"Hi, Will. Did you call to talk about kissing me?" That took me by surprise.

"Well, yeah. I did."

"What's up?"

I was developing a philosophy that I should just get to the point.

"Lily, I'm just going to get to the point. I feel like we're such good friends that if we keep doing that, it might lead to a relationship of some sort. And I don't feel like I'm in a place right now to be with somebody."

She paused, briefly. "Will, is there something wrong?"

"There's a lot that's not right."

"Do you want to talk about it?"

I thought for a minute. "I probably should."

"Do you want to come over?"

"Yeah. I'll be over in a minute."

I pressed the button on the phone and walked back out past Khan and Skeeter.

"I'm going to see Lily."

"Squeeze them knockers once for me," Khan yelled as I closed the door.

The air was starting to turn cool as I walked down the steps into the parking lot among the mountains. The only sound was the distant and steady wail of tractor-trailers steaming down Route 83. It was almost autumn, and the air had hints of it.

Lily's apartment was in the building halfway between mine and Costigan's. I walked up the wooden steps to the second floor and knocked on the door. I put my finger over the peephole.

"Who is it?" Lily asked from behind the door. I didn't answer. She opened it, wearing her thick brown hair up in a loosely drawn bun held in place with a pencil. If she moved her head one way or the other, it flopped like a buoy of sorts. She smelled of perfume, applied sparingly. She was in sweatpants and a girly V-neck T-shirt—study clothes.

We went straight into her room, and I sat on her bed. She sat at her desk and faced me.

By this point in the semester, we had kissed a few times.

"So what's up, Will?"

"Lily, I need to talk. But I'm sort of afraid to, because I have to tell you some awful things."

"Oh my gosh, Will, what's going on? Is it drugs?"

"No, it's not drugs. What makes you think it's drugs?"

"I don't know." She seemed a little embarrassed. "You live with Skeeter, I guess."

"True. It's not drugs, though. It's worse, though, I think. I wish it was drugs. I guess the best way for me to tell you this is just to tell you this. There's no delicate way to put any of it."

"Will, you can tell me anything."

"I know, Lily." I took a deep breath and looked around at the artwork she had hung on the wall—a perspective painting she had done in our freshman year, a copy of Sargent's *Street in Venice*, a small crucifix by the door. "You probably know that Kristen and I did a little hooking up, right?"

"Of course."

"Well I know you probably know that we had sex."

"Yeah."

"Well, that continued a lot throughout the year, if you didn't know. In June when I got back home, I got a phone call from a girl from school, and I thought it was you. It turned out it was her, and she was pregnant with my baby."

I expected her to gasp or put her hand over her mouth or something, but she didn't. She just looked at me and listened. I looked over at the wall.

"So, we did some talking about it, and I did a lot of thinking about it. Because I was working so much, I didn't get the chance to talk to her. I decided it was best that we put it up for adoption, but she decided she wanted an abortion. I tried to talk her out of it, but I couldn't. I drove her there and gave her money, because I thought it would give me a chance to try to change her mind. I waited for four hours, and she did it. We aborted our baby." I stopped and looked at the wall behind her. I tried very hard not to cry, and it was difficult.

"Over the summer...I...didn't talk to her again. I tried calling her a couple times, but she didn't call back...and I'm in the worst place I've been in my entire life. I think I had a nervous breakdown. I avoided my family; I got in a huge fight with my brother. I punched him in the face, which we never do. I got really drunk and slept with some girl from high school."

"How do you feel?"

"Lily, like, it's so hard to explain. Over the summer one morning I walked by myself to church, which is right across the street from me. I made myself go. I sat in the back and didn't look up the entire time. I felt so sick inside that when everyone got up for Communion, I left. When I got home I thought to myself, 'If God exists and loves me like the Church says he does, he would have saved my baby. So God must not exist. Or if he does exist, he doesn't love me, and he is a lot different than I thought he was. Or, he exists just as I was taught, and I got what I deserved, and my baby died because of my actions or omissions and so I belong in hell. Because if hell is built for anybody, it's built for people who do that sort of thing.

"So I belong in hell. And Lily, that's what's right. Look at me. I don't eat, because I don't have an appetite. I've lost so much weight. And I don't care to eat, because I don't deserve food. I don't like it. I can't enjoy anything when I'm supposed to be sharing it all with my little girl. Every joy I have is one I robbed from her. I can't think of another thing a person can do that is more evil."

"Will..."

"No, and it's like, I barely care. I'm not worth my own concern. I feel awful all the time, but it doesn't hurt. I don't cry—I don't have any emotion anymore. I don't feel like I have a soul. I used to feel it, and I don't anymore."

I tapped my pen on my thigh and looked at the tops of my socks, and decided to speak again before she could try to comfort me.

"So things got weirder this weekend. After you left our party, I was standing on our back porch. Maggie, Kristen's roommate, showed up. She was so wasted, she could barely talk. I was drunk myself. Anyway, we were talking and things were starting to get flirty and she started slurring, like...

"'I doan care abowt whah happene with Kristen thiss summer.'

"I stopped and said, 'What did you say?'

"She said, 'I doan care wha happene with you ann Kristen this summer.'

"So I said, 'She told you?'

"And then, like something snapped in her brain, she stepped back and started saying, 'Will, you have to go talk to her....You have to go talk to her.' She wasn't slurring anymore or anything. She told me, 'Every night she locks herself in her room and cries. She won't talk to anybody, because she says nobody can understand. She's hurting so much, and we can't do anything for her.' She made me promise. I told her I would just so she would stop it.

"And so I haven't been able to think straight since last night, or really since June."

I glanced at Lily for a second, then looked at the foot of her bed.

"Lily, I feel so awful telling you all of this. You would never get yourself into something like this kind of crap. You're so much better than that. You must think so much worse of me. I'm sorry."

"We all sin." She paused a minute. "Are you thinking of going to talk to her?"

"Yeah. I feel like I have to. I was thinking of going tomorrow."

She was quiet for a minute, while I stared at my feet.

"Will?"

I looked up, and she had her hand on her chest, and she was a little teary-eyed.

"Yeah?"

She spoke slowly. "One day you will feel so blessed."

I looked away toward the wall and tried to hold back the tears. That was a lot to take. I didn't want to cry in front of her, though. I got it under control after a minute and wiped my eyes. When I was sure I could talk, I looked up.

"How could you say such a thing after hearing all of that?"

"I just feel it. One day you will feel so blessed."

CHAPTER 42

There wasn't much to say after that. She told me she was sorry that I was going through it, but that things would get better, and she thought it was a good idea for me to go talk to Kristen. I gave her a hug and walked across the parking lot above the town below to the apartment. I went out on the back porch and smoked a couple cigarettes to be outside. I went inside and tried to do a little work, but I didn't get very far.

The next day I knew I was going to do what I had to do. It was related to this new thing that was developing, of just getting to things. After class I walked to the steps in front of our main building made of bricks, named McKinley. The quad stretched out before it with buildings on either side in a pretty much symmetrical layout. The grounds were kept well, as usual. The campus was so beautiful, it gave me hope. I looked out past the quad, which sloped down to Main Street, past the row of houses facing me to the far-off mountains that presided above.

Countless times already I had looked out to the mountains, and seen how the clouds rested upon their shoulders, or how the sun had glared in its red majesty during the last moments of the day, and asked God to take me then, because I wanted to be where things actually were that pretty all of the time.

That day it was just blue skies, white clouds, green grass, and orange-and-black butterflies on their way south. I sat on the steps outside McKinley and spent probably an hour watching the clouds pass, the girls walk by, feeling the sun. I smoked a couple cigarettes and then walked behind McKinley toward the buses.

I continued on my way down across the road winding through campus, down the steps to the train track. There was a freight train rolling by, and as it passed I watched the wheels roll and the tracks sink into the ground below them. I didn't grow up anywhere near any trains. Or mountains, for that matter. The big steel sights and sounds, the scraping and the booming and all that were fascinating.

When it passed I walked down to the bus and waited. Today it was the driver who listened to Metallica tapes all day. Today it was *Load*, which I didn't own and had no plans on owning. I endured it as the bus lumbered up the giant hill to the Campus Commons apartments. I walked back to our building, walked up through the parking lot and up the steps to the third floor. It was late afternoon, and when I got in I kicked off my shoes and put on some music. I lay on my bed and stared at the ceiling. I felt the urge to pray again, but I didn't feel like I had the right. *Help me be strong, Lord*, I thought. I continued to stare and watch the fan, sometimes trying to keep my eyes on just one of the blades.

I fell asleep for about an hour, and when I woke, it was getting to be about sunset. It was then that I made up my mind to do it. I went into the common area, sat on the couch, and put on my shoes. While I was tying them Khan came out, sat down in the chair next to me, turned on the TV, and started flicking through the channels.

"Where you going? You getting something to eat?" he asked after a minute.

"Not hungry. I think I'm going to go talk to Kristen." I had told each of the roommates by then, but not Kevin, the new guy.

"Really?"

"Yeah, dude."

He didn't say anything else. I went into the kitchen and poured myself a glass of Gatorade. Khan flipped through the channels and settled on a documentary about a man who had killed several abortion doctors in the South. They were going into his writings and journals. It was causing me a lot of distress, and I almost snapped and said something bitchy. Instead I paced a little faster and watched a bit of it. I couldn't tell if he was doing it to piss me off, if he thought I might want to watch it, or if he just wasn't making the connection.

The pacing lasted about forty-five minutes. Finally I told myself I would move and there would be no more thinking and no more hesitation, and if I couldn't breathe then I couldn't breathe.

I turned around and watched the TV for another minute, then turned back around, walked quickly across the kitchen, opened the door, and made it out.

I had to walk fast down the stairs, and down into the parking lot and to my car. I kept repeating "just go" in my head to keep out any thoughts. My chest and stomach were tight; my breaths were shallow. I got to Bess, got in, and began driving to her apartment, about a mile and a half away on the other side of the main road.

I lit a cigarette and drove, continuing to repeat "just go" in my head. I got stuck at a red light and almost turned around. My breaths were forceful on the way out.

When the light turned green, I sped through it, and came up almost immediately to the development cleared out of the trees on the left. I pulled in and parked, got out of Bess, and stomped out my cigarette. I was underwater again, and the air again felt heavy. I felt like I would collapse.

I got to their ground-floor apartment among the buildings with gray siding and a white door. I stood in front of it and stared at it. My lungs felt heavy—it was the resistance again, like at the clinic and at the threshold of the womb. But for me there were no security guards or high school wrestlers and their cheerleader girlfriends or reluctant patrons to clear the way. There were no contractions. It was me and a white aluminum door as thick as eternity. I had gotten myself into this mess, and I had to get myself out.

I had had a million dreams like this, like getting into a fistfight but with my arms too heavy to swing. I put all of my might into it but it wasn't enough.

God, please help me.

I lifted my arm and closed my eyes. I knocked three times as though I intended to break my knuckles. Nobody answered, and part of me was ready to give up for now. Instead, I knocked again.

I heard footsteps, and the door opened. It was her roommate Maggie.

"Hey!" She looked stunned—completely stunned—but talked like it was the most natural thing in the world for me to be there.

"Hi, what's up?"

"Nothing! Come in!" She turned around and started walking through the little kitchen into the common area. As she did she looked over her shoulder and whispered toward me: "I'm glad you're here."

I walked in toward the common area. The apartments were laid out precisely as ours were, with an extra half bath because they had been built later. Kristen was situated on a couch. When I walked in the room, she looked shocked, but she pretended like it was the most natural thing in the world for me to be there.

"Hi, Will! What's up?"

"Nothin', just thought I would visit."

Their apartment was less dank, brighter, and more colorful than ours. They had been to the furniture chain and bought some shelves, on which they had arranged some pictures; there were candles in maroon and olive green—some of them lit. They had a large television, and it was on.

I sat on the couch with Kristen to the right of me with a cushion in between us. Maggie sat on the chair to my left. We talked about the apartment and how much rent was, and how it was nice that there was the extra half bathroom. We talked about classes, the new dining facility, the new apartment buildings going up across the street from them—that was crazy, wasn't it? The decorations were nice, weren't they? Pottery Barn? Yes, but most of it was from Walmart. We buy everything at Walmart; I hate it because malls make me nervous. Kristen's car has been giving her trouble. She's going to try to get her dad to buy her a new one. What does her dad do? He's an accountant. That was cool, I was in the business program for a semester and took accounting but hated it things seem to be going fine in the English department. He's a partner in his firm. Wow, that's really impressive. It pays well but he works a lot. That sucks.

When we all ran out of things to say, we looked at the TV for a minute.

"I have to go to the bathroom," Maggie said. She got up and went into her room, closing the door.

On the television was an HBO Cher concert special. She was wearing a sort of headdress and a gold sequined bikini.

"What is she wearing?" Kristen asked.

"I can't stand Cher."

"Me neither."

We watched another minute, and again I knew it was my turn to speak.

"Kristen, I didn't come here to talk about Cher."

"I know."

"Do you want to go back to your room?"

"Yes."

She closed her books and we got up. She had the large room at the back of the apartment, like mine. Her bed was set up jutting out from the middle of the wall facing the door. It was covered in pillows and a few stuffed animals. It was extremely orderly.

She sat on the left side of the bed with her back against the collection of pillows, and I lay on my stomach with a pillow under my chest looking up at her.

"How have you been?" I asked.

"Okay."

"How have you been really?"

"It's been hard."

"Maggie told me you come in here and cry every night."

"I've been crying, a lot, yeah. It just doesn't feel like anyone can understand what I'm going through."

"I know how you feel." I felt it was time to get to the point, in case I didn't have the chance again. "Kristen, I don't know if you're Catholic or not, but I came here because I wanted to know if you wanted to try to make things right with God. If he would have it."

"Yes, I do."

"The priest at the campus ministry is really good. His name is Father Bob."

"I've been to a couple Masses with him. I like him."

"Did you want to make an appointment?"

"Yeah."

"Alright. I'll set it up."

"Thanks."

I stared at the pillow situated inches in front of my face. I inched down a little bit to get a better view of her.

"What was the summer like?"

"It was awful, Will. *Aw*ful. A week afterwards we had to go to a baby shower for my cousin, and I couldn't take it. I locked myself in the bathroom, and I cried the whole time. People kept coming to see if I was okay and I had to pretend like I was sick. I've lost a bunch of weight, because I can't eat. And I cry. Every night."

She started to tear up a little. "I used to have dreams about a girl, and then I woke up and I would be holding my stomach."

I looked at the pillows in front of me for a minute and let her cry a little. I started to tear up.

"Are you mad at me?" I asked.

"I've been a little angry, to be honest. Like, 'Look what he's done to me...' It doesn't make any sense, but you know. I've been angry at everybody. Myself, my parents, you, my friends. I've just been so...hateful and sad. I'm mad at life for it being so hard."

"I'm sorry, Kristen."

"I'm sorry, too, Will."

"I'm sorry that this happened, and I'm sorry about how I treated you."

"Will, both of us did that. It wasn't just you."

"Maybe. But it doesn't make me feel any better about it."

"It's been a long summer," she said.

"I've been in this class—developmental psychology—and they're showing a film on the abortion debate. It shows the whole development and everything."

"Yeaahhh....We're watching that too!"

"It's been awful...to pretend like it's no big deal."

"I know."

"I've been a real asshole lately," I said. People are saying stuff about me being so negative all the time. I clench my teeth and my fists all of the time." I turned over and sat up against the pillows. "But I think we're doing the right thing—going to see a priest."

"Me too."

CHAPTER 43

I got in Johnny's jeep, which was about fifteen years old and drove like it would rattle to pieces. But it was a fun car to drive, and he didn't mind other people using it while he was in Beijing for the semester. I never heard that from Johnny's mouth, but I was willing to believe it. After a minute, I got to Kristen's apartment and knocked on the door with my kidneys still rattling in place.

We had been in touch over the week and had hung out the night before. Our appointment with Father Bob was for that Friday, and so we decided we would go to church together on the Sunday in between. She came out dressed nicely in a white sweater with a sundress. She got in the passenger side door, which creaked and clanked as she yanked it closed.

I drove out of the parking lot and onto the main road. The ancient engine toiled in a near-futile roar. Along with it, the wind rushing in over the windshield blocked out any sound.

Apart from that, we drove in silence. We were both nervous to be going to church. It was difficult to get my head around the whole thing.

We arrived and walked past the bus stops up the steep hill, up the steps to the student center, around that building to the convention hall. It was the five o'clock Sunday Mass, which

Father Bob said on a portable stage with the congregation seated on fold-out chairs. It was crowded, as this particular Mass always was.

I always listened intently during Mass, especially the readings. The Gospel and the homily were what I looked forward to the most, but this time I made sure I was paying attention to everything that was going on.

Things progressed through the procession, the opening prayers, the first reading, the responsorial psalm, the second reading, and then it came time for the alleluia and then the Gospel. Father Bob walked across the altar to the pulpit:

"A reading from the Gospel according to Matthew."

"Glory to you, oh Lord," we all said, as we made little crosses on our foreheads, lips, and hearts with our thumbs. He spoke, saying,

"Jesus said to them:

The kingdom of heaven is like a landowner who went out at dawn to hire laborers for his vineyard. After agreeing with them for the usual daily wage, he sent them into his vineyard. Going out about nine o'clock, he saw others standing idle in the marketplace, and he said to them, 'You too go into my vineyard, and I will give you what is just.' So they went off. And he went out again around noon, and around three o'clock, and did likewise. Going out about five o'clock, he found others standing around, and said to them, 'Why do you stand here idle all day?' They answered, 'Because no one has hired us.' He said to them, 'You too go into my vineyard.' When it was evening the owner of the vineyard said to his foreman, 'Summon the laborers and give them their pay, beginning with the last and ending with the first.' When those who had started about five o'clock came, each received the usual daily wage. So when the first came, they thought that they would receive more, but each of them also got the usual wage. And on receiving it they grumbled against the landowner, saying, 'These last ones worked only one hour, and you have made them equal to us, who bore the day's burden and the heat.' He said to one of them in reply, 'My friend, I am not cheating you. Did you not agree with me for the usual daily wage? Take what is yours and go. What if I wish to give this last one the same as you? Am I not free to do as I wish with my own money? Are you envious because I am generous?' Thus, the last will be first, and the first will be last."

He paused and looked up at the congregation. "The word of the Lord."

"Thanks be to God," we all said.

We sat down and Father Bob stepped from behind the podium. He was probably 6-foot-6 with gray, well-groomed hair and glasses. He didn't look very athletic, but he wasn't out of shape. If he hadn't been a priest, he might have been a high school or middle school biology teacher. He did his sermons in front of the altar, walking back and forth, using sweeping arm gestures, sometimes getting so excited that a profanity would come close to slipping. He wasn't a fiery kind of preacher, but he spoke like it was his job to save people's souls.

He stood at the front of the altar and asked for three volunteers from the audience. My sensei in karate growing up used to do this, and then make the volunteers do push-ups for not asking what they were volunteering for, so I didn't raise my hand.

He picked three people from the audience and had them stand up front with him facing the crowd. He reached into his pocket and pulled out some money—a few bills. He handed one to each of them.

"Here. Take it. It's yours."

Stupid Eastern philosophy. The kids looked at the bills—ten dollars each—and two tried to give them back to him.

"No. Absolutely not. Take it; it's yours. I know you guys are worried about a priest running out of money, but I'll be fine."

One by one the kids sat down, red-faced.

"So what was the point of that? For them to go on a beer run for me?"

Laughs.

"Immediately our reaction to something like that might be, 'Hey, what did they do for that?' or, 'Wow, they're really lucky. I wish I got ten dollars for coming to church.'

"Immediately, we start thinking about whether that money is deserved. Right? We think about what the people did for it. If they didn't do anything, they're lucky. Certainly they're not *entitled* to it. In America, we work hard for our money. It's that simple. You get what you deserve.

"With our justice system it's the same thing. If you speed, you get a ticket. If you drink and drive, you get your license revoked. If you shoplift, you get community service. If you kill someone, you might end up dying yourself as the penalty.

"And here, in the Gospel, we have three groups of workers. One group works all day, another half the day, and the last only a couple hours. Yet they all get the *same wage*.

"I'm sure a lot of you are thinking to yourself what I thought when I first read this: What the heck?

"Isn't the worker in the first group right? He worked *all day*! In the sun and the heat! While the guys in the last group were taking a siesta, he was busting his back in the fields. Once the dirty work has been done, the sun is low in the sky, the air has cooled, the last group comes in for cleanup duty, and they get the same amount of money.

"What is going *on*?

"This is justice? This is fairness? Is this what these workers *deserve*? How does this make any *sense*?"

He paused and looked around at the packed auditorium. The congregation was still.

"Think about it, guys. Think back to the first reading from the prophet Isaiah."

He walked back behind the podium and flipped to it in the reading book.

"This is what the prophet writes: 'Let the scoundrel forsake his way, and the wicked man his thoughts. Let him turn to the Lord for mercy; to our God, who is generous in forgiving.'"

He paused briefly and enunciated each of the next words:

"'For my thoughts are not your thoughts, nor are your ways my ways, says the Lord. As high as the heavens are above the earth, so high are my ways above your ways and my thoughts above your thoughts.'"

He let it sink in, looking at several of us directly.

"Guys, *this* is why this passage troubles us so much. Because when we think in terms of what we deserve, we think as men think."

He stepped from behind the podium back to the front of the altar.

"God is telling us that he's doing it better than we are. Far better. Miles—light-years—better. I don't know about you, but to me that's comforting!"

A few laughs.

"He's not thinking in terms of what we deserve. If he was, we'd be in trouble, because *none* of us *deserve* heaven. None of us! Priests included! In fact, if we were to think honestly about how awful our sins are in the sight of God, if we could see the damage we do with one sin, we would all come to the conclusion that we deserve hell." He paused to let that sink in.

"But God, according to the way we think, is too good to be true. He gives freely what we do not deserve. He gives us life. He gives us love. He gives us beauty. We did not do anything to *deserve* these things. He gives us life itself. What did you all do to get born? Nothing! But most importantly, guys, he gives us forgiveness when we mess it up, even though we don't deserve it.

"It's the lesson of the money, guys. I gave the money and I didn't ask what they had done for it, and I didn't consider whether they deserved ten dollars or not. It's a *gift*. God gives us the Kingdom of Heaven as a *gift*. He gives it to us freely, and all he asks of us in return is that we love him, and in that spirit of love we do his will. It doesn't matter what you were doing in the past, as long as you are doing his work today. And you know, his will is always going to be the best thing we can do for ourselves."

He continued slowly, "As high as the heavens are above the earth are the ways of God above the ways of man. The sacrifice of God's only son—of Jesus' sacred body and immaculate blood—is a *gift*. It's given to us freely, and it's present here in the Eucharist. Do his work, and you will receive your gift, beyond anything you can imagine."

He paused, and there was silence, which continued as he walked across the altar and sat on his fold-out chair. I glanced over at Kristen, who was staring at her lap, and had a tear running down her cheek. I did, too.

CHAPTER 44

That Friday neither of us had class. I had emailed Father Bob and told him that I hoped to speak to him about something very important. He suggested Friday for a meeting, which we could both do. It was 10 a.m., and Kristen and I pulled up into the driveway in back of the campus ministry building at the bottom of campus in Bess. Standing at the back door, Father Bob greeted us warmly in a plain button-down shirt and khakis. I introduced myself and Kristen, and he said he recognized us from church. Neither of us had been in the building, and as he took us to his office he pointed out a few things—the kitchen, the large meeting area where Sunday-night Mass was held, a small room that served as a chapel devoted to Our Lady. Icons, candles, prayer books, and missalettes gave the otherwise sparse interior an unmistakable purpose.

He led us to his office, which had a scarlet rug that was fading in spots. The blinds were down and angled in a way that didn't admit too much light, but it wasn't dark. One wall was a large bookshelf full of books—Vatican documents, Augustine, Aquinas, St. John of the Cross, St. Theresa of Avila, St. Thérèse of Liseux, St. Francis de Sales, Pope John Paul II, Cardinal Josef Ratzinger, Tolstoy, Plato, Aristotle,

Descartes, Kant, Heidegger, Hemingway, Waugh, Green, Newman, Sheen, a pictorial history of Harley-Davidson, and many, many others.

Kristen and I sat next to each other on the couch. He pulled the chair from behind his desk to the front of it and sat before us, reclining with one leg crossed over the other, but not like a woman. He was wearing running sneakers.

"Hi, guys. Glad you could come."

Again, it was my job to speak.

"Thanks, Father, for taking the time out of your schedule for this."

"Hey, it's why I'm here."

I stopped for a minute, trying to think of how to start. The crucifix above the door was all wood and larger than usual. It was carved in a way like Jesus' arms were nailed too close together, so his shoulders couldn't rest against the cross. His arms and shoulders and chest were bent and he was looking more uncomfortable than he usually did. "There isn't any good way to put this, so I'm just going to talk."

"That's okay."

I took a deep breath and, before I had a chance to hesitate, I talked as it left me.

"Kristen and I were sort of involved with each other last year, Father Bob." I paused and thought about how to put what came next. "Part of that relationship was sexual, and we discovered over the summer that Kristen had become pregnant." I took a deep breath. "We did a lot of thinking about what we should do, but we were really scared, and we decided to have an abortion, and then we did."

The "A" word got caught in my throat a little, and my voice was shaky in general. Already I could hear Kristen crying. I waited a second to choke things back.

"And we're here because we feel like we've done a terrible thing, Father." My lip was trembling a little. "We feel like we've killed our own child. And we want to know if there's anything we can do to make things right with God." It was hard to continue talking, and I stopped for a second. But I didn't want him to jump in just yet, so I pressed on.

"But before you say anything, I want to ask you, please don't sugarcoat what this means. I am fully prepared for you to tell us there's nothing you can do for us. And if that's the truth, then please, that's what I want you to tell us."

He uncrossed his legs and sat forward, putting his elbows on his knees, with his hands folded and up against his chin. He looked straight ahead, which was to the left of me. He sat up again to speak, and put his elbow on the arm of the chair, and with his right hand he added gestures to some of his words.

"First of all, guys, I want you to know that, although I'm sure you feel bad right now, and it may not feel good to be here, I want you to know it is extremely important that you are here. It is extremely important. It's hard to make this step, and unfortunately a lot of folks aren't making it. But you know, this isn't the type of thing that's going to go away on its own."

"I think I'm realizing that," I said.

"The healing that you came here for is going to require God's help, so you are doing the right thing. And you need to know right now, guys, that although the baby is lost to you, he, or she, is *not* lost to God. She is *not* lost to God." He shifted a little bit and paused.

"Think"—he looked up second—"think about a famous person. Abraham Lincoln. George Washington. Queen Elizabeth. Whoever. And think about a not-so-famous person, like your grandparents. Unless they're famous, then think of someone else. Think about the effect each of those lives had.

It's like pebbles thrown into a lake with waves that stretch out to all the lily pads and water bugs on the surface and all the way to the shore, where those disturbances become waves. Some of the pebbles are rocks, some are boulders, but they all make waves that reach out all the way across the expanse and affect everything they touch. A frog might decide to jump in the water when a wave hits his lily pad, then get eaten by a fish that wouldn't have had lunch otherwise. Who knows? But the point is that all of the effects reach far beyond and last long after the pebble breaks the surface. That's what each person does on this earth, isn't it? We make waves that affect the world far beyond ourselves.

"I'm Irish. If my great-great-grandfather had died in the potato famine, I wouldn't be here, and neither would a few dozen other people, and we wouldn't be having this conversation. One life affects the world forever. And my point is, with your help and your faith, God can still make those waves for your baby. That life can still touch many, many lives in a different way. That's not to say that it makes no difference that the baby is here or not. But that life was not lost to God, and I want you guys to think about that and pray on it, and find comfort in that. But remember that only God can make those waves.

"And you will come to see as time goes by that God allowed this to happen for a reason, and God will give this a purpose in your life. As long as you remain faithful, he will use this to bring you closer to him, and he will bring good out of it."

"It doesn't feel like that's possible right now," I said.

I could tell this riled him a little. Not in a bad way, but in a way that made it difficult for him to sit still.

"That might be true, Will. But there's something else there, or you wouldn't be here, would you?"

"I guess not."

"Would it be wrong for me to say there is something that made you feel like this was the right place to be?"

"No," we both said.

"What might that something be?"

"I'm going to guess it's God."

"I'm going to guess that's what it is, too. It's the Holy Spirit. And I'm sure the reason he wants you here is to remind you of what he can do—make the impossible possible. Think about it, guys. What is the central symbol of our faith?"

He stopped and waited, because he expected one of us to answer. I couldn't think of the answer he was looking for off the top of my head.

"The cross, isn't it? And what is the cross? To us, it's a symbol of Christianity. But when we really think about what it *is*, we remember that it's an instrument of death. It was how the Romans killed their criminals. It might as well be a rifle or an electric chair.

"So here we have this dark, dark image that to so many, including Our Lord, meant a painful, humiliating death. And we decorate our churches with it. We put it on every steeple. We put it in our rooms and around our necks, and why? It's because of what God did through the cross. That act of murder became the path to eternal life. With God's help.

"To humans, that's impossible. But to God it is possible, and he did it. The impossible becomes possible through God. And even though things probably don't feel this way now, guys, God brought you here to show you that, and you will understand it someday."

"What scares me, Father, is that this is too much. Maybe God could forgive us, but I can't see how he would want to forgive us for this."

"There is *no* sin that is unforgivable. And remember, it's like the Gospel reading on Sunday—it's *free*. God isn't keeping score. There isn't a limit to his mercy, and there's nothing you can do to earn it. It's a *gift* from a God who loves us. All we have to do is trust in it. You guys came to the right place, and you're doing the right thing."

We all sat in silence and thought about this for a minute.

"It's really embarrassing talking about this to you, Father."

"That's understandable. But Will, you have to remember, I've worked for the past ten years at a *college*. And I live just a stumble from Greek row. You kids don't realize it, but on a night when my windows are open, I can hear *everything*. I've heard it all, Will."

"Didn't think of it that way."

"Just the other night, a group of guys were walking down this little street here behind the convenience store. They were talking about one girl and some of the situations she found herself in with some of the frat brothers. Let me just say I said a few prayers for that poor girl."

"Geez."

"This is only the second time, though, that somebody has come to me about this particular issue, and not because it doesn't come up. It's just that people are afraid to talk about it. Which is the complete opposite of what needs to be done in this situation. It says a lot about you two that you came."

"Thanks," we said.

"In the other situation, the couple came before they had made a decision about what to do. We talked about it, and they asked me what I thought. It was pretty simple, because there's only one choice to make. I told them that I would be there to help them with whatever they needed, and then I never heard from them again. So I guess they decided to have the abortion. The worst part, although the abortion is certainly tragic, is that they didn't feel like they could come back afterwards."

We sat in silence for another minute. He spoke up again.

"So, did you guys want to set up appointments for confession?"

I had thought that *was* confession.

"How about right now?" I asked.

"Well, usually the Church doesn't do group confessions. We should make separate appointments for the two of you."

We both said yes. Kristen set hers up for late morning, and I set mine up for mid-afternoon the next day.

"Are you sure you have time, Father? The weekends are probably the busiest time for you."

"It's not a problem at all. Don't worry about that. I have a robot who looks just like me and can take care of things when I'm not around. Usually people can't tell, especially when it's giving sermons."

The two of us laughed. He got up and walked us to the door. Kristen was being very quiet. We thanked him and said goodbye, and walked to Bess, which was parked out back.

I pulled out of the parking lot around the building and the convenience store next to it. I took a left onto Main Street and stopped at the light.

"I feel *so* good right now. I don't think I've ever felt this good in my life," Kristen said.

I thought for a minute.

"Neither do I, Kristen. And if we feel good now, there's no reason we should ever feel bad about this again."

"You're right."

CHAPTER 45

I came alone to the rectory the next day. Father greeted me at the back door, this time in his collar. He walked me back into the office, where he draped a purple stole over the back of his neck and we situated ourselves in pretty much the same place we had the first day.

"It's been a while, Father."

"It's easy. It's like riding a bike. 'Bless me, Father...'"

"Right. Bless me, Father, for I have sinned. It's been years since my last confession. Too long to remember. These are my sins."

I took a deep breath, held it for a minute, and talked on its way out. When I began speaking, he closed his eyes, in what seemed to be an effort to listen better.

"Well, first of all, I paid for the abortion of my baby, which...would mean that I have helped commit murder...of my own child. I can't think of anything a person can do that is worse than that."

I took a minute to catch my breath and blink back tears.

"Obviously, then, I've had sex before marriage, a few times with a few girls."

"How many?" he asked.

"Three. I have also done...other...activities that aren't quite intercourse that are close and also probably sinful. And I have done that with many girls. I know that God disapproves of this because it disrespects women and turns them into objects for the purpose of what I can get out of it. I thought I was respecting who they were. It seemed almost like it was innocent in a way; we were sharing something beautiful and intimate and hopefully maybe pleasing each other. But I wasn't...in that way I was dishonest with myself, and part of me knew it. Not only do I objectify women in the way I fool around with them, but also in the way I look at them. I try not to, but all the time I find I'm looking at girls and judging them on certain body parts, or on how attractive they are, which I know is shallow and mean. Among us guys it's really easy to get caught up in talking about girls and how they look or which body parts...catch our attention. There really isn't any excuse for it; it's just something we all do. I also look at porn every once in a while, which objectifies women as well. Among us guys, it's sort of expected that we look at porn. It's almost like all of us are supposed to have it. And, well, along with that goes—we also joke about—self-gratification, which I do also occasionally. I've been doing it since they taught us about it in sex ed. That was in fifth grade.

"All of this isn't just disrespectful to the women God created, it's disrespectful to me, and to God, who loves us. It's just so easy to get caught up in it all.

"I've stolen from the grocery stores and convenience stores in town, beer and cigarettes. A friend of mine pushed me while we were drunk and I fell backwards into a window at the gas station. The whole thing shattered, and the storekeeper took me inside to wait while he served some customers. When he got behind the counter, I ran back to the dorm. It probably cost somebody hundreds of dollars to repair....Uh, we stole a couch from a frat house and put it in my dorm. We stole supplies from our dorm building, pulled fire alarms, and we destroyed all sorts of stuff, with no reason except that we thought it was fun. It's all just a general disregard for the people around me, which is the same sort of thing that I got into with girls.

"I disrespect my mother and father. Not just in the way I yell at them and stuff, but by acting the way I do. They didn't raise me to be like this. I disrespect my little brothers by setting a bad example.

"I use the Lord's name in vain constantly. And I'm not sure if it's a sin or not, but I curse constantly. It gets so bad that it leaks into everything my roommates and I say to each other, like 'pass the *effin'* remote.' For no reason, we just curse. It just feels like it's sort of a form of violence. It's so...caustic. And again, I guess it ties into the other things I brought up. It's weird, because the whole time I thought of myself as such a peaceful, laid-back guy, but it seems like in reality I've been really violent. It's the last thing I wanted to be, and the furthest thing from who I thought I was. Uh, I've been in fights. They were for no reason, either. Just the stupidest of things. Really, it was just because my friends and I wanted to fight. I remember bragging to them that I had a perfect weekend one time—I got drunk with my buddies, I got in a fight, and I got laid.

"I've done some drugs and I smoke, which I'm not sure if it's sinful, but I guess isn't that good either. Just disrespectful to myself. I've also thought about killing myself. A little bit over the summer, and a lot when I was sixteen or so.

"I've missed church. I do that constantly. And there's no good reason for it. And if questioning your faith in God is a sin, I am guilty of it."

"Questioning your faith is not a sin," Father Bob interjected.

"Hmm."

I sat, looking at the ground for a minute.

"One thing I am pretty good at is that I don't tell outright lies. Not even small ones. I've worked hard on staying truthful, and I've kept to that." Later I remembered I was wrong about that, with all of the lying I did about the abortion and why I was feeling so bad. I searched for more but I wasn't finding anything.

"Is there anything else?" I asked.

He looked up and smiled. "You haven't been worshipping any golden calves, have you?"

"Yeah, I have. Drinking. I mean, in the way that I put it above so many things in my life, like my health, my schoolwork, sleeping right. I'll even spend money on beer when I'm not sure I have enough for food. And charity isn't even really a thought. I put it way before going to church. I guess that's it. Putting it all together, I guess I've been a pretty rotten person lately."

He looked at me, then up at the ceiling, then back at me again.

"Will, first of all, I want to tell you that I am both impressed and humbled by how well your heart, your soul, and your mind are connected."

"Are you kidding me?"

"No, Will, I really am impressed. You didn't give me a laundry list. I can tell you've really thought about these things and how they are affecting you and how you are affecting others. And it's going to lead you to a very deep relationship with God if you nurture it."

"I hope so."

"So do I, Will." He shuffled in his chair a little, sitting back with his legs crossed. "Now from your confession, I can tell you are someone who is very considerate of what he says and what he does, and who probably has a strong sense of right and wrong, but things have sort of gotten out of control."

"That's true."

"There's something I'd like you to keep in mind. There's an analogy I like to make, and it's this: think of yourself as standing on two logs that are parallel, and you are floating on them down a river, and it's moving pretty quickly." He motioned with his hands. "One of them is your actions, and one of them is your values. As you go down the river, you'll find that it tends to pull those two things apart. If you don't do something to bring them back together every once in a while, you'll find they'll get so far apart that you're forced to jump off one and float down the river on just one."

"I guess that's about where I am."

"But Will, you're on the right track. Confession gets us back floating comfortably and safely on those two logs. Prayer keeps them together. Will, there are a lot of good things ahead for you. I'm confident of that."

"That's really hard for me to hear right now."

"I understand. But you've gotta trust me. More importantly, you have to trust God. He makes the impossible possible; all we have to do is ask and believe. And you can be assured of my prayers."

"Thanks, Father." We sat in silence for another minute.

"Did you want to say an Act of Contrition?"

"Yeah....Oh my God, I am heartily sorry for having offended you, and I detest all of my sins because of your just punishments. But most of all, because they offend you, my God, who art all good and deserving of all my love. I firmly resolve, with the help of your grace, to sin no more, and to avoid the near of occasion of sin. Amen.

"Now, Will, for your penance, I'd like you to do something. Do you have a Bible?"

"I have one in Jersey."

He looked over at his bookshelf to his right and pulled a green one with canvas binding off the shelf. *The Catholic Study Bible* was on the front in large gold letters, from Oxford University Press.

"Here, take this one."

"Are you sure?"

"Yeah. I've got a few around. They go with the job. I'd like you to take this Bible, go to a place where you won't be bothered or distracted, and spend a half hour thinking about nothing but God."

I laughed a little bit. "I thought you were going to tell me I had to build a church."

"No. This will prove to be much more important. You don't have to read anything at all. You can flip through the pages if you want, but just make sure that for a half hour the only thought in your mind is God."

"Okay."

He sat forward again and raised his right hand with two fingers in a peace gesture with the fingers together, but with the side of his hand, not his palm, facing me.

"God the Father of mercies, through the death and resurrection of his Son has reconciled the world to himself and sent the Holy Spirit among us for the forgiveness of sins. Through the ministry of the Church may God give you pardon and peace, and I absolve you from your sins, in the name of the Father, and of the Son, and of the Holy Spirit." He brought his hand down and made a sweeping cross in the air.

I crossed myself and said, "Amen."

"Your sins are forgiven, Will. You're as good as the day you were baptized. Go in the peace of Christ."

"It almost seems too easy."

He smiled. "It wasn't easy, Will. It took three thousand years of Old Testament history and the torture, death, and resurrection of God's only Son for it."

"Right."

"And Will, this isn't magic, this is reality. There will probably be times when it's not very easy."

"You're right. Thank you, Father." I was starting to tear up a little bit.

"Thank God."

CHAPTER 46

I removed the Bible from my lap and stood up, putting it under my arm. I shook the priest's hand after he stood up, and I ambled toward the back door, losing my direction at one point. My knees were a little wobbly, and the floor beneath me felt like liquid.

He walked around me and guided me toward the door. We said goodbye and I got in Bess and sat for a moment, looking at the back door of the campus ministry building. My mind, for the first time since I'd hit puberty, was entirely still. My soul was like a lake on a calm day.

I got the keys out and started the car, backed out, and headed past the convenience store toward South Main Street. I took a left, and while stopped at the light noticed the clouded sky ablaze in pinks and oranges. The buildings on the corner across the street were all silhouetted. The light changed, and I drove the speed limit the rest of the way home.

When I arrived at the parking lot, I got out of the car with the Bible. I stood and leaned against the passenger side of Bess and enjoyed the coolness of the mountain air that was signaling the beginning of fall. Behind me the sky was already sinking into twilight, with the moon and the brightest stars out among the scattered clouds. I stared and inside I half prayed that I could stay there, that I could blink and on the other side of my eyelids would be eternal peace. It felt that close.

It was night before I walked up to the apartment. The kitchen light and the television were on, and the volume was up loud, clashing with how I was feeling. Everyone was in his room or perhaps somewhere else. I turned off the lights and then the TV and walked back to my room, closed the door, and turned on the lights. I took out my journal, sat on my bed with my back against the wall, put the Bible on my lap, and began paging through it. I concentrated on God, like Father had told me. I opened my journal and began to write:

I hope that the person I lost, my child, can see me, and see how sorry I am. I wonder what she would think—would she be angry at me?

At that moment, a thought that didn't come from my own mind poured through me in a sudden, almost violent sort of way, and immediately I began to sob. I picked up my pillow and buried my face in it so my roommates could not hear. The thought repeated a few times, and each time it did I cried a little harder until it wrung out my whole body. It was a long, long time before it stopped.

The thought was actually several thoughts that didn't unfold in a logical way, but together flooded my mind at once—that God had been there at the worst times in the past few months, and he was speaking straight to me through my friends. In particular were the conversation with Kat the night before the abortion, and the conversation with Lily the night before I went to talk with Kristen. "Will, you are a good person, and you would make a wonderful father," and "You will feel so blessed one day." In both instances they were the last things in the world I expected to hear.

CHAPTER 47

December had sunk into our hearts and our minds. Finals were done or mostly done for most kids. Most of us were looking forward to going home. Some had gone home already, and some were lingering for one last weekend. Our apartment was clean and had a twenty-four-inch artificial tree made in China with crappy plastic decorations on it. We had a plate of sugar cookies that our girls had baked for us and were nearly gone.

The night before, the girls had a Christmas party that required a tie. It was an excuse for them to get out nice dresses. It was a small get-together, and they actually cooked for it and bought us gifts. They were girlfriend material.

I went down the steps into the late morning in early December. I got in Bess, who was a little cold, but I didn't mind. The sky was frozen and covered in clouds, in shades of gray, with a bluish tint in places. The sunlight was spread evenly across the backs of the clouds, and some was getting to the other side.

On the way down the hill I could see most of the rest of town stretched out beneath the winter sky. Even though the students typically complained about it, Bristol was a beautiful town in a lot of ways. At the bottom of the hill I turned right at the entrance to the campus, just because I liked driving through it.

I took a right onto Main Street, where there were wreaths on many of the streetlamps and lights stretched across the street with greetings such as Happy Holidays, Season's Greetings, and Joy to the World. A few businesses had lights in their windows, and one or two had Christmas trees.

I parked in a parking garage across from Sparky's, which was one of the best-known sandwich places in town, although I hadn't been there yet.

I was a little bit nervous about the meeting, but I was sure it was going to be a good time. Inside I found Father Bob, who was wearing a khaki-colored zip-up coat, gray slacks, and a blue checked shirt. He looked like a high school biology teacher, of course. His face lit up at seeing me.

There was a bar with a couple TVs and pictures all over the place of rock stars and sports figures, but only a few were signed. That was sort of funny, I thought. It made the place look interesting, at least. Some of the decorations were old comic books and clippings from the newspaper about weird occurrences. Somebody had certainly put a lot of time into them.

The waitress came up and was friendly and cute. After she took our order, it was time to talk. This is what made me nervous—feeling like I had to have something to talk about. But I had prepared a few topics in advance.

"So, Father, how did you decide to become a priest?"

"Well, I can give you the short version or the long version."

"I'm in no rush."

"Then I'll tell you a short version of the long version."

"Okay."

"I went to school at Boston College. At that point, becoming a priest hadn't really occurred to me."

"What was your major?"

"History. I finished, though, and I ran into the same difficulty that a lot of kids that age run into, that they're not sure what they want to do with their lives." He paused and waited for me to chuckle, and I did. "So after that I moved out to Malibu, California..."

"Did you know anyone out there?"

"No, I had just heard of it. It seemed like a nice place, so I went."

"What did you do out there?"

"I worked in a surf shop."

"Really?"

"Yeah. You seem surprised."

"I don't know...I just...it's not what you imagine a priest doing before he enters the seminary. Where did you learn how to surf?"

"I lived in Florida from the time I was eight to the time I went to college. We were near the beach, so I picked it up as a teenager. The waves were always awful, though."

"Same in Jersey."

"So I was there for a couple years, then I got bored with that and decided to move out to Hawaii."

"Hawaii?"

"Hey, I'm tellin' you, this was a major crisis! I needed to be as comfortable as possible to sort things out," he said with a smile. "So I lived on the island of Maui for three years."

"What did you do?"

"Surfed and drove a delivery truck."

"Wow."

"It wasn't bad. I'd be lying if I said I didn't enjoy it. But all those hours by myself in the truck is when I started thinking about being a priest."

"You were called."

"Sure I was called. But it's not like something where you look up one day and you see the sun spinning in the sky or you get the stigmata or something. It's actually an unglamorous process, for me at least. You just get the idea and slowly things sort of reverse, so it seems like it doesn't make sense anymore for you *not* to be a priest."

"So what was the day like when you finally decided to take the plunge?"

"It's pretty funny, actually....My boss for the delivery truck business was a real hard case. He used to work us like slaves. That wasn't a problem for me, because I didn't have any family down there, and I didn't really have any friends either. A few guys that I worked with, but mostly I just kept to myself."

"That's weird. You seem so outgoing."

"Well, that wasn't a natural thing for me. If I'm outgoing, it's only by the grace of God. I used to keep to myself quite a bit. But anyway, I had been thinking long and hard—and praying, of course—about the whole priest thing, and I was just about there. Then one day, one of the few friends I had there—his mother died. I wanted to go to the funeral, and this was around Christmastime, which is the busiest time for delivery people. I needed to take off for the funeral, and the boss wouldn't let me. So I said to him right there, 'That's it. I'm going to the funeral, and you're not going to stop me. After that, I'm going back home and becoming a priest, because with people like you out there, the world needs them.' And I slammed the keys to my truck on the table and left the office, and left Hawaii right after the funeral. Six months later I was in the seminary."

"Wow. How dramatic."

He chuckled a little bit. "Looking back, it's a little uncharitable. But it felt great at the time."

We both laughed, and at that our food arrived. The turkey sandwich was all it was cracked up to be.

"Well, I have to tell you, Father Bob, you do great work. Sometimes it looks like you're glowing."

"Like in the comic books."

"Well, not exactly. But you know what I mean."

"Yeah—it's funny—we're Irish, and my grandmother was very close to us. I come from a family of six kids."

"Wow."

"She had been getting up there in years, and she was very sick for a long time. I hate to say it, but it was almost like she was lingering. Then, within three months I graduated from seminary and my brother had a boy. Then, right after that—like, two weeks after my nephew Kyle was born—she died. It was like she had been sticking around to make sure that one of us was a priest, and that one of us would make sure the family name would carry on."

"That's pretty funny. I mean, sad that your grandmother died, but funny in a way."

"Yeah."

We both took a minute to eat some of our sandwiches.

"So how have you been, Will?"

"I've been alright. I got stood up a couple weeks ago, but other than that, things have been alright."

"A lesson in humility."

"The worst part is that I have class with her," I said. "But aside from that, I'm doing alright. I haven't been drinking as much, I've been working hard in school, I've been getting to church. I've been happier."

"But how do you feel about what happened?"

I sat back and took a sip of my drink. "I don't know. It's very raw, Father. I believe in what happened at confession, and that God loves me and he forgives me. But when I think about it, I hurt a lot."

"That's alright, Will."

"I know. I mean, I'm not blaming God or Kristen for what happened. I forgive her, and I did from the moment it happened."

"What about the abortionist, the workers?"

"I forgive them too, although that's harder."

"But you don't forgive yourself."

"No."

"You have to, Will."

"If you say so, then I suppose I do, Father. But I wouldn't be honest if I said I felt that way even one bit. I knew better all along."

"Will, promise me one thing."

"Depends."

"Promise me you'll pray for it."

"If you promise me you'll pray for it."

"Deal."

"Alright then. Let's start right now. Lord, I pray that someday I can forgive myself."

"Amen."

"Amen."

We sat for a minute and I stared at my hand, which was playing with a straw wrapper.

"It's going to be hard, Will."

"It is."

We sat quietly for another minute, then I grilled him for the next hour on all the questions I had about the faith: Why would a loving God demand the sacrifice of his own son? Aren't artistic portrayals of Jesus as a pasty white guy inaccurate? Do Jews and Muslims go to hell because they don't believe in Jesus?

I was tough on him, but these were burning questions. He fielded them convincingly and with patience.

CHAPTER 48

I woke up and my lower half was cold. It took a while to assess what had happened. I looked ahead at the white plaster wall, at the steps descending down before me, and at my feet, which were wearing my sneakers. I remembered that I was in Italy, but where in Italy, I was not yet sure.

After a few moments I realized I was in the stairwell to my flat. To the left of me was the hallway, with white wooden doors with windows and an old latch with the key in it.

I jolted awake when I realized what day it was, and where I was supposed to be around then. I looked at my watch and it was 7:03. The bus would be leaving in forty-two minutes. I sprung up and gingerly sprint-walked down the hall to the room on the left. Sam was at the foot of his bed standing over his open suitcase. He looked up from his packing.

"Did you get laid last night?"

"No. I passed out at the top of the steps there."

"Where?"

"At the end of the hall."

"Are you kidding?"

"I wouldn't say that unless it was true."

"I guess I just meant I can't believe it."

"Neither can I. It was a long night."

By that point I already had my suitcase on my bed and was stacking clothes into it. I was starting to get the feeling back in my legs. I didn't have a lot of time to make sense of what had happened. We were out the door within five minutes.

We walked out the large wooden front doors where the cold was waiting for us, through the tall gate, down the street, through the piazza, past the flower stand to the bus stop, and waited.

"So what happened?" he asked.

"I don't know. I guess I was tired from walking. And Jägermeister."

"I told you to come home."

"I would have, but you saw how Melanie was flirting."

"Did you two hook up?"

"I don't know. I just walked her back to her house. Then I walked home and I guess I couldn't make it to the room."

"I can't believe that," he said, and seemed a little annoyed.

"Neither can I."

"Your bed is, like, ten yards away from the steps."

"You've got a firm grasp on a great many things." I looked at my watch. "Well, I got some sleep, and that's all that matters, right?" I said after a minute.

"Not really."

We got to the bus stop with enough time for me to grab an egg sandwich with zucchini on focaccia at the corner trattoria with an espresso. After my little breakfast I stood smoking on the corner in the cold early morning with the other students, who were showing up a few at a time. Word was getting around where I had slept. People were asking me about it, and I didn't mind. It was pretty funny. Melanie was there and she was not making eye contact.

We loaded the undercarriage of the bus with our stuff, and I was among the first aboard. I grabbed a window seat and hoped Lily would sit next to me. I was surprised to find that she did. Melanie and Ella sat behind us.

It wasn't long until I started dozing off. It had been a long night.

When I woke up, Lily's head was on my shoulder. I looked out the window and wondered if she had done it before she fell asleep or after.

CHAPTER 49

We arrived in Siena, where we got off our tour bus at the city gates, since it was difficult to maneuver a car in the city and there weren't that many places to park. There were laws there preserving the city's medieval authenticity, and the people there had to get permits to do anything. There we met our tour guide. He was a short man, completely bald, with round, black-rimmed glasses and a round face. His name was Francesco, and he had a friend, not a tour guide, named Ricardo, who was taller and had brushed-back hair and a long coat and a scarf. He looked like a thespian.

Francesco started off with a humorous tale of the rivalry between Florence and Siena, that in medieval times everyone's loyalty was to their city, not to their country, because their city was their country. That was interesting, I thought. I was exhausted, though. I lit a cigarette to wake up.

We began walking on the cobblestones between buildings built of earthy brown brick, a few stories high on each side. As we walked he explained some of the features and told the stories of some of the structures. It was only about five minutes' worth of slow walking before we made it to Piazza del Campo at the city center, which is pretty vast according to piazza standards. It is laid out in a slightly concave shape of red brick almost like an amphitheater, with the city government hall at the bottom and a white fountain at the top. Once every summer they fill it with dirt and have a horse race—Il Palio—where the riders don't wear saddles. Since it's such a short track, he explained, it is a raucous time and often people get hurt. But supposedly there are people who devote good portions of their lives to doing well at this competition.

The afternoon was ours to roam around the city. Most of us began in the shop at the top of the piazza in the city center. I lingered at the back of the crowd.

We had some time in the afternoon before we took a short tour of the civic building. Inside was a huge, graphic mural of soldiers running babies through with swords, and mothers with faces twisted in every conceivable expression of horror and distress. The painting was of the Slaughter of the Innocents, which was painted there to remind the civic leaders of what happens when the government abuses its power. The rest of the building failed to catch much of my attention.

We then headed back to the hotel, which was outside the city about five minutes and was originally designed to be a nursing home. One could sort of tell. It wasn't a situation a group of students could complain about, though.

Later that night we piled in the vans and drove once again to the gates of Siena. From there we walked along the cobblestone street about half the distance to the center, and entered a small archway with a wooden door that filled it, which led to steps descending down past a main dining room into a cellar. This was where we would be eating dinner.

It seemed to be an old wine cellar. The walls were brick, and the long tables were made of coarsely hewn, darkly stained wood, and were situated in different places among the archways and pillars. The whole place was lit with lanterns and candlelight. It was an authentic medieval experience, or it felt that way at least. I sat on one side of the room and Lily on the other, at the same table as Dr. Sellier, whose spouse and children had stayed at the hotel.

The tables were already set with bread, olive oil, and pitchers of wine. It was really how every dinner should begin. Before I sat down, I poured myself a glass of red.

Dinner was five or six courses—ribollita; linguine in pesto; roasted hen and potatoes roasted with salt, pepper, and rosemary for a main course; sweets for dessert; dessert wine; then cheese plates with fruit.

I drank about a pitcher of wine. As dinner was winding down, people started milling around and talking. I walked toward the bathroom, which was up the steps.

On my way I passed Lily, who was talking to Dr. Sellier. She was wearing a black V-neck sweater and black stretch pants with a pink belt, the candlelight in her eyes. She had her right arm across her stomach, with her left elbow resting on it, and she was playing with her necklace.

As I passed, I heard him say to her, "Your eyes—they speak," and I saw her reaction. She put her hand flat on her chest and said thank you and looked very flattered. I sort of wanted to tap him on the shoulder and punch him. Instead, I continued up to the bathroom.

I came back down and didn't look in her direction. I just wanted to get back to the table. I poured myself another glass of wine and kept to myself. After a moment, there was some noise coming from a back room. What emerged was a group of the restaurant workers dressed in medieval garb playing a recorder and a mandolin-like instrument. The music was cheerful and had a beat to it. I was angry and getting tipsy, so I figured what the hell. I started clapping my hands and waving my arms with the music and making a bit of a fool of myself from my seat. After not long I got up and grabbed one of the cloth napkins, hopping up and down, hooting, waving my napkin, and clapping. The people around me, especially the girls, were pretty amused. Some got up and joined me. The guys playing the music came over to our side, and more people began dancing along as well. Soon all thirty-five of us were clapping and stomping our feet, twirling our napkins.

After dinner, Dr. Sellier told us one bus would go back to the hotel, another would stay until 1 a.m. He would be waiting for the later one, naturally.

Most all of us stayed and followed the professor to a pub with two floors of bliss. I ordered a stout down below and went up the steps to the second floor. There the crowd had staked out a long table, and there was a seat across from Lily. It was good to see the good professor was nowhere in sight.

"Hey," I said as I took out my cigarettes.

"Hey," she said. "Have you seen Bruce?"

"You mean Dr. Sellier?"

"He prefers 'Bruce.' Have you seen him?"

"No, why?"

"He asked me to hold his jacket while he went to the bathroom. I wanted him to know I was up here."

"He's coming on to you," I said.

"Will, that's gross. He's married."

"Have you, like, been drinking?"

"No," she said, then caught herself. "A little."

"It's true, and you better watch yourself."

"It's not true," she said.

"Are you being stupid, Lily, or just ignorant?"

"Don't be a dick, Will. Have you seen him?"

"No."

She got up and left. I lit my cigarette and stared at the table. Doodles was next to me, talking about some fraternity business, about some guy from Ki Theta Beta or whatever having sex with the girlfriend of some guy in his fraternity, and so they had spray-painted the other frat's mascot or whatever.

"Will, have you been ta any AKL pahrties?"

"No, Doodles, I don't need to spend to make friends." He made a face like he was wounded.

"Here you are," I continued, "a good-looking, intelligent guy with some money, apparently. With an Australian accent. And yet it appears that you feel the need to spend hundreds of dollars to meet other men."

"Yeah, but we get sorority chicks."

"Not worth it." Several sorority chicks were sitting at the table, but none were listening. They were literally talking about shoes.

Doodles joined the conversation. I liked the guy, but I could tell his favorite sex act was and likely always would be masturbation. I finished my stout and decided I would go get another.

Down by the bar I found Lily wearing the professor's jacket and standing next to him as he talked to several of the girls from the trip. I walked by them, hoping they wouldn't see me. Sam was at the bar getting a drink, and I asked him to do a shot with me. He said no at first, but I ordered two and made him drink one of them. Then I ordered a stout, and he walked over to the crowd that had Lily in it. I really didn't want to be a part of it, but I figured I had nowhere else to go.

The professor was asking with interest about the hometowns of the girls and making jokes and speaking Italian and correcting mispronunciations, and the girls were all so delighted. I smoked and stared, and at one point Lily's eyes caught mine. She mouthed, "What's wrong?" to me, but I just looked away out the windows and blew my smoke out.

There were some people we knew outside, so I drank the rest of my beer quickly, ordered a shot at the bar, and went out there. It was a nice night—cool but not cold. These were a few of the more bookish girls. I had a real soft spot for them, because they lacked pettiness. They were talking about the tour and how amazing it was to be in a city that hadn't changed in centuries. In America, they were saying, everything was all about being new, and here there were laws that said you couldn't change anything.

Slowly more congregated outside, and it was becoming time to go. As the professor and Francesco led the way, Lily walked beside me.

"Is something on your mind?" she asked.

"No."

"You don't seem like yourself."

"Sorry about that," I said.

"I want my friend back."

I looked at her, because I really thought she was being a bit daft. I shrugged my shoulders and didn't say anything, just kept smoking and walking up the slight incline.

"He's right where he's always been," I said finally.

"Where's that?"

"Not here."

She just looked ahead, and I could tell from her face that she didn't want to play any games. That was great, because I didn't either.

The group of us stood at the gates of the city. The only van would have to take two trips. Francesco would drive and was perceivably drunk, and it made me quite nervous for us all. I said a few prayers for the safety of my classmates as the first load piled into the van, Lily among them.

I sat with the rest and listened to the conversation, not having much to say.

CHAPTER 50

The next day we spent in Siena, where we took in the other sites aside from the civic building. The main attraction was the cathedral, which was huge and beautiful. As the guide explained a lot of the imagery, it made me realize how little I knew about my faith. After the tours we had some free time to roam about the city. Most of us were tired, though, and so we lingered around the fountain in the main square.

In the late afternoon we went back to the bus where we had already loaded our bags. I sat in a window seat alone this time and put my headphones on but didn't listen to music. Instead I just stared out at the countryside passing by.

As we drove along, I watched the sun retreating slowly out of the sky. There was a thin layer of clouds, and the sunlight was a rich red and orange. It looked to be at the bottom of a lake shining up, and like there was blood in it, as from some upstream sacrifice.

As the bus descended from the mountains into the valley, something that had been creeping up on me decided now it would not be ignored—that my baby would have been born around then. There wasn't anything I could do about the fact that it was all I heard, all I saw, and all I felt. There was an awkward silence where there should have been breath and light and motion.

There simply was nothing more dastardly and insane than having lost her like I did. I didn't forgive myself, and I didn't see any way that I could. I was sure there was more I could have done, but I was blind and I was a coward. But it was enough just to have lost her.

I breathed on time that belonged to her, and I wanted her to have it back. I guessed my punishment was that she wouldn't take it.

It wasn't the sun at the bottom of the lake; it was me, I realized.

CHAPTER 51

I had been planning for Valentine's Day since we had gotten to Italy, really. I had figured that by then Lily would have come around, and we would be able to spend the rest of the trip together in Florence.

I had a date set up in my mind. We would get a bottle of white wine and go up to Fiesole in the hills right outside of the city, and drink it from an outlook where we could see the sun set on the city below. At nightfall, we would head back down into Florence and get some gelato, and I would read her some of the letters I had written her. She would tear up, and we would kiss by the Arno and wonder why we hadn't gotten together sooner.

It fell on a Monday that year, and it was pouring out. This was especially annoying because I had lost my umbrella at a bar over the weekend. On the way to school Sam let me share his. Our first class that day was Italian. I did a good deal of watching Lily. Sometimes she would catch me and I would smile or look away.

Break time came, and my routine had become one cup of instant cappuccino and one cigarette. The girls went off and talked in their corner. Some of them had boyfriends who had called the night before or sent them this or that in the mail. I stood against the wall and thought about whether I should take the long shot and ask her if she wanted to get some dinner or a coffee or something. At that point, Doodles walked up to me.

"'Ey, mate, can I get a cigarette?"

"Yeah. No problem."

"Sorry about the news."

"What news?"

"Ya didn't 'ear?"

"No."

"Remember whoile you and I were at Dante's on Saturday noight, the girls went aut to Dolce Zucchero?"

"Yeah."

"You said you didn't want ta come, because ya didn't feel loike dancin'."

"Right."

"Well, the girls met a pack a blokes from Oxford, and one of them walked Lily home."

"Yeah?"

"What d'ya mean 'yeah'? 'E smooched 'er, mate."

"What does that have to do with me?"

"Ah, don't give me that shite. The Brits are movin' in on our territory. One of 'em smooched Crystal too."

"You're the one who decided Lily is off limits to everyone, not me."

"Piechfuzz, what d'ya taike me for? Ya follow that girl around loike a puppy dog. If ya weren't such a stand-up guy, I'd think it was pathetic. But I know all ya got in your heart is pure intentions, so it bothahs the 'ell outta me to 'ear this shit."

"Look, she's hot. We both agree on that."

"Certainly."

"There was a time when for a little while it looked like we meant something to each other, and I would have liked that to continue, but really, I don't give a shit what she does."

"Piechfuzz, you'll make a great 'usband one daiy, because you're an awful liah, mate."

"I'm going into the priesthood."

"A priest? Yer jokin', roight?"

"Break's over. Gotta go."

"Roight."

After class, we did what we normally did, which was check our email. I got there first, and Lily occupied the computer next to me. I didn't say anything. I finished my email as quickly as possible and left. I descended the six flights of stairs and walked out into the rain, and then laughed to myself at how it seemed to be there for effect.

CHAPTER 52

Doodles and I walked through Piazza Navona. It was a Friday night, and it was warm for that time of the year, so the cafés along the perimeter were full of people dining, drinking, smoking, and laughing, all in dark clothes it seemed, with candles on the tables and strands of lights illuminating their features. The two of us didn't say anything. We were scanning the crowds for the girls we had lost.

We found them after a while—Lily, Crystal, Amy, and Maria—at a long table with a bunch of men in kilts. Rome was playing Scotland in the rugby championships. Every bar in the Eternal City was full of Highlanders in kilts taking shots and singing songs.

Doodles and I approached the table, and the oldest gentleman asked us to have a seat. I sat at the end of the table, with Doodles to my left, next to an older gentleman and two other younger men. To my right were Crystal, Amy, Lily, and Maria, and three more young men.

The older gentleman introduced himself as the coach of a rugby team. He asked if we had heard of the Scottish Rugby Union, and I said no. He explained that in Scotland, it was the equivalent of the NFL in America. These were his players, and at the end was the rookie. When he said the word "rookie," the guy stood up reluctantly, put his hands behind his head, and started swiveling his hips, singing some rhyme in a high-pitched voice. When he was done he put his arms out in front of him, and thrust them back and his hips forward at the same time with a grunt. Then he sat down and chugged the rest of his glass of wine.

"What was that about?" I asked.

"This being his first year in the SRU, he's our little cocker spaniel, you might say. Of the female variety. I'm being delicate on behalf of the ladies, here. He does what we tell him to do. And anytime we say the word 'rookie,' he has to do the rookie dance."

The guy at the end got up and did the dance twice. I had developed a protective instinct toward the girls, but these guys were completely harmless, and could demolish me anyway.

They were genuinely interested in the fact that we were young American kids. They wanted to know about our lives and what we knew about Scotland, and to talk about their brief visits to the States. They were interested in getting us to come up to see Scotland before we left Europe. They were as interested in talking to us guys as they were in talking to the girls. It was refreshing to be around people who were decent.

They were also interested in getting us very, very drunk. The coach apparently had some money, and made sure every glass at the table was full at all times, especially ours. The girls didn't drink very fast, but Doodles and I did. He ordered bottle after bottle, and after he had gotten us well pissed, he ordered us each a snifter of Sambuca. It was at that point I blacked out.

When I came back to, I found that I was sitting on a bench, in front of one of the fountains that makes the piazza famous. To my left was Lily, and we had lost the rest of the crowd.

"People don't have any respect anymore. They don't understand beauty. They have it all around them, and when they see it they just want to fu...to fornicate with it. They don't want to honor it. I want to honor beauty, Lily. I want to be worthy of beauty, like you."

"That's sweet, Will."

"I hear people compliment your eyes....I write you all kinds of poetry, dammit. They can't talk about your eyes. I can talk about your eyes, because I'm not just trying to get into your pants. He can't talk about your eyes. I'm trying to be a good person to you. A friend. Someone who gives you the respect you deserve. Here." I reached in my pocket and gave her the folded-up poems I had written her. I had been carrying them around since Valentine's Day, trying to find a good time to give them to her. That wasn't it.

"Thank you, Will." She opened them up and started reading the first one.

She looked up at me for a moment, then back down at the poetry.

"Excuse me," I said.

I got up and walked around the bench toward the fountain and urinated in it. She was yelling at my back, but I continued until I was finished. When I finished, she came up to me and grabbed me by the arm.

"You're so beautiful."

"C'mon, Will. We're going back to the hotel."

I blacked out again.

CHAPTER 53

When I woke up I found I was in all of my clothes on top of the bed at the hotel. I got up to urinate, and when I walked past the mirror I noticed something odd. I did a double take and found a Scottish Rugby Union cap on my head. I was happy to find that.

When I finished, I brushed my teeth. I had showered late the night before, and I felt like hell, so I didn't bother to take another. I lay back down on the bed, and Sam was stirring.

He sat up and looked at me intently.

"Peachfuzz."

"Yeah?"

"What is the gayness that has landed upon your head?"

"It's a hat."

"That's not a hat. It's a blue diaper."

"When in Rome."

He chuckled and got up and went into the bathroom. I got up and looked through my bag for something else to put on. I changed while Sam took a shower. The room was starting to steam up, so I got up and left to sit out in the lobby, where a couch, a coffee table, and several chairs were laid out.

There I sat down and looked at the etching of Rome above the couch opposite me and tried not to think.

Doodles came out of his room and sat across from me. He had his headphones on, listening to a CD player. He turned it off and put the earphones around his neck.

"'Ow are ya, mate?"

"I'm in the middle of something."

"Telepathy?"

"No. Never mind. I feel like hell."

"I'm feelin' alright. Those Scotsmen were troiyin' to get us pissed."

"A resounding success."

"Roight. 'Bout the only thing about the Scots they are successful at."

"What's that supposed to mean?"

"Ah, shit. I dunno. Don't know the first thing about Scotland. I might be descended from Scots for all I know. What didjew an' Lily do last noight?"

"Don't really remember. I remember talking to her a little bit, but I don't remember most of the end of the night."

"Hm. Me neithah. I guess I didn't get in Crystal's pants yet."

"Hmm."

"Where did you get that 'at?" he asked.

"Rugby guys gave it to me, I guess."

"Where in the 'ell is moine?"

"I don't know. Guess they thought I drank more."

"Bullshit. Scotsmen are liars."

"Maybe they just thought I was better looking."

He tilted his head back and he smiled widely, like the notion struck him as funny. "Well, then. That's it, i'n it. They felt bad for ya."

"Whatever works."

Sam came out and he sat on the couch with Doodles.

"Mornin', Sam."

"Morning, Dudley."

"Will."

"Yeah?" I asked.

"Did you talk to Lily yet?"

"No, why?"

"She's pissed off, dude," he said.

"For what?"

"Supposedly you pissed in one of the fountains in Piazza Navona."

"She's pissed about that?"

"A little. But then she had to walk you home and neither of you guys had keys."

"Yikes."

The first and last thing—and several other things besides—the manager told us when he met us was that we had to make sure we stayed with somebody who had a key. If we forgot our key, he would not get up in the middle of the night to let us in.

"So what happened?"

"Apparently you were singing really loud in the stairwell to piss the manager off. Then you got to the top of the stairs and you passed out. Lily didn't have a key, so she had to knock on the door and ring the bell for twenty minutes. The guy came and he was really pissed off, and then Lily had to ask the manager for help to wake you up and pick you up off the stairs and put you to bed." By the time Sam finished the story, Doodles was in tears laughing.

"How do you know all of this?"

"I got in right after Lily did."

"Great."

"But at least you got a free hat."

"Right."

"Willie boy, you are a gentleman and a scholah. Looks like you'll be floggin' the dolphin a bit longah, mate!" Doodles said, still half laughing, his face bright red.

"I hate blacking out."

When he stopped laughing finally he said, "Whoiy, ain't it good for ya every once in a whoile?"

"No," Sam said.

"Whoiy not? I figure, ya got ta bend your perception every once in a whoile, yannow? Let the wind blow ya where it wants ya."

"That's ridiculous," Sam said.

"Yeah, that's pretty stupid, Doodles."

"Ah, shit. I'm just riffin'. But what's the use in doing the same thing over and over again?"

"Like drinking?" Sam said.

"No, like going where you're supposed to and thinkin' and doin' what you're supposed to. Sounds like a poile a dung to me."

"It just freaks me out that last night I completely erased myself from my own body. If I wasn't in control, who was? That freaks me out."

"Then stop," Sam said.

"I wish it was that simple," I said.

"It is that simple."

"I stopped drinkin'," Doodles said. "At about two o'clock this morning."

He and I laughed. At this point, more people began coming into the lobby. I was bragging about my new hat; Sam and Doodles were talking about their nights and the fact that I had pissed in a famous fountain and forgotten my key the night before. Lily came out and looked angry at me. I walked up next to her.

"I'm sorry, Lily."

"That was disappointing, Will."

"I'm sorry."

"Do you know what it's like for someone my size to carry around a two-hundred-pound boy?"

"One hundred and ninety."

"Whatever. And no, I did not hook up with anyone from Oxford. Do you believe everything you hear?"

"What?"

"You don't remember? You were asking me if I hooked up with some guy from Oxford. You told the manager I did." Doodles shrugged.

I sighed. "I really am truly sorry, Lily. Sometimes I can't control myself."

"No kidding! What are you going to do about that, Will?"

"I'm sorry."

"I worry about you, Will."

By then, the whole crowd was in the lobby, including the Sellier family. Dr. Sellier came up next to me, and I turned to him away from Lily.

"Good morning, Will."

"Good morning, Dr. Sellier."

"That's a nice hat."

"Thank you."

"Remember how you got it?"

"Not really."

"How is that?"

"I was hanging out with several Scotsmen last night, and they decided they wanted to get me and Doodles drunk. Then I woke up with this hat on my head."

"Interesting. Did you do any sightseeing last night?"

"Not that I know of," I said.

"Didn't see any fountains?"

"Nope."

"That's odd, because there are lots of them in Rome. Particularly in Piazza Navona."

"Well, that's funny. I don't know. Sometimes I look and I don't see things that are right in front of me," I said.

"Try to be more attentive. We don't budget for bailing students out of jail."

"Sure."

Once everyone was in the lobby, Dr. Sellier explained that there were a few Masses at St. Peter's if we were interested in that sort of thing, and then early in the afternoon we would be meeting at the Roman Forum for a tour. Sam, Lily, Amy, Melanie, and I decided to go to Mass. I asked Crystal to go, but she said she wasn't Catholic. You don't have to be Catholic to go to Mass, I said, but she wasn't interested.

We left our hotel and walked mostly silently through the piazzas and waking streets and by the cafés. Some streets were crowded with little cars and *motorini* despite the hour. We walked across the bridge spanning the Tiber River, and on to St. Peter's Square. I had been there once a few years before. This time, though, for the jubilee year, the basilica with its huge dome had been power-washed and was gleaming white in the sun. Even though I had seen it before, it was still quite impressive as I walked up to it. It was hard to believe its size, even though it was right in front of me. The piazza, with the columns and the statues of the Apostles reaching out around the sides, was crowded with people coming in for Mass. Because of the jubilee, the huge metal doors to the right of the main huge metal door were open, and if you walked through them, you would get some special graces and a break in the punishment for your sins. When my mother was telling me about them, I thought it was sort of a silly-sounding thing. But in line, I was a lot more willing to believe it. The crowd was large and getting a little pushy, especially as we came up to the door. It was inscribed in Latin all around. On the doors were relief depictions of man's sinfulness throughout creation—from Cain and Abel on. I prayed that it would work, and it would reach into all the filthiest things. And when I walked through the door, I actually felt some of the forgiveness that Father Bob told me I received when I had gone to him for confession.

I thought to myself that I couldn't believe that it was that easy, but I couldn't deny how I felt. So I just thought about not messing it up. We walked and stood among the crowd. The Mass was in Italian, but I understood most of what was going on. I thought it was interesting how even in a different language, the cadences to the prayers were exactly the same, like the words seemed to have the same sound, like they had the same number of syllables. I thought about how much I wanted to be forgiven for all I had done, and that I wanted to be able to forgive myself.

I walked up to receive Communion and got pushed around, because there were no pews, and Italians don't believe in lines. I didn't know what the rush was about, because everyone would be getting the Eucharist. As it got closer to the priest, two lines formed.

I received, then stood in the back with the others for closing prayer. We waited for the crowd to clear out, then we took in the sights. We started at *La Pieta*, which had so many new connotations for me. I stood in awe of it for about twenty minutes. It was behind bulletproof glass, which was a shame. People's flashes glared off it as they took pictures.

After a while, I caught up with the others. They were walking around the perimeter, taking in all of the artwork and the tombs. We walked by the statue of St. Peter and touched his foot. The light was coming in the side of the building, and streaming in slanted columns down from the giant windows to the middle of the marble floor. We took pictures of each other standing in the sunlight. It was a good effect.

It was getting near noon, so we went out to the square to hear the Papal Blessing. There were so many things I didn't understand about the figure of the pope. I knew him to be a saintly and Godly man, and since I was little I had always felt proud that he "belonged" to me. But lately I had become so suspicious of power. I had a feeling that this guy is just a person like all of us, so why do people make such a fuss? But I figured I wouldn't have the chance again. We walked out the giant doors of the giant church and into the square. When we got to about the middle, surrounded by people, we looked up in the direction everyone else was looking. I couldn't figure out what everyone was looking for, but finally saw the open apartment window.

We waited for about ten minutes, and when he finally appeared, a little white dot in the huge window, the crowd cheered, including me. There wasn't a thing wrong with the pope, I concluded, after seeing him. The Holy Spirit was pouring out of him, and I could feel that from the middle of the square. I snapped some photos and tried to understand what he was saying, which was in Italian. Whatever it was, it wasn't very long. He gave the blessing, I crossed myself, and then he disappeared. But I felt a lot better than I had that morning.

CHAPTER 54

It was St. Patrick's Day, and we didn't know where we were going, so we just walked in the direction of Piazza San Marco. Although the conversation was raucous during dinner, the walkways and canals of Venice demanded a sort of reverence, like it was a place intended for solemn prayer—the streetlights like votives. The eight of us hardly encountered anyone as we clomped over the cobblestones among the illumined displays in the glass and jewelry shops that lined the streets. Glass in every shape and color decorated the storefronts, arrayed in the Italian way of doing things—that is, with intention. From one of these streets we entered San Marco Square, entering on the opposite side of the San Marco Basilica. It loomed before us like a slumbering lion, to awake at the eschaton.

Nobody spoke much. We all seemed to be taking it in. Once we had walked the length of the great piazza and come close to the basilica with its ornate Byzantine mosaics and archways, we turned to the left into the tangle of alleys and canals.

Down one alley that seemed a mile beneath the rooftops, we stumbled upon a welcoming din. It was a crowded Irish pub, and we entered. We positioned ourselves near the bar, where the bartenders spoke English and served the stout with a clover stamped in the head, which we all agreed was a fuzzy gesture.

We all talked and drank heavily, and I was in charge of ordering the drinks, since I was positioned in front of the bar. This was an irksome lot. It was so crowded in there, I couldn't turn around fully.

At one point, a girl squeezed up until she was standing in front of me.

"Excuse me?"

"Yeah?" I was surprised she was American.

"I'm trying to get some food but I can't get to the bar. Will you order it for me?"

"Sure. What do you need?"

"I don't know. I haven't had any dinner." She stood on her toes to look past me at the goods behind the bar. "I'll take a pack of Hits."

"Cookies for dinner?"

"It's better than a pack of gum," she said.

I ordered and she handed me her money. I wanted to strike up some conversation and keep her around for a while. She was cute.

She just looked past me with her arms crossed. I paid and handed her the package of cookies and her change.

"Thanks," she said. She gave me a half smile and turned around.

We resumed the conversation among the few of us, then I excused myself to go to the bathroom, where there was a line.

"So what's your deal?"

It was the cookie girl. It took me a second to answer, because I had never been a party to a conversation that began in this manner.

"I'm waiting in line for the bathroom."

"No, I mean what are you doing here?" she said.

"Drinking." I reached in my pocket to get a cigarette. "To forget."

"No, in Italy."

"I go to school in Florence, if that's what you mean."

"So what, did your mommy and daddy pay for you to come here?"

I wasn't sure if I was going to dignify that with a response, so I lit my cigarette and blew the smoke just above her head. It bothered me that I looked rich to her.

"I pay for what I can with loans and put the rest on my effin' credit cards. I also work here."

"In the bar?"

"In Italy. I got a scholarship to be a Resident Advisor."

"That's special," she said.

I took another long drag and squinted down at her. She was only about chest height, with blonde shoulder-length hair pulled back tightly. Not in a practical way, but in a way that was meant to be stylish. She was wearing a blue cashmere sweater with a deep neckline and black stretch pants.

"Are you done?" I asked.

"Sorry. There are a lot of rich college boys running around Europe."

"Well, I'm a lot of things, but I'm not rich."

"So you're one of the good ones," she concluded.

"Don't judge me."

She looked behind me for a second, then at my chest, then past me again with her arms folded.

"Well, I'm sorry again."

Sam walked up and told me the rest of them were going back to the hotel. I told him I was going to stay. I didn't know how to get back to the hotel, but she was pretty, so I was staying. Sam asked me a couple more times if I wanted to go back, probably because he knew I didn't know how to get there, and he knew how much I had already had. I waved them off. My turn came up in line.

"When I get out, can I buy you a drink?" I asked.

"Sure, if you can afford it."

"I just won't eat tomorrow."

Inside I spent some time—a few puzzled moments—considering the name of the toilets. Dolomite. Like the pimp? Like Snoop Dogg in *Nuthin' but a G Thang*? *Pimpin' hoes and clockin' a grip like my name was Dolomite.* Who names their toilets after a pimp?

I went back up to the bar and kept an eye on the bathrooms to see when she came out. I ordered a stout so I didn't look like a lush, but ordered a shot at the bar. I noticed she had gotten us a table as I came back.

"Who are you here with?" I said as I sat down.

"In Italy?"

"In this bar."

"Behind me and to my left, at the table by the bathroom there is a man sitting by himself. His name is Taha and he is from Bahrain."

"Is he your boyfriend?"

"No. I met him in Paris the first week I got here. He told me he's from the royal family and that he wants to marry me. He's paid for everything since then. We've been all over Europe."

"Are you going to marry him?"

"No."

"So, how much money does he have to spend before you tell him that?" I asked.

"I told him already. He says he doesn't care. He says he'll win my heart."

"With money?"

"Yes."

"Are you for sale?"

"No."

"That's some crazy shit."

"I know."

"Only in America. Does he try to do stuff with you?" I was probably looking at him too much, on account of the Jägermeister.

"No. He gets me a separate room everywhere we go. He doesn't want to offend my honor."

"Why doesn't he come over here and sit?"

"He doesn't drink, and he gets very jealous when I talk to other boys."

"Well I don't want to get in the middle of something."

"Don't worry, dear. I've told him that I will not be obeying his rules. If he wants to take me all around, that's fine, but I'm not going to be forced to do something for it. He pouts about it, but I'm not going to feel bad."

"I can't believe that. And you were giving me hell because you thought my parents paid for this?"

"I came here with my own money, and that's the only money I intended to spend. At the same time, I'm not going to be an asshole and refuse to let a guy pay for me."

"Sounds a little opportunistic to me."

"I come from the Land of Opportunity. Weren't we talking about you?"

"You're far more interesting."

"I'd much rather not talk about me right now. It's St. Patrick's Day. It's time to drink up, isn't it?"

"Are you Irish?"

"I'm American," she said. "May I have a cigarette?"

I reached into my pocket to get the pack. "Are you Catholic, at least?"

"I'm a recovering Catholic."

"What's that supposed to mean?"

"It means what I said. I was Catholic and I am recovering from it."

"Recovering, like from a car accident?"

"More like an addiction."

"Oh, right. Let me guess—to opiates."

"Exactly."

"Genius."

"I thought it was pretty clever, myself."

I handed her a cigarette and lit it. I took one out and put it between my lips, then looked around the room for a minute—red walls with dim lights and candles at each table. They weren't quite sitting still for me.

"That's where it begins, isn't it?" I said as I lit my cigarette. "With the thought that you're clever."

"Where what begins?"

"The whole no-religion thing. Apostasy."

"Have I offended you?"

"No. Just...no. Seems a little typical."

"What religion are you?"

"I guess I'd be a recovering apostate."

"To Catholicism?"

"You betcha."

"So you've fallen off the wagon?"

"I never quit drinking."

"I meant your religion."

I looked around the room for a minute more. This was all very interesting—her inquisitiveness and her faked refinement. She sat very straight and blew her smoke out in a particular way. She almost talked with an accent. It was endearing, even, but I didn't know if I wanted to continue along these lines.

"I know what you meant. I just decided I don't want to get into it. It's Saint Patrick's Day, and I'm going to enjoy my drink," I said.

"Oh, come on, now. You're Irish Catholic, or at least you hold yourself out to be."

"So?"

"That's not conduct becoming a good Mick is it?"

"Having a drink on St. Patrick's Day?"

"No, I mean not getting into a tiff. You seem to have the drinking down pretty well," she said.

"I'm just trying not to have a bitchfest over religion. I was enjoying the thought that you're being flirty, not...like... snotty. Have pity on us, the dolts who haven't outsmarted the Church. And my thirst is Irish, not my temperament. Usually."

We sat for another minute and smoked in silence. I stared down into the candle on the table. The wax had all turned to liquid.

"So when did you have this epiphany?" I asked.

"About the Church?"

"Yeah."

"Somewhere between my mother leaving and my dad dying when I was sixteen."

"I'm sorry."

She looked past me again. "Well, I've had a lot of time to get over it. It just is what it is."

"And you blame God?"

"Who better? A loving God wouldn't put little girls through the nastiness I've encountered."

"You seem to be doing alright."

"That's because I did it my damned self. You learn a hell of a lot living in New York City by yourself at the age of sixteen.

Everything I have I got myself, ever since then. And according to your thinking, it was God who put me there."

She didn't look that hardened, and I suspected she was exaggerating. She just looked like a college girl. I was falling in love.

"You sound a bit entitled." I wouldn't have said that if I wasn't so hammered.

"We're all entitled to a childhood."

"That's what your twenties are for."

"Oh, excellent."

"Sorry, but what if God wanted you to be tough?" I asked.

"What if I didn't want to be tough?"

"Maybe God needs you to be tough."

"He could have found another way."

"Maybe." We sat for a minute and smoked. "I think a lot of people find comfort in the Church," I said, finally.

"Superficially."

"What a pain in the ass. How do you know? Maybe it actually comforts people."

"Look, I have my doubts about people who find comfort in the thought there's a big fairy in the sky handing out candy canes and snowflakes to the good little boys and girls."

"We've established that. When's the last time you've been in a church, though?"

"We're in Italy!"

"When is the last time you've attended Mass?"

"What is this? Are you trying to proselytize me?"

"No, you brought it up. But seriously, if you don't ever go to church, and you don't read the Bible, you are criticizing something you never understood."

"Do you go to church?" she responded.

"When I can."

"Do you read the Bible?"

"Sure, but mostly I hear it at church."

"Then aren't you believing in something you never understood?"

"No, I wouldn't say that."

"Of course you wouldn't."

"Well, look, I had a decent religious education and some profound religious experiences. And I go to church. That counts for something."

"Profound religious experiences? Tell me about them." She leaned in, and sounded actually interested.

I paused for a minute. This was a rather frank conversation to be having with a girl I had met minutes ago. Of course, if the conversation was about whether or not I had a condom, it wouldn't be so odd. Which was odd. In a way, it was refreshing to be having it.

"I think I'll pass."

She leaned back in her chair. "What? I must say you puzzle me. Since we've met you have told me I should get to church more, and as a reason you cite your profound religious experience, but you're sneaking shots at the bar, chain smoking, cursing, and trying to pick up chicks."

"A mystery wrapped in an enigma."

"Indeed."

I smoked for a minute. "You know, I am guessing that at the top of your list of reasons not to be religious is that it's too judgmental."

"True."

"Yet you seem to have it down pretty well."

"True again. I'm sorry."

"I'm going through a little rough patch, not that that's a good excuse," I said.

"I'm sorry."

"We're all sinners, all of us. I don't see it as wrong or hypocritical to be Christian and a sinner, just Christian and unrepentant. I was just calling you out on some fair-weather Marxist bullshit. It's so tired. And I only chain-smoke when I drink."

"Fair enough." She took a drag of her cigarette and squinted at me when she did it. She blew it out in her way and then spoke. "But tell me something. What is Christianity doing for you?"

"I didn't know I was going to have to write you an essay."

"Take your time."

I looked past her into the array of tables, red light coming from the sconces on the wall, candles glowing on the tables, silhouettes against the red light with outlines painted on their features with the blonde candlelight. The place was still crowded.

"I guess the short answer is that it gives me hope—that the people I've hurt will have peace. That I will have peace. Sometimes I'm allowed to feel that peace, the peace of knowing and loving Jesus. Always I'm trying to get it back." I took my cigarette from between my lips and crushed it in the ashtray. "Usually I'm failing."

Her expression softened a little. "I hope you get it back." She was being sincere.

"Thanks."

We sat in silence for another minute. It was a long minute, and I didn't want us to get all emotional, so I thought I should talk again.

Instead, Taha came up from behind me and put two pints of stout on the table. I thanked his back as he walked toward his corner. I had forgotten he was there.

"Look, I'm gonna go back to the hotel."

"No, don't," she responded.

"I feel really weird about this."

"This is our arrangement, and if he is unhappy about it he can go back to Bahrain anytime he wants."

"Isn't drinking against his religion?"

"He isn't any more religious than I am, except when it comes to bitching about the Jews. He's a saint in that regard. I'm convinced that half the reason he keeps me around is because he can't get me to listen to him. He's fascinated by the way an American girl thinks. Really, he's jealous of it, I think."

"What's the other half of the reason he keeps you around?"

"Same reason you're still around."

"And what would that be?"

"He thinks he can get into my panties."

I took a drag of my cigarette. "You're not the only blonde in Italy."

"I'm the only blonde talking to you."

"I've got morals."

"Really? That would stop you?"

I smiled. "I'm not getting into hypotheticals."

She smiled back. "Let's assume for a moment that it's not a hypothetical."

"What, would Taha sit in the corner?"

"Don't worry about Taha. I know how to deal with him."

"From your experience having other men take you home from bars?"

"Will you stop being a prick and answer my question?"

"Well, no way if Taha is involved."

"No Taha."

"To be honest, right now if you wanted to take me back to your room, or to an alley, or to one of these bathrooms right here, or even probably under this table, I would be game."

"What of your morals?" she asked.

"You're messing with them."

She smiled, took a sip of her beer, and looked at me. "Why 'right now'?"

"What do you mean?"

"You said 'right now' you would be game.' Why 'right now'?"

"Because I'm drunk."

"What if you were sober?"

I thought for a minute. "I probably wouldn't do it."

"Why not?"

"Beer goggles."

"Excuse me!"

"No, I'm kidding. You're definitely a lovely lady. No, we hardly know each other. It would be out of respect."

"For whom?"

"Myself, God."

"What about me?"

"I was getting to you."

She thought for a minute. "It's not me messing with your morals, then, is it?"

"No, it's you."

"No, it's the drink."

I happened to be taking a drink at the time. I paused, drank a little more, then put it down. Those words hit me hard, like a locomotive.

"Don't sound so offended," I said after swallowing the beer.

"Oh, I'm not. Just makes me think."

"About?"

"I don't know. Like...what are we doing here?"

"Drinking, talking, smoking," I responded.

"But why? Haven't you been talking to me just to...have a liaison?"

"No. That would be icing on the cake."

"But if I was a sixty-five-year-old crack whore, would you be talking to me?"

"Probably not."

"Why?"

"The crack, the whoryness."

"A sixty-five-year-old nun, then."

"I don't know."

"Why didn't you go home with your friends?"

"So I could talk to you."

"Why me and not the nun?"

"I would probably talk to a nun in a bar."

"But why me? You didn't know anything about me."

"Well"—I thought about how not to admit it—"because you're attractive."

"Thank you."

"But you started talking to me. I was just going along with it," I said.

"Because you think I'm attractive."

"Yes."

"And because you thought you could have a tryst."

"I hadn't thought about it."

"Part of you did."

"Probably, but not the part that thinks."

"So what then? It's come down to whether we can find some reasonably quiet place for you to have your world rocked, if I'd be willing."

"Not anymore. You've made me feel bad enough about my morals." I smiled again. "Although when you put it that way, not as bad."

"Then we should just go our separate ways," she said.

"I was enjoying our talk."

"But really, hasn't it been very shallow?"

"We've talked religion."

"We've barely scratched the surface."

"True."

"Isn't it really the sex keeping you here? The possibility of it?"

"We can learn something from each other."

"You go to university to learn. You don't go to a bar to learn."

"I go to a bar to drink," I said.

"Me too, and the entertainment," she said.

"What about the sex?"

"Not so much."

"But sometimes?" I asked.

"No, not since I was eighteen, and then only once."

"So why did you start talking to me? Entertainment?" I asked.

"I don't know."

"What seemed entertaining about me?"

She took a sip of her beer. "I'm not sure you want to hear it."

"No, I do."

She looked past me like she was thinking, then back at me. "You looked sad."

"Give me an effin' break." I took a drink and looked around, then at her. "And that was entertaining to you?"

"No, I was just curious."

"Well, I didn't know it was that obvious."

"I'm not sure that it is. I was watching you for a couple minutes while you were at the bar."

"Because you thought I was something to look at."

She smiled, and I did, too. "Perhaps."

"Well, thanks, that's nice to hear." I took a sip. "As for the sadness, I don't know what to say. There was a death in the family."

"I'm sorry. I know how that can feel."

"And I feel like...I could have done more to show her I love her. And so yeah, I do have a lot of sadness. I don't think I'll ever make any sense of it in this lifetime." I looked past her. "And so that's where God comes in."

"To help you make sense of it?"

"To help me live with the fact that it will never make sense, and that it will always hurt, until I die. Once I am dead it will make perfect sense."

She took a drink. "Hmm." We sat in silence.

"Well," I said finally, "I don't know. Maybe this was about panty-raiding. If it was, I'm sorry."

"Don't be. I'm fine with that. You had no chance."

"Well, let's pretend I did have a chance. Don't be fine with it...being about panty-raiding."

"Alright."

"But maybe it was just about you. And me. You and me, having a drink together and talking. That's good in itself, I think," I said.

"I like that."

"And drop the Bahraini."

"Soon," she assured me.

"Looks like we all have our addictions, right? I have to go, because I'm probably going to get lost."

"I'd like to keep in touch."

"Me too. Do you have a pen?"

"Yeah."

She reached in her purse, and I got out a receipt. I tried to write my email down, but I couldn't write. I was too drunk.

I had never been too drunk to write and known it. I wrote it three times. The third attempt looked mostly legible.

"So I guess I'll be hearing from you."

"Sometime."

We both stood up and gave each other a hug with a kiss on the cheek. I waved in brief acknowledgement to Taha, then walked out through the thinning crowd into the cool and silent cobblestone alley, gray stone on most sides of me, the smell of the seawater, and white light coming from the street at the end of the alley. I walked straight a block, then turned left at the first street, over a canal, where I noted the boats and gondolas parked for the night. I headed straight through a small piazza with a church, and took a left at the next street, where I found my hotel. It was, surely, a miracle that I found it. I said a prayer of thanks before entering. She never wrote.

CHAPTER 55

I slowly became aware of the fact that I was opening my eyes and closing them. The pain in the soles of my feet and my knees came next. My eyes opened again, and I saw the stainless steel doors and the unlit elevator buttons in front of me and to the right. I closed my eyes briefly and opened them again. I straightened up, and felt that my back, knees, neck, and arms were all cramped. I blinked hard a few times and watched the silver doors as I felt the elevator stop. They slid open, and an old couple stood on the other side of it. They looked at me and stopped, looking startled. I stared at them, but I was confused and it didn't register what was going on. If someone would have told me at that point, I wouldn't have believed them. The doors slid closed again, and the elevator didn't move. I didn't know where I was, but I figured that in order to get out, I had to go to the lobby. I looked at the buttons and pressed "L."

I picked up my legs one by one to stretch out my knees. When the elevator stopped and the doors opened, I tried to walk as quickly as possible past the two workers behind the front desk out the front door, and I tried to look like I wasn't the guy who had passed out in their elevator. It was difficult, though, because my feet were numb and cold. They stared at me the entire time I walked across the expansive lobby.

I exited and stood in the morning sunlight, looking at the bare trees in Piazza Indipendenza across the street. I was in Florence, at a hotel. There was no reason for me to be in a hotel in Florence. I turned around and looked at it, then looked across the street at the piazza again. I wondered why I had not been arrested. I looked at my watch, which said 7:56 a.m. This was Via Nazionale, the street where the hookers hung out. I always felt so bad for them, wondering what had led them to finally decide to sell their bodies. My guess was that my stay at the hotel and the hookers were unrelated, because if I had gotten horizontal at any point the night before, I would have stayed that way. But I had definitely slept standing. I pulled the box of cigarettes out of my pocket and pulled out the last one, which was bent at nearly forty-five degrees but hadn't broken. I lit it and smoked in amusement. There wasn't anything else I could be but amused.

But my knees hurt, and the sun—gray and strange—hurt, and it was cold and I had no jacket. I had lost it in a bar in Perugia. I was enjoying the cigarette immensely, though.

I began walking. The sun hadn't yet reached the street. It just lit the backs of the gray and yellowish clouds above the buildings on the other side. This was getting bad, and I needed to get some help. But I didn't speak the language.

When I got back to Signora's, I opened the doors with care and walked quietly into my room. It was Saturday, and she wasn't around. Sam had gotten up early that morning to go on a day trip to Pisa, Anna was cleaning in the office, and Gabriele was in his room. I stripped and climbed into bed, and before I slept another few hours I said a quick prayer.

There are four corners on my bed, a pillow for my little head. Matthew, Mark, Luke, and John, bless the bed I sleep upon. Amen. God bless everybody. My God, please save me from myself.

I woke up around noontime to hear Anna vacuuming Gabriele's room. I got up, put on some clothes, and went into the kitchen, which had some bread and jam left on the table. I could tell I was interfering with the flow of things, because the preparation for dinner had already begun on the other side of the table. I poured the cold coffee out of the carafe and drank it, and that with the bread and jam and alcohol still in me made a pretty fiery mixture. Today I was meeting with Lily to have dinner with her parents. I had met her parents briefly on two occasions—once when they were moving her out of her dorm room in freshman year, and once right before we left for this trip.

I took a shower that was only lukewarm, so it had to be quick. I got dressed and knocked on the door for the Signora's child-like grown son Gabriele.

"*Pronto?*" he asked from inside.

"*Forse insieme facciamo un pó di lavoro.*"

"Sí, sí, sí," he responded enthusiastically, and went into his closet to pull out coloring books and some crayons. With Signora's permission, I had previously initiated activities on Saturday with Gabriele and sometimes Sam. There was no set program; sometimes we would go for walks, sometimes we would just sit and color or craft something. We took him once to help at the flower stand, cutting ribbons. We even took him to the movies once to see *Fight Club* in the theater. That was probably a mistake, but we weren't thinking.

Today he had selected some choice coloring books from the latest Disney movie, which I think was *The Hunchback of Notre Dame*.

Gabriele was overjoyed to have this time together with his "*amici.*" He even became somewhat affectionate, kissing us on the cheeks and such, which took some getting used to from a forty-year-old man. It gladdened the heart, though, and simplified life, which seemed in other ways to get too complex. I can't speak for Sam, but I know I felt I was getting more out of it than Gabriele was.

After an hour and a half of some serious coloring and crafts, I lay down and did some of my art history reading, then fell asleep again. I woke up at 5 p.m. and fixed my hair, brushed my teeth, and put on my blue sweatshirt with two T-shirts underneath, since it would probably be cold.

I left the loft, walked to the bus stop, and got on the bus. This was going to be a disaster. I was shaking pretty badly, and my stomach was cramping sharply. This was normal. I did not want to eat, and I did not want to feel like I had to impress parents. I always felt nervous around older people. I got off at Piazza Santa Maria Novella and walked down toward Piazza Repubblica. On one of the benches I found the three of them. It was five forty-five, and I was supposed to meet them at five thirty. Her parents had to leave early the next morning to catch their flight.

Both of her parents greeted me with a handshake; Mrs. Marconi gave me a kiss on the cheek.

Lily's father had gone to America from Italy to study at Yale, which is where he met Mrs. Marconi, whose parents had both gone to America from Italy when they were small. Mr. Marconi had worked for the CIA for many years, then for a law firm, and then was the American diplomat to the Vatican. He was slightly less than average height with an athletic build, like a wrestler. His dark hair was slicked back, and he had dark features and a dark complexion. He was mild-mannered and genteel, but had a twinkle in his eyes. He would punctuate many of his comments, made in his Italian accent, with a wink. That night he was wearing gray pants and a navy blue blazer with a white shirt and no tie. He looked like a diplomat, who could easily take me in a fight.

Mrs. Marconi had been a buyer for a department store in New York City, then had quit to become a teacher. When she had Lily, she quit teaching to stay at home with Lily, and later James. She was an inch or so shorter than Mr. Marconi, with her hair pulled back and clipped in a bun. She had a wide, warm smile, and was wearing quality, fashionable clothes. Her skirt was light gray wool, her sweater was pink and looked like cashmere, and her jacket was white leather, and went down to her waist. She was wearing very high heels and stockings. She had a decent amount of jewelry on that looked very expensive.

"So, Will, I hope you are hungry," Mr. Marconi said with a smile.

"Well, to be honest I've been feeling a little sick."

"What's wrong, sweetie?" Mrs. Marconi asked.

"I'm not sure. I just feel a little sick to my stomach."

"Well, maybe you'll feel better if you eat something," she said.

This situation was simply not ideal. I was shaky, and I had to impress the parents of the woman I loved, without having any sort of romantic reason to have to do so, since I wasn't dating her, and it didn't look like I had a chance. All pain, no gain.

As we began walking, I put my hands in my pockets. It was getting a little cold as the sun went down. Her mom took notice.

"Will, where's your jacket? It's cold out here."

"I lost it."

"Where did you lose it?"

"If I knew that, it wouldn't be lost." I said that with a big smile so she didn't think I was being a jerk.

"Well you can't walk around without a coat. It's freezing out here."

"It's almost spring," I said. She sighed and we walked.

"Oh, I can't wait for dinner! The place we're going has the best gnocchi in the worrrld!" Lily said. She was walking arm in arm with her mom. From Piazza Repubblica the four of us strolled east, where the streets and alleyways grew narrower and more irregular. After a little while we came upon a restaurant with a glass door at the corner of a building. There were potted plants on either side of it. From the street you could see the inside, which was lit with a soft, bright light. Inside was a sizable dining room with white plaster walls, dark wood trim, and tables with white tablecloths, each set already with a basket of Tuscan bread.

The four of us sat down, and the two girls started chatting. Lily's mom was her best friend, and that was something she wasn't afraid to admit. It was, by far, one of the most attractive things about her.

The family was happy to be with each other, and happy to have me. I, on the other hand, continued to feel quite uncomfortable, because I figured they could tell I was shaky. But I decided I would try not to let it bother me, and just let myself have a good time with them.

"So," Mr. Marconi said as we were looking at our menus, "I hear they already know you in every bar in Italy." He said this without looking up from his.

"I'm sorry?" I said.

"You know, the *discoteca*?" He looked at me and was smiling. He had dimples that made him look more like a ballbuster. "I hear you can ruin a good bit of liquor."

I wasn't sure if he had really heard this or not. "Oh, I'm sorry I...I didn't know if you were talking to me or Lily."

"Oh!" he said, like he was greatly amused. "Her too? Well, that is no surprise. She is just like her mother."

Both of the women exclaimed, Lily saying, "Dad!" and Mrs. Marconi saying, "Enrico!" at the same time. Mrs. Marconi reached over and smacked him on the arm. I was laughing, too. At that, a man with a mustache who was dressed in a chef's shirt and pants with tiny black and white checks came up next to Mr. Marconi. "Enrico!" he said in a loud voice.

Mr. Marconi looked up. "Marco!" He stood up and enthusiastically hugged the man, kissing him on the cheek. I looked at Lily, who was sitting to my right. "*Cugini*," she said, like this happened all of the time.

They spoke for a few minutes in Italian, and I couldn't follow along. The rest of us looked up at the conversation. Soon the man's attention turned to us. Mr. Marconi was pointing in our direction, apparently explaining who we were. When he gestured toward Mrs. Marconi, she said a few words in Italian, like it was a pleasure to see him. He leaned over and gave her a kiss on the cheek. After a few minutes, they finished up.

Mr. Marconi sat down. "That's the son of my mother's cousin," he said to me.

"Do you have a lot of family here?"

"Oh, yes," he said. "You know Marconi, the radio man?"

"Yeah, you're related?"

"No, actually."

I looked at him, puzzled.

"I am joking. Yes, yes. Lily never told you?"

"No."

A waiter came with a bottle of red wine, which he presented to Mr. Marconi, who nodded, and he opened it, filling each of our glasses. When the waiter finished, Mr.

Marconi raised his glass. "To youth," he said. "They waste it on the young," he said, smiling.

"To youth," we said, clinking our glasses.

When it came time to order, I decided on a pasta dish. Mr. Marconi asked me a few times if I was sure that was all I wanted. I told him yes.

"So, Mr. Marconi," I said.

"Please, call me Rick," he said.

"My mother was very strict about addressing adults properly."

"Whatever you please. Just not Dick," he said, then he smiled and winked.

"You were diplomat to the Vatican?"

"Oh, yes, a few years back. It was very nice. Very interesting."

"He has a lot of great stories," Mrs. Marconi said.

"Really?" I asked.

He smiled. "Well, I met with the pope many times."

"This pope?" I asked.

"Oh, yes. This one."

"What is he like?"

"A very warm, very holy person. Likes to joke a lot. I remember one time, we were having dinner at his residence. He would always call me by my last name. 'Marconi,' he would say in his Polish accent. So we were eating and he says, 'Marconi, how do you like the dinner?'"

"In English?"

"Oh, yes. He speaks many languages. So I reply, 'Oh, it's very good, Your Holiness. Almost as good as the food at Cardinal O'Connor's.' Everyone was looking down at their plate, because they didn't know what he would say. They thought I had offended him. I was just joking," he shrugged.

"What did he do?"

"He just laughed and said, 'You are a tough customer, Marconi. Next time, we will serve the beef.' Then everybody laughed."

"That's cool."

"Yes, we are lucky to have him. He is a living saint, I think."

Lily's parents started asking a lot of questions, as older people tend to do to younger people, about the program and my position as the Resident Advisor. They were also asking about what I planned on doing in the future, which was always a sore subject, since I didn't know. I was able to divert the talk to our classes, which were interesting enough to describe.

Dinner arrived. Once it did, Mr. Marconi asked me if it was enough. I told him yes, that I wasn't feeling too well. He didn't seem satisfied with my answer, so he called back the waiter. He asked me what else I wanted. I told him roasted chicken. I ate the pasta. There was a long pause while everyone ate their dinner.

"So are you two an item?" Mr. Marconi asked, breaking the silence.

"Enough, Rick," Mrs. Marconi said. I could see Lily giving him the evil eye in my periphery.

"I'm just asking. There is no harm in a little question." I could tell he was trying to get a rise out of the girls. He was embarrassing the hell out of me.

"No, Mr. Marconi; we're just friends," I said in between bites of eggplant pasta.

"Well, you know Lily dumped the sailor boy."

"I heard, Mr. Marconi."

"ENOUGH, Enrico," Mrs. Marconi said again.

"I am just asking; that is all. You two would bring us some very good-looking grandbabies."

I started smiling, because he was succeeding in getting a rise out of the girls.

"That's true, Mr. Marconi. I am hoping for the opportunity to impregnate your daughter." I was trying to be inappropriate back to him, but regretted saying that the second I said it. Mrs. Marconi started laughing immediately, though. Lily was very red in the face.

"See? How do you like it?" Mrs. Marconi said, still laughing.

"I cannot blame him. He is a man; she is a pretty girl. It's how these things work." He looked at me. "Just marry her first, or I'll kill you." He wasn't smiling as hard at the moment, and he kept looking at me. Before I could react, he broke out laughing again. I was pretty sure he meant it, though.

"Dad, enough! You're ruining dinner."

"What? What did I do?" He leaned back in his chair and put his hands up. He was all smiles.

She just shook her head and stabbed her gnocchi with her fork. My chicken came, and it was around then that I realized I was actually becoming hungry. The shaking was getting a little better.

"So how is your gnocchi, Lily?" I asked.

"They're unbelievable. You want to try some?"

"No, it's okay. Eat your food."

"You have to try it." She scooped a few up with her fork and put them on the edge of my plate. I put them in my mouth and they melted away. They were very good.

The discussion was light and comfortable after that. Mr. Marconi made sure my wine glass was filled the entire time. After dinner he ordered us all cappuccinos, and limoncello for him and me after the coffee. As we were getting up, Mr. Marconi's cousin came back and gave him, Mrs. Marconi, and Lily a hug, and me a handshake. We then strolled down via de' Calzaiuoli to Piazza della Signoria, which was lit up nicely. People strolled around in an aimless sort of way.

The clothing shops had lifelike mannequins dressed like nobility, and in styles that would not arrive on Yankee shores for another two years. There were several sunglasses shops, and shops with wallets, purses, and belts. Others had stationery or pastries of every conceivable variety, arrayed with the greatest precision. Interspersed were *gelaterias*, cafés, money exchange shops, and *tabaccherias*, and even these achieved at least a sense of order, and the vestiges of a life chosen, a vocation pursued. We stopped and looked at the shops and wondered out loud at this feature, although we didn't quite succeed in putting it into words.

After a nice evening, we walked the Marconis back to their hotel, which was one right on Piazza Repubblica, which meant that it was very expensive. Mrs. Marconi gave me a hug, Mr. Marconi a firm handshake and slap on the shoulder. I waved to Lily, then walked out to the piazza myself. Some people were making art with spray paint—extraterrestrial scenes, planets and stuff. A guy was juggling various things, and had a few people watching him. After watching him a few minutes, I put a little money in his hat and walked home.

CHAPTER 56

Class went by quickly the next day. Four of us—Doodles, Ella, Melanie, and I—went out to dinner at the only Mexican place we knew. It was a passable approximation, except they used mozzarella for the cheese. Afterward, we walked around looking for wine shops, and found one down past the *duomo* near the Arno. Each of us bought a bottle of cheap Chianti. We went back to Melanie and Ella's apartment, which was closest to us. There we uncorked the bottles and started drinking out of them. We played a game in order to make it go quicker.

After about an hour the room was getting hot. The girls hadn't gotten very far into their bottles; Doodles and I were each about three-quarters of the way done. We decided to leave for Dante's Inferno, since it was almost 7 p.m. By the time the girls had touched up their makeup and checked out their outfits, Doodles and I were done with our bottles.

We all started walking to the bar, which was about a quarter of a mile away on the other side of the *duomo*. We got there at about seven thirty, which made me angry, because it was all you could drink for 10,000 lire starting at seven and lasting only until nine. I paid my 10,000 lire and got my first plastic cup of beer. The girls got a table outside, because they didn't want to bring their wine where the bartenders could see them. A few of our friends, including Lily and her roommates, showed up as well. Everyone was happy to meet up, because none of us had planned on seeing each other. The rest of our crowd met some other Americans who were there randomly. I was introduced briefly but didn't care much. Together all of them were sitting inside at a long table.

I joined the outside crowd. Melanie was sitting across from me, and was holding her head.

"I'm sick of this wine. Do you want it?"

"Sure," I said.

"It's giving me a headache."

I finished my beer and drank the rest of the wine as the conversation went on around the table. They were playing "never have I ever," which is a game where a person names some sort of activity, usually a sex act, and anyone who has not done it has to drink. The person who doesn't drink is revealed as having done it. We played this a lot, because we liked talking about sex, because we were all young and most of us were attracted to each other. One round, the topic was whether anyone had had sex before they were fifteen. Only Amy didn't drink, and when Doodles asked her about it, she said she had sex when she was fourteen with a guy who was married and was an Episcopal priest. Doodles told her she was going straight to hell. It was supposed to be a joke, but she didn't laugh. I got up during an anal-sex question to go to the bathroom. I ran into Lily and asked her what was up. She looked like she had something to tell me.

"Will..."

"Yeah."

"See that guy there, with the blonde hair?"

"Yeah."

"His girlfriend is sitting next to him. They've been going out for a couple years."

"Yeah. I met them. He seems like a tool."

"Well I was sitting next to him, and while we were talking he put his hand on my thigh and started rubbing it. While he was sitting next to his girlfriend!"

"What a douche."

"I didn't stop him."

I took out a cigarette, looked past her, and lit it.

"Maybe you should have, Lily. In any case, congratulations."

She twisted her face a little, because I had said it like a jerk, and she also didn't like cigarette smoke. I didn't feel the need to listen to her anymore, or explain myself, so I continued on my way to the bathroom.

When I came out, I met Doodles at the bar. We ordered a shot of whiskey. Then I ordered us another one and a beer, and went back outside.

I approached Crystal. "Wanna get some more?" She nodded and the two of us went to the bar together. Crystal was tall. She had brown hair and blue eyes, and was outgoing and very good looking. She was probably the funniest girl on the trip. She laughed hard and easily, and poked a lot of fun at herself. She was brutally honest about most things. But there seemed to be a lot she wasn't saying.

The two of us stood at the bar and chatted with the bartenders. One of them had a thing for Crystal. The Italians typically fawned over her. Doodles joined us for a few rounds.

"Crystal, you are looking quite hot tonoight, by the waiy," Doodles said.

"Thanks, Dudley. It's the beef. I've been eating a lot of beef lately."

"Getting your hot beef injection?"

"Yeah."

"Perhaps I could help out with that."

"Perhaps," she responded.

On my end, things were starting to get blurry. The bartenders weren't collecting money for the shots we were ordering, nor for many of the beers. We were good customers. So during the time at the bar, I had a few more beers and another shot. I also blacked out around then.

When I came to, I was walking back. It was about 2 a.m., and I had no cigarettes, and the sole thought in my mind was that I needed one. One thought was about all I could manage. On Via Nazionale, I walked along the park, on the same side as the girls. It was a little quicker that way. I passed one who was tall, wearing a grayish fur coat and red stilettos. She was older, and wasn't very attractive. I was in the habit of asking random people for cigarettes, and I figured there wasn't a hooker on earth who didn't smoke. So I stopped, turned around, and walked back a few steps toward her.

"Excuse me, do you have a cigarette?" I asked in Italian. I figured she didn't have to be on all of the time. I was wrong, though.

She walked up toward me, and in a throaty voice said something in Italian too quickly for me to understand. When she got up close to me things quickly became inappropriate.

"No, no, no, no. Stop. I don't want this. Do you have any cigarettes? I want only a cigarette." My Italian was bad, but was better the drunker I got.

"*No, no ho cigarette.*"

"*Grazie.*"

I turned around and started walking again. Doodles was right that red wine makes one sentimental. So being inebriated as I was, I became overwhelmed by the feeling that somebody should do something. Every night I walked by them, and it troubled me how they felt they could or should give themselves up for money. So I decided I would do something about it. Not the project to undertake in that state.

I stopped and turned around. Something, somewhere, hesitated. I walked toward her, and stopped a few feet away to keep her hands off me. With the best Italian I could muster, I started:

"Excuse me."

"Yes, handsome?"

"Stop this life."

"What?"

"This life. It is not good. You must stop. Do another something."

She stopped and looked at me with interest and puzzlement, like I was a talking cat.

"Excuse me?"

"I don't know. You are a good person. You are pretty. You should not do this...I don't know what the word is. Do another something. Maybe you may be a teacher or something."

She looked at me for another moment, and seemed to step out of character.

"Come here."

"No. I must go home." My consciousness was faltering in a way. I would be aware of some things, but not others. At times, I knew that I was talking to a woman, and that she was a professional, and that I was in Italy. At other times, I forgot the profession, or that this was occurring in Italy.

"No, please, come here." She waved her hand toward herself. The street spread out behind her, with puddles reflecting the streetlights. There were no cars, no people, and no sounds. Our voices carried a little. I walked toward her.

When I got close enough, she put her hands behind her back and kissed me on the cheek. She took my hand and we began walking. I had forgotten for the moment that she was a professional, and that we were in Italy. I also forgot who I was and where I had to go. I forgot about my baby and Kristen, about Lily, about her parents. School, money, Jersey, and everyone in it were gone. I forgot about the cigarettes and about eternal damnation. I was walking with a woman, holding her hand, which was about the dandiest thing in the world. We came to the door of an apartment building, which didn't look any different from the others. We went in and ascended some stairs. She opened an apartment door, and walked in, turning on a light.

The dingy little room had a king-sized bed against the middle of the wall to my right, which was made neatly. Right next to the door was a dresser with a mirror. Straight ahead was a television angled toward the bed, with a room behind it that I supposed was a washroom. The windows were across from the bed, with streetlights coming in through some blinds. The curtains were red. It looked like a moderately cheap hotel room.

"Is this where you keep your cigarettes?" I asked.

She stepped past me into the room and opened her coat, which revealed that she was not wearing a whole lot. It was nice lingerie, or so it seemed, which made sense, because Italians did that sort of thing well. Or rather it seemed nice, but I was pretty banged up, so who knows. The facts of the situation didn't come crashing in at that moment, but later began to whisper in my ear.

We stopped for a second, and she tapped the bed with her fingertips. I sat down and she walked around the foot of the bed, taking her coat off and throwing it on a chair next to the

TV, which she turned on. It was porn, which reminded me where I was.

She sat down on the other side of the bed, leaned over toward me, and began kissing me.

"Stop."

"Why?"

"I don't have any money." I figured this was the polite way to handle the situation.

"It's okay."

We started kissing again.

"Stop, please."

"Why?"

"Because I don't have any money."

"It's free, I told you."

We started kissing again, and I forgot where I was, and I wanted to forget where I was. When I remembered again, I knew I had to leave, and I did.

CHAPTER 57

I woke up and looked at the alarm clock. It was ten thirty. On Fridays, we had only art history, which all of us had to take. Today, we were taking a tour of Palazzo Pitti. It was our last tour with Signora Vitelli, one of our Art History professors. She was a taut, aristocratic, older woman who seemed to be the type who never had to worry about money, but that hadn't gotten to her. She had a straight back, perfect English, expensive clothes and jewels, full makeup every day, and if there was a part on her seventy-something-year-old body that was out of joint, she wasn't letting it bother her. She loved art, she loved life, and she loved youngsters. She called us *bambini*—babies—and always seemed dazzled by everything. It could be a scarf one of us was wearing, or any one of our questions. She was the type of woman who would have listened to all of my problems, patted me on the head, and said, "Cheer up. It will get better soon." She was a sliver of light.

Our last tour with her began at eight thirty. I remembered that first, and sat up cursing at myself. What a loss. I then realized that I was still drunk, which led me to remember what had occurred the night before. I sprang out of my bed, and I was still in my clothes. I went into my pocket and took out my wallet. I counted my money several times, and it was all there. I couldn't make any sense out of it.

I took a long shower. I knew I had to get down to the school. I had a lunch appointment with Theresa, the other Resident Advisor, and Dr. Sellier, who wanted to thank us for everything. I left the flat, and it was a pretty day. I walked fast even though I was achy all over, especially in my stomach, and I was dizzy. The sun was bright and spring-y, and in the piazza the trees had started sprouting buds. Florence in the spring could be a beautiful place. It just depended on your state of mind.

I didn't wait long for the bus. When it came I boarded and sat down and felt very hot and sweaty and uncomfortable, like I did when I drank too much. I watched the stones pass by on the shaded side of the street. I didn't let myself remain on one thought for too long.

I got to the huge wooden doors at the school, and Melanie was there having a cigarette.

"Will, where were you?"

"I overslept. Can I get one?"

"Ugh. Will—you smell awful."

"I took a shower."

"You smell like Giadda." Giadda was our History teacher, and an alcoholic.

"Great. I have lunch with Dr. Sellier."

"You better smoke a cigarette. You smell."

"Al*right*. Do you have one?"

She took one out—Gauloises. I lit the cigarette. "I feel awful."

"You look like you're still drunk."

"It's all the same." I took a couple drags of my cigarette. "How are you feeling?"

"I'm alright. You drank most of my wine."

I sighed and smoked hard. I began apologizing to God in my mind.

"Well, I have to go meet the doctor."

"You know he came on to Lily."

"What...what does that mean?" I asked.

"She was checking her email, and he sat down next to her, sitting sideways and straddling her chair."

"How do you know this?"

"I walked in on them. He just got up real quick and walked away."

"How was Lily?"

"White. She said he had his hand on her thigh."

"I have to go," I said.

I walked and smoked and prayed and seethed, with the sun glaring off my shirt and everything else into my eyes. The restaurant was about a block away, on the sunny side of the street. I put out my cigarette and walked in to find Dr. Sellier and Theresa already seated at a table, with the seat not taken in the sun.

"Hello, Mr. Ferguson."

"Hi, Dr. Sellier."

"Hi, Will."

"Hi, Theresa."

I sat down and picked up my menu and began perusing, but the words seemed to skip around on the paper. I squinted, but I couldn't think straight.

"Dr. Sellier, I wanted to apologize for missing the lecture this morning. I was really upset to miss Dr. Vitelli."

"I know that sometimes we...get so absorbed in our studies that we just...have some trouble waking up in the morning."

"Right."

We sat in silence for a minute looking at our menus, me trying not to smell too much.

"So I just wanted to invite you two out to lunch as a token of my appreciation for all you have done this semester. I think we've all had a wonderful time, and we've all learned a lot. You two have been incredibly helpful, and I just think we made a wonderful decision in having you two as our Resident Advisors."

We both thanked him. I looked down at the menu, and I could not read it. I could see the words, but I could not focus long enough to figure out what they were saying and comprehend it. The Lily situation flashed through me on and off, but I couldn't get beyond the fact that the seams were splitting. I felt that if I could only talk to them, I could feel better. But I swallowed it back and stared down at the menu.

The waiter came and I ordered a pasta and eggplant dish.

"So I thought I would ask you two about the trip—what sorts of things we could do differently in the future, what the highlights were, what things we could have done without."

"Excuse me, Dr. Sellier. I apologize." At that, I got up and walked to the bathroom. I went in and stood in the middle of it, in front of the two urinals. I looked at the tiled wall below them, and stared. I took a couple steps toward the sink and washed my hands. I dried them without looking in the mirror.

I went back out to the table. "Is everything okay, Will?" Dr. Sellier asked.

"Yeah. I just had too much coffee this morning."

"Okay, Theresa and I were just talking about what the program lacked that we thought we could improve. Did you have any thoughts on that?"

"Mmm....What did you say, Theresa?"

"I sorta thought things went well. I think some people had some problems with the families they stayed with."

"Yeah...I, uh, I don't know. I think there were a lot of things the students avoided that were sort of, in general, things that could have been better for them, from an educational standpoint, for them not to avoid, generally."

"Uh-huh. Like what, Will?" he asked.

"Like, I don't know. Students sometimes seemed to fool around too much. So if there was anything wrong with the program, it was us. The complaining people did about not going to Capri was a bunch of shit...excuse me...was silly...in my opinion. Otherwise, I thought, umm...that we all...I had a great time. I very much enjoyed getting to know my fellow classmates and my professors and your family, Dr. Sellier. It was a fantastic experience and I'm very grateful. I've learned a lot about myself."

Theresa concurred.

My plate arrived, and I ate and tried to ignore things. We talked and reminisced, and it was a difficult time all around.

I was happy to leave, and I went immediately to go get some cigarettes at the tabaccheria on Piazza Repubblica.

I returned to the school and sat on the small step outside the front door. I was less drunk but still shaky and having a hard time keeping it together. I sat and packed my cigarettes, unwrapped them, and pulled one out to smoke it.

I had arrived at rock bottom, or at least as far down as I was willing to go. I was sick of knowing what was right and wrong and knowing what I wanted for myself and for others and desiring the good things, and then, like I was outside of myself, watching myself blow it. I believed in God and I believed in beauty and I believed in lucidity and sobriety, and I believed in love, and there seemed to be something in between me and all of that and it was me.

My God, I prayed, *please forgive my sins, and then take me. You have given so much to me and I keep failing. Save me from myself, Lord. I don't feel like I have anything I can offer, Lord. Please don't allow me to die with all of these sins on my heart.*

I finished smoking the cigarette and threw it out a few feet in front of me and sat and watched it burn on the stones. It was enchanting for a minute. I stood up and walked slowly up the six flights of stone steps.

I walked past Chiara looking lovely as usual and to the computer room. Dianne was the only person there, quietly emailing. I sat down and checked my mail. There weren't any messages. I started writing to the person I thought would be a good idea to write to at the time, Father Bob. I had to blink back tears, and since Emma had come in and started waiting for the computer to open up, I had to write quickly. I told him that I needed to get things off of my chest, and that I felt like things were out of control. I wrote that my drinking was becoming very dangerous, and I was getting very drunk four times a week. I told him I was blacking out repeatedly and finding myself asleep in the streets, and other things that were best left for the confessional. I was especially upset about the drinking, since it was at the root of my problems in the first place. I told him that I was upset about not being with a girl, but that I knew that what I was most upset about was the abortion. The would-be birthday had passed, and I hadn't felt right since. I told him that I knew that God had forgiven me, but I did not feel so great about that now, and I supposed that this was because I didn't know how to forgive myself, but in any case, I just missed my baby. I finished by saying it felt better that I got these things off my chest. I also told him that I would be home soon, and I asked him to pray for me that I didn't self-destruct before then.

After I sent the message, I did an internet search for mass times at the duomo. I had gone a couple times, and wanted to make sure I went the next time I had a chance. I wanted to get to confession, but didn't know the word in Italian, and didn't know if it counted if the priest couldn't understand you and you couldn't understand the priest.

I got up and left the building, and took a walk, first to Piazza Repubblica, up past the duomo then through San Lorenzo market toward Via Nazionale. I walked up Nazionale past Piazza Indipendenza and finally to the Fortezza da Basso. Next to it was a park with benches and trees and a walkway all the way around it. It was a place where I was sure nobody would find me, and where I knew there were a few trees. I walked around and found a bench near the fortress walls and looked out at the trees and stray cats before me. I folded my arms across my stomach and didn't try to think of anything. I had a feeling of general disbelief at how rotten things had become. I felt like a disgrace to my family and to God. I asked him to forgive me. I asked him to give me the strength to stop disappointing him, and to gain control of my life.

That night I went out looking for other people, but found nobody. I went to Dante's to see if anyone was there. Nobody had arrived yet, so I ordered a beer and waited at a table. I was staring at nothing when a group of American kids noticed me. They called me over to their table but I declined, finished my beer, and left.

I wandered down to the Ponte Vecchio lined with jewelry shops, but that had an opening halfway across, with a monument and a place for people to congregate and look out on the Arno. I walked to the opening and looked down at the water passing below, then out at the Ponte Santa Trinita, with the lights along Lungarno Acciaiuoli and Guicciardini reflecting off the surface of the black water, and the tiny lights from the villas peering down from the mountains far off. I thanked God for the beauty and lingered for nearly an hour, then began the long walk home.

CHAPTER 58

The next day I woke up around 9 a.m. I went into the kitchen and ate the bread and jam at the table. I walked the distance to noon Mass at the duomo, with Vasari's depiction of The Last Judgment painted on the inside of the giant dome. The Mass was in Italian, but I got the idea. I felt bad and apologized to God for my baby and for all of the things that had followed after that. It had never gone away—the feeling like I could tear open my chest, I had to weep so bad. I figured it never would, as long as there was that awkward silence. I felt so much in me that I had caused her pain in her little life, and there wasn't anything in me that would ever want anyone to feel pain on my account, and my God, did that hurt. I just couldn't believe I had somehow gotten tangled up, and I couldn't hold on to how much I missed her. I prayed that she could see, that she could know how much I loved her somehow.

CHAPTER 59

Another week passed. I left the flat at about six forty-five at night. I had a long walk ahead of me, but I had been planning this one for about a week. It was a free weekend; some of the others were going on a day trip somewhere. I had actually planned on joining the trip, but Lily had informed me of this unique...opportunity. In some ways, I was amused; in some ways, I was deeply saddened. More the latter.

Since arriving at some rough idea of what I thought I might do, I had been praying about this. I managed to go to bed early the night before, which was a Friday, because in some ways I was pretty shaky. I had never done anything like this.

I walked hard from the outer regions of the city down past the train station through San Lorenzo market, past the duomo. I prayed for the Virgin Mary's intercession as I passed her likeness on the facade. Across the Ponte Vecchio I went through some narrow streets and into the small piazza that we had crossed at our first meeting here.

In the middle I found Doodles, who had been champing at the bit for this moment to arrive since I had told him about it two nights before.

"Yew ready, partnah?" he asked.

"Ready as I'm going to be."

"Let's do it."

"Just me, Doodles."

"I knew you were going ta try an' pull this shite, Peachfuzz."

"Because you knew it had to be me."

"Then what did you call me down 'ere for?"

"I'm going to call if you're needed."

"Don' I get ta watch?"

"I'll tell you all about it."

"Shite. I shoulda gone ta Milan."

I rang the bell to Casa Verità. Dr. Sellier rang me up.

I opened the door and walked up the stairs. The door to his flat was slightly ajar. I sighed deeply, and with some hesitation, I walked in. I looked around a little bit, and didn't see him. Straight ahead in the kitchen was a table made up nicely for two with candles and a bottle of wine. I came a little closer and looked at the bottle—Chianti, 1979, which happened to be the year I was born. It was uncorked, so I figured there was only one sensible thing to do—I poured myself a glass, took a sip, and replaced the cork. Something was in the oven, and it smelled succulent. I was hungry.

I sat down and waited, sipping more of the wine. I heard him coming down the long hallway. He spoke as he walked.

"You're early, Ms. Marconi. I'm sorry for the delay; I had to get decent. I was just out of the shower when you rang," he said as he walked.

He came into view on the other side of the table wearing a white button-down shirt tucked into jeans. The top buttons of the shirt were unbuttoned, and his sleeves were rolled up. His hair still looked damp from the shower.

"Mr. Ferguson," he said, puzzled but collected.

"Dr. Sellier," I replied.

"You know that I prefer 'Bruce.'"

"I know, Dr. Sellier, but my upbringing advises me otherwise."

"What brings you here?"

"I need to talk."

"Is this something that can wait until Monday? Now is not a good time." He chuckled a little as he said the last part.

"No." I looked around the room. "I see you have some food in the oven. Were you expecting the missus? I had thought she was leading a day trip to Milan."

"No, Katherine is away. I have some private business to attend to. Are you...enjoying the wine?"

"Very much. It's delicious." I took another sip. "Please, Dr. Sellier, I only need a minute of your time." I looked at him for a minute, his noodly frame. I began to see in him the bearded man in the Porn Storm movie eyeing up Kat. I saw Ms. Daphne from fifth grade and her awful socks and her fake sanctimony, our illustrations of us in our innocence in hand. I saw the shadow of the doctor lingering for a moment at the sight of Kristen's parted legs before he took the only thing that had ever been truly hers, or mine. I saw the thousands and tens of thousands of doctors, judges, educators, administrators, and the talking heads. I saw Dr. Sellier—Bruce—and saw in his eyes the way he looked at us, at the girls, at Doodles.

But this time, I saw something that I had never seen before in any of them, and now I saw it in all of them.

"Dr. Sellier, Lily Marconi will not be joining you tonight."

"I don't know what you are talking about."

I shifted in my seat. "She forwarded me your invitation." I took another sip of wine. "She told me about the rose, about the time you...put your hands on her."

"And what are you going to do about it, William?"

I paused to let the emotion flash through me and then subside before acting. "Mr. Ferguson," I corrected him, finally. I stood up and chugged my glass of wine and looked at him. I grabbed the bottle of vino, then spat on his plate. Looking back at him, I walked past him and out of the flat, down the stairs into the piazza.

There was still a little daylight left. Doodles had his back against the apartment building wall, smoking.

"Let's go to the bridge and drink this," I said, handing him the bottle.

"Shit yeah," he said, looking at it.

CHAPTER 60

Lily and I had been planning on spending this day together shopping. She would be shopping for a birthday outfit, and I would be shopping for gifts for my parents. Since our Art History excursions were over for the semester, our Friday would be free after a short general meeting in the morning. The two of us sat next to each other, and she leaned over to me during the meeting and whispered that she wanted to leave before we got talking to the others.

The meeting was just a recap of what sorts of things had to be put in their proper place before the end of the trip, what our last events would be, questions, and I had to hand out the final meal allowances. It was over in less than an hour. Once the meeting adjourned, the two of us slipped out the door before most of the others had gotten up.

We dashed down the steps and giggled a little bit. The stones inside the building were still a little cold. The spring air on the other side of the giant door was considerably warmer, though. Warm but not hot.

It was mid-April. The sunlight nowadays reached further down into the streets and piazzas, and the stones seemed pleasant in the sun. Flowers sat on windowsills and in pots, and blooms sprouted on the few trees in the city. Classes had now drawn to a close, and we were making travel plans for the weeks following the end of our program. As charming as the city had been, leaving it was something I awaited with great zeal and anticipation.

We turned the corner out of our building and headed toward Piazza Repubblica, which was full of people and sunshine. We stopped at Giubbe Rosse, which was a café known for the anarchists and writers who used to congregate there. I hadn't heard of any of them. I got a cappuccino and she got a caffè Americano, which we both drank standing, since we expected people from the trip to come by, and we were trying to avoid them. She got one cookie to go.

We finished our drinks and walked out into Piazza Repubblica, where the sun was high, bright, and warm on the gray stones. People walked in every direction; some *ragazzi* kicked a soccer ball around. We first walked under the Romanesque arch to the east toward Dante Alighieri's haunts. I had my hands in my pockets, and she munched on her cookie with a guilty grin on her face. As we walked east, the streets became narrower. We walked past the tripe stand into the American Express offices. It was a clean and open space that smelled like a bank, and operated much like one. We stood in line, which these days tended to be longer than it had been in the past, on account of tourists who came during the spring. We looked down on them with a similar disdain as did the locals, and we all acknowledged how funny it was that we felt we owned the place. But right then we weren't in a hurry, so we weren't too bent out of shape over having to wait.

The two of us talked and reminisced about our favorite parts of the trip, and how fun it was going to be to head out of the city. We had seen Florence for what it was—a work of art and a gem in the crown of Western civilization, but also a harsh city where the sun didn't really reach the streets and the grass and the trees for the most part had been buried in stone.

While we were there we both got ourselves a few hundred dollars in traveler's checks and train tickets to Vienna. We would buy the other tickets there. We stepped out into the sun and walked back west toward Piazza Repubblica. We stopped in some stores—Coin first, then Benetton. There Lily spotted a purse and almost bought it for her roommate Molly back home. She decided against the purchase, though, because she would probably end up keeping it for herself.

After Benetton we decided to get some lunch. We took the short walk past the shops and chapels through Piazza della Signora to Lily's favorite place, Il Gatto e la Volpe—the Cat and the Wolf. We sat down at the wooden tables below the bottles of wine lining the top of the wall below the ceiling. I ordered a quarter carafe of Chianti, and we both ordered a bowl of ribollita. We didn't say much, just watched the people walk by outside and dipped our bread in olive oil. I didn't feel like there was much I had to say.

"Florence has been great, but I'm ready to go home," she said.

"Me, too," I said. "But I think I'm more concerned about getting out of this city."

"Yeah."

Each of us ordered a shot of espresso after our soup. We got up and walked over to a department store, then to a couple more of Lily's favorite boutiques—Rinascente, Mattucci. In between we stopped at a tie shop and got my dad a couple ties and a nice new Italian leather wallet, and at a football hooligan store, where I got Zack a nice Italia goalie shirt. Our last stop was Liu-jo, Lily's favorite shop. She had some credit from a pair of pleather pants that had melted at the dry cleaner, plus her parents' money. The first items she took a look at were the bathing suits. She tried on a couple and asked what I thought. I thought a lot, but just said they were great. She settled on a light blue one with orange edges, and it was quite the sight on her with her dark hair.

She moved on to birthday outfits, and tried several of them on. Many of them were a little more daring than she was used to, and that was something I could get used to. She settled on a pink V-neck top that was sort of like a thin sweater, and some dark jeans with flowers and vines and such embroidered on them. It wasn't a bold declaration on the state of fashion, just a statement that she didn't need to make any statements. The price tag was far above any amount I had ever thought of spending on clothes, but it was her birthday and I was sure there was a lot I didn't know about such things.

After that we took a walk to the bus stop at Piazza San Marco. There was a bus there that went up to Fiesole, in the hills on the outskirts of the city. I had learned of it when I came once a few years before. The bus ride was about ten or fifteen minutes winding up the mountain in the steepest sort of way.

Fiesole was the last stop, and we got off. It was a small village with a few villas, a small square, and a few restaurants and shops. I stopped and bought a bottle of wine and asked the cashier to open it. There were some Roman or Etruscan ruins—most notably a small amphitheater that our Civilization class had visited before. We walked on a street toward Florence, which was down in the valley below. The road led to a trail, like a small park except that it was on the side of a mountain. There were a few trees with buds sprouting. We climbed onto a rock and sat looking out onto the red clay rooftops below in the late-afternoon sun. It was hard from that distance to see any of the movement in the city. The streets were too narrow for the most part.

We looked out at Florence, and I sipped from the bottle. I passed it to her and she took a couple sips.

"That's good wine," she said.

"It's Vernaccia."

"From San Gimignano?"

"Yeah."

I took another swig.

"I miss my family," she said finally.

"Yeah. I miss mine, too. I feel so bad, because I know my parents have been putting money into my account, and I know they don't have it, really."

"But it will get better when you guys move, right?"

"Yeah. It will."

"Then don't worry about it. I'm sure they're happy to do it for you."

"You're right. I just don't know. I feel so selfish, like I don't deserve it."

"It's their gift to you, Will. They do it because they love you."

"You're right." Then after a pause, "I'm having a tough time in general, I guess."

"I know you are, Will. I'm sorry."

"It's alright." I looked out at the rooftops. "More wine?" I smiled at her to let her know I was being funny.

"I'll have a little more. I don't want much more, though. I don't want to fall off this rock."

"I won't let that happen."

I took out a cigarette and lit it.

"Want a cigarette?"

"No, thank you."

"Live a little."

"I don't smoke, Will, it's gross. My body is my temple."

Hearing that, it sounded more than a little corny. I had probably heard that saying many times before. But it still felt a bit astonishing. I knew it in a million different ways, but she put it more concisely than I had ever put it to myself. It was new and it was old. I put out my cigarette on the rock and looked out on Florence.

We sat in silence and in awe at the city stretched out before us, the silver river bending through the middle visible in places. In the hills the yellow, orange, and brown buildings in random places with red roofs reflected the afternoon sun and didn't look real among the dark green grass and cypress trees. Across the way we could see some of the white and green marble stones of the basilica of San Miniato al Monte, a shrine to the first martyr of Florence. The Romans cut off his head during their persecutions, and the story goes that he picked it up, walked across the Arno, then up to his hermitage in the hills, where he died finally. The church there now was built on the spot where his body rested. During a war, Michelangelo had the church wrapped in mattresses to protect it from enemy fire.

"I wish we could stay here," I said.

"Yeah. We should go, though."

"You're right."

We were meeting some people and Lily had to change. We climbed off the rock, and I threw the rest of the wine out. We walked back to the bus stop and didn't have to wait long for the bus.

In a little while we made it to the place she had been staying. It was an old palace just on the other side of the Ponte Santa Trinita, with massive wooden doors that opened up to a courtyard. It was a registered historical site.

She planned on being a while. She wanted to drop her stuff off and get changed for our dinner later with some of the other girls. I told her I would busy myself and we could all meet at the duomo. I walked to the middle of the Ponte Santa Trinita and climbed over the side of it onto a triangle-shaped stone structure that hung over the water. I sat Indian-style and smoked a cigarette in the sun, which was getting a little lower and longer. I looked down at the water passing by below, then across at the traffic and the miniature people in the distance. I told God that I was grateful for that moment, and for things in general. I asked for strength.

After a couple cigarettes I started getting cold, so I got back up and crossed the rest of the bridge toward the center of town. I had about an hour to kill, so I walked the few blocks to the school and checked my email.

Father Bob had written me. He told me that it sounded like I was struggling with something very big, and that I should keep the email I sent him. It was interesting, he said, how sometimes it seems like people should be having a great time like they tend to do abroad, but it turns out that inside they're hurting badly. He had a lot of hope for me, though. He could see I was in a bad place, but that I was doing the right thing. I wrote him a quick note to tell him I was feeling better and I would write some more when I had time. There were other people waiting to use the computer.

CHAPTER 61

At five thirty we all met in front of the duomo. I was sitting and waiting, watching the tourists go by and studying from afar the intricacies on the doors of the baptistery. They were covered in panels of bronze relief sculptures depicting Bible scenes in considerable detail and depth for the medium. The doors were set against alternating green and white marble blocks that formed the facade of the building, which was octagonal in shape. They had at their unveiling traversed all the frontiers of what people thought art could achieve. The artist was Brunelleschi, the same fellow who had designed the duomo of the cathedral after centuries without its having a permanent roof. The Florentines had built the cathedral with the hope that God would lift up someone who could figure how to cap it. Providence obliged, in time.

Lily and Crystal arrived first, both laughing and joking about something that had happened back at the flat. They wouldn't tell me what it was, so it was something that probably had to do with passing gas or menstruation, or one of the two or three other things that girls tend not to reveal to guys, but that ended up getting revealed in circumstances that had the two groups living close by for extended periods of time. I would get it out of them later.

Joined by the others, we walked down the street that led off the space between the baptistery and the cathedral, and down a couple blocks to a Mexican place. Typically, or rather all the time, I suppose, they had a happy hour from five to six. The girls had it in their mind that they wanted to go there to get some strawberry daiquiris.

I didn't buy a beer. It was too early in the evening, and more important, I was cutting down on drinking, because, well...I shouldn't have to say it. I had had the Vernaccia earlier. They, on the other hand, were buying pitchers of daiquiris. This was not going to be pretty. None of these girls were big drinkers.

The girls were gossiping like they, excepting Lily, usually did, and Lily managed to direct the conversation to the travails of the day's survey of Italian fashion. This led to the now familiar conversation about how the fashion in Florence was two years ahead of America's, and anything any American purchased there, they would be able to use for two years, at least. Which led to talk about how they had to do more shopping, which led to a discussion of how many clothes and things Doodles had bought, which led to more gossip and reminiscing about the other people on the trip.

The pitchers kept coming, and it was becoming a girl-bonding thing. I sat near them at the bar drinking Coke, smoking cigarettes, and listening or tuning out as I wanted. They were starting to draw attention from the bartenders and some of the other customers, since one of them, Ella, was a particularly loud drunk. At this point, it was amusing, but I knew we would be arriving at annoying without delay. But who was I to judge?

Lily, who had a low tolerance for both alcohol and the behavior it inspired, stepped out of their circle and walked over to me. She was in jeans and a pink V-neck shirt. She was electromagnetic. Intergalactic. Phenomenological.

"Will, can I talk to you for a minute?"

"Have at it."

She hesitated. "I don't know what I want to say."

"Then maybe you should start again in a little while."

"I mean, I know what I want to say, I just don't know how to put it."

"Well, you know me, I'm in no rush."

"I know..." She had both hands on her glass, holding it just above waist level. She never seemed to fidget or anything. "Thank you for today. I was thinking about it while I was getting dressed, and I wanted you to know I really enjoyed everything. I love spending time with you and feeling like there is a person in my life with whom I can feel, like, completely comfortable. With you I feel like I can be myself, and to you, that's wonderful. I love spending time with you and your sense of humor and everything." She put the fingertips of her right hand on the center of her chest, where a necklace would hang down. She would do that when she was saying something important.

"Thank you, Lily."

"And, you know, I know that you've expressed to me that you might like to have our relationship be something more than it is..." She paused and looked up a little bit, like she was thinking of the right words to say.

"Maybe," I said with a grin.

"Well, I just hope that you understand that I think it's really important that we just stay friends at this point in our lives. Your friendship is really important to me."

I had a thought at that moment, but none I thought I should share. I wondered if she could see my insides leaking out.

"*Just* stay friends?" I asked. "I think being friends with you is a real blessing. I'm a lucky man."

Her chin quivered a little bit. "That's so sweet, Will. I just...wanted you to know how great a friend you are to me."

"Well, thank you. You're a great friend to me, too."

I put my right arm around her and pulled her in close for a second. I let her go and she joined the other girls. I joined, too, to put my mind elsewhere. I lit a cigarette. I meant what I had said.

As the daiquiris flowed, Ella grew louder. She started talking about Melanie, which made her curse as well. Crystal and Amy weren't much better. The bartender came up to me and asked me to tell them to quiet down, which I did. It lasted for all of thirty seconds, after which I told them again. They did again, and they all started whispering hoarsely to mock me. I hated babysitting drunks, but knew I was getting my just desserts.

I asked Lily to keep an eye on my stuff and went to the bathroom briefly, and when I returned Ella was yelling, "Kiss my big white ass" at the bartender. He told me if she didn't quiet down, we'd have to leave. I relayed the message to Ella, who told me she didn't care, and tried to sit down on her barstool. She missed it for the most part and slammed down on the floor, the stool falling on top of her and her glass breaking. The other girls were laughing and slapping their legs and telling each other they were going to pee in their pants. I picked up the barstool and then Ella, apologized to the bartender, picked up my backpack, and herded them out like drunken geese.

On the street they were laughing and cursing and falling on each other, and I was getting mightily pissed off. Doodles was walking toward us as we exited the bar.

"Are these girls alright, mate?"

"Bite me, sailor!" Ella yelled from a few feet away.

"Thanks, love. You're looking tip-top tonoight," he replied.

"They're drunk and sentimental," I replied.

"Nahsty mix there, ayde say."

"I'd agree."

I tried to keep walking as the girls flopped into each other and dropped their bags and whatnot. It was one of the nicest nights yet, temperature-wise. People were out strolling beneath the twilight, and with spring baring her ankles, it was more than usual for a Friday night. So they were attracting quite a bit of attention.

"Are yew going to get a bit of brew tonioght?"

"A bit of what?" I asked.

"Beeah, mate."

"Right. I thought I might get one or two."

"Noice. We just have to shayke these bitches, roight?"

As we walked past the duomo toward Piazza Repubblica, Lily and Amy decided they needed to sit down, which they did on a curb. Lily started holding her head and saying, "I just want to lie down for a second. Just for a second."

She flopped onto the sidewalk, on her back, and Amy followed suit.

"Lily, Amy, get up."

"Juss for a seconnt," Lily replied.

"No, get up."

"Pleease. Juss for a seconnt."

I couldn't believe how drunk these girls had gotten, right under my nose. They all had the tolerance of a finch, except for Crystal maybe, and I knew that. I should have paid more attention.

"No. Get up, now. You girls are lying on the filthy sidewalk. People are looking at you. Get up. You girls have to go home."

I grabbed Lily's hands and pulled her up. Amy saw that and crossed her arms and put her hands in her armpits, so I pulled her up by the lapels on her red coat.

"Get off me, Will. Stop being a dick."

"Walk, Amy, or I'm going to drag you."

"C'mon, Amy, you can lean on me," Crystal said.

Doodles was watching the whole thing in amusement.

"You could help, you know."

"Not my style." He took out a cigarette. "These girls are wrecked. What were they drinking?"

"Daiquiris."

"Which means they'll be peukin' latah."

When we got to Piazza Repubblica, I told the girls to go home, because I was going to the Inferno.

"I want to come," Ella said.

"You can't Ella; you're cut off."

"Don't tell me what to do."

"Ella, you're just going to get us thrown out of the next place."

"Fine. I didenne want to go withhe you anyway."

"See you later."

The three others lived near each other, so they were all heading in the same direction, and Ella tagged along with them. Her house was in the other direction, but she wasn't my problem anymore.

Doodles and I started walking eastward toward Dante's Inferno, which was in the vicinity of Dante's house and the chapel where he used to pine for Beatrice.

We entered and sauntered up to the bar and ordered our drinks from Maurizio and Donatello. They weren't in a very talkative mood that particular night. We sat at a table for four.

"This moight be one of aur last toimes drinkin' togethah, mate."

"It's a shame; we're real artists."

"But I'm ready to get tha hell autta this plaice. It's a stinkin' rathole dogshite-smellin' plaice. Just filthy stinkin' stones and filthy stinkin' Italians."

"All I want is a hamburger."

"Shit yeeah, mate. We should see if Mickey Dees is open."

"Maybe."

"Well, I'm goina grab me anothah. I see you won't be needin' one."

He got up with a smug smile on his face. This was a challenge. I had drunk enough with him before to know I could drink him under the table, so I finished mine and followed him to the bar. I would decide later whether I would see this through to completion. It was innocent enough—just me and Doodles.

"Ya gotta come to Amsterdam with me," he said.

"Too late. Just bought the ticket to Vienna."

"You're a little wankah, yannow that?"

"There isn't shit there but weed and hookers."

"Aye know, brothah! What in the nut d'yew think I'm going for?"

"Sounds like a doomed endeavor."

"Listen to you. Are yew the effin' pahrty-like-a-rock-stah Piechfuzz, drink-till-ya-pass-out-in-a-random-'otel-elevator, 'ook-up-with-every-fine-piece-of-ass-in-'is-general-vicinity man I grew to know and love? Wheah is that man?"

"I don't know. I hate smoking weed, and I'm not interested in getting warts on my dick." I took a sip of beer. "Or going to hell."

"Shit, man, what's it there for?"

"To remind us of our vulnerability."

"Don't get philosophical on me, mate! I'm gettin' anothah beah."

"I've been waiting for you."

We walked up to the bar, and I kept my eye on my bag.

"So when are you going to go back to Australia?"

"Not until after I graduate. I'm going back and livin' in the house for the summah."

"Do you miss it?"

"Shit, no. Not while American girls loike an Australian accent."

"Is your dad going to have any problems financing this madness?"

"My dad's a true wankah. He just puts money in my account. 'E's such a poile a dung. Just before aye left we got in a foight an' 'e told me, 'Yannow whut, you were supposed ta be a puddle on the small of ya mothah's back.'"

"Did you hit him?"

"No. I stahrted cryin' like a whelp. Then aye told 'im I was glad aye was aloive ta give 'im 'ell."

We stood and drank for a minute. I was sorry to hear that.

"Did he lose any money last week?" The stock market had endured a historic crash. Bubbles were popping and wealth— their word, not mine—was evaporating everywhere.

"Probably lots."

We walked back to the table.

"I can't believe people didn't see that coming."

"Most people did, but they were too greedy ta cash aut in time."

"It's unbelievable. We should just stay in Italy and open a bakery and drink wine. Learn Italian and marry some Italian girls."

"Sounds loike a plan ta me, brothah. But it moight be a little tough for you, yannow. On account of my looks. Ya moight be pickin' up scraps."

"Dood, I don't love you for your vanity. I love you in spite of it."

"That's tha truth, brothah."

I smiled and took a sip of my beer.

"I wouldn't be able to stand it."

"Neithah would I."

I got back up and went to the bar, and he followed. They gave us two cups each along with a shot of whiskey. We took them back to the table. We clinked glasses and took the shots.

"Aye got a question for ya, mate."

"What's that?"

"D'yew believe in God?"

I took a sip of the beer. "Yeah, I do. What about you?"

"Aye dunno. I figeure, 'ow can ya be sure?"

I took out a cigarette, as did he, and lit it.

"It's like, or it is, loving someone."

"Aye don't know that aye've evah loved anybody."

"I'm sorry to hear that."

"So am aye, mate."

We sat and smoked in silence for a minute.

"It seems dishonest to think that this universe behaves in such an orderly fashion without some sort of force driving it. Otherwise, where would the order come from?"

"That's interesting."

"But the more important thing is what I've experienced. There are times when I've known that what I was experiencing was God, and that it could only be God."

"Experiencing God how?"

"Like a person whom you love face to face. God's shown himself to me, in that he gave me peace at times in my life when I didn't believe in peace....It's like you're born in a house of glass with a door, but it's closed. You hear about the wind, and you're not sure it's there. You can watch people outside getting their hair blown around and the trees shaking, and people can describe it to you through the glass, but you won't understand the wind unless you step outside. God is the wind."

"Ya feel it aul the time—the peace?"

"No. But I'm always trying to get there."

"Aye 'ope ya get there, mate."

"I hope you do, too."

We smoked in silence a little more.

"Hmm. Well, maybe I'll take a stroll one day autsoide my glass 'ouse. What 'bout you?"

"I've been outside, but I don't know where I am right now. You never know, I guess."

"Bullshit. I know I'm not autside tonoight. Tonoight I'm gettin' waisted."

"Hmm."

"I'm takin' a piss. Get us beers while I'm gone."

We competed until about midnight. It was a draw, to the severest degree. When we left the building, he went in the opposite direction. I began walking, and it was very difficult. The spring air was like bathwater as I walked alone past the duomo toward San Lorenzo, then toward Via delle Belle Donne. The streets were full of people, the weather being so nice and it being a Friday night. I focused on the building at the end of the street, which had a white marble sun on it that spit water into a trough. Two girls usually hung out there.

I walked toward them, and found that focusing on them helped me walk in a straight line. When I got up near them, one started laughing at me. I continued and walked straight up to a phone booth, stopped, took out my wallet, took out my card, and called home.

"Hello?"

"Hi, Mom."

"Hi, my baby!"

"What are you doing?"

"I'm watching the news."

"Oh yeah. Who won?"

"Will, are you drunk?"

"Yeah. I'm a little drunk. Sorry."

"It's okay, baby."

"No it's not. I'm just calling because I missed you guys."

"We miss you too, Son."

"So what are you doing?"

"Watching the news."

"Oh. I already asked you that."

"That's okay."

"You need to open a flower shop," I said.

"A flower shop?"

"Yeah. There's a guy near our apartment who sells flowers."

"Okay, Son. We'll open a flower shop."

"I'm sick of it here, Mom. There aren't enough trees. It's been great, but I want to go the hell home."

"I want you home. I miss you terribly."

"Alright. Well, I should go home I guess. I mean, to the lady's house."

"I know what you mean, baby."

"I miss you. Tell everyone I love them."

"I will, baby. I love you."

"I love you, too."

I woke up in the phone booth. It must have been an hour or so later. I looked at the phone, then I checked my pockets. Everything was there. But I realized that I was not wearing my backpack. I looked down by my feet and there was nothing there. I stepped outside and I looked around for people, but the street was empty. I couldn't believe this. It had my train ticket to Vienna in it. It had my passport, my journal, and all the gifts I had bought for everybody that day.

I started walking back toward the bar. I knew it was a waste of time, but I figured I had to do it. When I got there, about fifteen minutes later, it was closed. I looked through the window down on the floor to see if I could see anything, but there was nothing. I still had my cigarettes.

I walked, smoking again, past the duomo. Just before San Lorenzo square, I decided I would sit down to finish my cigarette. I sat down and smoked in a storefront with my back against the front door and leaned up against the jamb.

CHAPTER 62

When I woke up, two young kids were looking at me—both blonde with blue eyes. The boy was bent over shaking me on the shoulder, speaking to me in Italian.

"Wake up! Wake up! It's time to go. Go home. You fell asleep." He looked a little concerned, but amused.

"I am home."

"No, no. Go home. You fell asleep. You don't belong here." He smiled at me and waited until he could tell I was awake.

"Okay. Thank you."

I got up and looked at my watch. It was six in the morning, and the light was gray, even, and dim. When they saw I was standing, they sort of skipped away giddily, hand in hand. I had no idea what two kids were doing out at that time in the morning.

I was cold. I reached in my pocket and pulled out another cigarette, even though I didn't want one. I lit it and walked through Piazza di San Lorenzo by the merchants as they pushed their carts full of leather goods and cheap tourist T-shirts into place and unlocked them. I felt very embarrassed for myself. I tried to stare at the ground, so as not to get any looks, but I was the only person on the street not wearing a jacket, and I was walking crookedly and slowly down the middle of it, and I was taller than most of these fellows, in wrinkled khaki pants with my button-down shirt out, so I had some trouble blending.

In any case, I was really grateful to the kids.

I started to feel bad, but I figured, what was the point in beating myself up? I was going to do the only thing I could do, which was try to gain again what I had lost. There was only one way to go from where I was. I would be back home in two and a half weeks. I just needed more strength. *I'm trying, Lord. Please look past the fact I'm failing. Thank you for today.*

CHAPTER 63

We left on Good Friday. I had bought another ticket to Vienna, got a temporary passport, bought other gifts for my family on my credit card, and paid the library for the books I had lost. The souvenirs from every place and the journal were just losses. I posted notices here and there, but it was all gone. I wasn't going to let myself get too bent out of shape over it.

The group had had a nice dinner at a nice restaurant the night before, where we all said our goodbyes. I got a special mention in Lily's speech, which I thought was special. I made a joke about having something prepared to say but losing it, then I thanked Dr. Sellier's son for being a model of how to act, and made another joke about this being Dr. Sellier's last chance leading the semester abroad.

Before our smaller group left, we had one more dinner at a nice restaurant near the Arno. We took a few pictures from the Ponte Santa Trinita with the Ponte Vecchio behind us. The sunset was brilliant in the west, and was casting nice pinks and oranges onto the water and the bridge. We then took the walk up to the train station, which took us a few minutes with all our bags. It was me, Lily, Amy, and Ella.

We walked up to the platform and sat on our bags. Ella was the only one who said anything about being sad leaving. The rest of us felt that way, but talking about it seemed a little redundant. For all its harshness, we'd had a good time. We just sat, and some of us smoked in the sunset next to the tracks.

I slept through the night but tried to stay awake as much as possible once it was light out. I watched as the train moved past villages and farmland, as the terrain became more mountainous with green grass, cherry blossoms, forests, and wildflowers. Even though I was on the train, I felt I could breathe easier.

CHAPTER 64

Amy and I were both up early, so we went to the dining car and got some pastries, soft cheese, and espresso. Afterward we stood in between the cars and had a cigarette. We chatted about things we remembered, our families back at home, though she didn't like talking about hers much, and music. We went back to our seats and found Lily awake, talked for a few minutes, then watched the scenery pass by through the window. It made me wonder why more people didn't take trains.

We arrived at the station and unloaded our stuff. Amy and Ella had sent the bulk of their things home through the mail. Lily and I had all of our stuff. When we got to the escalator out of the train station, which was quite a ways up, it was broken. So I brought her bags up first, then walked back down and got mine. She thanked me, and Ella made a comment about my being a gentleman. My mother raised a gentleman, I said.

At the top of the steps, the street was wide, paved, and clean. The sidewalks were large and lined with trees in bloom. The sun was shining brightly and was warm. I was wearing a black Jack Daniel's T-shirt, so I was hot, but I didn't mind.

We had to get our bearings to find our hostel. Ella took charge of that effort by consulting our guide. I was the man in the group, so I had a tinge of an idea that I should be in charge of our direction, but if she wanted to step into that role, I was more than happy to let her.

We sat on our bags in the sun while Ella flipped through the thick guide that was written for young backpackers in Europe. I felt the sun on me and breathed the fresh air.

When Ella finally figured out where we were going, we started walking. We went first to the tram stop. Here, rather than buses or the subway, they had trams that ran on tracks but looked like buses. Our stop was right in front of city hall, which was one of the Vienna landmarks. It looked like a giant palace, with a low wrought iron fence and a well-maintained lawn and well-placed trees behind it.

When the tram arrived, I carried our bags onto it, then sat down and watched as we rode down the wide boulevard, shops on either side.

When we got to the stop, it was late morning. Following Ella's direction, we began wandering down a well-shaded street. Except for the other language on street signs, it looked like it could have been a street from a residential area in any well-planned American city—like a prelapsarian Brooklyn. After walking a few blocks, we arrived at the door where the hostel was.

The outside was unexceptional, as was the lobby—just a desk, a bulletin board, a pay phone, and a couple chairs. The rooms were separated according to sex, and there was one bathroom for each sex. There was a light breakfast served, and a courtyard, and we slept six to a room. I got my key from the receptionist, and we decided to put our stuff down and head out for some lunch in an hour. That way we could freshen up and take a nap if necessary.

I walked down the hallway and entered my room, which was just a white room with six bunks with white sheets and a desk by the window. I was the first guest in that particular room, so I had my choice of which bed to take. I took a bottom bunk so I could hide my stuff under it. I changed into some clean clothes, took out my alarm clock and set it, then lay on top of the sheets with my hands behind my head. I thought of Lily and the first night we kissed.

It had been the first night we spent out after the summer before. Brandon, "our girls", and I were out at a few parties in our apartment complex, and she had been rather flirty. I knew she had broken up with her boyfriend over the summer. She was wearing a short blue skirt and a white shirt with tiny straps and a black, thin button-up sweater over her shoulders. She was holding my hand throughout the night, and as we stood and talked she would hold onto my arm.

The parties had turned out to be pretty lame that night, but I went out long enough to get sauced enough to pick up on Lily's signals and believe they were signals, not just some sort of mistake. After going to a few parties, Lily had told me she was getting tired, and she asked me to walk her home. She had held my hand the entire way, then once we got into her apartment, she went to her cabinet to get some chips and to the fridge to get some dip.

"Do you want some?"

"No, I can't eat that shit."

She dipped one chip and ate it, then hopped up on the counter at a corner with her legs crossed.

"It's okay if it's only once in a while." She dipped another chip and put it in her mouth. With the chip still in her mouth, she said, "You want to kiss me, don't you?"

"Yeah."

She uncrossed her legs but kept them together, flipped her hair behind her shoulder, then held up her finger for a second while she swallowed the chip.

"Okay."

Then we kissed for a minute, and I pulled back and said, "I've been waiting for two years to do that."

She smiled then and kissed me a little more. When I moved my hand down from her back to her leg, she suggested it was time for me to go. I protested, and she said no, it was time for me to leave.

Soon those memories gave way to sleep.

CHAPTER 65

I woke up to the alarm clock. I sat up and put my shoes back on, then went out to the courtyard in the back. There were flowerbeds, a bench, and a few tables with a fence. A tree in the corner provided shade for half of it. It was a pleasant place. I lit a cigarette, and toward the end of it the girls came out.

We left the hostel and walked back to the tram, which was about a block away. We boarded and got off at the stop near a castle that had become a museum. We walked up the road toward what seemed to be the city center. The shops were very posh—even the pastry shops. We were all hungry, and we found a place with beer and what we figured was probably Austrian food. We didn't know, though, because we couldn't read the language.

I ordered an item on the menu that I was most certain I could not pronounce or translate in any way, and a Coke. The girls asked the waiter first if he spoke English, which he did, and then which items were the salads.

We didn't have much to say to each other, because we were all so tired and hungry, and we had been through most of it before. We talked a little about how different this was from Florence. It was clean, the air was fresh, the streets were wide, but hardly any people were around, it seemed.

Our food arrived. It turned out I had ordered a thirteen-inch fried sausage on a bed of sauerkraut. It wasn't exactly what I was in the mood for, but I was starving. The girls had all ordered some variation of a salad, so they thought it was pretty funny that I was eating that.

After lunch we ambled around. We looked in a few shops and staked out a few places that looked like they might be good to return to that night. To our surprise, it didn't seem like there were many nightclubs or anything. We came across a hip coffee bar playing some Eurotrash techno. We took a seat and ordered coffee, which was supposed to be good, this being Vienna, but wasn't that special. Afterward, we walked toward the imperial palace, which was an endless white building with hundreds of windows and a great lawn spread out before it for what seemed like miles. We all lay in the grass, like it seemed most people were. I dozed off for a little while, as did the others.

CHAPTER 66

When we woke up, we went back to hostel. We all wanted to get showers, and that night we went to a bar where the theme was chairs. Each of them was different, and many of them were unique designs. All of us except Lily ordered beers, and we talked about nothing. A couple Austrians, one looking like a lieutenant from the S.S., the other with hair like a court jester, invited themselves to our table and immediately started bitching about the Freedom Party and the possible end of socialism in Austria, and how stupid America and American culture are, except for *The Simpsons*. They drank vodka martinis and smoked unfiltered cigarettes. "If you could imagine, there is no poor. No poverty. Healthcare for all. And they want to destroy that." It was as if the word "destroy" had been invented for Austrians to say with their accents, or at least for these two particular Austrians. Captain S.S. then asked me if I was Christian, to which I said yes. He told me he was sorry for me.

They suggested we all go to another bar, and us not knowing where to go, we followed them. We found a table and they immediately began rolling a joint. We asked if that was legal. They said no, but nobody was going to bother them there. I didn't smoke the weed.

The jester started asking Lily how she kissed with lips so thin, and I wanted to beat the hell out of him, but just let her handle it. She could be tough when she wanted to be. She told him to shut up, and we decided to leave.

The next morning was Easter morning. We woke up and I insisted we try to get to church. We took the tram to the center of town and walked by several churches. We couldn't read any of the signs, though. It was about noontime. We got to one cathedral and everyone was leaving. We found another one with giant spires and busy Gothic architecture and entered that. Inside there were a string quartet and an operatic soloist performing. We sat down, and I couldn't tell if it was a Catholic church or not. It seemed like it, but I didn't know enough to look for statues of saints. There was no service, and it wasn't likely we would find one. The music was haunting and breathtaking, and I could feel that God appreciated the effort. I told him I appreciated the effort, too. I prayed hard and listened intently to the music. Several times the girls wanted to go, but I asked to stay a little longer.

We left after about an hour and looked for something to eat. Finally we stopped at a bakery that seemed to be some sort of Austrian chain. Behind glass cases were a variety of pastries and breads, squeezed juice, and coffee. We sat and ate and chatted. Afterward, we strolled around, found Mozart's apartment, which was closed, and then went back out to the lawns in front of the imperial palace and lay down. We were done with the sightseeing business, and all of us longed for home.

CHAPTER 67

O n the plane ride home, after our stay in London, which was like America with high prices, I sat next to Lily, with Crystal on the other side of her. There was a university cricket team or something in the back of the plane, all in shirts and ties. Crystal got the idea that they should go talk to them. So the two girls after a little while went back to sit with them. That left me in my place to stew.

It was enough for me. I had to get away from her and put my mind to other things. I took out my new journal and began to write to her. What came out was a nasty letter that said, essentially, good riddance, I was done. After writing for a bit, I stopped and read it over. I was thinking of giving it to her, but I knew it would be a mistake. It wasn't an honest letter. I was just hurt, but it wasn't because she was doing anything wrong.

I decided to write another one. It took me just as much time, and it was just as long as the other one. I told her that I was tempted to give in to frustration, but I was just going to accept things as they were. I told her I didn't understand why things were the way they were, but I could not help how I felt, and I still loved her, and I could not imagine how I could ever love another girl. I told her I also understood that she couldn't help how she felt, and that I hoped she would come around, but if she didn't, there was always the priesthood. I had a lot to learn, though. I ended by telling her she always had a friend. I tore out the second letter and slipped it into her journal, then looked out the window down at the sea to see if I could spot any ships.

Soon afterward, she sat down next to me.

"Hi," she said.

"Hi. Did you need something?"

"No. I just wanted to sit with my friend."

"Oh." I was a little startled at that. "Thank you."

"You're welcome."

She stayed in her seat the rest of the ride home.

CHAPTER 68

My parents met me at the airport in tears. I gave them a hug, and they excused me for being quiet, since I was so tired. I told them that the first thing I wanted them to do was take me out for some good Mexican food. We went to a popular chain, and it was pretty bad. It was good to see my parents, though.

I asked them about the new house, when we would be moving, when we had to start packing. I asked them if they'd had any luck finding construction people who needed laborers. Dad had a few ideas. I wanted to work outside with my hands. We drove home, and I talked for a while but was tired, so I listened to my headphones and enjoyed the scenery outside the windows.

Over the next several days my parents kept repeating to me how happy they were that I was home. Mom kept asking me if it was alright that we were moving out of Chelsea. I knew it was the best thing for our family, so that made it alright. That was the most important thing. My local friends Eli and Tony came back on the same day from college. Eli was busy with his family, but Tony came over to see me. I walked with him along Fifth Avenue, where the most traffic would be if it had been the summertime. I told him a lot about the trip—a lot of the bad things.

"Willie," he said.

"Yeah."

"I'm not joking when I say you have a drinking problem."

"I probably do."

"No, you do."

"Alright. I do. I'm not going to be drinking much in the near future. I'm not twenty-one yet."

"I worry about you, buddy."

"I know. I'm fine."

"Alright."

I managed to get a job as a bouncer at a bar in the next town up four nights a week, along with the waiter job I already had, a construction job, and a job tending to the grounds of a doctor's office.

The job at the bar was particularly good for me, because it gave me the opportunity to watch people get drunk and smoke cigarettes while not participating myself. It was a good perspective to get, because it made me pretty much disgusted with the whole business.

As for Lily, the two of us corresponded by email soon after getting back from Italy, and frequently, for about a week. I decided I wasn't doing so well at keeping my mind off her, so I figured I would stop emailing her, no matter how much I wanted to do so. I wouldn't call her either. I would make her miss me.

After a long month, she emailed me. She talked about how her summer was going, that she had gone to the beach at Rehoboth with her family, and that was a nice time of togetherness that she hadn't had with them in quite a while. She updated me on her parents and her brother, and talked about what classes she would take next year. Her bathing suit was working out well, she said; she was spending a lot of time with her *nonna*. She wanted to know all about what I was doing. "I guess I just miss you," she wrote. I was quite satisfied with myself that it had worked.

Toward the end of the summer, Father Bob stopped at our house on his way back from a continuing education class in Boston. It was out of his way; he was probably stopping out of concern for me. We didn't have a lot of time to talk seriously about anything, because when we were hanging out, Mom was there. Dad was working. I had wanted my friend Dave from high school to meet him, because we had debated religion over email several times. He came over for a while, but we just had a polite discussion. We didn't discuss religion much.

He had to leave the next morning. I walked him out to his car.

"I just wanted to let you know, Father, that I'm alright."

"Are you sure? Things seemed a little rocky, there."

"I've had a lot of trouble forgiving myself."

"Do you believe God has forgiven you?"

"Yes, Father, but I don't know why."

"It's because he loves you without conditions, Will."

"I know that."

"Did you want me to hear your confession?"

"Right here?"

"Sure."

"Okay. I didn't know you could do that."

"You absolutely can."

"Alright."

I confessed that I had fooled around with a few other girls, that I had missed church, that I stole an expensive bottle of wine from a sleazy professor and ruined his dinner, that I judged a sleazy professor for his being sleazy, that I had drunk myself nearly to death on several occasions, that I hadn't been suicidal, but that I really didn't care if I died, whether the abortion was my fault or not, that I had mistrusted or misunderstood God's forgiveness, and I had refused to forgive myself for creating the circumstances. I told him I was sure there were a few things I was forgetting. He said the blessings, and my sins were forgiven.

CHAPTER 69

During my senior year at school, I lived with Gallo and Skeeter in a townhouse built in the seventies with ugly blue carpeting throughout. I partied less and usually limited myself to a few beers a night, and it was working. I made it a point to apologize to some of the people who had to deal with my bad behavior.

It turned out that Lily and I spent time together nearly every night. I was doing a teaching internship, and I had no iron for my dress shirts. Rather than buy one myself, I would go over to her apartment and iron there. When we hugged hello and goodbye, she would linger for an extra minute. I noticed she had a framed picture of the two of us together in her room.

After about a month of this, I had to go back home for a weekend, and I wrote her an email right before I left. I told her that it would be silly for us to deny that we were seeing each other a lot more, and I felt that if I were to move on to another girl, she would get jealous, and vice versa. I told her I thought we complemented each other nicely, and that we would be great together, and it wouldn't make any sense to me if we didn't end up together. But if she wasn't interested in me, I needed her to tell me, and I needed us to spend less time together so we could move on.

That weekend I went to church with my family and prayed that whatever was supposed to happen would happen—either we would start going out, or we would go our separate ways and I would find the woman I was supposed to be with, if I wasn't supposed to go into the priesthood.

I drove home and figured I would be patient again, and refrain from contacting her. That Tuesday night Lily called and told me she wanted to talk. I told her okay, to come over. While I waited for her I said a few prayers that it would go well. I was nervous but not too jittery.

She knocked on the door, and I went down the steps of our new townhouse to open it.

She wasn't dressed to impress anyone; she had clearly been studying. She was in a white V-neck T-shirt and sweatpants, and her dark, curly hair was pulled up into a bun. I was still quite impressed. I asked her to come up to my room, and I sat on the edge of my bed; she sat on my desk chair a few feet away.

She would be sitting me down to tell me either that we needed to spend less time together, or that we needed to get at least a little more serious.

"So what's up?" I asked.

"I've been thinking a lot the past few days."

"Okay."

"I got your email," she said.

"Good."

"And..." She looked up at the ceiling, and I couldn't tell if she was dragging it out for effect or because she didn't know what to say. Finally, she looked at me. "I like you." Her voice went up on "like," so it sounded extra cute.

"Like—*like* like?"

"Yeah. Like, like-like."

"Wow."

She got up off her chair and sat next to me.

"Is it alright if I kiss you?" I asked.

"It's *very* alright."

We smooched for a minute or two. My mind was doing backflips; I was living something that I thought would never happen but had always hoped would. I had thought several times in the past several years that it might, or that it was supposed to, but for it to actually happen seemed—well, too good to be true. She put her hand on my chest and pushed back slightly, so we could talk again.

"I love you," she said.

"I love you, too, Lily."

"I hope it's not too soon for me to say that, but I do."

"It's not. I just am surprised to hear you say it. I mean, I can believe it, but it's just—I can't believe it. I...uh, I was wondering when it would be alright for me to tell you that."

"I'll tell you again. I love you."

"I love you, too, Lily."

We smooched a little more, but there was no undressing. She had a lot of work to do, so she went home. We married a year later.

THE BEGINNING

ACKNOWLEDGMENTS

I give thanks to God, my family, to the good people at Liberty Island Press, and to all of the people who helped me along the way in this endeavor and others.

ABOUT THE AUTHOR

E. Scott Lloyd is an attorney who resides in Virginia with his wife Ann and their seven children. In addition to his work as an attorney and as an author, he is a songwriter and the vocalist / guitar player from the band Day of Salvation (dayofsalvationmusic.com). *The Undergraduate* is Scott's first novel. You can find him on Twitter at @escottlloyd

Learn more about new and upcoming titles at

LibertyIslandMag.com